Three Pearl Buttons

A novel by

Beverley Shenoy

To Simone,

Much love,

Beverley Shenoy

This is a work of fiction. Some real life experiences have been utilized as a guide to build the storyline. All characters, names and incidents portrayed in this novel are the work of the author's imagination. Any resemblance to actual events and persons is merely coincidental. The localities mentioned within the book actually do exist, although the author has taken certain liberties with their depiction in the story.

Book Cover designed by First Water.

Printed and distributed by LSI.

ISBN 978-0-615-29717-0

Printed in the United States of America

For my mom,
For the tough choices and the endless sacrifices

And
For every woman who truly understands tough.

Three Pearl Buttons

Chapter One

Super Band Aid Girl

Sophie opened her eyes. Her brain jolted awake. Rudely. Like a slap in the face.
What was that?

She had been dreaming a happy dream. Sophie had climbed to the top of a very tall mountain. She had started out on what had seemed to be a fairly easy trail. It was obvious she had done this before. So many times before that it was second nature to her. Sophie hiked along the path, everything she needed strapped securely to her back in her favorite green backpack. In it, she had a yellow water bottle, filled to the brim with cool water, a small packet of crackers and another packet of chewy fruit gummies in case she got hungry, a six pack of small juice boxes, a map of the mountain she was attempting to climb, a little flashlight and a small face towel. She was in a happy mood.
Sophie loved the outdoors and jumped at any chance to be outside. Hikes on trails, swimming, riding her bike. She was always game to try anything. Her father encouraged her to try

new things. He was always taking them to new places where she could learn about nature. She would observe nature and would make notes and stick pictures of the things she had learned about in the nature journal given to her by her father. She was very proud of her latest acquisition. Even though it had only been in her possession a few months, she had enthusiastically filled up a number of pages already.

This particular trail, she noticed had some interesting vegetation along the way. There were all sorts of trees and shrubs and little plants, each so different in its own way. There were several different species, and many trees of the same species. Its not that they looked very different from each other because they really didn't, Sophie observed. Each tree looked more or less like its counterparts. And yet they were different in their own subtle way.
Upon closer scrutiny she realized what it was that made them appear different from each other. It was really their *attitude* that set them apart. Each had its own personality that was different from the others. Some had branches so high, they touched the sky. Some had thick wrinkled gnarled barks. Aged, each wrinkle seemed to denote milestones in their lives. Some were bowed and bent over like an old woman with an abnormal spine curvature that left her looking down to the ground, never up. Some grew straight up and then changed their minds along the way, choosing to twist sideways instead. Beautiful trees. Thick barks, thin barks, peeling barks. Big leaves, small leaves, brown leaves, green leaves. New branches without leaves, old branches with dusty leaves. Each tree grand in its own lofty majesty.

Even though they were different, they shared two things in common. The first, they were all really tall. They seemed to go on forever and ever. Sophie squinted and looked up. She could barely see the top of the trees. In some cases she couldn't see the tops at all. The leaves and upper branches of the trees formed an enveloping shelter from the sun, though every once in awhile, the sun would find a gap in the trees and wink down at Sophie as she went on her way. Rays of sunshine streamed downward in straight lines, highlighting the dust particles in their path, making them sparkle. The chosen sparkling dust particles basked in the sun, trading their inconspicuous existence for a moment of golden magic. Even if it was only for a moment. They returned to their perpetual state of inconspicuousness the instant they were shoved aside by wannabe sparkling dust particles, ready for their own fleeting moment in the golden sunlight.

The second thing the trees had in common was that they had lived together in these woods for a really long time. Eons ago, they had taken seed and germinated into young bright green saplings expecting to be nurtured into maturity. However, it appeared that they had been left in the woods, abandoned and forgotten. And yet, despite their abandonment or maybe because of it, they continued to grow stronger and taller every day, achieving new heights, growing upwards as if in search of something. They continued to mature, growing so many new branches and leaves, that they formed a dense umbrella over the earth below. Almost as if the trees in these woods had something to prove, their defiance underscored by every new leaf that sprouted, every new branch that emerged.

But they were not really abandoned, even if at first they appeared to be so. The gentle ageless hand of Mother Nature had cared and caressed them every step of the way. Always there, nudging them in the right direction. And so they grew up and up and up, tall and strong under her tutelage.

Taller and Older. The trees in the woods, as timeless as they were tall. Timeless in their stature, statuesque in their beauty.

Sophie continued on her way. She had to get to the top of the mountain but she was taking her time about it, reveling in the glory of the day. She picked her way carefully, making sure to test how securely each rock was lodged into the mountain side before placing her foot squarely on it. Just like daddy had taught her. There were little shrubs along the way that offered her blueberries to munch on. She could recognize blueberries anywhere. But there were all sorts of other berries too. Some big, some not so big and some down right tiny. They presented an arresting array of color too. Deep red, orange red, blue, purple, green and even some yellowish white ones, tempting Sophie to taste their sticky sweetness. But she was not tempted. She was unfamiliar with them, so she shied away. Adventurous little Sophie, not quite so adventurous with new foods. She knew berries could be poisonous just like the splayed orange and dark red mushrooms wildly sticking out everywhere on the forest floor.

Sophie observed the woods around her. It was quiet and peaceful, her feet making crackling sounds as she stepped on twigs and fallen branches. Her footsteps were the only sound for miles around. She used the tree trunks for support as she stepped gingerly from rock to rock. The trunks were so thick she couldn't put her arms around them entirely. There would have to be at least three Sophies to do that, she thought to herself. The thicker the trunk, the older the tree. She had read that in her nature book. It was a beautiful day. There wasn't a breeze blowing, but the ground was shaded and cool, rays of sunlight twinkling through the lofty tree branches. Sophie took a moment to delight in the dappling sunlight. But she didn't have all day, so she pressed on.

She was on an important mission. As she climbed the rocks along the path, she realized that the path was getting steeper and harder. She was panting now, her mouth dry. She came to a clearing in the woods and decided to rest a moment. She took a long cool sip of water from her bottle and consulted her map to make sure she had not strayed off the designated path. Yes, she was fine. She was a good map reader. She looked around her. The tree barks were getting thinner and the over head foliage was sparser now, allowing the sun to shine strongly through. She knew she was getting closer to the top. A few minutes later, Sophie got up and continued on her way.

Soon she came to a fork in the path. Which way now? She knew, having just consulted her map. She had to look for the path with rounded rocks. A dried up stream. Water had flowed over the same rocks for hundreds of years, rounding off their edges and dulling their sharpness before veering off to seek a new path of its own.

Sophie was on her way to a super secret meeting. A Super Secret Meeting of Super Heroes. Sophie was the one and only *Super Band Aid Girl*. She had been transformed into a super hero because she took care of those who needed her. If someone was hurt, Super Band Aid Girl was quick to the rescue, ready to give a hand up, apply ointments, wrap bandages and cover bruises with her Super Band Aids. And because she knew of its benefits from personal experience, Sophie would hand out Super Juice Boxes to the injured victims. Juice made everything better. Super Band Aid Girl Sophie knew that. She firmly believed in the powerful elixir of the Super Juice Box.

Sophie went about her average day, doling out band aids, bandages and juice boxes to all in need of her careful ministrations. She had been busy on her mission to save the world, one band aid at a time. Alonzo had observed her good deeds and had written to the Society of Super Heroes, extolling her virtuous deeds. He had secretly written his letter, so it came as a total surprise to Sophie, when Alonzo informed her that she, Super Band Aid Girl Sophie, had been invited to attend the next secret meeting of the Super Hero Society. Sophie had been ecstatic. She would get to meet other boys and girls who were super heroes just like her.

Alonzo would be going with her, of course. She had thought long and hard about who should accompany her to this important occasion. She had wanted to take Zackki along as well, but the invitation was for two persons only. Sophie reasoned that if it wasn't for Alonzo and his secret letter, she would not be going in the first place. So, it was decided that

Alonzo would accompany Sophie to the meeting. True faithful Alonzo. He had come to her aid a couple of years ago not too long after Papa Robbie had gone to heaven. She had been feeling sad and lonely and missed her grandpa. Mummy often said talking things over with a close friend helped in difficult situations. Sophie had friends in school, but no best friend. Alonzo had mysteriously appeared one day when she had needed him most. She never had to explain anything to Alonzo because he always knew how she was feeling. He was a great friend to her. What made him extra special was that he was invisible to the rest of the world, as though he had singled her out to be the only person who could see him. She talked to him and included him in all her adventures. He was always there when she needed him. He was always by her side. He was her best friend in the whole world.

Sophie had climbed to the top of the mountain. It had been a long and arduous climb. What might have proven to be too much of a challenge for most, Sophie knocked out with surprising agility, coming away with just a few scratches from the low lying shrubs. But then she was a Super hero. She could do it. Undoubtedly.
She was to attend the meeting in full Super Hero attire. Sophie looked down at her clothes. She was in need of a spruce up as the climb up the mountain had left its unwelcome mark. She dusted herself off and combed her fingers through her long dark brown pony tails. She critically surveyed the rest of her super hero attire. Her purple sparkly tunic had a little twig caught in its fibers which she pulled out slowly, careful not to fray the fabric. Her black Lycra tights and sneakers were a little dusty. Nothing a good stomping wouldn't get rid of. So she stomped her feet till little clouds of dust rose from her sneakers. She counted the band aids in her heart shaped silver pocket, centered on the chest of her purple tunic- *one, two, three, four, five, six, seven, eight, nine...* where was the tenth one? She had left home this morning with ten band aids, like she always did everyday. One had probably fallen out of her

pocket during the climb. Sophie shrugged. Nine band aids would just have to do. She quickly put on her shiny silver eye mask. She had taken it off earlier and placed in it her green backpack to avoid ruining it with her perspiration as she climbed the mountain. Also, she admitted, the sparkles were a little rough and scratchy around her eyes.

There was only one final item to check. Her Super Hero Cape. It was long, extending all the way down past her back, the hem ending mid thigh. It had been crafted from a silver fabric. It was shiny and sparkly and swished this way and that when she walked. It was attached to the purple sparkly tunic at the shoulders. Sophie didn't have to worry about the tie ends of the cape scratching her neck since this was not the kind of cape one tied around the neck. Thankfully, it wasn't. Her cape attached to her tunic with two pieces of velcro. Sophie loved her cape. She thought it was the best part of her costume, so she wore it proudly. She adjusted her backpack under her cape. One final flick of the voluminous shiny silver fabric sent the cape fluttering like a giant sparkling butterfly. A butterfly flapping its wings, making a breeze on the still and breezeless day. Sophie squared her shoulders back. She was ready for the meeting.

She had not far to go now. The map had said so. Alonzo who had parked himself on her shoulder as usual, stomped his feet impatiently.

"No time to tarry Super Band Aid Girl Sophie. Tardiness is frowned upon by the Super Hero Society!" he said.

"Oh, alright, Alonzo, I was just checking my costume," Sophie replied.

"I can't arrive at the meeting looking like a dusty old dish rag now, can I?" she added properly.

"No of course not, Sophie," returned a chastised Alonzo.

Still, they both realized the need to get to the meeting on time. Arriving late at anything was just plain bad manners. What a terrible first impression it would make! Sophie was doing her best to be well mannered. So, with Alonzo's tapping feet keeping time on her shoulder, they continued on to the secret meeting place.

Wait.

What was that sound?

Sophie stopped to listen. Silence.

There it was again!

Sophie turned around slowly.

"What is it?" asked Alonzo looking scared.

"Some kind of animal crying I think. It might be hurt. It's coming from down there," said Sophie pointing to the mountain below.

"*Aaaahhhhh*"

She was jolted awake. Rudely. Like a slap in the face.

She looked around her, disoriented and confused. The room slowly coming into focus as her eyes adjusted to the darkness. She could make out the shapes of familiar things in front of her – her toy chest not quite closed as Eddie, her stuffed caterpillar was sticking his tail end out the top, an armchair barely visible beneath a pile of hastily thrown pieces of clothing, a pair of sneakers that had been flicked off her feet the night before to land casually beside a lopsided doll in a lopsided rocking chair. As her eyes swept the room slowly, they came to rest on little Zack asleep in his bed. His steady and rhythmic breathing was a sure indication that he was soundly asleep.

That strange sound, did she imagine it? Probably. She couldn't hear anything now except for Zack's gentle snores. She stopped to listen. She definitely couldn't hear anything. All was quiet. And yet she felt something amiss. What was it that had suddenly roused her from her happy dream?

Silence.

Maybe she did imagine it after all.

"Figment of my imagination," thought Sophie (She had heard Uncle Josh say that to Auntie Amy before, though she had no idea what 'figment' meant. Something to do with a fig? Figs and imaginations? Maybe figs with imaginations? Could figs

have imaginations?) Anyway, it seemed appropriate to use it now. But she couldn't shake the figment away.
She could not shake the feeling that something was amiss. What could it be?
She sensed something was wrong. Very wrong.

Sophie tried to quiet her beating heart. She lay down again, forced her eyes shut and slowly counted to ten, just like her Nana Lynette had taught her – she took a deep breath and counted- one, two, three, four, fiv---
"Ahhhhhh"
There it was again!
Sophie bolted upright in her bed. She had not imagined it this time. It was real. Definitely real. Not a figment of her imagination after all.
"Ahhhhhhhh"
That sound again!
Louder this time, not so muffled. It was familiar yet not so familiar. It was a sound like she had never heard before. *And yet she knew that sound. That voice.*
That voice she would know anywhere.
That voice she loved.
That voice she had known even before she was born.
It was mummy's voice.
Her mummy was crying.
It was a strange sound. It was mummy for sure and yet it sounded different somehow. As though an animal had climbed inside of her and was screaming to be let out. A really growly sound. A growly sounding animal. In pain.
"Was mama hurt?" Sophie wondered. She swung her little brown legs to the side of the bed, her feet not quite touching the floor yet. She jumped off the bed hastily, her elbow making contact with an empty stainless steel milk tumbler on the bedside table. The cup crashed to the tiled floor making a clanging sound. Not too loud, but loud enough to wake Zack.
He raised his torso to look at his sister through sleep-filled eyes.

"Huh? What happened?" he asked groggily.

"Get up, Zackki. I just heard mummy crying. I think she hurt herself," said Sophie impatiently.

"Maybe she stubbed her toe," said Zack, yawning. "You know she can't really see her feet any more," he added matter-of-factly.

"Let's go see if she needs a band aid or something," Sophie added.

"Do you think there will be blood everywhere?" Zack asked, suddenly awake and very interested.

These days Zack was very interested in icky sticky substances like glue, body lotion, cream, toothpaste, ketchup, petroleum jelly, snot and of course, blood. Blood was at the top of his list because it was not as easy to come by as the other icky sticky stuff. He jumped out of his bed hurriedly and followed Sophie out of the room. He was very interested to know if his mother was bleeding. Maybe she would give him some blood for his collection.

The tiled floor felt cool to their little feet, bringing some respite from the sultry still air of the October night. As they walked down the hallway to their parent's bedroom, Sophie and Zack could here other voices. Muffled sounds. Grown ups trying to be quiet and not doing a very good job of it.

There it was again. Funny crying sounds.

Gut wrenching. Guttural.

More clear. More real. More terrifying.

Sophie's heart skipped a beat. Zack sensed something bad was happening, his interest in all things icky and sticky waning for the moment. She stretched out her hand and took her brother's little hand in hers. Zack squeezed her hand tight. Sophie squeezed back. Drawing comfort from each other, they walked on, unsure of what they would find at the end of the hallway. The hot October night was thick with dread. The hallway seemed longer than usual. It was exactly thirty-one steps to mummy's room and yet it took them forever to get there tonight, dread mounting by the second. They reached their parent's room. The door was slightly ajar. Sophie could see her mother sitting on the bed. Her shoulder length brownish black hair was in total disarray. Their mother was wearing her favorite dress that daddy had given her. She was wringing the hem of the dress between her hands. She was sobbing, making those strange animal sounds. Auntie Amy was by her side with her arm around her sobbing sister, tears flowing freely down her own face. Uncle Josh was sitting quietly in a nearby chair, looking uncomfortably at the two sobbing women. Sophie and Zack watched the scene in front of them unfolding, unobserved, from the other side of the slightly ajar bedroom door.

Sophie felt a chill enter her body. It seeped in through her toes and slowly permeated the rest of her body, insidiously weaving a chilly spiral to her heart. She stopped breathing. She stood very still, frightened now. Something was definitely wrong.

She knew it.

"Mummy does not look hurt. She has no booboos anywhere. No blood," Zack said frowning. He had studied his mother intently for a few seconds and come to his conclusion.

"Why is she crying like a big baby?" he whispered to Sophie. He couldn't make any sense of the scene in front of them.

Distracted by their whispers, Amy looked up and saw her niece and nephew at the door. They had been discovered. Sophie and Zack were feeling a twinge guilty for eavesdropping and shuffled their feet in shame, still holding onto each other. Uncle Josh rose from his chair and came toward the children. Up close, his eyes were red rimmed too, as though he had been crying for a while. Angela looked up too. She saw her precious babies, looking confused and bewildered, and drew them close. And then she did the strangest thing. She started crying even harder.

Zack took a closer look at his mother in case his previous scrutiny of her condition had missed something. Even up close she didn't look hurt. No blood or anything of that sort.

Definitely no blood, he noticed disappointedly. And yet mummy was crying. The tears were spilling down her face faster now. One tear bounced off a pearl button on mummy's dress and landed on her tummy where it quickly got absorbed into the cotton fabric, Zack observed detachedly.

Amid tears and broken sentences, Sophie and Zack were told that their daddy had been involved in an accident at work. A very serious accident.

He would not be coming home again.

The service was held the following Thursday afternoon. The year was 1993. Oppressive, stifling heat seemed to be the order of the day. Like every other day this month. October was shaping up to be yet another hot month. The month of May is technically regarded as the hottest month in Bombay, India. (It was still known as Bombay back then. The name changed to Mumbai in 1996.) The month of May is undisputedly the hottest month of the year, but October is close on its heels. Bombay could boast about the consistency of its weather patterns, except that the weather itself is nothing to boast about.

The year is divided into three seasons – Summer, Monsoon and Winter (or so the Meteorology books will have you believe.) But truth be told, it basically has two seasons – The summer season and the monsoon season. Its inhabitants face a monsoon season from June to September, characterized by torrential rain and subsequent flooding. The air is hot and humid during the monsoons as a result of the incessant downpours. December, January and part of February offer slightly cooler temperatures before sun rise and after sunset, the day itself being fairly warm though not unbearable. This period technically makes up the winter season mentioned in weather books. The remaining nine months of the year typically experience very high temperatures. Bombay in general is hot and humid as it lies along the coastline of the Arabian Sea and is subject to the salty, sticky air blowing in from the west.

The memorial service for Frank Machado was held in the afternoon on October 13th. Sophie was dressed in a hot black velvet dress with hot black patent leather shoes and hot black nylon socks. Sophie sat quietly trying not to fidget, only wiping the sweat trickling down her face when it was too much to bear. Zack was dressed in a hot black two piece suit with a stuffy white collared shirt with hot black leather shoes and hot black nylon socks. He was fidgeting. He was fidgeting with the stuffy white collar, sticking his fingers between his starched collar and his neck reddened by heat rash. He was yanking on the collar, trying to loosen it. He fidgeted and fidgeted.

So sticky. So humid.

So very hot.

A huge number of people had shown up to the memorial service at St. Andrew's Church. After the service they had followed the family to the huge hall next door to the church. Little groups of people stood around the large room engaged in conversation.

"Poor children. So small. To lose their father at such a young age," said Mrs. D'silva to no one in particular.

"And Angela, *bechare,* what is she going to do now? Two little kids and six months pregnant," joined in Mrs. Patel, shaking her head sadly.

"What about their house? Who will pay the maids? The house bills? The fancy schools? How will she manage financially?" said Mrs. Sharma, clucking her tongue.

"Maybe her sister Amy will help her out," chipped in Mrs. Patel.

"No, no. they are not doing so well," added Mrs. D'silva, knowingly. As though she had the inside scoop on the family.

"Really? How do you know?" asked Mrs. Sharma never one to miss out on anything.

"I know, because their son, Gavin told my son, Bradley that they couldn't send him to America for summer vacation this year," Mrs. D'silva said, lowering her voice.

"Oh, I see," replied Mrs. Sharma not sure what one thing had to do with the other. All the same, she listened intently to the other two women.

"Anyway, Frank was a pilot with Air India for so many years. They were quite well off. Maybe she doesn't need hand outs from anyone," continued Mrs. D'silva, now an authority on Angela and Frank's finances.

"Yes, they must have a decent nest egg stashed away, I'm sure. Lucky for Angela," said Mrs. Patel. She thought for a moment, and then said, "But still, Angela should think about getting married again."

"That is a good idea. I mean she is still young and not bad looking," piped in Mrs. Sharma.

"I'm sure she could find a widower or a divorcee. Somebody who won't mind that she has kids, you know," said Mrs. Patel unknowingly condescending.

"Actually, Angela will get a good settlement from Air India. After all, her husband died on the job," said Mrs. D'silva, now assuming to be an authority on Air India's policy for bereaving families.

"Oh, really?"

"You think so?"

"Do you know how much?"

Cruel, idle talk.
Evil, gossiping women.
Gossiping and paying their respects to the dead.

Sophie and Zack were seated on either side of their mother. She was crying as she accepted condolences from well wishers. Mama Machado was seated to the left of Zack. Stoic. Not a single tear in her eye. All four dressed in black. The blackest of black. Like four black ravens.

How did that superstition go?

One for sorrow, two for joy. What about four ravens?

Four for deepest darkest despair.

So many people. So many faces.
So many people pinching Sophie and Zack's cheeks. (Their way of consoling grieving children.)
So very annoying.

The line of well wishers seemed to go on forever. People were milling in and out of the room. Sophie didn't realize that her family knew so many people. She had never laid eyes on most of the people here. Some she did know. People who lived in their apartment building, on their street, those who went to their church and school. Like Mrs. D'silva, Mrs. Sharma and Mrs. Patel gossiping about her family at one end of the room.
But who were all these other people? So many people, so many faces. People streaming in and out of the room. People, faces, swimming people faces, people swimming faces, people, faces, so hot, so very hot.
Sophie fainted.
A commotion. People ran forward to help, glad to have something to do. Someone picked Sophie off the floor and carried her to a chair at the refreshment table. Someone got her a glass of water. Yet someone else splashed her face with the cold liquid. Sophie came to. She looked around her. One second ago she was at her mother's side across the room. How did she get here so fast? Sophie tried to get up, but Auntie Amy held her back.
"You fainted from the heat, Sophie," Auntie Amy explained to her bewildered niece, putting her arms around the little girl.
"Sit here awhile till you cool down. Have some lemonade, sweetheart. It will make you feel better," said Auntie Amy kindly, handing her a glass of the sweetened chilled liquid.
Sophie sipped her lemonade and looked around her.
There seemed to be a large gathering of people around the food table. The refreshment area had been set up for the well wishers. Cool drinks and snacks –*Limca*, Seven Up, Coke, *Thumbs Up,* Lemonade and *Frooti* mango juice packs sat in cooling vats of ice. *Samosas, Chicken Patties and Ribbon Sandwiches* were arranged on huge rectangular trays. Mirabai

kept refilling the trays, the contents of which seemed to be disappearing at an astonishing speed.

The refreshment area was crowded with cheek pinching well wishers. Sophie noticed one particular group of people, none of whom she recognized. They had dutifully stood in line to pay their respects to the grieving family and now their duty executed, felt entitled to the cool libations and tasty edibles being offered. Plates heaped with the offered refreshments, they made small talk about the weather, about the cricket test match India versus Australia, about the latest bollywood movie.

They munched on the delicious *samosas*, (fried triangles of dough stuffed with spicy potato) *the East Indian patties*, (flaky, buttery, rectangles of puff pastry filled with ground chicken and flavored with curry spices) and the *ribbon sandwhiches* – four slices of white bread, (crusts cut off) each separated from the others by way of three fillings – at the bottom, a green coriander-coconut chutney mixed with butter to make it creamy, in the middle, a cheese paste filling also mixed with butter to make it creamy, and finally on the top, an orange-ish brown meat paste. Also mixed with butter to make it creamy. Of course. *Amul Butter. The best butter in the world.* This mountain of bread and fillings was then cut in to smaller more manageable bite sized pieces.

Replete with snacks and cool drinks, the group in question continued with their small talk. Mindless chatter. Noise. Some of the well wishers were winding down the small talk, getting ready to make a hasty exit. They had done what they had set out to do. It was time to leave. Suddenly they observed new activity at the refreshment table. Dinner was being served. They decided to wait a little longer.

Mirabai laid out a stack of paper plates with paper napkins separating them. She placed them at one end of the table and laid out some trivets for the hot dishes. Tall plastic glasses held a collection of disposable forks and spoons neatly grouped together. She set up another tray with paper cups which she began filling with cool icy water from a big plastic jug. The water cups filled up, she placed huge platters of steaming food on the table. Mirabai went about her business, little knowing that several pairs of beady eyes were following her every move as she got the table ready. The table was finally set. The several pairs of beady, greedy eyes made their way to the food-laden table, all thoughts of departure dissipating entirely, their interest freshly renewed by the presented offerings. The *samosas, patties and ribbon sandwiches* were quickly relegated to the rank of appetizer, now that dinner was on the table.

Mutton Biryani with Raita.

From *Lucky Restaurant* near the *Bandra* train station.

The fragrance of the Biryani spices wafted through the air, tickling nostrils, stirring gastric juices and reviving salivary glands awake from their sonorous slumber. As the well wishers immersed themselves in the fragrant layers of basmati rice and richly marinated mutton (goat), topped with spoonfuls of cold *Raita* (yogurt sauce), their minds were totally absorbed in the moment. Oblivious to all else.

Poor dead Frank Machado forgotten.

Not even a distant blimp on their radar.

Sophie sat on her chair and listened to the conversations around her. She knew about the tradition of serving food to guests at a funeral. Her mother had explained it to her at Papa Robbie's funeral. In times gone by, refreshments were served to mourners who had traveled from far off locations. Sometimes they traveled for days on end, on bullock carts no less, to attend the funeral and were exhausted and tired from their journey. They would often spend a few days with the grieving family and rest before they made the same long bumpy journey back home. To Sophie, it made sense that they be provided with food and drink. But today, with modern means of transportation, people could get to where they were going in a matter of minutes in most cases. (Those traveling from out of town not withstanding.)

 Most of the people here were from *Bandra* itself or the neighboring suburbs, some even from the same street or same building they lived in.

Freeloaders.

Who *were* these people? Eating and drinking like tomorrow would never come.

Why were they here? Free food? Mindless small talk?

Did any of them even care about my daddy?

Sophie got up disgustedly and made her way back to Angela and Zack. Sitting at the refreshment table was only just slightly better than having her cheeks pinched. But mummy and Zackki needed her. They needed her to be strong. They needed her to care for their hurting hearts. Her place was with them. As theirs was with her. They only had each other now. Sophie looked up at mummy as she took her place beside her. Mummy smiled down at her. Her eyes full of love. Her eyes full of tears. Yes, mummy definitely needed her. Sophie smiled back and assumed her place beside her family, bravely offering her cheeks up to be pinched.

The line of well wishers was never ending.

"So sorry for your loss," cheek pinch, handshake, cheek pinch.

"If there is anything we can do," cheek pinch, embrace, cheek pinch.

"So sorry Angela, kids," cheek pinch, pinch.

"So sorry Mama Machado. Such a tough cross to bear," pinch, pinch.

"Sorry," pinch, pinch.

"Sorry for your loss," pinch, pinch.

"Sorry to hear about Frank," said Mrs. Patel. Pinch, pinch.

Idle talk.

"Call me if you need anything," said Mrs. Sharma. Pinch, pinch. *Cruel.*

"Oh Angela, I am so sorry," said Mrs. D'silva. Pinch, pinch. *Know it all, gossip.*

"Sorry,"
"Sorry sorry sorry sorry sorry sorry sorry sorry sorry sorry."

Sorry.
Such a silly sounding word.
It wasn't going to bring daddy back.

The line finally ended. The ordeal over.

Chapter 2

The Many Faces of Death

Sophie did not need Alonzo tonight.

The house was quiet. Only the immediate family members had returned to the house after the service, the well wishers long gone. It had been a long day and most of their extended family had retired for the night. Only those closest to Angela and her children had returned to the house. They sat around the living room, tired, spent. It had been a long day for everyone.

Nana Lynette had arrived from *Goa* earlier that day, rushing to Bombay on the first available train when she heard about Frank's death. She could not handle the bus trip from *Goa* to Bombay anymore. The bus ride had always been treacherous for as far back as Lynette could remember. The drivers were reckless as they swerved dangerously close to the edge of the narrow curved mountain roads, paying no mind to oncoming traffic that just as dangerously paid no mind to them. The new Volvo bus drivers were no different in their driving demeanor inspite of their specialized training. If anything, the ride seemed significantly more dangerous to the passenger, who now had an IMAX view through the panoramically widened front windshield as the possibility of death loomed perilously three dimensional.

Anyway, the train was faster, and Lynette wanted to get to Angela and the children as quickly as she could. She had packed hurriedly, throwing a few things into a suitcase and had left home. She was exhausted from the long trip up the *Konkan* coast to the city of Bombay. It had taken her a total of eleven hours to get here, nine hours of it, spent on the train. She was still wearing the dress she had traveled in. Lynette had only just made it in time, not having had the chance to change before the service. As she sat in Angela's living room now after the service, she slipped her shoes off her swollen feet, her only concession to comfort today. As if her sufferance would somehow lessen Angela's. Her heart was bleeding for her newly widowed daughter.

Amy's husband Josh was in an armchair, smoking quietly. He had released the top two buttons of his beige long sleeved shirt and rolled up his sleeves. He had taken off his black suit coat and hung it on the back of the armchair he was sitting in. Amy was seated on the sofa with Sophie squatted at her feet. Sophie had changed into an orange cotton sleeveless dress, glad to have replaced the black velvet one she had on earlier today. Amy dressed in a white chiffon *sari,* stroked Sophie's head, occasionally twirling strands of hair around her slim index finger.

Next to her on the sofa, in a simple black maternity dress, Angela sat crying softly. Zack had discarded his stuffy suit but had left on his white cotton undershirt and white cotton underpants. He was curled up in Angela's greatly diminished lap, his head resting lightly against her breast. Angela's unborn child sensing the somber mood outside its warm and cozy home, lay sleeping quietly.

Angela's mother-in-law Mama Machado, also clad in a black dress, was not crying. Still stoic. She stared ahead yet saw nothing. She was seated in an upright chair brought over from the dinning table. She couldn't sit on the sofa anymore. It sank too low, like a sink hole opening up and sucking her in, making it hard for her to get up and out of it. Each left to their own thoughts, they drew comfort from each other's presence, saying nothing. The room was silent except for the whirring sounds of the ceiling fan blades as they rotated at a frenzied speed, circulating cool air in to the hot and stuffy room.

Mirabai walked into the room, her slipper-less feet making no sound on the tiled floor. She placed a tray on the table. The tray contained several stacked ceramic cups and saucers, a spouted pot containing warmed milk, a sugar bowl and a pot steaming with tea. The bag-less tea leaves had been steeped in boiling water for a few minutes and then strained into the teapot, the aromatic liquid making its descent into the warmed pot leaving the spent tea leaves behind. Their purpose served, the tea leaves lay cold on the stove ready to be discarded. Two stainless steel tumblers of warm milk and a plate of snacks left over from the afternoon memorial service rested on the tray along with an unopened packet of *Parle glucose biscuits* (Indian cookies).

Mirabai poured the tea, mixed in the milk and sugar and handed out the *chai* in tea cups on saucers to the adults in the room. Sophie and Zack took the tumblers of milk from her. It had been a busy day, none of them having had the stomach to eat any thing earlier. The *ribbon sandwiches* and the reheated *samosas* and *chicken patties* left over from earlier that day were a welcome sight.

Mirabai unloaded her tray and left the room as quietly as she had entered it. It had been a long day for her too. She had been on feet all day serving the people at the funeral. She had been crying too, mourning the loss of Frank *baba*. She was done for the day now. The kitchen had been scrubbed clean, things had been washed and put away, and the family had been served. She had reheated the *Biryani* for their dinner and had left it warming in the oven. Nana Lynette had informed her earlier that she could retire for the night after she had served the tea. Mirabai put on the slippers she had left by the front door when she had come in earlier that day and left the house quietly. She would be back tomorrow to take care of the Machado family. She headed home now, to take care of her own.

"Mummy, what's a widower?" Zack asked suddenly, shattering the silence.

He had said ' wi – do –er', slowly and carefully. As though he had practiced it many times before actually saying it out loud. *He had.*

He had obviously overheard the gossiping ladies at the funeral service. It was an important question and he had wanted to make sure he got it right.

"Are you going to marry one?"

"Is a wi-do-er like a daddy?"

"Are we getting a new daddy?"

Hoping to influence his mother's decision against getting a new daddy, he added in a small voice,

"Coz I really like my old daddy."

Angela looked at her son. She took his little face in her hands and said,

"No Zachary. I am not marrying anyone and you are not getting a new daddy. You and Sophie and this little baby in my belly are all I have. All I need. All we need. Just the four of us. No matter what anyone says or whatever you may hear. I want you to know that."

Zack nodded. He understood.

"Do you think Jesus will send daddy back? I'll say extra prayers every night for two weeks," Zack promised, considering extra prayers a fair trade for the return of his daddy.

"No my love, I don't think that is possible. Jesus needs daddy by his side," Angela replied with a laden heart.

Zack was quiet for a few seconds. He nodded as if making up his mind about something.

"Well, I guess, I am the man of the house now," said Zack solemnly. As solemnly as a three year old can muster up solemnity.

"Yes, my son, you are now the man of the house," Angela replied, matching his solemnity, trying hard not to cry.

Her three year old boy who liked icky sticky stuff.

Mama Machado glanced over at her grandchildren. Adventurous little Sophie was so grown up and yet only seven years old. Frank had adored her. He had been very lenient with her, incapable of punishing his little girl. It was Angela who had had to be the firm disciplinarian in their family. She would really feel the void her father had left behind and would have a hard time coming to terms with his death. Sad little Sophie, her sad saturn eyes were in stark contrast to the brightness of the orange dress she had changed into after the memorial service. The radiant orange was the only splash of color in a room full of people in the somber colors of mourning. The bright cheerful hue somehow seemed to accentuate their grief. Instead of brightening their moods, it underscored their sadness, its warmth and cheer lost in the surrounding blackness of sorrow.

Mama Machado turned her gaze to Zachary, her precocious grandson snuggled in his mother's lap. She watched him dissect a ribbon sandwich, tasting a tiny bit of each filling on the tip of his tongue. He tasted the cheesy ribbon first followed by the meaty ribbon. They both passed his taste test. The green chutney ribbon did not fare so well. He scrunched up his nose at the chutney, wiping his tongue on the back of his hand. He probably thought it was too spicy, thought Mama Machado. He quickly devoured two thirds of the sandwich, leaving the chutney ribbon in the corner of his plate.

Zachary was a bundle of sweet innocence and quenchless curiosity. Just the other day, he had come to her, questioning her decision to put red *Kashmiri chillies* in the *Pork Sorpotel*. "It gives the curry a deep red color and tons of flavor," she had replied.

He had considered her answer thoughtfully and had offered an alternative.

"How about ketchup instead of red chillies?" he had quipped matter-of-factly.

"It would take care of both issues – color and flavor. This way, the curry won't be so spicy and I could eat it. A whole big bowl of it," he had laughed gleefully.

A child's logic. Simple. Hard to refute, difficult to explain. She had been making *Sorpotel* in the exact same way for more that seventy years. Along comes three year old Zachary Jason Machado to question age old tradition handed down from generation to generation. A treasured recipe, a well guarded secret, tossed aside nonchalantly in favor of ketchup! She smiled at the memory. Her mother and grandmother would probably roll over in their graves at such a notion.

Zack was always asking questions and offering solutions that made sense in his little world. Sometimes, they even made sense in the real world. Three years old. So young and so oblivious to the challenges that lay ahead of him. He was untarnished by the harsh realities of a cruel world. But he would not come away from this tragedy unscathed. Mama Machado knew that. The loss of a loving parent at such a tender age would surely manifest itself in time to come. It would rob him of his sweet innocence. She only hoped it would be later than sooner.

Right now, he seemed more interested in the food, helping himself to another ribbon sandwich. This time he licked off the cheese ribbon and then proceeded to do the same to the meat ribbon taking his time to savor the flavors. Once the fillings were gone, he quickly gobbled up the slices of bread he had just licked off, leaving the chutney ribbon discarded on his plate beside the previously discarded chutney ribbon.

Mama Machado knew what it felt like to lose someone she loved. She would do her best to protect Zachary and Sophia, but she knew life could be merciless sparing no one in its path of destruction. She too had heard those women gossiping this afternoon, planning Angela's future, her husband not yet cold in his grave. It had irritated Mama Machado to hear them making assumptions about Angela's needs. Determining her future for her, presumptuous in thinking Angela was incapable of making her own decisions. A brainless puppet whose strings they could pull, twisting adversity into cruelty to satisfy their own perversity. Human nature, always looking for something to chew on. A juicy tidbit to gnaw on. Thriving on her misfortune.

Ugly heads rearing. Yes, green ugly twin heads. *Jealousy and Envy.*

The need to dissect the remnants of her life. Swooping in for the kill.

Like the vultures at the *Parsi Tower of Silence,* waiting, watching, swooping in to decimate a carcass to shreds till there was nothing left to shred.

Looking at Angela still crying inconsolably, Mama Machado knew she had to help Angela get back on her feet. Frank would have expected that of her. Angela had been a good daughter-in-law, a loving mother to her children, and a devoted wife to Frank. Her son would have wanted her to take Angela into her fold, to help her.

She would, for Frank.

She would, because she would have done it anyway.

She would, mostly because Angela had brought out the best in Frank.

Yes, she would help Angela. She needed time to think about it, to come up with a sound plan. Angela was in shock now, but she would get out of it eventually. Life had to go on. She had three children who were depending on her. Angela had depended on Frank. But he was gone. She could depend on Mama Machado from now on. She would help Angela figure things out. But not now. Not here. Not today. She needed to concentrate on something else first.

Too many painful memories crowded her mind. Memories that she had shut out for years, never allowing them to see the light

of day. Never allowing her mind to open that rusty box sealed tightly shut. Over the years, she had distanced herself from those memories. It was the only way she could have survived. But in blocking out the memories, she had also blocked out her ability to feel. Her heart was numb to pain just as it was numb to joy. To her, it seemed like a small price to pay. Anything was better than experiencing that kind of pain. Now, she felt nothing. It was easier to bear, easier to deal with.
Her feeling heart had been replaced by a huge gaping void. A big black hole. Bottomless. Empty.

The numbness had slowly allowed her heart to heal over the years, to form scabs around the wounds, to mend. But today was different from other days. Today, those memories pounded at the door, not asking anymore, but demanding to be let out. She had resisted them for years, fending them off at every turn till they acquiesced to her determination. She had been victorious for so long. Since Frank's death two days ago, her memories had resurfaced stronger this time. For two days she had forced them to recede. But today was different. Today she had said goodbye to her son for the last time. Her memories surged forward, clamoring for her attention. Clamoring to be heard. To be freed from their prison. She was tired of fighting. She could not stave them off any longer. She gave in to them. Just this once.

Mama Machado was the only surviving Machado of her generation, her husband having passed away twenty-two years ago. Joe Machado had been one of six children. Three of his siblings had followed him to their graves in the years subsequent to his death. Two had passed away before he did. All their spouses were gone too. Mama Machado turned ninety- two years old this year and was the only survivor of her generation in the Machado family. She had been mother to nine children, eight girls and one boy. Five still alive, three dead – death by miscarriage, death by illness and now death by plane crash.

Mama Machado had survived three of her nine children.
No mother ever wishes to outlive her children.
Every mother prays to be the one to die first.
Mama Machado, like most mothers, had prayed for God to take her first, but God had not heard her prayers. He had taken three of her babies, cruelly allowing her to live.
She would have traded places with any of them.
In a heart beat.

The first – death by Miscarriage.
Amelia Fernandes married Joseph Machado when she was nineteen years old. He was thirty-two. At that time, it was an age difference nobody thought to be too wide. Her parents thought they had found their daughter a good, dependable husband with a secure future, wise in the ways of the world, someone who would nurture and pamper their beautiful little Amelia.
They were wrong.
His parents thought they had found their son a good, god-fearing wife, young and healthy to have his children, a pillar he could lean on.
They were right.
Two months after the wedding ceremony, she was informed that she might be pregnant. Every one else in the family seemed to think so anyway. She had been feeling a little sick but dismissed it lightly, thinking nothing of it. At nineteen, but a child herself, Amelia had not known what signs to look for, so the ladies in the family quickly enlightened her. Based on her newly acquired knowledge of the signs and symptoms of pregnancy, she thought she might be pregnant too.
Upon medical examination, her doctor pronounced her six and half weeks pregnant. Both baby and mother were doing well. Members on both sides of the family were very pleased, slapping each other on the back, and shaking each other's hands as though each of them had a personal hand in the outcome. Amelia was bewildered and frightened by the pregnancy and what lay ahead, not knowing what to expect.

She was overwhelmed by all the attention that came her way as a result of it. The ladies of *Ranwar* (the hamlet they lived in) took turns stopping by the house, bringing her sweets, milk, home made pickles, fresh juices, dried fruit and nuts. They knitted socks and crocheted blankets for the baby. They sang to her, rubbed her feet, answered her questions, allayed her fears, cast aside her doubts. She was cosseted in every way possible. A baby chick to their mother *hen- ery*. Under their ministrations, her confidence grew stronger, her anticipation of the birth of her first child greater. Her belly grew bigger every month, the baby inside of her kicking and moving. The bigger her belly grew, the happier she got. She swelled with pride, awed and astonished by the miracle of life she carried inside her.

She was in a happy bubble. Nothing could change that.

She felt invincible.

She had been seven months pregnant with Violet (they had baptized her just before they laid her to rest in the family grave at St. Andrew's cemetery. She had never thought she would bury her own child there.) Amelia, who much later came to be known as Mama Machado, had been visiting with her sister in *Borivili* and had been returning to *Bandra* on the 5:52 pm train. The train had just pulled into the station, the commuters disembarking at the platform. She had been at the top of the bridge and knew that if she wanted to make that train, she needed to hurry. It had been a super fast express train that would get her to *Bandra* in twenty-four minutes. If she wanted to get home to prepare Joes' dinner on time, she needed to get on that train.

 Amelia had quickened her step as she had begun to descend the flight of stairs leading to the platform. The heel of her shoe had caught in the metal stair nose. She had plummeted down the staircase, landing at the bottom, a pile of broken bones and gushing uterine blood, having lost her shoe, her consciousness and her baby.

Several days later, Amelia had come home from the hospital in a cast, shattered, a piece of her missing. Something had died inside of her that day. She had felt like she had been stabbed in the heart.

Life snatched from her womb.

Little Violet, who never had a chance to bloom.

The second – death by Illness.

Annabelle had been two years old. She had been a carefree, happy baby, like all babies are, till she got sick one day. She had been Amelia and Joe's fourth child. They had had three girls before her. Her sisters before her were, Violet (who had not made it to her birth. She would have been ten years old) eight year old Genevieve and four year old Allison.

Annabelle had charmed her way into everyone's hearts with her dimpled smiles, her mop of curly brown ringlets and her contagious giggles. She had resembled the little cherubs Michelangelo had painted on the ceiling of the Sistine Chapel, except that she had been a brown cherub with brown hair and brown eyes, as though Michelangelo's brush had painted over her in sepia tones. She had begun crawling at an early age and was walking by her tenth month. She would scurry by as fast as her chubby legs could carry her. Annabelle would spread her arms out for balance and walked with her legs spread apart, her chubby thighs and diapered behind getting in the way. A little waddling penguin with a human head.

Genevieve and Allison had played with her, dressed her, and arranged her hair in pretty ribbons as if she had been their little doll. She had enjoyed her sisters just as much as they had enjoyed her.

One day soon after her second birthday, she had become sick. The flu had been making the rounds, so Amelia had thought nothing of it initially. But her symptoms had been persistent. She had not been able to shake them. She had been listless and had been running a temperature, refusing to eat. She had been coughing incessantly too. Amelia had taken little Annabelle to see Dr. Shah on *Hill Road*. He had examined her and had run some tests. Diagnosis–Bacterial Meningitis.

There are two ways to get meningitis: by virus or by bacteria. Hence the terms - Viral Meningitis and Bacterial Meningitis. Viral meningitis, more commonly occurring, is easier to cure. Bacterial Meningitis on the other hand, is the more deadly of the two. If not treated in time, could result in brain and spinal damage even resulting in death.

The next few days had been a nightmare for the Machado family. Amelia had not left Annabelle's bedside. She had replaced cold compresses, changed wet clothing, stripped down bedding, fed her soup and had administered her medications while praying the entire time for her daughter's recovery. The illness had ravaged her body, her face pale, drawn and bloodless, her body, gaunt, thin and frail. Her fever would not subside, the antibiotics not working. They had laid Annabelle on a bed of ice blocks, but the fever stubbornly kept rising. Until, one day it could go no higher. Her tiny little body had caved in to a mightier entity. She had succumbed to her illness, Bacterial Meningitis emerging the victor. Annabelle had died that day. Amelia had died inside too. Stabbed in the heart again.
Annabelle. Meaning 'gracefully beautiful.'
Gracefully beautiful Annabelle. Not so cherubic anymore.

The third death – death by Plane Crash.
Frank. Frank had been her only boy, her only son. Frank, gentle natured, even tempered, loving, caring Frank. He had been her youngest child. After having had eight girls, Amelia had given up any hope of having a son. Infact she went so far as to think that she would not bear any more children after Rowena, who she had birthed at forty-two. Nine years later, she had discovered that she was pregnant with Frank. Amelia was fifty-one years old. She had already become a grandmother to Carl and Caroline (Genevieve's children) and

Stephanie (Allison's daughter), when she had become pregnant with Frank. Her final pregnancy had come as a total surprise to all in the family.

It had been a smooth, uneventful pregnancy and an equally smooth and uneventful delivery. Frank had come into the world three weeks before his due date. He had come very quickly, eager to get a head start on life. 'Frank' had not been the name she had had in mind for her son, but Joe had wanted to name him after his great grandfather. He had wanted no arguments. She had given him none. It was useless anyway. She had learned to pick her battles with Joe. That was how Frank had received his name.

Genevieve, by that time had migrated to Australia with her husband Bryce and their two children, Carl and Caroline. Allison and her husband Andrew and their daughter Stephanie had relocated to Singapore. Her four younger daughters – Bernadette, Jeanne, Bridget and Rowena still lived at home. Her girls had been a great help with little Frank. Amelia had learned to rely on her girls. She had trusted her girls. She had loved her girls. And they had all loved Frank. They had each loved Frank just a little more than they had loved the others. He had been their baby. He had belonged to them all. Frank had had an easy life. His sisters had been at his beck and call. They had doted on him and he had loved them for it.

A peaceful life. A violent death.

Surrendered to his watery grave.

Knife stabbed in her heart and twisted over and over again.

Where was that bottomless hole she had come to rely on? That hole that took her pain and her emotions and hurled them into nothingness so that she did not have to feel anymore? Why had the bottomless hole not claimed her?

She had been ready to die.

Ready to join her dead children.

Mama Machado slipped out of her trance. Dazed. The pain fresh, the wounds raw and bleeding, the scabs wrenched off their wounds. As though it had all happened just yesterday.

The pain plundered her heart, tearing at her soul. Mama Machado was feeling again. After sixty-three years of self imposed numbness, Mama Machado was feeling again. The efforts she had made after little Violet's death, to keep the pain at bay, useless now in the face of her own personal hell. Her barriers were no match for the tumultuous onslaught of her pent- up emotions. She could take no more. She was ninety-two years old. She had cried a lifetime of tears. She had thought she could cry no more, that she had no tears left. But she was wrong.

The tears came, like water surging out of a burst dam.

Today she finally cried.

But her tears were tears of blood.

Angela had been very worried about Mama Machado. She had accepted the news of Frank's passing with deathly calm, but Angela alone had seen the light go out of her old myopic eyes. Since then, she had gone about the day like nothing had changed. She attended the memorial service and was gracious to all, not a tear in her eye. And yet Angela knew how much Frank had meant to his mother. He was her life line, her reason for living. When she saw Mama Machado finally give in into her catastrophic loss, she breathed a sigh. Mama Machado needed to let it all out. She needed to cry, to grieve. Everything would be okay. Eventually.

Angela went over to Mama Machado's chair and stood in front of her. She put her arms around her weeping mother-in-law and cradled her frail, aged head in her breast, like she had done with Zack just moments ago. Mama Machado raised her arms and locked them behind Angela's waist, resting heavily on Angela. Their roles were reversed temporarily. Mama Machado, who for most of her life had been the pillar of support most people leaned on, was now leaning on Angela, her young daughter-in-law. Angela, who had been protected and sheltered all her life, was now the rock Mama Machado was leaning on. They stood there for a long time soothing each other, rocking gently back and forth, crying together, holding

onto each other, mourning the loss of a man they both had
loved so differently and yet so deeply.

Amy got Sophie and Zack ready for bed. They had drunk their
bed time milk earlier in the living room. They changed into
pajamas, his green with blue and white stripes, hers yellow
with purple stars on it. Daddy had bought them on a previous
trip to Bangkok. They brushed their teeth and rinsed their
mouths. Potty was the last thing to do before bed. She went
first, sitting down demurely. Then it was his turn. Zack faced
the pot and aimed his stream into the center of the pot. Zack
concentrated on his task. Daddy had shown him how to keep
the pot clean, how not to sway this way and that. He was
careful not to wet the toilet seat. After he was done, he
inspected the rim of the pot. Clean. Zack smiled. Daddy would
be so proud of him.

Amy tucked them into bed. She hugged and kissed her sister's
children. They loved their Auntie Amy. She was almost as
good as mummy. Mummy came first of course, but Auntie
Amy was a close second. She always knew what to do to make
them feel better. Amy dimmed the lights and settled into the
only armchair in the room, moving aside the pile of clothes
resting on its arm. She planned to sit with them till sleep came.
But they were restless and cranky and would not settle down.
They wanted their mother.

Mama Machado had calmed down after her torrential outburst
and Josh had taken her home. Angela had retired to her
bedroom, not really wanting to be there but drawn to the room
at the same time. She felt closer to Frank in this room more so
than any other room in the house and yet there were too many
memories to haunt her. She was restless too. Amy poked her
head in the door and said to Angela,

"Zack and Sophie cannot sleep. They need you Angela. Do
you think you can handle it right now? Or would you prefer to
be alone?"

"It's okay. Amy. I need them too. Let them come to me," she
relented.

Sophie and Zack had been hanging onto Amy's *sari* out of sight behind the door. But the moment they heard their mother consenting, they wasted no time in climbing into the big bed, lest she change her mind. Sleeping in the big bed cuddled up to mummy and snug under the sheets was the best thing ever, Zack and Sophie thought. Angela lay in the middle with Zack and Sophie on either side of her, one arm around each child. Sophie snuggled into Angela. Zack did the same on the other side, burrowing his head into the side of her ribcage. They were with mummy tonight. Mummy was so soft and so warm. She smelled of Oil of Olay soap and Fa deodorant. The perfect mummy smell.

That is why Sophie definitely did not need Alonzo tonight.

Chapter 3

The Aftermath

The children were tired and soon drifted off to sleep. Angela was tired too. It had been a long day, but sleep would not come. She thought about her babies asleep beside her and about the baby kicking in her womb. How was she going to take care of them? Frank was so good with the kids. Frank *had been* so good with the kids, Angela painfully amended. He had patiently answered Zack's never ending questions, so generously tolerant of Sophie imaginative meanderings.
Widowed at thirty- two.
Widowed and pregnant.
Never worked a day in her life. How was she going to feed them?
So alone.
Angela cried. She couldn't think clearly since she had heard about Frank's plane crash. There was so much to do, so much going on....Over the past two days, she had walked about in a daze most of the time. She walked from room to room, touching things here and there, lost in her world of pain. It seemed as though she had left her own body and was living

someone else's life. Living outside her body. The only thing that grounded her experience and forced her to acknowledge it, was the excruciating pain. She was so tired but she could not sleep. Only tears. Her eyes were red and swollen, but the tears kept on coming.
River of tears.

Frank Machado's body was never found.
He had been a pilot with India's leading airline for nine years. Air India had employed him a few years after he had graduated from flight school and he had never felt the urge to leave. He was dedicated to the job and never regretted his choice to stay with the nation's foremost airline instead of opting for a higher paying job overseas. The job came with its innumerable perks, but what cinched it for Frank, was that he could stay in Bombay and raise his family. He could have the life he was used to and still have a well paying job. Not such an easy feat in Bombay, when Frank had to choose his career path in the 80's.

Frank left home on October 10th for the last time. He had a scheduled short haul flight to Bahrain and Dubai, with a layover in Dubai for one night. He would return home the following evening.
BOM- BAH-DXB-BOM
He had flown this route many times before. Quick. Easy. Nothing to it.
Sophie was in school the day he left. Zack was playing with his friend, Ritesh from next door. Angela had helped him pack an overnight case for the layover in Dubai. Frank had kissed Angela and Zack and left home that October afternoon. His world had seemed as right as rain.
The flight took off as scheduled and everything went as planned. He stayed over in Dubai for one night. He had a few hours to shop for Angela, Sophie, Zack and for their unborn child. The next day, they took off just as scheduled. Everything was working like clock work. Frank was a

methodical man and was pleased that everything was moving along like a well oiled machine. He was looking forward to a nice dinner with Angela and the kids. She always made something special for dinner when he returned home after an over night flight. Dinner on such occasions was usually a surprise, so it made it all the more interesting.

Frank thought about his children. Sophie and Zack would squeal with delight at their new toys. Angela would love her new dress with its matching high heeled shoes. He bought lots of beautiful things for his family because he could, but he did it more because he loved to see their faces light up at the things that he had lovingly picked out for them. He was glad that he had a job that could provide a few luxuries for his family.

Frank had been thinking of his family. He had been happy in his last few moments before all hell broke loose. On the last leg of the flight, approximately thirty minutes before landing into *Sahar International Airport* in Bombay, they experienced engine trouble. The airplane was over the Arabian Sea, when a flock of seagulls flew directly into the aircraft's engines.

Frank had taken the aircraft to a lower altitude in readiness to start his descent into Bombay airport. Suddenly out of nowhere, (or so it seemed) a flock of birds slammed into the aircraft, some splattered on the wind shield of the cockpit, their guts and bloody feathers smearing the glass, obscuring the view of the cockpit crew. Others were destined for greater disaster as they were sucked in by the powerful engines. Frank was jolted out of his pleasant reverie. He and his co pilot did everything they could, applied every emergency procedure in the book, but it was of no use. There was not enough time.

According to experts, in such a situation, the force of the impact is dependent on three things: the weight of the animal, the speed difference and the direction of impact. A low speed impact of a small bird on a car windshield causes relatively little damage. On the other hand, a high speed impact as in the case of Frank's jet aircraft can and did cause considerable damage to the aircraft. The impact of a 12 lb/ 5 kg bird at the speed of 150mph/240kmph equals that of a half ton (1000 lbs) weight dropped from a height of 10 ft/3meters.

When the sea gulls flew into the engines, (known as *Jet Engine Ingestion* in aviation terminology) they caused serious damage to the rotation speed of the engine fan. It caused a *Catastrophic Failure,* a sudden and total failure of systems from which recovery was impossible. The Catastrophic failure resulted in a *Cascading Systems Failure.* As the sea gull struck a fan blade, that blade displaced into another blade which in turn displaced into another and so forth, causing a cascading failure.

It is a failure in a system of interconnected parts, where the service provided is dependent on the operation of its preceding part and the failure of its successive parts. This type of failure, common in power grids, occurs when one of the elements fails completely or partially and it shifts its load to a near by element in the system. Those near by elements then become overloaded and shift their load to other elements. Cascading failure is a common effect seen in high voltage systems, where a single point of failure on a fully loaded or slightly over loaded system results in a sudden spike across all nodes in the system. This surge of current can induce the already overloaded nodes into failure, setting off more overloads, thereby taking down the entire system in a very short time.

Captain Frank Machado, his co-pilot, fourteen cabin crew and 294 passengers crashed into the Arabian Sea, just a few minutes away from home.
The humungous man- made bird was no match for a small flock of God- made birds.
Massive search and rescue efforts were organized. Most of the bodies were recovered among floating pieces of airplane debris and dead fish.
Captain Frank Machado's body was never found.

It was 7:43 pm Indian Standard Time.
October 11th, 1993
He was 41 years old.

Officials from Air India arrived at the Machado residence two
and a half hours later to deliver the news.
"Sorry to inform you Mrs. Machado, but Captain Frank
Machado's plane crashed…"
News that brought their world crashing down.
They could not arrange a funeral and subsequent burial service
as there was no body to bury. Instead, a memorial service was
held two days later.

The first two weeks after Frank's death, passed by in a daze
for Angela, Sophie and Zack. Family and friends poured in
from everywhere, the phone rang incessantly. There were the
arrangements to be made, church and legal documents to be
signed. There was no death certificate as Frank's body was
never found. He was deemed 'missing'. Indian law dictated a
seven year waiting period following which he would be
declared legally dead.
They had family visiting from everywhere. All the Machado
children made it to the funeral. Genevieve and Jeanne flew in
from Australia for a week and had stayed with Bridget in
Santacruz, a few miles to the north of Bandra. Allison came
down from Singapore for two days only as she had no days of
leave to spare, having been to Bombay on vacation less than
two months before. Bernadette arrived from Kuwait for a day.
She had to rush back as her husband was leaving on a business
trip and the kids were in school. Rowena came from
Mazagoan, in south Bombay.
On Angela's side of the family, Amy was with her the entire
time. Like Angela, Amy lived in Bandra too, on St. Paul's
Road, not too far from Angela's home. Their brother, Alastair
arrived from Canada the night before the service. He stayed

with his in- laws in *Mahim*, one train stop away from Bandra. Their other brother, Adrian, from New Jersey could not make it. His wife Shayna was in labor and expected to give birth to their third child very soon.

The first two weeks after Frank's death were busy for everyone. Family members had stayed and helped out in any way they could. Well meaning friends and neighbors dropped off all types of food preparations for Angela and her children. They had received so much, that even after she had sent Amy and Mirabai home with food packages of varying sizes, she still has enough to feed her family for a week. Angela asked Mirabai to freeze the food in smaller meal size portions. Angela was grateful for their thoughtfulness. Even the simple act of cooking seemed like such a chore these days.

Eventually life returned to normal. Everyone had returned to their normal routines. Mama Machado's home was just a stone's throw away in *Ranwar*. Just knowing she was close by was a huge consolation to Angela. Nana Lynette was staying with Angela for a while, before she too had to return to Goa. She had initially planned to come up to Bombay a few weeks before the baby was due, to help Angela with the new baby. But her plans had changed with Frank's death. She had come up to Bombay three months earlier than planned. She would not leave Angela in this frail state, so she had decided to stay a few months, till Angela was back on her feet after the baby was born. Amy, of course was right around the corner. With everyone else gone, the house seemed empty. If the first two weeks had been tough on Angela and the kids, the toughest was yet to come.

Learning to live without Frank.

Little things reminded them of the man they all loved. A book here, a song there, the sports section of the Times of India newspaper, the tea cup he used, his favorite meal. Time heals all wounds, they say (*Who is they?*). Amy and Josh stopped by everyday, doing what they could, helping in anyway possible, dropping Sophie off to school or driving Angela to the doctor, running errands, stocking groceries. The baby was due in less than three months and Angela was tired all the time. Her mind was vague and unfocused. So, Amy and Josh pitched in whenever they could.

Mama Machado stopped by their home often. She couldn't make it everyday. Her old bones would not allow it. She had asked Angela, Sophia and Zachary to live with her for a few months, at least till the baby's birth, but Angela had refused, wanting to stay in her own home. It made her feel closer to Frank, to be around his things all the time, to be in the home that they had shared together. Angela spent sleepless nights, worrying, crying, thinking, hurting. She slept with the lights on at night. It was easier that way. The doctor prescribed sedatives to help her sleep, but she didn't take them. They could harm the baby.

Her baby. *Their* baby.

Her last link to Frank.

His final gift to her.

She was fiercely possessive.

The kids were asleep and Amy and Josh had returned to their home on St. Paul's Road. Mirabai had left for the day and Nana Lynette had turned in for the night.

Angela showered and changed into an old comfortable night gown. From under her pillow she pulled out the shirt Frank had worn on his last day home. She had meant to wash it that day, but had not got around to it. Now, she was glad she hadn't. Every night, she held that shirt, burying her face in the folds of the soft fabric, breathing Frank in. She lay down on her bed and closed her eyes willing herself to sleep, to transport her into dreamless oblivion. But sleep would not come. What came to visit instead were her nightly fears. Her thoughts took over...

Frank, my love, where are you? Can you hear me? Can you see me? What's it like being on the other side? Is heaven as beautiful as they say? Are you happy there? I have so many questions for you, Frank. Are you going to answer me? You left us so suddenly. I have so many things I want to say to you. We didn't even have a chance to say good bye.

The kids really miss you. Sophie is back in school now, but she is distracted, she doesn't do her homework. Sometimes when she isn't looking, I catch her starring sightlessly, like she is lost in some far away place. She talks more than before to her imaginary friend, Alonzo. I thought about keeping her home from school for a few more days, but I think the sooner she gets back into her routine, the easier it will be for her to adjust. I wish you were here to help me with her. You always knew what to do...

And little Zack considers himself the man of the house now. So much responsibility for his wee little shoulders. But he seems to be taking his role seriously. I often find him looking at me out of the corner of his eye. He doesn't know that I can see him checking up on me, making sure I have eaten, that I am not crying. I try very hard to appear happy when he is around, even though all I really want to do is curl up in a ball and die. He was so worried that he was going to get a new daddy. But I assured him that would never happen. How could anybody replace you in our lives? You were everything to us. Everything to me, my darling.

Everyone has left. They have all returned to their lives and to their families. But our family still waits for you. Wherever you are Frank, I hope that you are happy. We had a wonderful life together and now that you are gone, I don't know what to do. I don't know how to go on. Who will fill the void you have left behind? It is only now that I realize how dependent I was on you. You took care of me, of the kids in every possible way. I feel so helpless now. I am always second guessing every decision I make, wondering what you would do if you were me. I didn't realize how hard it would be.

I walk around with so much pain all the time. I expected to be mentally devastated, but the pain somehow feels so physical, so visceral. It almost seems like I have one less limb or one less organ. Like its there, but I can't feel it and my body does not know how to deal with the loss.

Thoughts of you in those last few deadly minutes inundate my mind. I keep wondering what it must have been like for you. What your thoughts were before disaster struck? Were you thinking of us? Of me? Did you have happy thoughts? And when all hell broke loose, did you have time to think about what you were going to do to save yourselves? When did you come to the realization that you were going to die? That you were going to crash and drown in the cold dark waters below? That must have been such a terrifying moment for you, my darling. I should've been with you. We were in this together for better or for worse. I should have been by your side. I should have died with you. Then we could have been together forever, even in death.

Did you have a chance to make peace with the Lord, to atone for your sins? Were you even thinking about yourself in those last few minutes? I cannot imagine what must've been going through your mind. It tears me apart to think that you were scared for yourself and for all those other people on the plane. I can only wish that you did not have even a spare second to be terrified, that it all happened very quickly, that you suffered no pain or fear.

Frank, can you hear me? I miss you so much, my love...

Oh Frank, how am I to go on without you? And what about our unborn child? I can feel our baby growing stronger inside me everyday. Our baby who will never know you, never know your adoring love. You will never hold our child and never have a chance to show our baby your love. How am I going to be mother and father to our children? I don't have your patience and your understanding.

I am so frightened, Frank. So scared of what lies ahead of me. Scared that I have to do it all alone. Scared that you will not be by my side. What am I to do? Who will I turn to in times of need? Whose shoulder will I cry on? Who will wipe away my tears? Who will caress me and hold me in his arms? Who should I turn to when my body yearns for you? What should I

*do? Am I destined to melt into a roiling heap, unsated,
unsatisfied? Grow into a bitter old crone who once briefly
knew love? Am I going to be lonely forever? Who is going to
love me? Am I never going to feel your body lying next to mine,
to feel your warm body throbbing next to mine? To smell you?
To touch you? To taste you? To love you? Frank, oh Frank...I
can't go on without you. Why did I not die with you? Why did I
not die instead of you? You left me Frank. It's not fair. You
died and left me alone! Frank, my love, my life, I am so alone,
so lost without you......*
I long for you, I yearn for you,
Touch me Frank...I miss you so much...
Frank, Frank, my love, can you hear me?
Frank, I need you, I want you...
My love, I need to feel you inside me...
Oh, Frank! Can you hear me?
Frank, Frank, why do you not answer me?

Yesterday marked the second anniversary of Frank Machado's
death. Sophie and Zack proved to be true examples of
childhood resilience in the face of tragedy. They were able to
bounce back and lead normal lives – school, homework, sports,
sleepovers, picnics, pillow fights, spit ball fights, every day
fights.
Angela did her best to make life normal for her three children.
They were busy with school and work during the day. Their
days were hectic and packed with activities. They were
constantly going until every ounce of energy in their battery
cells was fully expended. And then they would fall asleep
soundly. Deep sound sleep. Angela envied them their
resilience, their sound sleep.
Angela put them to bed like she did every night. She read
them stories, sang lullabies, said their night prayers with them
and tucked them snugly under the covers. She walked her
weary body over to her bathroom for a long hot shower before
climbing into her own bed. She was tired, but sleep never

came easily anymore. It was then that Angela's worst fears would return. The darkness of night brought back the pain, more a dull ache now than the searing pain she had felt with Frank's immediate passing. The pain accompanied by loneliness was always hovering on the fringes of her mind, waiting for the slightest opportunity to slink in. Like a thief in the night.

Angela still sleeps with the lights on. They have been on every night for the past two years. Sophie, Zack and the baby are used to the lights now. Sleeping with the lights on at night is more the norm, than the exception. The neighbors see their lights on. They are used to it too. They think nothing of it.
The lights are on, not because she is afraid of the dark.
The lights stay on.
Because Angela is waiting for Frank to come home.
Frank, whose body was never found.

Chapter 4

The Power of Potato Chops

"Mummy why is your bed wet?"

"Mummy?"

"Wake up mummy!"

Angela woke up. Sophie and Zack were standing by her bed. They had come to her room together tonight like they had done every night since Frank's passing. Sometimes it would be Sophie, but most often it would be Zack who would wake up during the course of the night, drag the other out of bed and make their way to Angela's room. They always came in together, like they did everything else together these days. Since their father's death, Sophie and Zack stuck to each other like glue. Joined at the hip. Two peas in the same pod. They played together all the time, which hadn't been the case before at all.

In the pre Frank's death days, Zack would knock down Sophie's painstakingly built bridges or towers of building blocks in one fell swoop or he would scribble in her carefully maintained nature journal or he would tease her or pull her hair and run away as fast as his little legs could carry him. They would both cry. She the victim and milking it for whatever it was worth, he the aggressor who knew punishment would be meted out. In such cases (as was more the norm than the exception), they were made to play separately. Peace and quiet would be restored temporarily till the ants in Zack's pants urged him to aggravate his sister again.

Not so anymore. Their dynamic had changed drastically. Now, they played together all the time, hardly ever fighting. Sophie would not leave the room with out her brother and Zack would not stay in a room unless his sister was there too. They had formed a little team that did everything together, each dependent on the other. They had formed a symbiotic relationship, each benefiting from the other's existence, much like the honey guide bird and the honey badger of Africa.

Both animals love honey and yet each seems to face hardships in acquiring some. The bird can find a beehive, but can't open it. The honey badger can open a hive, but doesn't know how to find one. So they work together to achieve their goal. The bird flies above the grasslands and noisily alerts the honey badger when it locates a honey comb. The honey badger in turn, tears open the hive with its sharp claws. In the end both bird and badger feast on the honey. It is a relationship that benefits both partners.

Angela had inadvertently overheard her children talking one day. Zack and Sophie had been playing in their room while Angela had been tidying up in the room adjacent to theirs. She had heard them talking.

"Sophie, do you think mummy will die too?" Zack asked his sister.

"You mean like how daddy died?" Sophie asked in return.

"Uh, huh," he nodded.

"I don't know Zackki. I don't think she would die in a plane crash like daddy did 'coz she doesn't work on a plane or anything. But she could die some other way, I suppose," Sophie replied, giving his question serious consideration.

"She said she was going to die," Zack interjected emphatically.

"Kind of…what she said was that if anything ever happened to her, then we should stick together, take care of each other. It's not the same thing," said Sophie.

"I don't want her to die," said Zack in a small voice.

"I don't want her to die either," returned Sophie.

"Yeah 'coz if she dies, then who will take care of us?" said Zack, ever pragmatic.

"I don't know. Auntie Amy and Uncle Josh I suppose," returned Sophie, chewing on her lower lip.

"I would miss mummy a lot," said Zack.

"I would too if she were to die and leave us," said Sophie.

"I don't want to be alone," he replied.

"Me neither," she seconded.

"What would we do then?" he asked worriedly.

"We won't be alone Zackki, 'coz we have each other," she soothed her little brother.

"Always?" he questioned.

"Always," she assured him.

"Okay, but just be sure, we should promise to be together forever," he countered.

"Okay let's promise," agreed Sophie, turning to face him.

"I promise, cross my heart and hope to die, to be with Sophie forever," said Zack solemnly looking up at the ceiling. He entwined Sophie's little finger on her right hand with his own after crossing his chest.

"I promise to be with Zackki forever," echoed Sophie, also looking upward, as though searching for confirmation that their promise had been heard by a higher power. She curled her little finger tighter around Zack's.

"Say cross my heart. You have to say it or it won't work," urged Zack.

"Cross my heart and hope to die," Sophie replied obediently, crossing her chest.

"Now that we've promised, we should be safe, right?" asked Zack uncertainly.

"Yes, I think so. I definitely think so," said Sophie strongly.

"That's good," breathed Zack heavily as though a weight had been lifted from his shoulders.

"Yup, it's good," said Sophie.

"Daddy should have promised too. He died 'coz he didn't promise. He went away from us and he was alone and *that's* why he died," said Zack emphatically, implicitly believing his words to be true.

"Yeah, he should have promised. Then he would be here and we wouldn't be so sad all the time," said Sophie.

"I don't like feeling sad," Zack said.

"It feels funny, like weird or something," she agreed.

"Yeah, weird," he repeated, sadness being too complex an emotion for his three year old brain to fully comprehend.

The truth of it was that they were afraid they would lose each other. Angela realized their insecurity, so she had allowed them to have their little team. It was their way of coping with their father's death. She had cried that day, listening to her little innocent children. She would talk to them about it in a few days, but for the time being she had let them be, not wanting to intrude on their private moment. She had waited a few minutes and then left the room quietly, not wanting to alert them to her presence.

It was the little bird and badger team that was now standing over her. Zack had climbed into her bed and had snuggled up to her, but he had quickly un-snuggled and climbed out when he had realized it was wet. He found a towel on a chair and was vigorously rubbing himself down.

"What is it? Sophie? Zack?" Angela asked as she raised her torso from its supine inclination on the mattress.

"What happened? Is everything okay?" she asked, rubbing the sleep from her eyes.

"Mama did you wet the bed?" Zack asked his mother in the gently reproachful tone she usually reserved for his occasional bed wetting incidents.

"What?" said Angela, feeling the bed sheet with her finger tips. Her skin came away wet and warm. She looked down and saw the dark stain on the beige sheet. Her water sac had just broken. She was going to have her baby.

"Zack, go wake Nana Lynette and Uncle Adrian," said Angela, all traces of sleep gone from her mind. She looked into the drawer of her bedside table and fished out a phone book.

"Sophie love, get me the 'phone. I have to call the doctor," she said.

"What's happening mummy?" Sophie asked, picking up on the urgency in Angela's voice.

"Your baby brother or sister is going to be here soon," she answered.

"Hurry, get the 'phone."

Zack left the room to rouse Nana Lynette while Sophie ran to do as her mother asked. Angela called Dr. Rodrigues, her obstetrician and explained her situation. While she was on the phone with her, Lynette had walked into the room soon followed by Adrian. She caught the general gist of the conversation and quickly took charge of the situation. Angela needed to hear what the doctor was saying to her, but the kids were being much too noisy. Adrian stayed with Angela while Lynette took Sophie and Zack by the hand and ushered them towards the kitchen. She poured each a glass of milk and set down in front of them a plate with *Good Day* cashew nut biscuits (cookies). Zack munched happily on his cookie, liking the idea of a night time snack. They should do this every day, he thought.

"Can we do this everyday, Nana?" he asked voicing his thoughts.

"Do what?" she answered his question with one of her own, her mind busy with thoughts of Angela and the baby.

"Have milk and cookies everyday in the night," he said.

"That doesn't make any sense Zackki," Sophie interjected. "You *may* have cookies and milk *every day* or *every night*, but you *may not* have them *'everyday in the night'*."

"Huh?" Zack said confoundedly.

"Your sentence, Zackki. That was incorrect English," she explained slowly.

"Oh. Can we still have them every day but only in the night," said Zack attempt to correct his English.

"Zackki, its still wrong," said Sophie emphatically.

"What's wrong about it?" he challenged.

Sophie looked to her Nana for help. Lynette added, "Sophie is right, Zack. You must use *'may'* when you need to ask permission to do something. For example, *'may* I go out to play' or *'may* I have an apple'. You use 'can' to show that you are able to do something. For example, 'I *can* fly a kite' or 'I *can* sing that song.' Do you understand me?"

"Uh… sort of," said Zackki, not sure he quite understood his Nana's explanation.

"Zackki, *'may* we have cookies and milk every day' or *'may* we have cookies and milk every night'," Sophie corrected.

"Okay, okay," he replied exasperatedly.

"Nana *may* we have milk and cookies every night?" he asked Lynette, mocking his older sister.

"You both should be in bed asleep at this time, not thinking about milk and cookies," Lynette replied.

"Okay, then why are you giving us milk and cookies tonight?" questioned Zack.

"Tonight is a special night, that's why," answered Lynette.

"What's so special about tonight?" he persisted.

"Mummy says our baby brother or sister will be born tonight," answered Sophie for her grandmother.

Angela entered the kitchen. She had changed into street clothes and had on her shoes. She carried a large bag with her. Sophie and Zack looked at her in surprise.

"Where are you going mummy? I thought you were going to pop out our baby," said Zack.

"Pop out? Good gracious child! You say the funniest things!" said Lynette incredulously.

"Well, I heard Auntie Rowena telling Auntie Jeanne that when she had Kevin, he just popped right out, no trouble at all. So Nana say what you want, but babies *do* pop out," Zack said indignantly.

"Babies don't pop out like toast out of a toaster oven, Zackki. You have to '*deliver*' a baby," added Sophie, wise for her seven years.

"Yes, honey. I am going to deliver our baby, but I need to get to the hospital so that Dr. Rodrigues can help me get the baby out," Angela replied.

Lynette looked worried. She said, "Did you call Amy and Josh? They can take you to the hospital."

"Adrian's on the 'phone with them right now. I'm sure they will be here in a few minutes," Angela said, trying to put her mother at ease.

"In the meantime, I think you should lie down. It will slow things down a bit," said Lynette wisely.

"I think it will be best if I do that," agreed Angela walking back to her bedroom.

"Sophie, Zack, I need you both to be very good now, you hear? I am going to get changed so that I can go to the hospital with mummy. Auntie Amy will stay back with you. Will you be good children?" Nana Lynette asked.

Sophie and Zack nodded, both sensing the gravity of the situation.

Amy and Josh arrived shortly thereafter. Adrian and Josh carefully walked, half carried Angela to the car. They laid her horizontally across the back row seats. Lynette sat with her daughter in the back of the car, cradling Angela's head in her lap. Adrian sat up front with his brother-in-law while Amy stayed back to be with Sophie and Zack.

Angela's doctor had been worried about her condition, worried for the baby and for its mother, worried that the baby would not make it to full term. Angela had refused medication to calm her shattered nerves for the last three months. She had not been sleeping well or eating well. Somehow she had made it to the end of her pregnancy. Angela was two weeks shy of her due date, but at least the baby was full term.

Dr. Rodrigues was thankful for that. Hopefully the delivery would be quick and easy for Angela. She was ready for her patient when they arrived at the hospital. Josh dropped them off at the entrance to the hospital and went on to park the car. Adrian registered Angela at the hospital reception while Nana Lynette and a nurse on duty assisted Angela in preparation for the baby's birth. They hooked her up to two machines, one to monitor her and one to monitor the baby.

Angela's cervix was fully dilated at ten centimeters and Dr. Rodrigues was urging her to push. She instructed Lynette to count to ten during which time Angela had to push the baby out. Angela pushed while Lynette counted slowly,

"One, two, three, four, five, six…."

"Seven, eight, nine, ten," said Angela in a rush unable to keep on pushing to her mother's slow count.

"You have to count faster mum, I can't push for so long," puffed Angela, out of breath from the exertion as she threw her self against the pillows.

"Let's do it again," said Dr. Rodrigues with a little smile.

Lynette started counting again, this time a little faster. Angela pushed to the count of ten.

They repeated this every time Angela had a contraction, but the baby would not come. Angela pushed and pushed, vomiting a couple of times from the effort into a hospital bedpan kept ready at her bedside for just such an eventuality. She pushed and pushed, but there was no sign of the baby. Angela was getting tired from all the pushing, but she kept going, doing as her doctor asked.

Dr. Rodrigues was positioned at Angela's legs raised up in stirrups when she noticed a drop in the baby's heartbeat on the fetal monitor. Every time Angela pushed, the baby's heart rate slowed down.

"Angela, stop pushing. The baby's heart rate is slowing down with every contraction. I do not want to take any chances with your baby being in distress. We should do a cesarean section."
"Please get my baby out safely doctor. Do whatever you need to do to make it happen," Angela pleaded.

The operating room was ready for Angela. She had been prepped for surgery by the nurse, and had been anesthetized locally. She was lying on a stretcher as they wheeled her into the operating room. Lynette was given a set of surgical garments to wear over her clothes and a pair of paper booties for her feet. She stood by Angela's head the entire time, holding her daughter's hand. Dr. Rodriguez and an assisting surgeon worked quickly to get the baby out.
"You should not feel any pain, Angela. Relax. Your baby will be with you soon," Dr. Rodriguez assured her.
"Do you feel this? Is it hot or cold?" She asked
"No doctor I don't feel anything. I can feel your hands but nothing else," Angela replied.
"Good. You will feel a great deal of pressure, but that is perfectly normal," her doctor informed her.
Angela lay strapped to the operating table. She had received an epidural injection in her spine earlier. As the anesthesiologist shot the drug into her system, she had experienced sharp pins and needles in her back and in her left thigh. Her leg jerked back and forth involuntarily as her back arched in pain. The nurse stood in front of her and did her best to steady Angela's body.
Finally the medication took over and Angela could feel no more pain. She could not feel her limbs. She knew they were there of course, but her mind could not control them. Her legs would not stay on the table together. When her right leg fell off the table, the nurse picked it up and put it back on the table. No sooner had she done that, than her left leg fell off the table. She picked up the left leg and placed it on the table, but then the right leg fell off the table.
Right leg off the table, left leg on.

Right leg on the table, left leg off.

Left leg on, right leg off.

Left on, right off.

On, off.

Noodle limbs.

A rubber doll. Boneless.

If Angela had not been so worried, she might have found the situation funny. Her legs were moving of their own volition. She had no control over what they did. She was a living breathing puppet with flailing arms and legs. All that the puppet needed was a few strings to complete the picture. After much limb picking, the nurse finally strapped her legs together first and then to the table. She also strapped each arm down to the extended wings of the table. Like Jesus on the cross.

"It's a girl!" Dr. Rodrigues exclaimed as she pulled the baby out from her mother's uterus, handing the baby over to a pediatric nurse. The new born baby came into the world with a loud and zesty cry.

Lynette hugged her daughter as best she could hug a strapped down Angela. Her tears gushed forth. She was thrilled to welcome another grandchild into the world, she was happy for the baby and for their family, but most of all she was just relieved.

The past three months had taken their toll on their family and Lynette was barely keeping it together. She had tried to stay strong for everyone- for Angela and for her children. She had worked hard to maintain Angela's home at even keel. She had taken care of Sophie and Zack as their mother had been too distraught to do anything. She saw to the daily running of the house, the cooking, the cleaning, the shopping, the school homework, the school lunches. Amy had helped whenever she could but she had her own family to take care of too.

Lynette had taken care of Angela and her unborn child. She had cooked nutritious meals and had practically force fed Angela for the baby's sake, ensuring that she took her prenatal vitamins and kept her doctor's appointments. She monitored Angela and kept a watchful eye on the family. The stress had worn Lynette down.

She worried constantly about everything, fearing that their family would crack wide open if they had to deal with another setback. She feared that if something bad happened to the baby, it would send Angela over the edge. She was walking a very fine line as it is. Their family was too fragile right now to deal with any more adversity. She lived with this fear constantly hanging over her shoulder day in and day out. It had pushed her to try harder to maintain a status quo, it had pushed her harder to do more.

So here and now in the hospital, hearing her grandchild's healthy lungs, Lynette was relieved. Like a tightly coiled spring finally un-springing. She cried and thanked God silently for blessing their family with a healthy baby. But mostly she thanked God for getting them through this trying time, for giving her the strength to keep going to get to this point.

Angela looked at her baby tenderly. Frank's baby, their baby, their little miracle was here at last. She cried, missing Frank more than ever at this very moment. Nobody had thought that she could carry this baby to full term, nobody had thought that the baby would make it. But mother and baby had proved everybody wrong. The little baby was here against all odds, against all expectations.

She had been advised to end the pregnancy on more that one occasion on account of her frail mental state and her rare blood type. What nobody seemed to realize was that this baby had been her reason for living. For a brief period, she had wanted to die after Frank had gone. She had wanted to end her own life so that she could be with him. She had lost all sense of reason and all sense of responsibility to Sophie and Zack. But being pregnant had changed everything for her. It had kept things real for her. She could go on only *because* of this life growing inside of her.

There was just no way she would let this baby go.
No way she *could* let this baby go.

Her doctor and her family had meant well when they had
asked her to consider ending the pregnancy. They had been
worried about her state of mind and about her ability to take
care of a newborn baby, about the added responsibility of
another child while dealing with her husband's death.

For her entire life, her family had coddled her, taken care of
her, sheltered her, at first her parents and siblings and then
later Frank. She knew that they secretly didn't think she could
handle adversity. She had just drifted along, allowing those
who loved her to take over. Maybe it was her fault that she
had let them. Maybe it was their fault for not giving her the
chance to prove otherwise. It didn't matter whose fault it was
now. Laying blame at anyone's door was not going to change
anything.

*The important thing for Angela was coming to the realization
that she needed to take charge of her own life. She had her
children who needed her, who depended on her and she was
going to steer her family down a path of her choosing. She
was going to be in control of her destiny.*

Nobody had thought she would be strong enough to have the
baby. She had doubted her own capabilities too. But the baby
was here and was living proof that she could do it. Maybe she
was a strong person after all and she just needed to let that side
of her see the light of day. In the past, she had been happy to
accept the way things were. She could recollect only one time
in her life when she had ardently sought something she really
wanted. It was the time when she had confronted Frank. If she
had allowed him to drift away from her, they would have
never shared the happiest years of their lives.

She felt a stirring in the pit of her stomach. Angela was
excited at the thought of taking charge of her life. The thought
of failure made her queasy and unsure, but the thought of
success dispelled the uneasiness. She did not know how she

was going to do it nor did she have a plan. She most certainly did not have it all figured out. There was only one thing she did know and it was that she *was definitely going to try.*

It was several hours before Angela could hold her new born baby. She had been placed in a recovery area under observation till the anesthesia wore off. The baby had been taken to the nursery for tests. After Angela was transferred to a room, a nurse on that floor brought her baby to her. Angela was tired from the pushing and the surgery, but sat up carefully to take her baby in her arms.

The baby was red all over. Her eyes were closed and her lips puckered to an 'O'. She had a head full of fine black hair and long fingers with well rounded cuticles. Angela stretched out her finger and touched her little baby's palm. The baby reflexively wrapped her hand around Angela's finger. She opened her eyes ever so slightly and looked at Angela for a moment and promptly went back to sleep.

Angela was choked by the emotions running amok in her pregnancy induced-hormone raging-emotional-mind and body. She held her little baby close to her body marveling at her baby's perfection. All her little parts so perfectly formed, like little mini miniatures. Her little fingers so long and graceful, her scrunched up little nose, her skin so translucent she could see the tiny blue veins beneath it. Her little chest heaving up and down as she drew breaths in and out, her umbilical cord all knotted up was still a few days from drying and falling off, her little legs thin now, promised rolls of chubbiness in the near future, her ten little sausage toes fanned out and wiggling. All her parts were just perfect little baby parts.

"Mummy? Mummy!" Sophie said as she stepped into Angela's hospital room the next day. Zack was following closely behind her.

"Oh look Zackki, mummy is holding our baby," Sophie said to Zack.

"Uh huh," Zack replied cautiously.

"Hi my darlings. How are you?" Angela asked.

"We're fine mummy. We came with Auntie Amy to see our baby," said Sophie.

"Come closer to get a better look," invited Angela.

Sophie crept closer, a look of awe in her eyes.

"She's so tiny mummy," she said touching her little sister's hand.

"Yes she is. Zack and you were tiny like this too," Angela said.

"Is she sleeping?" Sophie asked.

"I think so. Babies sleep a lot when they are this young," Angela explained.

"Oh look mummy, she opened her eyes. She's looking right at me!" squealed Sophie ecstatically, clapping her hands, her eyes alight with glee.

"She can hear your voice, I'm sure, Sophie, but she cannot see very well yet. Her eyes have to still develop," Angela said.

Zack continued to hover at the foot of the bed, not quite certain what to make of the baby. On hearing that she had opened her eyes, he inched forward to get a better look.

"Does she have a pee pee, like me? Will she have to pee standing up or sitting down?" he asked.

"Zackki, only boys have pee pees. Can't you see our baby is a girl?" returned Sophie in exasperation.

"What does she have?" he questioned.

"A wee wee of course! What else?" said Sophie matter-of-factly.

"Kids kids enough! Your mother is tired," said Amy hushing them while taking the little baby from her sister.

"She sleeps so peacefully," she said.

"Yes, she does. I hope she is a sound sleeper. She is going to have to be, if she wants to get any rest with Zack and Sophie's constant chatter," Angela said ruffling Zack's hair playfully.

"Can she do anything else beside sleep?" asked Zack.

"Not much right now. Why? What would you like her to do?" Amy asked.

"Well can she sit up or stand up?" he asked.

"Not yet," Angela replied.

"How is she going to go potty then?" he asked doggedly returning to his previous unfinished topic of conversation.

"She'll have to go in her diaper," answered Angela.

"Ugh. Gross," said a very recently potty trained Zack, scrunching his nose up in disgust.

Angela was happy to be home with her family again. Even though she sometimes felt that her life had come to a standstill the day Frank died, the birth of their little baby proved other wise. The baby had continued to grow and get bigger and stronger with the passage of time. And then before long it was time for her to make her debut in the world. The last three months of Angela's pregnancy had past in a blur of sadness and tears, grief and desolation. The only thing that kept her focused was the fact that she had been the sole caretaker responsible for the life growing inside her body: A little person blissfully unaware of the burdens of the outside world, a little person deserving the best chance to make it to that burdensome outside world.

The baby had become the center of attention in the Machado home. To each of them, she meant something different. To Angela she represented a miracle and a farewell gift from her beloved husband. In Sophie she stirred a latent maternal instinct to nurture and care for her little sister. To Zack, she was an enigma that he fully intended to poke and prod to discover more about.

To them all, the baby was a welcome distraction from their pain and suffering. To them all, she was a soothing salve to their hurting hearts. To them all, she was the binding force that kept their family from falling apart. She was only a little person and yet she exerted the single most cohesive force over her family. They each took for themselves what her sweet innocence could offer. They each began to hope that their lives would get better. She kept them focused on her and not on their grief, she enthralled them and fascinated them and awed them. And slowly she helped her family get past their pain and learn to accept their loss. She was their miracle baby.

Unknown to her, she had entered their lives and washed away their despair, filled their hearts with happiness leaving not much room for the sadness that had nested there for three months. They believed she would be the beacon that would lead them to the land of the living again. She lifted their collective depression, she brought promise and brightness to their dismal world. She took charge and arrested the downward spiral her family had been swept into. She steered them instead, in a new direction energizing them to slip out of their dungeon of misery.

She achieved her family's rejuvenation armed with nothing but a few smiles and a few gurgles. They nuzzled into her softness and she let them. They offered her a finger and she wrapped her own around it, they kissed her and stroked her hair and she allowed it, they talked to her and she listened not understanding any of the words. That was all it took on her part. It was all she could do. But it was enough. More than enough.

"Mummy, what are we going to call her?" Sophie asked her mother one afternoon.

It had been seven days since Angela and the baby had come home from the hospital. They had just put the baby down for a nap and were working on dinner in the kitchen. Zack was sitting at a small table peeling the skins off of boiled potatoes while Sophie was whisking some eggs in a big mixing bowl. Angela was stirring a pan with ground meat, sliced onions and spices on the stove. Angela turned when she heard Sophie's voice. She answered,

"I have actually been thinking about that for a while."

"What's wrong with 'baby girl'?" Zack wanted to know.

"It's not really a name Zackki," Sophie answered.

"So what? It's what we call her now anyway," Zack responded.

"That's only 'coz we haven't picked out a name for her as yet," said Sophie.

"She likes 'baby girl'. I'm sure of it. Otherwise she would have said so," persisted Zack.

"Don't be silly Zackki. She cannot talk yet, so how can she say whether she likes it or not?" retorted Sophie.

"I still think it's a good name. It is what we call her now. She is a girl and she is a baby, right?" returned Zack trying to make his point.

"Yes Zachary it is what we call her now, but she needs to have a name of her own," interjected Angela.

"Why?" he questioned.

"It will help establish her identity. Imagine if nobody in the world had names. We would all be baby boy or baby girl. If someone called out 'baby boy' then all the men and boys around would have to respond. You wouldn't be able to single anyone out. That would be very confusing, don't you think?" explained Angela.

"That's really funny mummy," Zack giggled picturing it in his head.

Sophie giggled too, also mentally picturing the image.

"Okay, I guess she needs a name," he agreed.

"Do you have any ideas, Sophie, Zack? Something other than 'baby girl' of course," their mother asked.

Sophie and Zack were silent for a few minutes. Zack felt that he had made a suggestion, now it was their turn.

"How about 'Gardenia'?" suggested Sophie.

"Too flower-y," vetoed Zack. Angela agreed.

"What about 'Maria'?" suggested Sophie again.

"Too common," vetoed Angela, Zack agreed.

"What about 'Brenda'?" suggested Sophie yet again.

"We already know a 'Brenda'," said Angela.

"So what?" said Zack, thinking that if he sided with Sophie, it would put an end to the name picking which was likely to go on forever. He wanted to get back to making potato chops and pan rolls.

"When daddy and I picked out your names, we tried to come up with a name we both liked and we wanted to make sure that we didn't know anyone with that name," Angela explained.

"Why is that important? So many people have the same name. What's wrong with that?" Sophie asked.

"There is nothing wrong with that of course. It's just that when I hear a name I automatically associate it with the other people I know who have the same name. You three children are very special to me, so when I hear your name, the only person I want to be thinking about is you," said Angela, hugging Sophie's shoulders.

"What about people born after us who have the same name?" questioned Sophie.

"It won't matter then. The first Sophie I ever knew would be you. When I think of the name 'Sophie' I will always think of you no matter how many times I hear it after," explained Angela.

Sophie digested her mother's comments while Zack allowed his mind to drift to the potato chops at hand. He had mentally distanced himself from the name picking a few moments ago.

"Do you have any names in mind, mummy?" Sophie asked.

"I actually do. I like three names, but cannot decide which one I like best," answered Angela.

"Maybe we can help. What are they?" questioned Sophie.

"Okay. Here are my three names: Megan, Olivia and Abigail," stated Angela.

"I like them all, but I like 'Olivia' the most, then 'Megan' and third 'Abigail'," pronounced Sophie.

"What about you Zack? Which one do you like?" asked Angela.

"I like 'Olivia' too," said Zack, returning to the present conversation for a brief moment.

"I too like 'Olivia'," agreed Angela.

"How about we name the baby, 'Olivia Megan Machado'?" asked Sophie excitedly.

"I like the sound of that," said Angela.

"Me too," agreed Zack.

"Okay. 'Olivia Megan Machado' it is!" said Angela smiling.

"Great! I'm getting hungry, so can we please get back to making the potato chops?" pleaded Zack.

Sophie and Angela laughed at Zack's one track mind. He really did love potato chops just like his father before him had, reminisced Angela. She had made a platter full on the evening of Frank's death. It had been one of his favorite foods and she had wanted to surprise him. Instead she was the one who had been surprised by the Air India officials at her door and she was the one who had been shocked to hear about his death. Just thinking about potato chops brought back the ghastliness of that day and she had been unable to make them ever since. Today was the first time she had agreed to make them for Zack.

This was the new Angela. She was taking charge of her life and doing her best to turn their lives around one little step at a time. So far she was doing okay. It helped having Zack and Sophie as helpers. Like her children, she too felt things were changing around the house. It felt as though the cobwebs of grief and misery were slowly being swept away, the curtains of sorrow were being lifted allowing the bright sunlight to filter through their home and warm their cold hearts. She finally believed that they could move forward even if Frank was not destined to be part of it. The past three months had been very hard on them all, but she could see a slim ray of light at the end of their tunnel. A ray that was getting bigger and brighter with each passing day.

"Mummy, it's burning!" cried Zack.

Angela snapped out of her thoughts and quickly took the pan off the stove.

"It's just a little dry Zack, not burnt," said Angela.

"Is it completely ruined now?" asked Zack dejectedly.

"No son. A dry meat filling is exactly what we want for potato chops and pan rolls," she said.

"Oh, goody!" Zack said clapping his hands together.

"Okay here is how we make them," said Angela.

Zack and Sophie watched their mother's actions carefully and listened attentively to her instructions. First she mashed up the boiled potatoes that Zack had just peeled. To the mash, she added a little melted butter and some milk, salt and pepper. She rolled small portions of the mashed potato mixture between the palms of her hand. She made golf- sized balls cupping her hands as she progressed. She then flattened the ball and placed a teaspoonful of the ground meat mixture in the flattened center. She deftly gathered up the edges and sealed them to each other on the top of the meat, making sure that none of the filling escaped. She placed the ball on a cutting board and with the assistance of a spatula, shaped the flattened meat filled ball (that didn't look like a round ball any more, but more like a hockey puck) till it had smooth edges. She repeated this procedure several times, stacking the neat little potato chops on a plate.

"Mummy can I do one?" asked Sophie

"Me too, me too!" piped in Zack.

"Sure you can try too. Here, take some potato and some filling. Go on try it," she encouraged.

Both Zack and Sophie tried their hand at shaping potato chops for the first time. It was tougher than mummy had made it look.

"Oh, mine is terrible! It doesn't even look like a potato chop!" Sophie exclaimed.

"Don't be discouraged Sophie. It takes a lot of practice to shape a good potato chop. It's not so bad for your first try."

"Here let me help you to shape it a little," said Angela taking the spatula to Sophie's version of a potato chop.

"See. That not so bad huh?" Angela said when she was done.

"Go ahead, try another one," she further encouraged, handing Sophie another ball of potato.

"Look at mine, mummy!" squealed Zack happily.

"It looks more like a pancake than a potato chop, but that shape works too," Angela replied affectionately.

They soon got through the entire potato mixture, managing to make quite a few potato chops, some of the mixture winding up on the floor and some of it finding its way into little smacking lips. Next, Angela dipped the chops in the egg wash that Sophie had whisked earlier and a final coating of breadcrumbs before they found their way into a hot frying pan. Angela flipped them over once, careful not to break them. She placed the ready potato chops onto a paper towel lined platter. Zack was impatient and couldn't wait for dinner.

"Mummy can I have one please?" he asked.

"What you should say is 'May I have one please'," corrected Angela.

"May I please have one, mummy? Please! Please, please, please!" said Zack join his hands to further emphasize his impassioned plea.

"Yes you may," said Angela placing a golden brown potato chop on each of two plates for her children.

They squirted a little ketchup on the chops and using the side of a fork as a knife, they cut off a piece of the chop. The potato chop was crisp on the outside and soft on the inside. They ate in silence, till it was all gone.

"Mummy you make the best potato chops in the world!" Zack exaggerated.

"May we have another please?" asked Sophie.

But she need not have bothered asking, as Angela was already reaching for their plates for refills. She was happy to see her children so relaxed. This was the first time they had actually done something together in three months. She had been so caught up in her grief and the kids had withdrawn into their own world. But today, they had come together. To make potato chops. It was wonderful to see their happy ketchup stained mouths wreathed in smiles and filled to capacity with potato chops.

"We can use the same meat mixture to make pan rolls," explained Angela.

"The only difference is that instead of potato on the outside, we use crepes," she continued.

She whipped up a flour batter quickly, not bothering to ask her children for help this time. They were too busy stuffing their faces anyway and would not want to be interrupted. She ladled the flour batter into smaller frying pans. She had three pans going at the same time and was done with the little crepes in no time. She rolled the ground meat mixture into each crepe, making sure to seal both ends by tucking them inward. Then she dipped them in the egg wash and breadcrumbs and pan fried them like she had done with the potato chops earlier. Before long, two platters were ready and headed for the dinner table.

She heard a whimper from the bedroom.

"Ah, perfect timing. Sounds like Olivia is awake. Zack go see if Nana Lynette is ready for dinner. I am sure Uncle Adrian must be hungry too. I will go and get Olivia," she instructed.

Dinner was a huge success. Zack put away so many potato chops and pan rolls, that Angela was sure he was going to be sick. It had been a good day. Angela had enjoyed spending time alone with her children and made a mental note to plan more of the same in the future. The kids had had a blast too and were settling down for bed. Nana Lynette was reading them a story. Angela nursed Olivia and settled her into her crib for the night. She tip toed out of the room and headed for some quite time with her brother Adrian in the living room. Nana Lynette would join them after she read Zack and Sophie their bedtime story.

After the kids had gone to bed, the three adults had got into the habit of spending an hour or so together every evening after dinner. Angela cherished these times with Adrian. She had always been close to him, but now that he was living in America, these occasions were few and far between. He had been unable to make it to Frank's funeral as his wife Shayna, had been in labor with their third child. He had been cornered between a rock and a hard place. Shayna on the one hand needed him by her side as she gave birth to their child and Angela on the other hand had needed him by her side as she had just lost her husband. In the end, Adrian had stayed with Shayna for the birth of their child and returned to India to help Angela with the birth of hers. She had been relieved to know that Adrian would be with her for her baby's birth.

Lynette had been a pillar of strength, helping out in every way imaginable over the past three months. But she had aged considerably after her husband Robert's death. She was still very able, but functioned at a much slower pace now, her age and her arthritic knees catching up to her. Angela was afraid that it had all been too much for her. She remembered a time when her mother could feed her entire family of six with a three course dinner, prepared single handedly, from scratch, in under an hour. Angela used to think she was super woman and than she secretly had two extra pairs of hands attached to her back that came out only when needed. Today, her mother was still very active for her age, but everything took much longer to do. Having Adrian around even if only for three weeks was a godsend to Angela and her family. She was glad to have her brother in her home.

She curled up in a chair with a bowl of fresh *sitaphal* ice cream (custard apple ice cream). Adrian was watching sports on television, but turned the box off, when Angela walked in.

"Its okay Adrian, if you want to watch TV," assured Angela.

"I was just passing the time. I would like to discuss something with you before I return to the States," he said.

"What is it?" Angela asked.

"I have not brought this up in the past because you and Frank were making a life for yourselves and your kids here in Bombay. But now that Frank's gone, have you given any thought to what you would want do?" he asked.

"Not really. I have been thinking about it of course, but I haven't made any concrete plans. So far, the compensation I received for Frank's death is paying our bills, but that will run out eventually. I have to come up with a plan in the meantime," Angela said worriedly.

"I'm sorry that you have to deal with financial matters at such a difficult time Angie, but the reality of it is that you have to confront it. You should not put it off any longer. Don't wait too long to cement a plan. Shayna and I constantly worry about you," Adrian said.

"We'll be okay, Adrian. It's just been a tough few months, but I will figure something out soon," responded Angela.

"I have something else to discuss with you as well," he added.

"What is it?" she asked.

"Would you consider moving to the States?" he questioned.

"To America? I don't know. I never really considered that as an option," said Angela.

"There are two ways to do it. One way would be to try to find a job there first, with a company willing to sponsor you. The kids of course would be dependant on you as they are underage. Once you get a green card you could apply for citizenship in a few years. You will have a job and the kids will be able to go to school. You could begin a new life right away. You could leave these painful memories behind and make a fresh start in a different country. Make some new happy memories," he explained.

"Hmm. That makes sense, a fresh start for us all. But who would hire somebody with no work experience? What would I do? I think securing a job would be very tough for me at this time. You said there was another way?" Angela asked.

"Yes there is. The other option is that as a US citizen, I could file papers with the US immigration for you and your family. However, it will be several years before it comes through. You could try to find work here in the meantime and when your immigration visa comes through, you could decide if you want to move to the States or whether you would rather just stay here in Bombay," Adrian said.

"That's a lot to think about," said Angela.

"Yes of course it is. The first option allows you to move to America right away and make a new beginning. The second option gives you a block of time to decide on what you want. It would give you a chance to plan for the future," he said helpfully.

"I would need to talk to the children. They have their friends and school here. Uprooting them now might just be more stressful. Olivia is too little as well. I think moving to another country now would just be too much to handle for all of us, especially me," she said truthfully.

"Then consider the second option," pushed Adrian.

"It will give you more time to decide what you want. In the meantime you must try to figure out a work situation here. If things work out for you here, you may not want to move, but if for whatever reason you do want to move, at least you have options. I can file your papers in the meantime. It takes a good many years to materialize Angie, but you have to make a decision sooner than later," he added.

"Okay I will think about it and talk to the kids as well," she said.

"Good. I brought the necessary forms with me, so if you decide to go with the second option, we can get them filled out right away and I will submit them as soon as I get back to New Jersey. Then we will wait and see what happens," Adrian said.

"I will think about it Adrian. Thank you for caring," said Angela with tears in her eyes.

"I know it is hard to make decisions alone, but it must be done, Angie. You have to think about yourself and the kid's futures. America will open up a world of opportunities for your children. They would have a shot at the best schools in the world and so many career choices. You and the kids would stay with us in New Jersey. Once you get a job and till you get on your feet, you could eventually have a home of your own," added Adrian.

A few days later, Adrian returned to New Jersey. He had been elated when Angela had taken him up on his offer. They had filled out the forms together after she had discussed the issue with Sophie and Zack.

The kids had been excited at the thought of living abroad. They were close to Adrian's children in age and got along extremely well. Angela did caution Sophie and Zack that it would be several years before their visas came through and that in the meantime they had to go to school here and life would go on as usual.

But the delay didn't seem to matter to them. Maybe they didn't fully comprehend what 'many years' meant. But the thought of just knowing that things were going to change for the better seemed enough. It warmed her heart to see their sad little faces light up in anticipation of a new life.

The same way they lit up when they had helped her make potato chops and pan rolls.

Chapter 5

Angela and Frank: The Beginning

Angela loved waking up before sunrise. This was her time alone, the calm before the storm. Her time to dwell on the day ahead of her, to reflect on her life, to think of the past, to think of the future. When Frank was alive, she had shared this time with him. They had both looked forward to their time alone. Sometimes they talked, other times they lazed in bed dreaming about their future. Sometimes they made love satisfying their desire for each other, nourishing each other's spirit, other times they just sat side by side watching the sun rise over the city.

No matter how often they witnessed the sunrise, it was breathtaking. If possible, it was even more breathtaking each time. The sun slowly extended each of its warm bright arms over the sleeping city of Bombay, inviting her to wake up, cajoling her and her inhabitants from their dormant state. It gently blew its warm breath over the city, much like a lover gently caressing his lady love's soft skin.

Angela and Frank would sit together, holding hands. They would listen to the sounds of the world waking up around them. The chirping birds cheeping to their young ones, the newspaper thunking on the doormat at the front door as the newspaper boy went about his rounds, car doors opening and slamming shut as the building *gurkha* (watch man) washed his quota of building cars, a bicycle bell tinkling as the *paowalla* (bread man) made his morning deliveries.

In the distance, they would hear the sound of the western railway trains starting up in readiness for their daily commuters. The city was waking up, slowly at first, picking up the pace as the clock ticked on and the sun rose higher in the sky with the promise of yet another sweltering day.

Even after Frank had passed on, Angela had maintained their little habit on the balcony. She didn't talk to anyone anymore or make love to anyone anymore or dream lazily about their rosy future together anymore, but she sat quietly in a chair on the balcony and contemplated life. This was her time alone, before the hustle and bustle of the day and its routines took over. Her time before Sophia, Zachary and Olivia woke up and demanded her undivided attention. This was her time alone.

For herself. For her spirit. For her soul.

Today was no different than any other day since Frank's passing. Angela woke up before the alarm clock went off. She turned it off like she did everyday. Almost as if she **was** there to do the clock a service and not the other way around. She slipped her feet into her comfy bedroom slippers and walked over to the kitchen for a cup of tea. She deftly poured the steaming liquid into a cup and headed back to her room.

Their home had two balconies (verandahs). The first one was adjacent to the living room. They had enclosed the space with tall windows, had broken down two non-load bearing walls and extended their small living room. The second balcony was attached to the master bedroom. Frank had wanted to reclaim that space as well, to expand their bedroom, but Angela had wanted the balcony. To her, it was a special place. Over the years Frank had come to share that special space with her and had learned to enjoy using it. Today it was hers alone.

Angela sat down in one of the two rattan chairs. She put her feet up on the matching rattan table in front of her and wrapped her hands around her warm tea cup. She sipped the hot brew, the fragrant orange pekoe tea leaves wafting to her nostrils. She took a sip, allowing the hot milky liquid to trickle down her throat, warming her body as it found its way to her stomach. Angela sighed. *Nothing like a good cup of chai.*

She sat a while enjoying her tea, absorbing the silence around her. The stillness calmed her, relaxed her, soothed her. She had no specific thoughts today. She allowed her mind to drift, to think of anything it pleased. Free to go anywhere, no ropes to rein it in. Random thoughts gradually gave way to more structured ones. Angela was thinking about happier times. The sun rose in its resplendent majesty, like it did everyday, turning the dark shadows of the night into liquid rivers of gold. But Angela missed the sun-kissed splendor of the day, her thoughts far back in time to her own golden days....

It had been a busy day for the Pinto family. Truth be told, it had been a really busy week. Amid a flurry of activity, Angela found a quiet moment to herself. She looked at her reflection in the mirror. Her long brown black hair had been carefully swept up and secured in a loose knot. The stylist had spent an inordinately long amount of time arranging her silky hair atop her head, to give the appearance of being casually tousled. To the untrained eye, it looked casual, but Angela knew there was nothing casual about the length of time it had taken to achieve this casual look or the number of hair pins that had been necessary to hold this creation in place. But it had been well worth the effort. Angela looked stunning. Thin softly curling wisps of hair framed her delicate features. Her dark brown eyes shone warmly through mascara fringed eyelashes, her eyelids defined expertly with kohl to enhance their almond shape. Her cheekbones were lightly dusted with a soft peach brown blush, accentuating their prominence. Her lips lush with promise, were brushed with a warm toned lipstick. Angela turned her attention to her long neck adorned with a string of simple pearls to match the ones in her earlobes.

Today was a special day for Angela. It was the day she would be united with her love. The day Angela Maria Pinto would marry Frank Anthony Machado. Angela had been waiting for this day. Not because she wanted to get married like every girl did, not because she had dreamed of this day since she was a little girl. She had waited for this day because she would be joined forever to Frank. Her one and only love.

Frank Machado was as ordinary as Angela was beautiful. He was a man of average height, of average build, with average features. He was neither ugly nor beautiful. He was someone who could very easily get lost in a crowd. He was not blessed with a charismatic personality or with a witty sense of humor or with a winning smile. And yet Frank was a special man. He had an uncanny way of affecting people with his quiet strength. Once you got to know him, you couldn't help but like him. He always seemed to be around when most needed, as though a beeper went off in his head whenever trouble was around the corner. He was sensitive to people's feelings, perceptive of their needs, a rock that they could lean on. He was a caring compassionate man who loved his family without reservations. He had an indescribable inner beauty that touched all those around him.

Frank was at his mother's home in *Ranwar*. He too was getting ready for his wedding day. He put on his black three button suit coat over matching trousers. He adjusted the knot of his tie and slicked his hair back with the palm of his hand. He had been waiting a long time for this day to come. Today was the day when Angela would become his wife. Frank considered himself blessed to have Angela in his life. That she had consented to be his wife was a constant source of wonder to him. At times he couldn't believe that Angela had chosen him over so many others. She had had no shortage of eager and willing suitors and yet she had sought him out. He had not had the courage to even try to win her love, considering himself unworthy of her attention. He thought back to the first day he had laid eyes on the girl across the street.

Lynette and Robert Pinto had moved their family into Bandra on December 17th, 1973. They had moved from *Byculla*, a small town towards the south of Bombay. Robert and Lynette had finally saved enough money to buy a small place of their own. They had been living with Robert's parents and his brother and sister since they had been married fourteen years ago. They had had a hard life with not much money to spare after the monthly bills were paid. Once their children were a bit older, Lynette began working outside the home and was able to increase their savings. It still took them fourteen years to accumulate enough money for a place of their own.

They had four children. When they moved to Bandra, Alastair, their eldest son, was thirteen years old, followed by Adrian who was twelve, Angela, their third child was eleven and Amy, their youngest was ten years old. The Pinto family didn't have much money growing up and saw some real hardships along the way, but they were happy and made do with what they had. They made do with borrowed school uniforms, hand-me-down clothing and second hand books. But Lynette and Robert were loving parents who wanted the best for their children. So they did what they could to set aside some money and were able to finally buy their own home.

The four Pinto children were excited to be moving to Bandra. They were looking forward to their new life and their new home. Finally they would have their own space and did not have to share a tiny cramped apartment with four other people. They loved their grandparents, but it was getting harder and the space was getting tighter as they got older. Lynette and Robert had bought a two bedroom flat (apartment).

In Bombay, most people live in apartment buildings. *Bombayites* use the term 'house' synonymously with 'flat' or 'apartment'. If invited to their 'house', it really means that you are invited to their 'apartment', even though technically a house and an apartment are not synonymous.

There were very few actual bungalows or cottages still in existence in Bombay, the city having grown rapidly to keep up with commercial expansion. Beautiful, quaint houses gave way to high rise apartment buildings in order to accommodate the exodus of migrants to the city. Bandra still had some free standing homes left, but they were slowly ceasing to exist as giant real estate developers flooded Bandra, offering sweet deals to the cottage owners. They demolished the old dilapidated homes and constructed tall shiny new buildings with many posh apartments in their ashes.

Lynette and Robert could not afford those fancy new apartments. They had bought a two bedroom apartment in an older building, something more suitable to their price range. The apartment was on the second floor of a three storied building. The building did not have an elevator as one was not needed for a building three stories high. The apartment itself overlooked Hill Road.

Hill Road is the main artery of Bandra (west). It is a hub of activity at all times of the day and even late into the night. Hill Road connects with the Bandra Train Station Road on the one end, progresses through the suburb of Bandra in a pretty straightforward fashion and connects with Mount Mary Road at its other end. The road itself is approximately one mile (1.6 km) in length. Parts of Hill Road are lined on either side with licensed stores of every nature imaginable as well as unlicensed hawkers selling everything from toys, tableware and fake jewelry to earthen pottery, lingerie and glass bangles. The busy shopping area is interjected with street carts selling *bhel puri* (a well loved Indian snack that can be assembled in several ways, using just a handful of ingredients), *Kiri kaleji* (grilled meats, livers, hearts and animal unmentionables), kebabs (grilled meats on a stick), fresh *ghanna juice* (sugar cane juice), *frankies* (a flat round piece of dough dipped in egg first, then rolled up with diced and spiced meat and pan fried), *kulfi* (Indian ice cream), *falooda* (a concoction traditionally made with rose milk and *kulfi* though variations are available). All sold among a host of other delectable edibles for the thirsty, hungry shoppers.

Hill Road also lays claim to the famous *Elco Arcade Shopping Center*. It houses hordes of tiny shops selling clothing and fabric among other accessories. Shoppers arrive here daily from all corners of Bombay to sample its wares. Hill Road is second in fame and size only to Linking Road (also located in Bandra). Linking Road was at one time considered to be the 'Shopping Mecca' of Bombay, similar in every way possible to Hill Road except that it is much longer and more famous, thereby attracting more shoppers.

Lynette and Robert's building was in the non commercial part of Hill Road. Still, a very busy road as it is the main road through Bandra (west), but not as busy as the commercial section of Hill Road. Their building was right across the street from St. Andrew's Church, the church they would soon become parishioners of. The little village of *Ranwar* (where Frank lived) was just a hop, skip and a jump away.

Frank was twenty-one when Angela moved into Bandra. She was eleven years old. From the window of his bedroom, he could look into Angela's new home. The day they moved in, Frank happened to be standing at his window. He watched the activity below distractedly, his mind on other things. He noticed the family busily unloading their things. They trudged up the flight of stairs and deposited their cargo into the vacant apartment clearly visible from his window.

Down below, in the building compound while everyone one was busy at work (the neighbors had chipped in to help), there was a little girl. She was skipping around the boxes and suitcases, her scrawny little legs jumping over the little boxes, skirting around the larger ones. She seemed really happy, oblivious to the labor being exerted around her. He watched her for a few minutes enjoying her childhood display of carefree elation. She looked to be about ten or twelve years old.

Suddenly she looked up in his direction, as though she had sensed that she was being watched. Her eyes made direct contact with his. Curious. Unabashed. And then very slowly, she smiled. Frank's heart missed a beat. It was the most dazzling smile he had ever seen. It lit up her entire face, as though her smile had started out in her toes and got bigger and brighter as it made its way to her eyes. Frank smiled back. She waved at him, her long ponytail jiggling with the vigorous motion of her hand. He waved back.

Over the years, he would often see Angela from his window either at home or in the compound playing. They would smile and wave at each other, sometimes saying a word or two. Frank was ten years older than Angela and their worlds couldn't have been further apart. He had graduated from college and was considering his options for the future, she was still in school dealing with sixth grade tests and homework.

Frank had decided to go to flight school abroad and left home for England when he was twenty-three. He stayed in England for the duration of his education and then extended his stay for a few more years, gaining experience in the field. He had carved out a comfortable life for himself, but missed home nonetheless. He missed his family and his life in Bandra. Most of his friends were still in Bombay, some having migrated to other parts of the world.

He missed his visits at the *Bandra Gymkhana*, where he would shoot a few games of pool or play a few sets of tennis. He would hang out with friends for a few beers every Friday night. The older folk would get together for Housie/Bingo weekly on Thursday evening. Mama Machado was a perpetual fixture at the weekly Housie Night. He missed the easy camaraderie of the people of Bandra, the sights, the sounds, the smells. Frank decided to return to India for good. He had several years of flight experience under his belt and decided to try his luck with Air India, India's national airline.

Frank returned to India after nine years in England. He was thirty-two years old. Mama Machado was overjoyed to have her son back. All her children had flown the coop. Genevieve and Jeanne had migrated to Australia, Allison had married and moved to Singapore, Bernadette was in Kuwait, Bridget and Rowena had married but stayed in India. Bridget resided in *Santacruz* and Rowena in *Mazagoan*. Frank had been gone nine years, but he was finally returning home for good.

Mama Machado was eighty-three years old. She was frail and was certain she would not be around much longer, but mostly she was just lonely. When Frank decided to give up his life in England and move back home, no one was happier than his mother. She eagerly anticipated Frank's arrival. She had been preparing for days. Everyone in *Ranwar* and some even beyond, knew that Frank was coming home. His homecoming was special. Mama Machado with help from some of his closest friends arranged a homecoming party for him. Frank was happy to be home surrounded by the people he loved.

The day after the party, Frank went to the 6:00pm Sunday Mass at St. Andrew's Church. He stopped to talk to a few acquaintances after the service before he headed to the Bandra Gymkhana for an evening out with friends.

"Hi Frank."

Frank turned around to see who had said hello. He looked confusedly at the young woman standing in front of him. He did not recognize her. She smiled. His heart skipped a beat. Only one person could smile and affect him so.

"Angela?" he asked tentatively.

She nodded, smiling back at him.

Before him stood a creature one only reads about in novels. Angela had always been a cute child destined for prettiness, but before him stood a woman so stunning, her beauty left Frank speechless. She was almost as tall as he was. Frank was mesmerized. Her hair shone, her skin glowed and her eyes twinkled. When she smiled, her teeth glistened back at him. Every perfect feature was in perfect proportion in her perfect face. Frank stared at Angela, like a school boy gaping at his first crush.

Her exhilaration at the effect she had on Frank gave Angela the courage to stand her ground, matching his stare, unabashedly, basking in his adulation. Several moments passed. They were lost in each other. They were caught up in a moment of their own making, all other sounds obliterated from their consciousness. It was their special moment, each secretly willing it to last forever. Eventually, slowly, the sounds around them infiltrated, impinging on their secret moment.

Angela. The scrawny legged girl had been transformed into this heavenly creature before him. Had he really been away that long? Where was little Angela? When had she blossomed into this beautiful woman? Frank knew at that very moment that he had made the right decision to return to Bombay.
Looking into Angela's eyes, Frank knew that he was home.

In the following weeks Angela ran into Frank often enough, that one could not chalk the run-ins down to mere coincidence. If Angela saw Frank on the opposite side of the street, she would cross the road to say hello, she made sure the windows in their living room stayed open so that she could wave out to him, she waited for him after the Sunday evening mass. She capitalized on every opportunity to see him. Many boys, Angela's age had tried to go out with her, but she had been uninterested. Let the Tom, Dick and Harry(s) of this world marry the Sue, Jane and Mary(s) of this world. She wanted Frank.

Angela had loved Frank for a long time. What had started out as a simple friendship between an eleven year old girl and a man ten years her senior, had blossomed in her mind. She had romanced about their first meeting embellishing along the way, till she believed that she had always loved him. All the fantasizing however, had not prepared her for their encounter soon after he had returned from England. She had not been prepared for the onslaught of her emotions as they played unchecked across her face. She was not prepared for the way her body reacted to his presence.

Just looking at Frank turned her legs to vermicelli. Her heart raced, pounding in her ears. Her back arched of its own volition, thrusting her hardened nipples forward as though she had been caressed. Her palms sweated. Her skin tingled. Her pores oozed pheromones. Her brain fired signals in all directions till she was quivering all over.

Most boys she knew would welcome any interest from her, would bend over backwards to go out with her. But Frank for some reason best known to him alone, was avoiding her like the plague. He stayed away from his bedroom window or pretended to have not seen Angela when she waved to him, he chose to attend a different church service on Sunday and generally did his best to avoid her. Angela could not understand why.

She had not thought her body capable of such intensity. Angela knew Frank had felt the same way. She had seen it in his eyes that day. She had seen his pupils dilate, had heard his sharp intake of breath, she had seen his nostrils flare, his shoulders go rigid. She knew exactly what he had experienced because she experienced it too. At first, she was afraid of her reaction, unable to comprehend its potency. But as time wore on, all she knew is that she wanted to feel it again. She needed to feel that chemistry again. And again and again.

Angela tried to engage Frank for weeks, but Frank was never around no matter how hard she worked at arranging 'coincidental' meetings. It seemed like the harder she tried, the further he ran. Finally, she realized the only way she was going to see Frank was if she confronted him directly. She had never acted so boldly before, but she felt as though she was being pushed to do so from within. The following evening, she stood outside his home and waited for him to show up. He had to show up at sometime, she reasoned. She waited two long and impatient hours before she caught sight of him. Frank looked surprisingly pleased to see her, greeting her cautiously. "Hi Angela. How are you?" he said.

"Why are you avoiding me, Frank? Have I done something to offend you?" blurted Angela bluntly to the point, ignoring Frank's casual greeting.

"I am not avoiding you. I have been busy settling in, looking for a job, interviews, that sort of thing," said Frank

But Angela would not be dismissed so easily. She had every intention of getting to the bottom of this.

"Yes you have. You have been avoiding me and I want to know why."

"Angela, it's hard to explain," he replied, knowing that she would not let it go, that he would have to explain.

"I want to know why Frank. You have to tell me why you are avoiding me," Angela pleaded.

Frank guided her to the stoop on the side of the building and sat down beside her. He was quiet for a few minutes. Angela waited patiently beside him.

"You are young and beautiful Angela. You have so much going for you, your future in front of you. You have only just graduated from college, you need time to explore what's out there. The world is at your feet. You are at a very exciting point in your life. You need to grab every opportunity and live it to the fullest."

"But I am, Frank. I am going after what I want. I want you to be a part of my life," she said.

"Angela, I am ten years older than you. At thirty-two I have lived on my own, worked abroad, had relationships. I have had good and bad experiences, but the important thing is that I have had the chance. You will feel stifled if you don't allow yourself to fly now. You will get over these feelings you have for me and move onto other relationships. I don't want you to be hurt. I don't want to get hurt," he explained.

"But you are hurting me, by shunning me away, by ignoring me," she said.

"I don't mean to hurt you Angela," said Frank.

"But you are. And you are hurting yourself too in the process. Frank, please don't do this," Angela implored.

"It is not easy for me to say this to you Angela. It is not easy for me to turn you away, when all I want to do is hold you in my arms," said Frank, clasping and unclasping his hands in front of him.

"And all I want is you, Frank. Why not give us a chance? The ten year difference in our ages means nothing to me. What I feel for you is more than some silly infatuation. I want us to have the chance to explore our feelings for each other, to see where it takes us. Won't you give us a chance?" Angela asked of Frank taking his hands into hers as she spoke.

Frank and Angela went out on their first date soon after. Many dates followed that first one. They discovered a love so pure, so deep, so satisfying that neither one of them could deny it. Frank asked Angela to marry him two months later. There was never any doubt in either mind that they were destined for each other.

Angela lived just down the street, so Mama Machado knew who Angela was of course, but she had never spoken to her. She wanted to meet the girl who had captured Frank's heart. Angela was lucky to be loved by Frank because Frank's love was unwavering, solid as a rock.

She invited Angela and her parents to go with them to Housie/Bingo Night on Thursday at the Bandra Gymkhana. Lynette and Robert were pleased to be invited. Membership to the Bandra Gymkhana was not easy to come by. It was primarily a catholic organization that was managed by the East Indian Catholics of Bandra. There was a long waiting list for memberships and East Indians were given preference over other sections of the catholic faith. Lynette and Robert were happy to spend an evening there. They had only been there a few times before, always as guests of friends and neighbors.

They got to the venue promptly at 7:30pm. Frank signed them all in and they were quickly seated at a large table. The waiter came by to take their order before the game began. They ordered *chicken lollipops* (chicken wings that were prepared by pushing the meat to one end of the wing bone, so that it resembled a lollipop). They also ordered several plates of *spring rolls* and *kebabs*, both *sheek kebabs* (long cylindrically shaped and cooked on skewers) and *shammi kebabs* (pan fried patties of ground meat).

The Housie game was to begin at 8:00pm. The waiter brought them their food and drinks before the game began. A few volunteers distributed housie tickets to the gathered crowd. Each ticket was worth one rupee. Some bought two, maybe three tickets, other more ambitious players bought eight to ten tickets. Each pinkish-orange ticket was a rectangular piece of paper approximately two by four inches in measurement. The paper was divided into a grid of squares, some squares were filled with single digit numbers, others with double digit numbers and some squares were left blank.

There was a designated person at the head table who would call out the numbers. If you had the called number on your ticket, you marked it with a pencil or a pen or you made a hole in the square with a toothpick. There were five prizes: *Jaldi Five* (Quick Five - the first ticket to get five of the called out numbers). The next three prizes were *Top Line, Middle Line, Bottom Line* (the prize going to the first ticket to mark all the numbers in either the top, middle or bottom line) and the final prize was the *Full House* (the first ticket to have all numbers marked off.)

There was much excitement in the room as the players settled down and concentrated on the game at hand. The man at the head of the table spread a game board out in front of him. He shook the bag containing the plastic number tokens. He would select a token from the bag, call out the number and then place the token in its corresponding spot on the board.

Jimmy, a member of the Gymkhana, had been designated to call out the numbers that day. He cleared his throat, a sign to all that the game was about to begin. He shook the bag, displacing the current positions of the tokens. The plastic tokens jostled against each other. In an attempt to be fair to all (people and tokens alike), the tokens had to be randomly picked. He put his hand in the bag and selected the first token of the evening. A hush took over the room. All pencils, pens and toothpicks ready for the first number, eyes down on the tickets.

"Two fat ladies, eight and eight, eighty-eight!" Some lucky pencils, pens and toothpicks marked or poked a square on their ticket, most did not.

"All by itself, number three!"

"Unlucky for some, one and three, number thirteen!"

"Come on Jimmy, Shake the bag, *yaar*," Jimmy obediently shook the bag.

"Two hockey sticks, one and one, number eleven!"

"One fat lady, all by itself, number eight!"

"Top of the house, nine and zero, number ninety!" (pronounced 'nine-tay').

"Two little ducklings, two and two, number twenty-two!"

"Shake it, shake it!" Jimmy shook it. Jimmy shook hard.

"One and six, sweet sixteen!"

"Half a century, five and zero, number fifty!" (pronounced 'fif-tay'). Of course.

And so the game went on. Jimmy pulled tokens out of the bag. Some of the players happy with the numbers, some urging Jimmy to shake the bag, hoping their luck would improve with a good bag shake. Jimmy was careful to shake the bag each time he was asked to, lest he be pegged for favoritism. Lynette won the *Jaldi Five*. She had to take her ticket to the head table to verify the five numbers she had marked. They were good numbers. Lynette won the *Jaldi Five* prize. She pocketed the fifty rupee prize and returned to her table beaming. All eyes were down for the top, middle and bottom lines and then finally for the coveted full house.

After the game, they ordered Chinese for dinner. *Indian Chinese* is very different from Chinese food generally available outside of India. In India, the Chinese dishes available are adapted to suit the Indian palette. They ordered *Sweet Corn Crab Soup* (very much like sweet corn chicken soup except that the shredded chicken was replaced with shredded crabmeat), *American Chop Suey*, (a noodle creation, available in Bombay, but not found on any Chinese menu in America or China for that matter), *Mixed Fried Rice, Hakka Noodles, Manchurian Chicken* and *Schezuan Pork*. The food arrived piping hot to the table. The waiter assigned to their table, adroitly doled out portions of the food before retreating to the kitchens.

The Pinto and the Machado families got on well. Dinner was delicious and the evening was pleasant. Mama Machado liked Angela and her family. They were not *East Indian* like the Machado family was. Robert was *Goan* (from Goa) while Lynette was *Mangalorean* (from Mangalore). But at least they were catholic and Angela was a good, god-fearing girl, Mama Machado thought to herself.

She shook her head sadly. These days there were so many marriages that resulted in divorce. Religion and God played a non existent role in family life, leaving children direction-less and confused about God. Mama Machado sighed. Interfaith marriages were difficult and came with their own set of issues, but to be fair, she also acknowledged that marrying within the same faith had its own set of problems. She had been privy to so many unhappy couples who stayed together. They stayed unhappy in their marriages, hating each other and their own inability to escape from its confines. It seemed that they preferred to be with someone they hated rather than have to deal with the stigma of divorce.

So what was the better solution? Dealing with the fallout that a messy divorce usually came with? Or accepting an unhappy situation for the sake of appearances? In the end Mama

Machado acknowledged that choosing a marriage partner wisely was crucial to its success and that compatibility was the key to longevity of the union.

Mama Machado scrutinized Angela as unobtrusively as possible. Angela was beautiful, there was little doubt about that. Even a blind person would be able to see her beauty. But her beauty was enhanced more so by the fact that she seemed unaware of the effect she had on others. The most beautiful thing about Angela however, was not her physical beauty. Rather it was her ability to make Frank shine. And how he shone! Frank seemed like a different person around Angela. He drew his strength from her eyes, his confidence from her smile, his fortitude from her love. Mama Machado saw the love they had and knew it was special. Angela and Frank were meant for each other. They would be good for each other, to each other. They would have a good marriage. Her son had chosen his bride well. She could not have chosen better. Frank and Angela had her approval and her blessing.

Angela and Frank did not want a long engagement. They set their wedding date for a few months later. Both families rushed to get things done. Both families begged for more time, but Angela and Frank would not budge. It was bad enough that they had to wait out those few months. If it wouldn't have upset their families so much, Frank and Angela would have eloped. Instead, they waited impatiently while the wedding preparations took shape.

They signed up for a marriage preparation course mandated by the church, booked a venue for an open air wedding reception, hired a well known caterer to cater the rehearsal dinner before the wedding, made table centers and center pieces, bought craft supplies from *Crawford Market* in south Bombay, proof read and printed wedding invitations and rsvp cards, ordered flowers from a florist, made decorations for the church ceremony, chose hymns to be sung at the wedding mass, selected a choir for the church and a live band for the reception, chose menus, chose fabric for their wedding finery also from Crawford Market, got outfitted for tailored suits, fitted for shoes from the myriad of shoe shops on Linking Road, picked flower girls and a page boy, bridesmaids and groomsmen, best man and maid of honor, made the bridal bouquet, little bouquets for the women in the bridal party, corsages, wedding favors, got sized for wedding bands from the row of jewelry stores by the Bandra train station, and the list went on and on. There was so much to do.

Angela was the first to marry among her siblings while Frank was the last among his. She was the first girl in her family to marry; he was the first and only boy from his. There was excitement in the air and much anticipation of the occasion.

Chapter 6

The Anatomy of a Bombay Wedding

Adrian and Shayna his girl friend of fifteen months, settled down comfortably in their seats. He stowed their carry-on bags in the overhead compartment, first having pulled out two blankets and two pillows for Shayna and himself. The flight to Bombay was approximately eighteen hours in totality, counting their brief stop over in France's Charles de Gaulle Airport in Paris. They had both worked a full day today and had rushed to the airport, to make their 9:00pm flight out of JFK airport in Queens, New York.

Adrian and Shayna were looking forward to a well needed rest on the plane. Lately, it felt like they were always rushing to get to where they needed to go. Granted they both had busy lives and careers that demanded long work hours, so rushing was a necessary evil, but a break every now and then wouldn't seem so bad. There just never seemed to be enough time to relax, to put their feet up and unwind. So, they were looking forward to a few quiet hours on the plane in the hope of catching some shut eye. The family across the aisle thought otherwise, however.

They were a family of four, two parents and their two children, a boy and a girl. They boarded the aircraft immediately after Adrian and Shayna did. The heavily overweight boy bumped into the other passengers not bothering to apologize as he made his way to his seat. He shoved his way forward bumping passengers rudely with his backpack. When he got to their designated row of center seats, he raised his voice and said, "I don't want to sit here. I asked for a window seat."

"These are our seats, Anil. Please sit down," his mother said quietly, embarrassed by her son's outburst that had caused several people to turnaround and stare.

"But you said I could have a window seat," Anil said.

"I know *beta*, but these are the seats they gave us. We needed four seats and these are the only four seats together," replied his mother patiently.

"Why can't I sit by the window? You promised," he said petulantly.

By now a line of passengers had formed. They were waiting to get to their seats in the back of the plane. Anil, his rolls of fat and his bulky backpack were blocking the aisle.

"I want my window seat," Anil stomped his feet angrily.

"Anil *beta,* please sit down. Please," his mother implored.

"No. I will not sit down. I am getting off the plane if I don't get a window seat!" Anil stomped again, threatening.

The flight attendant came over to speak with them. The line of waiting passengers was longer now, extending beyond economy and business class and well into first class.

"Is something the matter?" She inquired politely of Anil's mother.

"No, no. Nothing is the matter," Anil's harried mother replied hurriedly, unwilling to admit that she couldn't control her bratty son.

"Please take your seats madam. There are other passengers waiting to board," said the flight attendant pointedly.

"This is not my seat. I want a window seat," Anil interjected.

"May I have your boarding passes?" the airline employee asked frowning.

Anil's mother handed them over. The flight attendant scanned them and looking at Anil.

"These are your seats. It says so on your boarding pass," she said a trifle sternly, immediately sensing the problem.

"But I want a window seat," insisted Anil.

"These are your seats. We have a full flight tonight. There are no vacant seats on the plane tonight. If you can find a passenger to exchange seats with you, then you can have a window seat. In the meantime please take your assigned seats. There are other passengers waiting to board," she said, very business – like.

"What about my window seat?" Anil persisted.

"You *do not have* a window seat. Please take your assigned seat," She stared Anil in the eye. She cocked her head to one side and raised her left eyebrow daring him to challenge her.

"*Chalo, chalo beta.* Come on son, take your seat," his mother pleaded.

Anil lost the eye match with the flight attendant, his false sense of bravado failing him. He huffily slid into his seat, his eyes promising his mother that she would pay for this later.

The line started moving and order was restored. The flight attendant walked away. The one-eyebrow-raised-look she had used on Anil, worked every time on her own nieces and nephews and it hadn't failed her now. She smiled to herself recalling the rude boy's pomposity deflating under her unfaltering stare.

Shayna observed the scene next to her as it was unfolding. The boy was pesky and in need of a good telling off. He stomped his feet every now and then, his rolls of fat jiggling rhythmically to his stomping. All attention was focused on the boy brat so his sister's actions went unnoticed. She had emptied the contents of her mother's handbag onto the seats. A few of the items rolled off the seats and fell onto the floor. She found a shiny lipstick tube, twisted it open and proceeded to paint her face with it. She smeared her lips with the creamy lipstick enlarging them to an invisible lip line just under her nose, she streaked her left cheek like a tribal chief setting off to war, and dotted her forehead with reddish spots that could easily pass off for an outbreak of the chicken pox to someone at first glance. She wiped her lipstick covered hands on her travel dress decorating the yellow seersucker fabric with random blotches worthy of an abstract work of art. Satisfied with her appearance, she turned the lipstick and her attention to the tray table in front of her. She managed to get quite a master piece going, before her already harried mother caught sight of her little Picasso. The mother wiped her brow with the end of her sari *pulloo* (hanging end of the *sari*) and attempted to un-paint her child and the tray table.

While his mother was cleaning up after her daughter, brat boy opened up his backpack and began stuffing his face with potato chips and candy bars. An obese bully, thought Shayna uncharitably. The father sat through the entire fiasco, unaffected by it all. He didn't correct brat boy's insolence or restrain his gorge fest, he didn't stop Picasso nor did he help his wife undo any of the damage their children had done. He just sat through it all, reading the *New York Times*, leaving the domestic issues for his wife to deal with.

Shayna sighed. All hopes for a sorely needed nap and a peaceful flight slowly faded from her mind. This was going to be a long trip. A very long eighteen hours. Not only were they confined to a people-packed aircraft for eighteen hours but they had to put up with the two little imps in the seats closest to them, who had been thrown in for good measure. Maybe they would change seats on the plane far away from her, thought Shayna knowing that was probably not going to happen. Maybe they would get off in Paris, thought Shayna knowing that was even less likely to happen. Oh, well. Shayna sighed again, resigned to the eighteen long hours ahead.

Adrian had left Bombay for the United States of America in 1983. He had completed a bachelor's degree in English literature and a certification in Media Communications from St. Xavier's College, Bombay. Subsequently he had applied for a scholarship to a master's program in journalism at NYU. He had been accepted into the program and was holed up in a tiny apartment with two room mates. Most of his friends in Bombay had full time jobs, but at twenty-two Adrian was still enjoying a student's life.

He enjoyed living in New York City and absorbed all it had to offer like a thirsty sponge. Blending in with the diverse ethnic melee of New Yorkers that pounded the streets daily, Adrian felt like he belonged. The hustle and bustle, the swarms of people, the busy streets, reminded him of Bombay. He felt at home even though he hadn't been in New York very long. His pulse thumped in unison with that of a city that truly never sleeps.

Adrian soon got into the habit of frequenting a café near the NYU campus. He visited the café every morning Monday through Friday on his way to classes. He didn't have classes on Saturday and Sunday, so he hardly ever came this way on weekends, the café being too far from his apartment to be considered convenient. He had not been much of a coffee drinker in India, preferring tea instead, but somehow in America over the past two years, he had acquired a taste for the freshly ground brew. Two years in and he *had* to have a cup of coffee every morning, craving the java like a junkie on crack. But he limited himself to one cup a day.

One large cup of coffee. One large cup of coffee in America was equal to at least three cups in Bombay he had noted. Shortly after arriving in the States, he discovered that everything was bigger in America, including the cup sizes. Especially the cup sizes. The food portions were larger, the soda cups taller, the streets wider, the cars bigger, the people fatter, the buildings higher, the buses longer. Yes, he had discovered that everything was definitely bigger in America.

He stopped by the café every day on the way to his 9:00am class. Jesse, the kid behind the counter (a fellow NYU student in his sophomore year earning a few bucks in between classes) knew how Adrian liked his coffee. Adrian would show up everyday at 8:45am on the dot and Jesse would have his coffee waiting for him. One large hazelnut coffee with a dash of milk and three sugars. Adrian had come to appreciate his morning routine and looked forward to his daily stop on the way to class. He nodded at a few familiar faces as he came in one morning. Jesse was nowhere to be seen. Behind the counter instead of Jesse, was a girl with short blond hair and an easy smile.

"Hey, what can I get you?" she asked smiling.

"A large coffee please. Hazelnut. Milk, three sugars," he replied, a little disappointed that his large coffee was not waiting for him. Having his coffee made just the way he liked it, having it ready and waiting for him upon his arrival, had made him feel special. It had made him feel important somehow. It gave credence to his meager existence in a city where anonymity ruled the day.

"Jesse is not in today?" Adrian asked casually, not wanting to show his disappointment. After all, it wasn't this blond girl's fault.

"That's right. Jesse had some personal stuff to take care of, so I offered to fill in for him," she said, placing the coffee cup on the counter in front of him.

"Ah, I see," Adrian said, not really seeing at all. What personal stuff? Jesse would've told him yesterday. They were friends. They talked about everyday things. Jesse should've mentioned that he wouldn't be in today, thought Adrian unreasonably.

"By the way, I'm Shayna. Jesse's sister," she offered as an explanation, extending her arm forward.

"Adrian," said Adrian, taking the extended arm in a hand shake.

"I know. Jesse told me to expect you," she said.

"He did?" Adrian was pleased, his faith in Jesse temporarily restored.

"Yeah. I am covering his shift at the café for the rest of the week," she added.

"He won't be back for a week?" Adrian's thoughts were on Jesse, but his brain somehow found a moment to register that the skin of her palms was soft, her grip warm, her fingers long, as they curled around his hand coming to rest on the back of his hand.

"Yup. See you tomorrow," she said casually.

"'Bye. See you," he replied like-wise.

That's how Adrian and Shayna met. Over the course of the week, he got to know her a little better, exchanging little bits of information about him for little bits of information about her. They talked for the thirty seconds they spent together each morning across the counter of the café. Shayna was in her final year, just like Adrian was. She was studying for an MBA in finance, he was studying for a masters' degree in journalism. She liked her coffee black no sugar, he liked his milky three sugars. She was Jesse's only sibling, he had three other siblings. Her family lived in New Jersey, his lived in Bombay. She liked Indian food, he liked Greek food. She liked the theater, he liked sports.

By the morning of the third day, he found himself looking forward to his brief interlude with Shayna. He got to the café fifteen minutes earlier than usual and decided to leisurely enjoy his coffee. He sat down at one of the café tables. He had convinced himself that it was much better to relax and enjoy his coffee than to gulp it down on the way to class as he did every morning. He surreptitiously watched Shayna working behind the counter as he pretended to read the book in front of him.

He appeared deceptively casual when she stopped by to chat for a few minutes in between customers. By that afternoon, he had convinced himself that he needed an extra dose of caffeine if he was going to stay up cramming for his finals in a couple of weeks. He stopped by the café that afternoon. Shayna was surprised but pleased to see him. From then on, till the end of the week he had a large coffee every morning and a large coffee every evening, including Saturday and Sunday.

Jesse returned to the café the following week. Adrian was happy to see him, but not so happy to not see Shayna. Deflated, Adrian returned to his regular routine of one large cup of coffee a day. The two large cups of coffee a day wasn't working out so well for his sleep pattern every night. He dumped the pretense, reverting to his single *cup o' joe* (he had heard Shayna call a cup of coffee, a 'cup o'joe'. He had to still figure out what that meant. He made a mental note to ask her if he ever saw her again).

Finals were right around the corner and it was crunch time. A few weeks went by before he saw Shayna again, accidentally bumping into her at a subway stop on Fourteenth Street. He was afraid he would not see her again, so he seized the moment. He asked her out on a date. She agreed. They went out a few times after that, and a few more times after that. They had been seeing each other for a few months, casually slipping into an unspoken exclusive relationship, neither demanding too much from the other. Each was happy to take what the other could give.

"Angela is getting married in a few months," Adrian told Shayna one day.

"Really? That's great! I'm happy for her," Shayna said.

She knew all about his family just as he knew all about hers even though they had never actually met each other's families. Adrian religiously called his family in Bombay every Sunday morning (Sunday night in Bombay). Shayna stayed over at Adrian's apartment every other Saturday night and was usually around when he talked to his family. She had even spoken briefly to Amy and Angela on the phone a few times.

"Are you going to go to the wedding?" She asked.

"Yes. I don't think I could forgive myself if I didn't. I don't think my family would forgive me either," he joked.

Shayna looked at Adrian, hesitant for a second, unsure if she should voice her thoughts. Before she changed her mind, she added, "I would love to go to India. I know we have only been together a few months and I am imposing in a way, but India is such a fascinating country, I would love to go with you."

"Sure," Adrian returned, a little taken aback by Shayna's request.

Maybe Shayna wanted to take their relationship to the next level. They had not talked about taking vacations together or meeting each others' families. She had never said or hinted at anything before. Maybe this was her way of addressing the issue. He would have said something himself, but he had not been sure if Shayna was ready to go there. Apparently she was. He was pleased. Pleased that she wanted more from their relationship, pleased that she wanted to go to India with him. He would show her Bombay and she would learn to see it through his eyes, not like some passing tourist.

The months flew by and Angela's wedding was only a week away. Adrian and Shayna were on the plane headed to Bombay. They settled in, ready for the long flight ahead. This was Shayna's third trip to Asia but specifically her first to India. She was excited to go and looked forward to the experience. She had insisted on buying gifts for his family, even though he told her that it was not necessary. She had packed them in her carry on bag that was stashed above their seats in the over head compartment of the aircraft.

The plane was filling up quickly, the last few passengers straggling in with their baggage. She pulled out a few pamphlets and brochures from her bag and plopped them down beside a tourist guide book to India and Bombay. She planned to catch up on her reading on the long journey to India.

The flight departed from the gate on time and they were airborne in a few minutes. The flight attendants offered them refreshments and dimmed the lights after the food service. Adrian plumped up his pillow and proceeded to take a well deserved nap. Shayna switched her reading light on and scanned the travel brochures briefly before settling in for a longer read on the history of India.

India. A sub-continent unto herself. A nation as ancient as the Himalayas that bordered her in the north. A people, proud of their rich heritage, their bitter struggle for freedom from foreign oppression, their multi-cultural adaptations, their invaluable contributions to the world. India, a country steeped in tradition and yet open to modern world influences. The land of many people. Literally.

It is home to approximately 1.13 billion people. (In accordance with the last available Indian Census estimate for March 2008). Her population is second in size only to China's. India houses one-sixth of the world's population. It supports 17.5% of the world's population in 2.4% of the world's land area. India has more arable land than any nation except the United States and is third in the world after the United States and Canada when it comes to bodies of water. Indian life centers around agriculture (and its allied industries), agriculture being the predominant occupation.

India's diversity is reflected in more than two thousand ethnic groups wherein, a total of 1,652 languages and dialects are spoken, 22 of which are recognized as official. Hindi is the national language of India. India's diversity is further reflected in the representation of every major religion. India demographically breaks down into approximately 80.5% of the population being Hindu, 13.4% Muslim (the third largest Muslim population after Indonesia and Pakistan). India also has the largest population of Sikhs (1.8%) and Jains (0.4%) and Zoroastrians (also known as *Parsi.*) Other religious groups include 2.3% Christians, 0.8% Buddhists and 0.5% Jews and Bahai's and others.

The people of India vary not only by the religions they practice or the languages they speak but also by the food they eat and the clothes they wear. In the south of India, rice is the staple diet of the region as much of the lower half of the country is surrounded by the Arabian Sea to the West and the Bay of Bengal to the East. Fishing, coconut and rice growing are major occupations. Coffee plantations are also a prevailing business in the south. In the north, the staple food is bread. Indian bread – *roti, naan, paratha* and similar flat breads. India is land locked in the north and agriculture is a major means of livelihood. Tea plantations in the north of India, Darjeeling Tea in particular, have acquired world acclaim.

Indians owe their origins to the Dravidian and Aryan Civilizations. The Dravidians entered India from the east from what is known today as south western China. They were considered the aborigines or native dwellers of India. While most of the tribes of the world were still nomadic, the Dravidians established the Indus Valley civilizations of *Mohenjo Daro and Harappa*. Ultimately the Dravidians settled down in the south of India. The Aryans on the other hand, were a semi nomadic tribe originating from southern Russia and central Asia. They entered India from the Indus valley and settled in the north western portion of India. They were brilliant story tellers and are credited with giving India the epic tales of the *Ramayana* and the *Mahabharata*. The *Ramayana* is a story of Aryan *King Ram's* victory over evil multi-headed *Ravana*. *The Mahabharata* is a tale of the five *Pandava* brothers' battles with the *Kauravas* and how they ultimately emerged victorious. Over the ages, the two civilizations mingled, sharing ideas, rituals and their cultures. Today, due to advanced transportation and migration to the big cities, inter-caste, inter-faith and inter-civilization marriages of bygone eras, there has resulted an amalgamation of traits and characteristics, a cross-culturalism and a broad acceptance of their differences, that makes the people of India *Indian*.

Though food tends to vary from region to region, almost all Indian food is prepared with a basic set of spices found in almost every Indian home. The round stainless steel spice box with its individual round containers and individual spoons hold the most favored spices of Indian cooking. The whole or finely powdered spices include *haldi* (turmeric), *chilli* (dried red chilli), *dhania* (coriander seed), *jeera* (cumin seed), *garam masala* (a blend of whole cloves, cardamom seeds, coriander seeds, pepper corns, cumin seeds, cinnamon sticks and bay leaves. Other variations are also available). It is the delicately blended balance of these spices that are responsible for the strong aromatic flavors of Indian cuisine. Other ingredients favored by Indian cuisine include ginger, garlic, coriander leaves (cilantro) and green chillies. In addition to the basic set of spices, there are hundreds of other ingredients and spices that make Indian food as flavorful and as aromatic as it is. The cuisine of each region preferring certain ingredients over others, produces its unique specialties.

The *sari* is considered to be the national dress of India, but is worn differently from region to region. It is manufactured in two lengths of six yards and nine yards. The length of sari chosen depends on the style in which it is draped. Saris are available in various fabric types, both natural and synthetic-cotton, silk, nylon, rayon, chiffon, organdy and blends of all these fabrics as well. Those worn for daily use are simple and in sharp contrast to the heavily embroidered *zari* (gold and silver thread) sari worn for special occasions. While the sari in its adaptations is still widely worn across the nation, other forms of dress have been widely adopted.

No summary of India would be complete without mention of the contributions India has made to the world we live in. India is credited with inventing the number system, the concept of 'zero' having been invented by *Aryabhatta,* an Indian mathematician and astronomer in the fifth century. India gave the world the techniques of algebra, algorithm, square root, cube root and calculus among other mathematical contributions. Computer languages use binary digits that would have been impossible without the number zero.
The game of chess (among others less well known) first originated in India. In addition to the innumerable contributions to the field of engineering, medicine, surgery and astronomy, India gave the world spirituality in the form of

Yoga. The first university in the world originated in India. The Sanskrit language is part of the Indo-Aryan family of languages and is the root of most languages spoken in the world today. While present day media coverage often depicts India's poverty, she was once the richest empire on earth before the invasion and occupation of the British.

Below, are some important trivia about India:

National language: Hindi

National Animal: Tiger

National Bird: Peacock

National Tree: Banyan

National Flower: Lotus

National Fruit: Mango

National Game: Hockey (field hockey)

National Emblem: *Chakra* (wheel)

National Flag: Saffron, white and green horizontal bands. Blue *chakra* centered on white band.

Shayna looked up from her book. She stretched her arms and neck muscles, trying to relieve the crick in her neck. She looked around her. The passengers on the aircraft had settled in for the night. The noisy family in the four center aisle seats had settled down. The general air of quiet ambience had extended its cloak over them too. Chubby brat boy was done with his private stash of junk food, empty candy wrappers strewn untidily on the floor by his seat. He was wearing an airline headset and was watching a Hindi movie on the tiny screen in front of him. A couple of bollywood's sexy sirens were gyrating suggestively to a catchy Hindi film song. He was bobbing his fat head to the music, mouthing the words of the song, off key, softly. He was quite obviously tone deaf and knew it. The little girl was asleep, her head resting in her mother's lap, faint traces of lipstick still visible on her serene baby face. The mother and father of the children were asleep too, her head resting on her husband's shoulder, his head lolling on the seat head rest, his mouth hanging open exposing a set of yellow teeth badly in need of a dentist's tooth whitening touch. Shayna turned her attention back to her book. She flipped the pages of the guide book till she came upon the section on Bombay.

Bombay is the capital of the State of *Maharashtra* (one of twenty-two states that make up India). It lies to the west of India, touching the Arabian Sea. Bombay is a melting pot of varied ethnicities, where real estate is a premium and opportunities for success are a plenty. More than 72% of the billion plus population of India lives in approximately 550,000 villages. The rest of the population lives in the 2000 towns and cities spread across the country, Bombay city being a major player. In an attempt to improve the quality of life for their families, thousands of villagers migrate to Bombay, in search of better jobs, hoping for a bigger slice of the prosperity pie. It is no wonder that Bombay is home to approximately eighteen million people (last available census taken). Most village migrants unable to afford the prices of Bombay's soaring real estate, set up slum dwellings around the city, *Dharavi* being the largest slum in Asia.

The city of Bombay was once a collection of seven little islands- *Colaba, Mazagoan, Wadala, Mahim, Old woman's Island, Parel and Matunga-Sion.* These seven islands were part of Emperor Ashoka's Kingdom. Subsequent to his death, the islands fell into the hands of the Muslim rulers of *Gujarat* (Bombay's neighboring state) for two centuries. The Mosque at *Mahim*, is the only standing proof today of their dominion over the region. In 1534, the Portuguese took Bombay by force. They built several churches in areas heavily concentrated with Roman Catholics. St. Andrew's church in Bandra, is the only church in Bombay today with a façade distinctly Portuguese. The Portuguese built forts (still standing today) *in Bassein, Sion, Mahim and Bandra* to strengthen their presence. They claimed their acquisition and named it 'Bom Baia' meaning '*Good Bay*' in Portuguese.

Over a hundred years later, *Bom Baia* was given to King Charles II as dowry when he married Spanish Princess

Catherine of Braganza in 1662. The seven islands, not considered of great value to the British Crown, were leased to the East India Company a few years later for the paltry sum of ten pounds in gold.

The East India Company shifted its trading headquarters from *Surat* (in Gujarat, Bombay's neighbor) to *Bom Baia*, putting *Bom Baia* in the forefront of trading. The British corrupted '*Bom Baia*' to '*Bombay*' and the name stuck till 1996, when the name was changed yet again to '*Mumbai*' after *Mumbadevi*, a Hindu deity.

The Parsi community though small in size, (making up only 0.5% of the population and sharing that number with other minorities), made significant contributions to the growth of Bombay. They first arrived in India in 1640. The Zoroastrians also known as *Parsi* originated from Iran. In an attempt to save their religion of Zoroastrianism, they fled to India to escape persecution from the Arabs who proselytized Islam. Along with the *Koli,* (fisher-folk of the islands) they warded off attacks to the region, they bought grasslands and allowed cattle to graze freely, thus relieving poor cattle owners from paying a 'grazing fee' imposed by the British.

They also funded the development of causeways between the islands. They built the Zoroastrian *Tower of Silence* (final resting place for the Parsi community) on *Malabar Hill* in 1672. Zoroastrians who are followers of *Ahura Mazda* (considered to be The Lord of Wisdom) and the prophet *Zarathustra,* believe in venerating the natural elements of Earth, Water and Fire. Upon death, they return their bodies to the elements by exposing their corpses to the elements and the flesh-eating vultures that inhabit the Tower of Silence.

The Parsi community made several contributions to India, but perhaps their most significant contribution, was to the realm of ship building. The Bombay docks are a vestige of ambitious industry and entrepreneurial initiative. In 1870 the Bombay Port Trust was formed and the Zoroastrians built innumerable war ships and merchant vessels. Several streets and buildings were named after Parsi philanthropists to commemorate their contributions, including the building that houses Mumbai's computerized stock exchange.

Previously, raw cotton was shipped from India to England, manufactured into cloth that was then sent back to India to be sold. India's first cotton mill was built in 1854, putting an end to this practice. In 1853, the first twenty-one mile long railway line was laid in Bombay, the first railway line in the nation. Subsequent railway lines were laid down in other parts of the country, opening up opportunities for travel and trade.

Bombay attracted traders, ship builders and manufactures alike. They set up bustling businesses in luxurious silk, chintz, muslin, spices, tobacco, corn, rice, glass, onyx, tin sheets, copper vessels, oils, clarified butter, sugar, dyes, camphor and pigments to name a few.

The traders would navigate the seven islands by boat. The swamps that separated the island were dangerous and unhealthy, the commuters often losing their lives in stormy monsoon weather. The swamps attracted insects and spread illness far and wide, killing several inhabitants of the islands. Major planning and development resulted in the construction of causeways that linked the islands together. Forts and a castle were built to protect the people. By 1845 the city swamps were completely filled in and the seven little islands that made up Bombay were rendered one big island as it stands today.

Bombay grew commercially, its population increasing exponentially. Churches, hospitals and a mint for the production of coins sprung up. Traders from neighboring regions set up shop in Bombay, making intricate gold jewelry, weaving fabric, embroidering brocade. Money lenders, traders, iron-smiths and ship builders found a place in the growing market.

Other trading centers in India were soon eclipsed by Bombay's prosperity. Serious importation and exportation of goods catapulted Bombay to the top of the pyramid of trade and commerce. She became the 'Gateway to India.' Bombay was a deep water port and large sea vessels were able to dock, to load or unload their cargo. But the city needed a fort and soldiers to protect it from foreign ships and pirates. Several forts were thus built. One area in Bombay today is still referred to as the 'fort' area. The Bombay Marine fleet came into being to protect Bombay from foreign ships, later coming to be known as the Indian Navy.

Bombay was ravaged by the bubonic plague towards the end of the nineteenth century, resulting is devastating loss of human life. The City Improvement Trust recognized the need to develop the suburbs of Bombay City, urging development for residential purposes to ease congestion in the city. The population of Bombay spread out to fill the newly developed suburbs.

The *Bombay Gymkhana* was formed as a place for Europeans to socialize and mingle with other Europeans and to play cricket (a sport they introduced to Indians that continues to be the most followed sport in India). Other communities soon followed suit building their own gymkhanas across Bombay, some still in existence today. Fiercely competitive sporting events were organized by the communities between the various gymkhanas.

Bombay continued to expand, gaining importance in world trading, but India was still ruled by the British. Mahatma Gandhi along with several other national freedom fighters, called for the British to 'Quit India'. This historic event took place at the *Gwalior Tank Maidan* (field) in Bombay. The British arrested Indian leaders, but they could not arrest the surging momentum of the Quit India Movement. They finally withdrew from India on August 15th 1947. The last British troops left Indian soil through the archway of the Gateway of India after 282 years of occupation.

Mumbai today is the epicenter of India, where the mind bogglingly rich, live along side the heart wrenchingly poor. While Delhi is the capital of India, Mumbai is her financial and business capital. It is home to India's entertainment industry known as *Bollywood* and consequently home to its celebrities and film stars. Bombay boasts a night life on par with other major world cities, a paradise for shoppers and a culinary experience of international ranking.

Shayna closed her book. She was glad to have read the information available in the guide book. At least she had some basics about India and Bombay to go on. Adrian had promised to take her to Agra to see the *Taj Mahal*, after Angela's wedding as well as some day trips around Bombay for the local sites. She looked forward to it. She was a little nervous to meet Adrian's family in person, unsure of her reception. Still, they were almost there, so there was no turning back now. Their flight landed into Bombay. Shayna was glad the long flight was finally over.

The Machado and Pinto families buckled down and did their best to complete the wedding preparations before the wedding festivities began. Angela chose Amy to be her maid of honor. Being her sister might have had something to do with that decision but Angela chose Amy mainly because they were best friends. They were just one year apart in age, so they tended to like the same things, go to the same places and watch the same movies. They had grown to womanhood together, sharing secrets along the way. Amy was the only person who had known about her feelings for Frank before they made that knowledge public to their families and friends. She had convinced Angela that talking to Frank was the only way she would find out his true feelings for her. Angela had taken her sister's advice and here she was, less than a year later, marrying Frank.
She chose two other bridesmaids, Marissa, a cousin on her father's side, and Greta a college friend. For his part, Frank chose his closest friend, Neil to be his best man. Neil had been like a brother to him all his life. They had together attended

St. Stanislaus School but had chosen to pursue separate disciplines in college and had parted ways. They hooked up again in England many years later when Neil's office in Bombay had transferred him to their offices in London. There, the old school friends reunited. Frank had returned to India permanently while Neil continued to live in England, returning briefly to Bombay for his friend's wedding. Frank's niece, Catherine (Bridget's daughter) was the flower girl and Kevin (Rowena's son) was the page boy. Angela's brothers Alastair and Adrian would make up the rest of the bridal entourage.

Both families had coordinated the wedding festivities. They were scheduled to have the rehearsal dinner on Thursday evening, the *Paani* and *Ros* ceremonies on Friday evening, the wedding ceremony and reception on Saturday evening and the *Porthopon* on Sunday evening. Four days of fun and making merry. Family members flew in to Bombay for the wedding. Frank's sisters who lived abroad arrived on Wednesday while Adrian and Shayna arrived from America in the wee hours of Thursday morning.

Thursday was to kick off the wedding celebrations. Both families and all members of the wedding party assembled at St. Andrew's church that evening. Fr. George Vaz was a close friend of the Machado family and was chosen to officiate the wedding. He had been a spiritual mentor to the Machado family and had been the chief celebrant for all the Machado children's' sacraments – baptisms, first holy communions, confirmations and weddings, last sacraments and funerals. It was only natural that he would have the honor of performing the wedding rites of the only remaining single in the Machado family. He had come to know Angela and her family over the years as they were parishioners of St. Andrew's Church. He had guided Frank and Angela in their pre-marriage courses.

At the church rehearsal, he spoke to the assembled gathering. He walked them through the details of the wedding, including the positions of the bridal party as they walked down the aisle,

Frank and Angela's individual roles, their seats in the reserved pews, the actual mass rituals, the vows they would exchange, the record book they would sign after the ceremony, the exit from the church, the hymns they had selected, and instructed the choir leader. They practiced their entrance to the church a few times until they were confident they would not bungle it up. Fr. George urged them to get to the church well ahead of time.

The formalities taken care of, the families and their closest friends headed out to the rehearsal dinner. Angela and Frank had rented a small location for the evening. The caterers had elaborately laid out the food on long canopied tables. They had set up a salad bar with assorted salad makings and waiters served appetizers on trays to the party guests.

They had assorted trays of *chicken tikka*, tiny *cocktail samosas* with a meat filling, mini spinach and cheese *quiches* and *pigs in blankets*. The dinner buffet offered numerous courses in *Moghlai* cuisine – *mutton rogan josh* (a goat curry), *tandoori chicken* (large chicken pieces marinated in spices and yogurt and baked in a clay oven), *saag paneer* (pureed spinach and small chunks of cottage cheese in a spiced gravy), *navrattan korma* (assorted vegetables in a curry), *dum aloo* (a potato preparation), *wedding pullao* (basmati rice pilaf flavored with fried onions and dried fruits and nuts) and a variety of Indian breads and pickles and yogurts. For dessert, the caterers laid out a buffet of *gulab jamuns* (balls of fried dough immersed in a sugar syrup), pistachio, mango and tender coconut ice creams and a huge chocolate cake.

The food was superb and the presentation spectacular. The disc jockey hired for the evening played old and new song favorites, pleasing guests of all ages, as they danced to the rhythm of the beat. They danced until midnight, the party winding down slowly in the last hour. It was a great start to what promised to be a greater celebration as the wedding day drew nearer.

Friday brought them a day closer to the actual wedding day. It was the day scheduled for the *Paani* and *Ros* ceremonies. The *Paani* (water) ceremony performed by the East Indian section of the catholic community is somewhat similar to the *Ros* (anointing) ceremony performed by the Goan and Mangalorean sections of the catholic community. The families of the bride and the groom have separate parties, each celebrating their own traditions, different from each other and yet very alike.

Angela's family had gathered together at Lynette and Robert's home. Only very close friends and family were invited to the *Ros* ceremony. Shayna was happy for the opportunity to meet the closest members of Adrian's family.

An aunt prepared the table, arranging little bowls on the table. Shayna walked over to the table. She wanted to know more about the ceremony that they were about to perform. She had attended an Indian friend's wedding in New Jersey, but the bride and groom in question had been of the Hindu faith, and she had seen a very different set of ceremonies. She had assumed that all Indian weddings were conducted similarly. Only very recently, she had found out that that was not the case at all. Christian weddings were different from Hindu weddings which were very different from Muslim weddings which were very different from Parsi weddings which were very different from all other weddings. As far as she knew, Christian weddings in Bombay most closely resembled Christian weddings in America, but there were exceptions as she was about to find out. Reaching the table, she said,

"Hello, I'm Shayna. Adrian's friend."

"Hello. Yes yes, I know," the aunt replied, smiling.

"Can I help with something?" Shayna offered, smiling back.

"No, no don't worry. You might spoil your beautiful dress," the aunt replied.

"Please. I would like to help," Shayna returned.

"Okay. Maybe you can arrange these flowers in that vase," the aunt said pointing to one on a nearby table.

Shayna took the bouquet of flowers and arranged them in the vase. She carefully arranged the pink and white roses among the green ferns and baby's breath foliage that she had been handed. She was done before long.

"Do you think this is okay?" Shayna asked the aunt.

"What a beautiful arrangement! Beautiful, beautiful!" The aunt said encouragingly.

"Thanks," said Shayna.

"Not at all. Not at all. You really did a great job!" the aunt replied, beaming and effusive in her praise.

Shayna cleaned up the floral stems she had trimmed and put them in the trash along with the cellophane wrapper they came in. She fluffed up some sofa cushions, dusted the coffee table and placed some coasters on each side table. There was not much else to do really as most of it had been done already. The aunt had been observing Shayna and smiled at her.

"Thanks for helping out," said the aunt.

"Sure, no problem," Shayna replied.

"No problem? I didn't realize there was one," questioned the aunt confused by Shayna's choice of words.

"Oh, no. There is no problem. That's what we say back home. What I meant was that I was happy to help," Shayna clarified, hoping her explanation was satisfactory to Adrian's aunt.

"Oh, I see, I see! That's quite alright then. I understand," said Adrian's relieved aunt, the frown quickly disappearing.

"Good!" said Shayna, not wanting to upset Adrian's aunt either.

"Yes, yes! So long as there is no problem," smiled the aunt in reply, shaking her head from side to side. Like a pendulum.

Shayna couldn't help noticing, and not for the first time since her arrival earlier that morning, that people in Bombay repeated the same word in the same sentence when they talked. 'No-no, no' or 'yes, yes, yes' or 'not at all, not at all' or 'of course, of course or 'I see, I see'. As though saying it more than once somehow emphasized its meaning. Shayna thought it was definitely different but quite endearing.

She had also noticed that some of the people she has met didn't dip their heads forward if they wanted to nod or answer in the affirmative. They titled their heads from side to side instead. Much like a pendulum swinging to an imaginary cord. She made a mental note to herself to keep an ear and an eye open for other such mannerisms.

The family was finally ready for the ceremony. Every one assembled in the living room. Angela and her three bridesmaids - Amy, Marissa and Greta were seated on stools across from the assembly. They were dressed rather simply in old tee shirts and sweatpants, thought Shayna. She had expected the ceremony to be slightly more formal and had dressed accordingly. She wore a celadon green silk dress that accentuated the hazel in her hazel brown eyes. She felt a bit over dressed for the occasion but there was not much she could do about it as the ceremony was about to begin. Shayna found herself sandwiched between another aunt and Adrian. The double worded aunt had positioned herself center stage along with a group of younger female family members in one corner of the room, clearly visible to Angela and the other girls.

"What are those ladies going to do?" Shayna asked Adrian softly.

"They are going to sing songs called, '*Voviyos*' during the ceremony," said Adrian.

"*Voviyos?*" Shayna asked, the word sounding strange on her tongue.

"Yes, yes. They are old, old *Konkani* songs," piped in the aunt on her left joining the conversation. Shayna couldn't resist a smile. Here was another aunt who repeated words in the same sentence.

"*Konkani* is the language spoken by *Goan* and *Mangalorean* people," Adrian offered helpfully.

The first double worded aunt and her entourage of singers began singing the *voviyos*. She would sing a line and they would repeat it.

"Why are they repeating the words? Why do they not sing together?" Shayna wanted to know.

"Tradition has it that an elderly experienced lady leads the younger singers. She sings one line and the younger women folk repeat it. This way, the younger women learn the words and when confident of the song and the cadence, can take the lead in the years to come thereby keeping the tradition alive," the aunt knowledgeably added.

"What kind of songs are they?" asked Shayna.

"They sing about a happy life and a bright future for the bride," offered an uncle behind them, also joining in the conversation.

The *voviyos* underway, Lynette walked up to Angela. She dipped her fingers in one of the bowls from the table and touched Angela's forehead. Then, Robert walked up to Angela and repeated the action.

"What are they putting on Angela?" Shayna asked, intrigued.

"They are anointing (*Ros*) Angela with coconut oil," Adrian said.

"What does it signify?" asked Shayna.

"The parents of the bride are blessing her in the presence of her relatives in preparation for her new life," the aunt explained.

The coconut oil anointing complete, Lynette and Robert dipped into the other larger bowl on the table.

"What's that?" Shayna enquired.

"That is coconut milk extracted from the flesh of the coconut," said Adrian.

Lynette and Robert applied a small quantity of coconut milk to Angela's cheek and then applied some to Amy's cheek, Marissa's cheek and finally to Greta's cheek.

"Coconut milk is a symbol of wealth and prosperity," offered the uncle behind them.

"But why are they applying it to the other girls?" Shayna asked.

"They are unmarried girls and part of the bridal party. So they are being blessed too," offered the aunt next to her.

"Lynette, what about Shayna, over here. You must apply coconut milk on her cheek too," the uncle in the back called out loudly.

Lynette walked over and touched Shayna's cheek with the milky liquid, careful not to spill any on her dress. Shayna was a little embarrassed to be the center of attention, but was happy to be included in the ritual.

After the parents had anointed the girls, older family members lined up to do the same. The main part of the ceremony was over. The younger cousins and friends lined up as well, but did so more for the fun of it rather than for tradition. They took larger quantities of the coconut milk and splashed it on the girls. They brought out other food items from the kitchen – flour, sugar, eggs, soda, milk or anything they could lay their hands on and doused the girls with them. Everyone laughed at the antics of the day including the four girls, partaking of the merriment. The air was charged with exuberance and festivity. The girls were barely recognizable; they had so much stuff on them. No wonder they had dressed so casually, thought Shayna. They knew what they had been in for and had been prepared. Finally, after the friends and cousins ran out of things to dump on their heads, the four girls left the room to bathe and change into nicer clothes for the rest of the party.

Shayna had learned so much today. She stood with Adrian at the balcony railing after the guests had gone.

"Did Frank have something similar at his house with his family?" She asked.

"Yes. Frank's family is East Indian. They have a similar ceremony. It is called, '*Paani*' meaning water. It is a little different from the *Ros*, but it essentially embodies the same spirit," Adrian supplied.

"Does this happen before every Christian wedding in India?" asked Shayna.

"At more traditional weddings, definitely. Nowadays, brides and grooms prefer to opt for a bridal shower or a bachelor party instead," answered Adrian.

"Tomorrow is the wedding ceremony followed by the reception. What happens after the wedding?" Shayna wanted to know.

"After the wedding, we have what is known as the *Porthopon*," answered Adrian.

"Is that another ritual of some kind?" asked Shayna.

"Actually, it is just a dinner party for the family members of both sides. It is the first time that the bride returns to her parent's home after the wedding along with her husband and her new family. It is hosted at the bride's parent's home and is a welcoming gesture. A joining of two families, if you will," explained Adrian.

"That's nice. It's a great way to recount the previous day's events too I'm sure," said Shayna.

"Yes it is. It also gives both family members a chance to get to know each other a little better," agreed Adrian.

"The *Ros* was fun. Very different from what I'm used to, but fun nonetheless," Shayna smiled at Adrian, returning to the present day's events. She linked her arm casually through his. Accepting her arm, he smiled back.

"Were you alarmed when my mother put coconut milk on your face? She meant well. She didn't mean to embarrass you," Adrian said.

"Actually I thought it was really nice of her to include me in the ceremony," Shayna answered back.

"I'm glad," said Adrian.

"Yeah. I think your mother and I would get along nicely," added Shayna.

"It's good to know that you feel that way," Adrian said.

"I was able to understand the purpose of today's ceremony. Thanks to the explanations from you and your family," Shayna said.

"Did it surprise you when you saw my mother putting coconut oil and milk on the girls?" asked Adrian.

"Not really. I knew before hand about the anointing. So I was okay with that. I'm not sure how I would feel about being drenched in soda or covered with flour and eggs though," Shayna grinned back.

"It can be a lot of fun. The girls seemed to enjoy it. They were real sports today," added Adrian.

"Yeah, thanks but no thanks," added Shayna.

They both laughed, enjoying their little moment together.

Chapter 7

The Wedding

Saturday promised to be a beautiful day. It was the day Angela and Frank would tie the proverbial knot and pledge their love to each other forever. They had waited impatiently for months for this day to arrive and now it was finally here.

The dinner after the church rehearsal and the *Paani* and *Ros* ceremonies had gone off with out a hitch. Everyone was excited and in party mode, the previous two nights of indulgence having only whetted their appetites for more. The exuberant guests had partied after the *Ros* into the wee hours of the morning, but Lynette had insisted that Angela turn in early. She had not wanted her daughter looking tired and drawn on her wedding day.

Before going to bed herself the previous night, Lynette had set the alarm for 5:30am. She had wanted to be up early to get a head start on things. Lynette woke from a fitful sleep when her alarm clock sounded at the appointed time. She pottered around, fixing this and that before she peeked into the living room to assess what needed to be done there. A few of the younger guests, cousins and friends had crashed at their house after the party that had been swinging till 3:00am, their parents having left shortly after dinner.

They were sprawled all over the living room floor and sofa, the room in shambles. Empty beer bottles adorned the window sill, crumpled paper napkins graced the floor and crumbs of food littered the tables. Shoes, some overturned, and other party paraphernalia lay about contributing to the colossal mess. Lynette noticed a sock hanging off the curtain rod, its partner finding a resting place on a nearby lampshade. She wondered what these kids had been up to last night. Mirabai most certainly had her work cut out for her. The room was desperately in need of a clean up, but Lynette left the cousins sleeping as they were. She had other things to take care of and could use the peace and quiet to get some of her chores completed.

She walked into her bedroom and from her closet, pulled out the *sari* she would wear for the church service. It needed a light touch of the iron. The *choli* (sari blouse) was wrinkled too. Lynette quickly ironed out the wrinkles and hung the *sari* and *choli* along with its matching *gaagra* (skirt worn under the sari). She then turned her attention to the burgundy gown she would wear for the reception. It appeared to be wrinkle free, but she pressed the iron lightly over the crepe chiffon fabric anyway just to be sure, and then hung it in her closet along side the recently ironed wedding *sari*.

She checked her husband Robert's suit and then searched for his cufflinks. Somehow it was these little things that always caused a delay, Lynette thought to herself. You could be dressed and ready to head out the door, when suddenly you would remember a pair of cufflinks, or a bracelet or a tie pin, or some other small thing that you just *had* to wear that day. Thinking it would take only a minute, you head back to retrieve it, only to find that it was not where you last put it (or, as is more likely the case, forgot where you last put it and expected it to show up in the places you decided to look for it.) A ten second long search quickly grows into a minute long search which escalates into a ten minute, twenty, thirty minute long search, thus causing a delay. There would be no delays today. Lynette was going to make sure of that.

She found the cuff links and placed them in the drawer of her dresser alongside the jewelry she would wear later today. She polished Robert's shoes and placed a clean pair of socks in them. She picked out his tie and hung it beside his suit on a hanger.

Going into the other bedroom silently so as not to wake anyone up, she checked Amy's bridesmaid gown. Shayna had offered to iron it the night before when she got her own clothes ready. Shayna, in a show of support had opted to wear a *sari* to the church service. Lynette had promised to drape the fabric for her. Right now, the sari and its accessories were neatly folded on a hanger beside the dress she would wear to the reception. Alastair and Adrian's suits were hanging ready in their closet, shoes polished clean and socks balled up in their respective shoes. She checked the clock ticking on the bedroom wall. She was on schedule.

Lynette went about getting breakfast ready for her sleeping family, making sure that there was plenty of food prepared. There was so much to do today and only a few hours to do it in. But she need not have worried as none of the sleepers surfaced before 10:00 am, sleeping off their exhaustion from dancing the previous night away. She was glad to be able to check off several things on her checklist before the first person woke up.

Lynette tip toed into Angela's room. Angela lay sleeping peacefully. Lynette decided to let her daughter sleep. She needed the rest thought Lynette. It simply would not do to look tired on her wedding day. She stood quietly for a moment looking down at her child's sleeping face. Angela was asleep on her side with both her palms joined as if in prayer, except that her hands were tucked under her cheek resting on the pillow. She was curled up like a fried prawn. Lynette smiled, her lips curving upward. Angela had always slept in that position, even when she was a baby. And here she was all grown up but she still slept in the position she had preferred as a child. Some things just never change, Lynette thought as she sighed softly to herself. She turned around and just as she was about to leave the room, Angela stirred.

"Ma?"

"Hi baby. Sorry, I didn't mean to wake you," Lynette said looking at Angela.

"Did you sleep well?" She scrutinized Angela's face. She looked well rested, no signs of fatigue.

"Yes, I did. But I'm up now. There is so much to do," said Angela sitting up in bed.

"Yes, there are lots of things to do, but I don't want you to worry about a thing. I will take care of it all," soothed Lynette taking her daughter's hand, easing her gently back into bed.

"Mum, please don't. You will overwork yourself. As it is, these past few days have been really demanding on all of us but more so, on you. And we are not done yet. We still have to get through today and then the *porthopon* tomorrow as well," Angela cautioned.

"You are not to worry my child. It is not everyday that my daughter gets married. It's the first wedding in our family. It is my job to worry about the wedding details and your job to be well rested and to enjoy your special day," Lynette smiled.

"Oh mum, what would I do without you?" Angela said, hugging her mother.

"I cannot believe that this day is finally here. My own child getting married! I am happy for you my darling, but I will miss you terribly," Lynette hugged Angela back.

"You won't have a chance to miss me, Mum. You know that for the time being, I will be right down the street in Mama Machado's house. I will come see you everyday. And when we find a place of our own, we want to live in Bandra, so I won't be far away from you at all," Angela consoled her mother.

"Yes, I am thankful for that. You are leaving our home, but at least you will not be far away," Lynette said, a tear slipping from her eye.

"Ma, please don't cry," Angela said, her own eyes welling up.

"Angie, I was just remembering you as a baby and now you are all grown up. How the time has flown! You are a woman on the threshold of a new life. Within a few hours you will be a married woman. I am very happy for you. Frank is a good man and he will take care of you. I wish you happiness, my child today and always," Lynette said holding Angela's face in her hands.

"Now dry your tears. You don't want your eyes puffy and red on your wedding day," Lynette continued, drying her own eyes, her wobbly voice gaining authority.

"Breakfast is ready. So hurry up and get out of bed," Lynette said, hugging Angela one last time before she left the room.

The rest of the family woke up little after 10:00am, each one trickling into the kitchen for their own preference of a wake-me-up beverage. The family was gathered around the dining table, the cousins included. They breakfasted quickly on the eggs, bacon and buttered toast that Lynette had put out.

Amid laughter and jokes about the night before, Lynette assigned tasks to all gathered around her table.

"Adrian, take two of your cousins with you to decorate the pews at the church. The decorations are in the box in the hallway. Pick up the fresh flowers from the florist for the altar at the church."

"Alastair, you must see to the reception venue. Make sure all is going according to plan."

"Robert, talk to the caterers, to the church choir and to the manager of the band for the reception."

"Girls, be ready to leave for the salon in a few minutes."

Greta showed up shortly after breakfast and joined the rest of the ladies in the house. Amy, Angela, Shayna, Lynette, Marissa and Greta headed out to the beauty salon for massages, facials, waxes, manicures and pedicures and hair styling. Angela was the first one to be attended to at the salon She had to return home in time for Zizi, her hairstylist who was expected at 3:00 pm. He would do the bride's hair and then his make-up artist / business partner Marketa, would do her face, leaving Angela enough time to get into her wedding dress and still be ready well in time for the house blessings and the wedding service.

While Zizi and Marketa worked on Angela, the rest of the family got ready too. The ladies had returned from their beauty treatments and the men had finished up with the last minute details that they had been assigned to that morning. The Pinto household was a buzz with activity.

 Lynette helped Shayna with the *sari* she had chosen to wear today. Lynette expertly handled the six yards of plum pink silk, deftly draping the fabric around Shayna's slender body. She pinned and tucked the fabric here and there and managed to get the seemingly endless length of fabric to obey her command and fall into place. When she was done, the sari looked like an extension of Shayna, it was so well draped. Lynette fanned out the loose end of the *pulloo* (the end of the sari that hangs over the left shoulder) and showed Shayna how to carry the swathe of intricately detailed silk on her arm. Shayna loved the feel of the soft *Kanjeevaram* silk against her bare midriff. She had never worn a sari before and was a little self conscious exposing her mid section. Lynette showed Shayna the various ways she could drape the *pulloo* around her body. Shayna practiced a few times, beginning to get the hang of it.

The *pulloo* was absolutely gorgeous. It was heavily detailed in silver thread. The threads were sewn in a complicated pattern weaving in and out of the fabric. Here and there it was flecked with bits of silver metal chips. The same silver thread was used as a border on the bottom part of the silk sari as well. What started out at the bottom end of the *sari* as a neat silver threaded border about four to five inches high, exploded into spools and spools of silver thread embroidered adroitly across the entire length of the *pulloo*. The swathe of fabric draped elegantly over her left shoulder and extended to the back of her knee. The fact that she had six yards of fabric draped on her body took a little getting used to, but Shayna was up for the challenge. She was going to wear the sari to the church and then (as was customary for close female members of the bridal couple) she would change into a formal evening gown for the reception.

It was just past 5:00pm, when Angela stood in front of the full length mirror in Lynette's room, surveying her reflection. Zizi had done a remarkable job with her hair. She only hoped that the hair style would hold till the end of the reception and that she wouldn't get a headache from the million (or what seemed like it anyway) hair pins holding it in place.

Angela was not in the habit of wearing much makeup. Her usage was limited to an occasional dab of lipstick for special events, other wise preferring to wear none. Today Marketa had used so many different tubes, pots, tubs, brushes and pencils that Angela thought she must surely look like a frosted birthday cake!

With great trepidation, she looked at her reflection. The woman staring back at her looked unreal. The cosmetics made her look ethereal, heavenly, delicate. Angela thought it had even managed to lessen the point of her pointy nose and deflate the puff of her puffy cheeks. Her eyes appeared to be larger, more luminous and her skin more translucent. Angela thought Marketa and Zizi had completely transformed her face and hair. It was well worth the arm and a leg they were charging her for their talent. She smiled, the trepidation quickly fading away.

Her wedding gown fitted her curves to perfection, undulating gently over the swell of her breasts, tapering inwards at her waist and then flaring out gently over her hips to fall in soft folds to the floor. She touched the sparkling tiara that Zizi had cleverly placed in her hair, the diamonds and pearls twinkling back at her. She adjusted the necklace at her throat and took one final look at herself. She thought she looked much better than she usually did. Angela hoped Frank would be pleased.

She wanted to be beautiful for Frank. For her husband. Her eyes glowed softly in anticipation of her lover's response to her transformation.

The day had been equally chaotic at Mama Machado's house. The entire family, Frank's six sisters, their spouses and children had assembled for the blessing. It was 4:30pm. The photographer and the videographer had set up their equipment and were ready for the family. The blessing ritual began.
Mama Machado walked up to her son and held his hands in hers. She whispered a small prayer and said to Frank,
"May you always know happiness with Angela," She said.
One after the other, the other family members walked up to Frank. They either said a small prayer or a blessing or simply just hugged him or kissed his cheek. The photographer and videographer captured every touching moment. Once the blessing was over, they packed up and left to set up shop at Lynette's house for Angela's family blessing before they finally headed to the church.

Both families arrived at the church well in time for the service. Fr. George Vaz was waiting for the wedding party. Neil lifted Angela's veil and kissed her cheek before handing her the bridal bouquet, as was customary for the best man to do. People cheered and joked that it was the best man's privilege to kiss the bride before her husband did. Neil returned to the interior of the church to stand by Frank's side, while the rest of the bridal party took their positions. The service began. The church organ started up.
Four year old Kevin the pageboy, was to lead the bridal party into the church. He wore a mini three piece suit complete with mini tie, mini vest and mini pocket kerchief. It was an exact mini replica of the suits the older men in the bridal party were wearing. He carried a decorated cushion for the wedding rings in front of him and walked slowly down the center of the aisle. He performed his part according to plan. He walked slowly placing one foot steadily in front of the other.

Suddenly, he noticed the crowded church. At the rehearsal, they had practiced his part several times, but nobody had thought to tell him that the church would be full of strangers, his family nowhere is sight. They had been assigned seats in the reserved pews up front with the rest of the family. Little Kevin panicked. He promptly turned around and pelted back in the direction from which he had come, throwing the ring cushion with an upward swish of his hand. Immediately an "oooh" and an "aaah" and a few giggles could be heard from the crowd.

Frank and his best man Neil, were standing at the half way point of the aisle and saw Kevin running to the exit, ring cushion tossed in the air. Frank was thankful that he had listened to his sisters and had asked Neil to keep the wedding rings in his pocket till they were needed. If not, they would be down on their hands and knees looking between hundreds of pairs of feet, searching for the rings that would surely have rolled into the crowded pews.

Catherine the flower girl, quickly caught Kevin as he torpedoed out of the church. He slowed down, but kicked and screamed to be released. Amy walked up to them and calmed him down. Seeing familiar faces, he settled down and finally agreed to go back in to the church if he could hold Catherine's hand. Crisis averted, the organist played the entrance song again. This time around, Catherine and Kevin made it down the aisle uneventfully, Kevin swinging the recovered ring cushion back and forth in his free hand.

Amy was up next. As the maid of honor, she had the privilege of walking down the aisle all by herself. Her partner for the evening was Neil and he was already in position beside Frank. Amy walked gracefully by the pews and assumed her position near the altar. She was followed by Marisa and Alastair and finally by Greta and Adrian. The bridal entourage in its place, all eyes settled on the bride.

To the music of 'here comes the bride,' Angela walked down the aisle on her father's arm. She radiated happiness and warmth as she walked to the altar. All eyes were on her, but she had eyes only for Frank. And he for her. Robert kissed Angela and handed his daughter over to Frank. He assumed his position beside Lynette as Frank walked with Angela down the short length of the aisle to the altar.

"My dear brothers and sisters, we have gathered here today to celebrate the union of Angela Maria Pinto and Frank Anthony Machado......" Fr. George intoned.

The wedding mass progressed, Fr. George taking them through the necessary rites and rituals.

Before long, they had arrived at the wedding rite.

"Do you Angela, take this man Frank to be your lawfully wedded husband, to have and to hold from this day forward, for better or for worse, in sickness and in health, till death do you part?" Fr.George asked Angela.

"I do," she replied, gazing into Frank's eyes.

"And do you Frank, take this woman Angela to be your lawfully wedded wife, to have and to hold from this day forward, for better or for worse, in sickness and in health, till death do you part?" Fr. George asked of Frank.

"I do," said Frank, his eyes locking onto Angela's.

Neil fished out the wedding rings from his coat pocket and placed them on the ring cushion. Little Kevin, ring cushion held firmly in both hands this time very carefully walked up to Fr. George. He executed his office with much dignity and poise.

"With this ring, I thee wed," said Angela placing a ring on Franks' finger.

"With this ring, I thee wed," said Frank, placing the other ring on Angela's finger.

"By the power vested in me by the church, I now pronounce you man and wife. You may kiss the bride," Fr. George smiled and shook their hands.

Frank lifted Angela's veil and saw her face for the first time since the rehearsal dinner. She looked more beautiful today than ever. He gazed into her eyes taking his time, savoring the moment, drinking in her beauty and then he dipped his head forward to kiss his bride.

Angela gazed into Frank's eyes, lost in its depths. Her husband. Her love. She lifted her face to meet his lips half way. A cheer went up in the crowd. Many a guest wiped a tear, moved by the love evident between the couple they had just witnessed being united. Lynette was openly crying tears of happiness. Mama Machado not given to displays of emotion anymore was nonetheless happy for her son.

Angela and Frank made a beautiful couple. They were destined for great happiness together. They were also destined for great sorrow, but they didn't know that on their wedding day.
Would they have married had they known what the future would hold?
Probably.
Would Frank have married Angela if he had known that he would die?
Probably.
Would Angela have married Frank if she had known that he would die so young, leaving her to face a lifetime of loneliness leaving her to raise their three little children on her own?
Probably. Probably not.

The reception was held at a beautiful open air location. The venue looked like a page out of a fairytale. The tall trees that bordered the enclosed area were decorated with millions of little white lights. They shone down from the branches, high enough that they resembled twinkling stars, low enough to cast a fairyland-like appearance to the guests below. The tables were covered with white tablecloths and an overlay of shimmery gold fabric. More of the same fabric adorned the entranceway, the gift table and the guest book table. They had carried the same theme to the buffet tables set up to one side of the area. Every decoration at the venue had been coordinated in white and gold. The decorated space had a dream like quality to it.

The guests started filtering in and soon the venue was packed. The live band had previously set up their musical instruments on a raised dais and was entertaining the guests. The wedding guests clustered around the tables chit chatting, awaiting the bridal couple. They did not keep their guests waiting long. The emcee for the evening announced their arrival,

"Ladies and gentlemen, may I present to you for the very first time, Mr. and Mrs. Machado!"

Angela and Frank made their grand entrance and walked around the periphery of the dance floor. People showered them with confetti and silly string as the band played lively music. They cut the three tiered wedding cake placed on a table in the center of the dance floor. The band began playing the 'Bridal Special', a romantic song that Angela and Frank had selected. The newly married couple performed their first dance together as man and wife. The emcee encouraged the guests to join the bridal couple on the dance floor a few minutes later.

A short while later, the emcee called for the 'Bridal March'. Angela and Frank were at the head of the line followed by other family members and guests in pairs. To music, the emcee had each couple move forward in a straight line till they reached the front of the dance floor. Then every alternate couple either went left or right to the back of the line where the left-going couples met up with the right-going couples. So now instead of one couple abreast, they were two couples abreast as they walked up the center line again to the front. They repeated these steps till they were four couples abreast.

Then the emcee had each couple face each other and make bridges with their arms stretched above them. A train of guests went under the bridge and in turn formed their own bridges. It was a very complicated process, but the emcee had obviously led bridal marches before and he knew exactly what he needed to do to ensure that the exercise did not result in a people jam. The guests enjoyed themselves and took advantage of the opportunity to mingle with other guests at the party. The band took a short break and the guests returned to their seats for refreshments and to catch their breaths before the next dance set.

Alastair toasted Angela and Frank saying a few choice words over the microphone. He raised his glass in salutation to the couple and the guests did the same.

Shayna was fascinated by the new things she had learned and by the differences in her culture and Adrian's. There were similarities of course, but she noted that there were just as many dissimilarities as there were similarities. She had followed the emcee's cues for the bridal march. Adrian had to partner Greta the bridesmaid, so she accompanied a cousin she had met at the *Ros*.

After the bridal march Shayna found herself sitting next to Mama Machado at the family table. She hadn't had much of a chance to talk to her since she had arrived in Bombay. Shayna had met so many people in the three days she had been there, that she was quite certain she would never remember all their names.

"That was fun," she said out loud as she dropped herself into a chair.

"Yes. Everybody loves the bridal march," Mama Machado replied tiredly as she had been part of the march too.

"It's a good way to get a party going, that's for sure!" returned Shayna.

"It is. The young and the old look forward to it," said Mama Machado.

"You looked great on the dance floor," Shayna complimented her.

"Thanks," She replied adding, "but that is about as much as I can do. My old weary bones cannot keep up to this new fast tempo that today's kids seem to favor."

Shayna laughed. "I'm not sure if I could keep up with teenagers myself," she added kindly.

They sat quietly for a moment taking in the sounds around them.

"So, Shayna tell me, are you having a good time in India so far?" Mama Machado asked.

"I am having a great time! And I've only been here three days!" Shayna responded enthusiastically.

"Weddings are fun, but you should try to see some sites of Bombay too," said Mama Machado.

"Oh, yes. Adrian has promised to take me around Bombay over the next few days. Towards the end of next week, we are going to *Agra* to see the Taj Mahal," Shayna supplied.

"That's good. Try to see as much as you can. India has so much to offer," Mama Machado said, loyal to her country's heritage.

"I would love to go to the south of India. I have heard so much about the beaches there. But unfortunately we cannot go. Maybe next time. We have just three weeks in India and even I know that three weeks is not enough to explore everything India has to offer. Besides, we already have a short trip to *Agra* planned next week. Adrian has not seen his family for two years so it is more important that he gets to spend time with them as much as possible," Shayna said.

"That's very thoughtful of you," Mama Machado said with a new appreciation for this blond foreign girl.

"Family is important. I know his mother misses him when he is away," she added.

"I'm sure she does. They are a very close knit family. I really like that about Adrian. My family is close too, so I understand if he wants to spend time with them. It's a great opportunity for me to get to know them as well," said Shayna.

Mama Machado nodded her white head slowly, thinking to herself that if she didn't know it already, Lynette would have another wedding on her hands very soon.

An older gentleman limped up to the table to talk to Mama Machado. Shayna was about to excuse herself, not wanting to intrude, but the aged woman waved her back into her seat.

"Shayna, I would like you to meet Michael D'souza. Michael, this is Shayna, Adrian's friend from America," she made the introductions. Michael shook her proffered hand, taking her hand in both of his.

"Pleased to meet you Shayna," he said.

"Pleased to meet you too Michael," she responded smiling.

"Please sit with us Michael," invited Mama Machado.

In response to her invitation, Michael pulled out a chair and sat down at their table. Not too many people said no to the grand lady.

"Michael is a very interesting man, Shayna. His stories can shed some light on Bombay's history. He used to work for the Bombay Fire Brigade and was actually involved in an incident at the Bombay docks many years ago," Mama Machado said.

Shayna was definitely interested. She asked,

"Really? What happened at the docks?"

"It happened in the year of 1941. A long time ago," he began reminiscing.

"I had been working at the Bombay port at the time. A fire broke out on a docked ship. She was called 'Fort Stikine'. I remember as if it happened yesterday. She had docked into Bombay to unload her cargo – cotton, timber, gun powder, ammunition, gold bars and some other cargo. I cannot remember all the little details now. Anyway, she was there to unload her cargo, when a fire broke out."

"Was it an accident or was it deliberate?" Shayna asked, intrigued.

"No one could really ascertain that. All that is known is that there were two explosions. After the first blast, the Bombay fire brigade responded to the scene first. Then unexpectedly, there was a second blast. Many of those first time responders lost their lives in the second blast. No one saw it coming. I am guessing that the first fire ignited the dangerous cargo of the ship, setting off the second blast. That is what I speculate happened."

"How terrible!" Shayna responded.

"Yes, it was terrible. Many lost their lives. I thankfully escaped with just the loss of one leg. Now I have a prosthetic leg instead. Even though I limp and I can only walk around slowly, at least I am not confined to a wheel chair or more importantly, I didn't lose my life. Some of the other members of my brigade were not so lucky," Michael shook his head sadly.

He continued with his story. "The blasts were so loud, they could be heard all the way in *Dadar* which was eight miles away."

"Unbelievable!" Shayna replied.

"Yes. It was really very loud. The newspapers reported that the gold bars that made up part of the ship's cargo exploded in all directions. Some of the bars landed in the sea off the docks, some in different parts of the city, one even landed up at a *Parsi* man's house a mile away!"

"Wow. Did he get to keep the gold bar?" Shayna asked.

"He actually returned it to the authorities. They recovered all the gold bars eventually, some even showing up intact thirty years later," Michael marveled.

"That's quite a story," said Shayna.

"It's true," said Michael.

Adrian had gone to the bar after the bridal march and returned with drinks for Shayna and Mama Machado. He offered to go back to the bar for a drink for Michael as he had not been at the table earlier.

"What's your poison, Michael?" Adrian asked Michael.

"What time is it?" Michael asked, also checking his own wrist watch.

"8:10,"obliged Adrain.

"Okay, I'll have a whiskey, please. On the rocks," answered Michael.

"Right. I will be back shortly with your drink Michael," said Adrian setting off for the bar again.

Shayna thought it strange that Michael would check the time before he answered Adrian's question. Another Bombayism? Like the repetitive words? And the pendulum nods? She would have to ask Adrian about that later.

What Shayna did not know was that 8:00pm is the hour most older generation Indians consider a respectable time to initiate the consumption of hard alcohol. Not 7:30 pm, not 7:59pm. Only after 8:00pm. Also, there seems to be a widely accepted practice of consuming beer in small-sized glasses at noon time. One could consume copious amounts of beer if one so desired, but if it was imbibed at noon, then the container of choice would be a small glass. Taller glasses were reserved for evening consumption.

Michael, Shayna and Mama Machado settled into an easy silence for a few minutes.

"So Shayna, which part of America are you from?" asked Michael.

"From New Jersey, originally. My parents live there. I work in New York, so I live there now. Just north of New York City," she replied.

"I visited your country four years ago. I stayed with my niece in Brooklyn," added Michael.

"Really? Will you be visiting again soon?" Shayna enquired politely.

"I have no immediate plans. But my sister visits her daughter, my niece every year," he supplied.

"That's nice. She gets to see her daughter often," Shayna said making small talk.

"Yes, today so many Indians have settled all over the globe, that it has been said that every family in Bandra, possibly even Bombay has at least one person from their family living abroad," Michael said.

Shayna was astonished to hear that.

"That's quite a statistic!" she replied.

"Yes it is. As it is we have a population of about a billion people. Can you imagine what it would be like if every Indian in the world chose to live in India? I don't think there would be room for everyone!" Michael laughingly joked.

"Yes, I did read up on some information about India. The book I read suggested that approximately eighty percent of the population is Hindu. I can see that, Hinduism having its roots in India. Before I met Adrian, I did not know that India had a Christian population as well. It is tiny in comparison to the Hindu population though. Only 2.3% if my memory serves me right," Shayna said.

"Yes that is a small number no doubt. But when you consider a population of a billion people, 2.3% is not such a small number. 2.3% amounts to over twenty million people," Mama Machado calculated.

"You are right. I never quite looked at it that way. Twenty million people are a lot of people," Shayna accepted.

"What about Bandra? I understand it is home to a large group of Christians," Shayna said.

"Yes it is. While Christians, predominantly Catholics, are spread all across the city of Bombay and its suburbs, there are areas with a strong concentration of Catholics. Bandra is one such pocket. Did you know Bandra is the queen of the suburbs?" asked Mama Machado.

"No, I did not know that. How very interesting. Can you tell me a little more about Bandra?" asked Shayna.

"Yes, I can. I have lived here all my life. Bombay was made up of seven islands. Bandra was part of the island of *Salsette*. It was made up of twenty-five *pakhadis* or hamlets. *Ranwar*, where I live, is one such hamlet. Life used to be very different in the good old days," said Mama Machado, her wrinkled eyes taking on a far away look.

"*Ranwar* residents used to be rice cultivators. The rice fields used to stretch for miles and miles. The people built houses on higher ground saving the best parts of the land for paddy fields. Also, it was a land rich in produce and was constantly raided by pirates, so safety was a concern too. As there were limited areas of high ground, they built houses close to each other with narrow streets winding between the houses. If you look at the old houses of the village even today, you will see what I mean," said Mama Machado.

"Don't forget about the vegetable gardens," interjected Michael. "Every house in the village carried the local produce-sweet onions, and mangoes and coconuts."

"Things are very different today in comparison to the days gone by. I was still a young girl when I married my husband and moved into *Ranwar*. I was only nineteen years old. It was such a long time ago. The people of *Ranwar* accepted me as one of their own and made me feel very welcome. I remember the days when we would leave our front and back doors open. Neighbors would stop by at anytime of the day. Everyone knew each other. There were no thieves, no strangers," Mama Machado reminisced.

"I remember those days too," said Michael. "We used to hold the doors open with little pieces of wood to prevent them from slamming shut in the wind," he chuckled.

"Gone are those days forever," lamented Mama Machado.

"Today things have changed so much. I would be afraid to leave my doors open now. The traffic through *Ranwar* has increased tremendously because people use the streets of *Ranwar* to take a short cut to Hill road," she added sadly.

Shayna listened quietly to the exchange between these two aged people who seemed to have regressed in their minds, yearning for an era long gone. They were so absorbed by their memories, it almost seemed as though they had forgotten she was there. Thankfully, Adrian returned with Michael's whiskey.

"Please excuse me, but I would like to steal Shayna away," he said to Mama Machado and Michael.

Taking Shayna's hand, he asked, "Would you like to dance, honey?"

She was happy to accept. She had hardly spent anytime with Adrian since they had arrived. They had all been so busy. She was happy to have her man back now that the wedding formalities were over. She rose from her chair and they headed to the dance floor.

The reception was well underway. Couples of all ages and all shapes and sizes were swinging to the up beat rhythm on the dance floor. The band played a lively set much appreciated by the younger crowd. They followed it with a waltz set for the older folks. Dinner was being served at one end of the venue and people lined up at the buffet tables to partake in the lavish fare. Angela and Frank were busy greeting guests and accepting well wishes. Every one seemed to be having a wonderful time.

Mama Machado now alone, Michael having left to greet someone else, was still far back in the past. She thought about the day she had married Joe. They had been really happy that first year. She had considered herself blessed to have such a wonderful husband. He seemed so worldly to her innocence, so experienced to her naiveté. She was an impressionable wisp of a girl. He was an impressive man. She was easily impressed. Impressed by the things he said and by the things he did. He treated her fairly. She treated him like a God. She cooked his meals washed and ironed his clothes and kept their home clean. He never expressed appreciation for her efforts, considering most of what she did his birth right. Their relationship was by no means on an equal footing, but she was happy. She did not have a yard stick of experiences to compare it to. The first year was blissful as far as she was concerned.

When she lost her baby in the seventh month of her pregnancy, Amelia (Mama Machado) had been devastated. She had longed for the comforting arms of her husband. She had needed him more than ever. But Joe had not wanted to be anywhere near Amelia. He had brought her home from the hospital and moments later he had slammed the front door shut behind him. He had left her to deal with her loss on her own. She had not understood why her husband had left her alone. She had cried for her dead baby and she had cried for Joe, but neither one had heard her. Neither one had heeded her pleas.

Two days later Joe had returned home, the sour smell of vomit and whiskey on his breath. He had looked ragged, his eyes bloodshot. He said nothing to Amelia and yet she had been happy to see him. He did not explain his absence caring nothing for her feelings or for the fact that she had been worried about him, sick with fear. He had eaten the food she had placed in front of him not looking at her once.

The silent treatment had continued for several days. Any attempt at conversation on her part had been met with silence. Ultimately when he did bring himself to look at her, she had been stunned to see the hatred in his eyes. He hated her. He hated her? Why? What had she done? She had been unable to comprehend why. They had both suffered the loss of their child. Why did he hate her so? What had she done to deserve his hatred?

Eventually things had settled down at home. They talked about daily things, never once mentioning their dead baby. They had skirted around the issue, willing it away from their lives. Less than a year later she had become pregnant with Genevieve. She had prayed things would get better with Joe once the baby was born. She had her own fears about losing this baby too, but she had kept them to herself, never once voicing her concerns to her husband. Her imagination had run amok with scary thoughts of the baby dying, but she bottled it all up. She had been fearful of losing Joe's love if she brought up her miscarriage.

One day well onto her second pregnancy, they were having dinner at the table. Amelia turned to her husband and said,

"Brenda from next door asked if I could help with the church fair next week. Would it be okay if I helped out in the evenings?"

"What for? Doesn't she have any other helpers?" Joe asked.

"I'm sure she does, but it might be nice for me to lend a hand too. I will make sure to get dinner ready before I go," Amelia said, her eyes pleading.

"Why do you want to take on additional work? Don't you have enough to do at home?" he asked.

"Of course I do. But it would be good for me to be around other people, to help the church. I would really like to go," she said.

"Why endanger the baby? Isn't it bad enough that you lost my first child, you want to lose my second one too? How much more do you want me to suffer?" he blurted out rudely.

Amelia had sat in her chair stunned. She could not believe the words that her husband had uttered. He thought that *she* had purposefully lost their child? How could he? He had known how much she had wanted their little Violet. He had known how desolate she had been when they had lost her. And what did he mean by 'his child'? Was Violet not hers too? Had she not played an important part? Had she not carried Violet for seven months in her body, feeling her every movement? Was she not carrying this child too and feeling it grow inside her? Did her husband see her as just a vessel to bear his children? Why did he think that she wanted to hurt him? Why did he think that she wanted him to suffer? And what about her suffering? Did it not matter at all? Did she not matter in his grand scheme of things?

Amelia had been stunned on so many levels. She finally understood why she had seen such hatred in his eyes.

He thought she was the reason that they had lost their child.

And he thought that she was trying to do it again.

Cold fingers had clutched her heart as she came to the realization that she had married an *egocentric, self centered, narcissistic monster.*

She had glimpsed her first peek at her husband's ugly side. There were many more to come. Over the next few days, she had tried to see the situation from Joe's point of view, tried to be fair to him, to his pain. But no matter how many times she had tried, she could not find a reason why he should have blamed her for what had happened to their baby.

She focused her thoughts instead on her life after she had married him. She had initially thought it had been rosy and idyllic, but, in the cold reality of their situation, she saw it for what it had truly been - *subservient enslavement.*

She began to blame him for Violet's death. She had rushed to make that train that day because she had had to make Joe's dinner. She had tripped and fallen down the stairs because she had rushed. Had she not been rushing for Joe, she would have been bouncing her baby on her knee. She had lost her baby because of Joe.

Joe was to blame for Violet's death.

Amelia and Joe had continued to live together each blaming the other, each skirting the issue, neither taking the initiative to make amends, each living in their own world, the hurt festering like a pus filled boil.

When Annabelle their fourth child, had become sick from meningitis, Amelia had kept vigil by her bedside, taking care of her sick child's every need. Joe had chosen to handle his stress over the situation differently. He had gone out and got himself drunk. When Annabelle had died, the neighbors had found Joe lying in a ditch by the side of the road smothered in his own filth. He had been gone for days. When he had returned home, he said nothing but his eyes had accused Amelia yet again for losing another of his children. His eyes had spewed hatred for her.

This time, her eyes had spewed hatred back.

Things got worse as the years progressed. He got drunker and drunker. They hardly ever spoke to each other. He demanded more and more, she felt further enslaved. He would come home drunk and force his unwanted attentions on Amelia. She never resisted. After Violet's death she had blocked out all feeling from her heart. She could feel no pain. When Joe made advances in the bedroom, it had been easier to lie back till he was finished. It never took long anyway. She avoided his alcohol-soured kisses. He was always too drunk to notice. She bore his advances with as much enthusiasm as one could muster out of a slab of meat. When he was done, he would roll over and fall asleep. She would get up and take a shower. When Joe died, it had made no difference to Mama Machado at all. She had not been relieved. She had not been happy. She had not been sad. She had stopped caring....

Frank shook his mother out of her reverie. She came back to the present, to the wedding. Frank was trying to get her to join them on the dance floor for the *Masala*. She looked at her son. He was nothing like his father. She thanked God for that everyday.

The *Masala* (translates to 'spice' in Hindi) is essentially a medley of songs strung together. The songs are from different Indian languages and an icon at Catholic weddings in India. It usually follows the birdie dance/chicken dance and is the last big hoorah before the end of the reception. People dance together, no partners needed. They wave handkerchiefs in the air and sing and dance with total abandon.

At Angela and Frank's wedding it was no different. People whistled and clapped and sang and danced, waving handkerchiefs and table napkins in the air. At the end, Angela was made to sit on a chair and four men each taking one corner of the chair, hoisted her in the air. Another set of men did the same with Frank. The crowd teased the couple bringing them closer to each other and then pulling them apart. This went on for a couple of minutes (or till the chair bearers got tired of their load) and then they brought Angela and Frank together for one final kiss mid air.

There was just one more thing left to do before the evening could end. Angela threw her bouquet to the single women. Amy caught it among cheers from the crowd.

Amid ribald jokes, Frank took off the garter strapped to Angela's thigh and flung it to the bachelors gathered. It landed in little Kevin the pageboy's lap.

Legend had it that the girl who caught the bouquet would marry the boy who caught the garter. That was clearly not going to happen in this case. Amy and four year old Kevin would not be tying the knot. But it had been fun to do it anyway...

Angela slowly slipped out of her reverie. She had relived one of the happiest memories she had had with Frank. She eased herself out of the rattan chair and picked up her empty tea cup. The sun had long since risen and was glowing hotly in the sky. Angela had missed its majestically lofty ascension this morning. As she headed to the kitchen, Angela mentally shook her memories away, giving in now to the more pressing demands of the day.

Chapter 8

Second Chances

If ever there lived a person who was truly content with her life, it was Angela's little sister, Amy.

As the youngest child, one would have expected her to be the pampered little girl, protected by her three older siblings and spoiled by her doting parents. And if she had been spoiled and pampered, no one would have thought anything of it. But Amy's personality had defied all preordained expectations. Her mother often wondered about her youngest daughter's tom boyish ways.

As a child, she had little interest in dolls and tea parties or frilly dresses and floppy hats, preferring instead to hang out with her brothers and their friends. When her family first moved to their new home in Bandra, the boys in their building were surprised that she had wanted to play their games. They found her enthusiasm amusing, fully expecting it to wane within a couple of days. A few days with the boys would show her a thing or too, they thought. Their games were rough and in their experience no girl wanted to get banged and bruised up.

As a result of their forecasted prediction, they allowed her entry into their hallowed inner circle. They were confident she would soon realize her folly and scurry back to join the girls in their game of hopscotch rather than play cricket or football (soccer) with them.

But a week later, they were a little concerned that she seemed undeterred. If anything, her enthusiasm at being accepted as one of the boys fueled her fires to new highs. She would plant herself in the middle of their games, she expressed opinions on how they did things and she questioned the rules of their games, much to the consternation of her two older brothers, Alastair and Adrian. The boys were not happy. It soon became apparent that little Amy was not going to play hopscotch. The thought of having a ten year old girl in their 'boys only' group was not an easy thing to digest for the members of the group. They hiccupped about it when she wasn't around to hear them.

"She's so bossy!" exclaimed boy one.

"And opinionated!" added boy two.

"Let's not forget how controlling she is!" said boy three emphatically.

"She always wants her way!" said boy four heatedly.

The rest of the boys in the group agreed. They simply had to put their heads together to find a solution to the problem at hand.

They devised a strategy to eject her from their inner circle. Plan A-Rejection. The boys collectively tried to ignore her. When she joined them the next day, they paid no attention to her, even going so far as to turn their backs on her. But it didn't work. Amy refused to give in. They deployed plan B-Dissuasion. They attempted to convince her that their games were rough and that she could get hurt, that she would have more fun with girls like herself. That didn't work either. Plan C-Temptation, went into effect. They introduced her to the other girls who tried to entice her to play with their fancy dolls and their colorful umbrellas. Amy was most definitely not interested. Finally they resorted to plan D-Bribery. They tried to bribe her to leave them alone.

"Amy, would you consider playing with the girls if we gave you a *Five Star* candy bar?" asked boy two.

"No," Amy replied, showing no sign of budging.

"Fine. We'll double it. One *Five Star* candy bar *and* one *Double Decker* candy bar," said boy one.

"No," Amy stood her ground.

"Okay okay. How about this? One *Five Star* bar *and* one *Double Decker* bar *every day* for two *entire* weeks," said boy three hopefully. If someone had made him that offer, he would have jumped all over it.

"No," echoed Amy, crosses her arms in front of her to emphasize her refusal.

"Come on, Amy. It's a great offer. It will wipe out all our pocket money for a week!" lamented boy four, exasperation lacing every one of his words.

"No," Amy said. She was having none of it. She stood firm in her decision to play with the boys.

She had proven to be extremely formidable to shake off. A lesser person would've succumbed to their tantalizing bribe. Who didn't like *Five Star* and *Double Decker*? The boys had run out of plans. They resignedly acknowledged that Amy wasn't going anywhere, so they might as well learn to accept this new development.

The other girls giggled and made fun of her. But Amy didn't care. She was not interested in their games or their dolls or their hopscotch squares. She thought that the boys played more interesting games anyway. So if the girls wanted to poke fun at her and make funny faces, she let them. It did not bother her at all. If they decided to up the ante and get nasty with her, she could easily escape. Amy was a fast sprinter and she was confident that she could out run them all. She could run really, really fast.

And the boys saw her do just that one day.

The boys and girls of the building were playing downstairs in the building compound early one evening. A group of six girls were playing with a hula hoop and a jump rope/skipping rope off to one side while the boys and Amy were sitting on the building wall a short distance away from them. They were deciding on a game to play that day.

Nearby, a family from their building was getting into their car. The father got behind the wheel and started the engine. The mother piled her little girl and their baby boy into the back seat of the car. She then proceeded to pile their several bags into the vehicle. Shortly after, she climbed into the car herself and slammed the door shut. The father eased the car into gear and the vehicle slowly rolled towards the building gate to make its way down Hill Road. The family had been in a tearing hurry to get going. Consequently, in their haste to hit the road, the little boy's milk bottle and his brown teddy bear had fallen out of one of their many bags. The family had not realized this as they continued on their way.

"Stop! Stop!" shouted the building *gurkha* (watchman) as he raised his arms to attract their attention. But the family in the car did not see him waving frantically.

The group of girls and boys playing nearby were distracted by the watchman's cries. Before anyone could react to the situation at hand, Amy jumped off the building wall in a trice, sprinted to the watchman who had by this time, picked up the milk bottle and teddy bear, grabbed both items from his hands and charged forward to catch up to the moving vehicle.

She whizzed past the boys, she whizzed past the group of girls and she whizzed past the watchman. She made it to the car in record time. The vehicle was just about to pull out onto Hill Road. She tapped on the window glass and handed over her cargo to a very startled mother. If the wailing she could hear emanating from the interior of the car was any indication that the little boy was hungry for his milk, Amy was certain he would be very grateful for her effort.

"Did you see that?" asked boy one incredulously.

"She sure can run!" said boy two reverently.

"She could probably out run us all!" added boy three, awestruck.

"So what if she is bossy and controlling, right? I mean, she can really run!" said boy four generously.

"Yeah, she can really run!" agreed boy three.

"Before I even realized what was happening, she was halfway to the car!" said boy one.

"Like the wind!" said boy two.

"Yeah, she can run like the wind!" agreed the boys.

Amy walked back to the group of boys at the building wall. Still slightly out of breath, she climbed up the wall and resumed her position. They played it cool around her.

"That was really good of you Amy," said boy two generously.

"What was?" asked Amy.

"You know sprinting like that to help that family," said boy one.

"Oh that. It was nothing," said Amy shrugging off the compliments.

"Where did you learn to run like that?" asked boy four.

"Nowhere. I just know I can," replied Amy.

Seeing little Amy run, had been the turning point for the boys. They would never be able to look at her without thinking about this incident. They tried to keep the awe and admiration at bay, but every once in a while it would surface. They believed that anyone who could run like the wind surely had to have redeeming qualities, even if it was just a slip of a girl. She could surely run faster than most of the boys in the group, but they were not likely to admit it publicly, to her or to anyone else for that matter.

From that moment on by unspoken agreement, they stopped plotting to get rid of the girl. They accepted her into their group. Be it *chor-police* (Cops and robbers) or *dubba ice-pice* (Kick the Can), when they set up teams to play, Amy was always the first team player to be selected. Every one wanted her on their team because she could run. Having Amy on their team more or less guaranteed them a win.

Amy was thrilled to be finally accepted as one of the boys. At last she had achieved her goal. Had she known that it would only take one short sprint on her part to convert the boys, she would have gladly dashed back and forth on her very first day in the new building. Still, she was happy with the way things had worked out in her favor. One day she said to the boys,

"I think we should set up an 'All boys Club'."

"A club?" said boy two.

"Yeah. All boys only," said Amy.

"And you of course," added boy three quickly.

"Of course," returned Amy, never once thinking that she did not belong.

"We could have secret meetings," said boy four.

"Yeah, and a special password to enter," said boy three.

"We could plan special 'All Boys' events," said boy one.

"And picnics and tournaments," said boy two.

"Yeah. It's a great idea Amy. An 'All Boys Club'!" said boy two.

"But what about Amy? I mean, she is a girl after all. If she is in our club, then the other girls will want to join too," said boy three.

"Good point," agreed boy one.

"Amy maybe a girl, but she runs like a boy and she dresses like a boy. I mean she wears jeans and shorts and tee shirts just like us," said boy two.

"If the girls want to join our club, then they have to dress like us and run as fast as Amy!" said boy four.

"That'll keep the girls away for a long time!" laughed boy three.

"That's settled then. We must now pick a Club Leader," said boy one.

"Let that be the first mission of our club. We must vote for the leader by secret ballot," said boy two.

They tore out pages from a note book and split them into smaller equal segments. Each boy and Amy was handed a piece of paper. They wrote out their choice and folded the scrap of paper before placing it in an overturned hat. Amy had been chosen as the first All Boys Club Leader by a unanimous vote.

As the years rolled on, Amy represented her school and her college in track and field events around the state. Her experiences helped bolster her confidence and her independence. She may have been the youngest of four children, but no one treated her that way. Before long she was applying to corporate jobs in Bombay. She accepted one of three offers. It would be a long road ahead as she carved a niche for herself in the business world. But Amy was happy to have the chance to prove herself, a chance so many others had been denied.

She met Josh on her first day of work at the new job. Their acquaintance grew into a deep friendship and an abiding love for each other. Three years after they first met, Josh proposed to Amy and she had gladly accepted. They enjoyed a steady and enduring relationship. No ringing bells and mighty claps of thunder, but just strong and quiet. Theirs was a forever kind of love. A lasting love.

They bought their own place in Bandra on St. Paul's Road and set up a home for themselves. Amy was content with her life. She had a loving husband, a nice home not too far from Angela or her parents and she had a well paying job. In short, she was happy with what she had. In time, they would have children of their own and her little world would be complete.

For now, she was happy with what she had and Angela's little Sophie filled her life with an indescribable joy she had not thought possible.

The years rolled on. Angela was pregnant for the second time. Lynette had taken one look at Angela's forward thrusting belly and declared the child she was carrying was a boy. They only had a couple of months to find out if her guess had been correct. Alastair and his wife Gwen had two beautiful little girls already and Adrian and Shayna were expecting their first child. They knew it was definitely a boy. The ultrasound had shown them so.

Unlike India, America had no law that barred doctors from revealing the gender of the unborn child. In India, female infanticide also known as sex-selective infanticide, had reached such alarming proportions that the government had been forced to intervene by passing a law that mandated doctors to withhold gender information. The law went into effect and subsequently the abortion rates for female fetuses decreased.

Amy had been happy for her siblings and their growing families. She had enjoyed her nieces and had been looking forward to the birth of her nephews. While their families had expanded, she had continued to remain childless. Josh and Amy had tried to add to their own family, but it had been an exercise in futility. No amount of effort or prayers on their part had resulted in the desired outcome.

Secretly, Amy pinned for a child of her own. She yearned to feel life in her womb. She longed to be able to share that experience with Josh and to revel in the miracle of their child, borne of their deep love. She wanted to be able to share in the joys of motherhood with Angela. To be able to watch their children play together, learn together and grow up together. She wanted to raise their children together that they might consider themselves to be brothers and sisters to each other rather than cousins.

She wanted to sit with her mother and discuss babies and baby related things. To be pampered and cherished by her mother when she was heavy with child. She wanted to witness her children being spoiled and loved by doting grandparents. To fill baby scrapbooks, save locks of baby hair and make baby footprints. To anticipate the first steps taken, the first words spoken, visits from the tooth fairy, the first day of school, the first date, graduation. To make memories that would stay long after her babies had grown. Amy longed for these things. She longed for them more than ever. But it was not to be.

Not yet anyway.

Amy and Josh lived their lives, happy with each other and content with what they had, but they both knew their life together was incomplete without a child. They had themselves tested, but the specialists could find nothing wrong with their reproductive make-up. They considered alternative methods, but they were too expensive and had no guaranteed outcome. Their lives were certainly comfortable, but they had to reconsider their options financially. In the end, they decided to wait a while to see how things panned out for them. Maybe they would conceive on their own, maybe they would find a way to finance the expensive treatments, maybe they would change their minds and not want a baby after all. Anything was possible with time. Amy and Josh decided to wait awhile. In the meantime, life went on as usual.

One morning, two weeks and four days after they had come to an agreement to wait on the fertility treatments, their lives changed forever.

Amy woke up and went about her routine as usual. Before she showered and got dressed for work, Amy habitually pottered about the kitchen getting breakfast ready for Josh and for herself. Depending on what she had planned for dinner that night, she would start the preparations ahead of time. If she had planned on something that was quick to assemble, then she usually prepared it when she returned from work. She preferred to make curries before she left for work, giving the curries a chance to mature over the day.

That morning she had planned on *Lonvas*, an East Indian curry made with beef or mutton and vegetables for dinner. Sometimes eggs replaced the meat in the curry. If Amy was making *Egg Lonvas*, she would break the eggs one at a time into a shallow bowl and gently ease it into the bubbling curry. The eggs would cook on a slow burner, absorbing the flavors of the curry. At other times, she would drop boiled eggs into the curry and allow them to simmer for a few minutes to absorb the flavors therein.

That morning however, she was making *Beef Lonvas*. Amy deftly cubed and washed the meat and placed it alongside the cubed green pumpkin pieces on the cutting board. She proceeded to mince an entire pod of garlic. She decimated the garlic into minute pieces by vigorously taking her chopper to the peeled garlic flakes. Before long, the minced garlic was frying in heated oil in a pressure cooker on the stove.

Amy pulled out a long dark brown glass bottle from the spice cupboard. She pulled out the cork stopper and tipped the bottle over the pot on the stove. Nothing poured out of the bottle. Amy looked into the bottle. She had been using East Indian *'Bottle Masala'* in her cooking since she had married Josh four years ago, but she still marveled at the ingenious packing methods employed by the east Indian ladies that made the masala.

They dried and powdered a special blend of spices and then packed the powdered spices into a very tall, dark brown beer bottle. They packed and they packed and they packed the powdered spice in, leaving no room for air. They then sealed the mouth of the eleven inch tall bottle by plugging it shut with a cork. The dark brown glass prevented sunlight from adversely affecting the contents of the bottle. The masala, simply called *'Bottle Masala'* for obvious reasons, stayed fresh for a very long time. Simple and yet ingenious.

Amy inserted a long wooden skewer into the mouth of the bottle and loosened some of the spicy powder. She tipped the bottle over the cooking pot once again. This time the loosened spices poured freely out of their glass container. As soon as the spices hit the hot oil and the fried garlic, a delicious aroma of frying spices wafted through the kitchen. Amy fried the masala and garlic together for a minute or two before she added the meat to the pot with some water. She covered the pressure cooker with its accompanying lid and placed its whistle on top. While the meat was cooking, Amy quickly cleaned up the kitchen, washing the utensils she had used.

"Smells so good in here, honey," Josh said sniffing appreciatively as he entered the kitchen. His hair was still damp from his shower, the ends curling slightly against the crisp collar of his striped blue button down shirt. He was dressed for work.

Amy looked over to her husband and smiled.

"*Lonvas* for dinner tonight," she said needlessly.

"I know, I could smell it in the shower," laughed Josh.

"That just means I fried the masala well," added Amy a little defensively.

"You're fantastic, Amy. You've learned how to cook all my favorite dishes!" said Josh happily, quick to reassure his wife of her well appreciated superb culinary talents.

"I had a good teacher," Amy returned.

"Yeah, my mother really was a very good cook. She taught you well," he said.

"Yes, she did," Amy agreed with her husband.

When Amy married Josh, she had been well on her way to establishing her ease around the kitchen, but she had never cooked an East Indian meal before. Her mother-in-law had taken her under her maternal wing and taught her how to make her son's favorite foods. Years later after much practice, Amy, herself half *Goan* (from Goa) and half *Mangalorean* (from Mangalore) could make East Indian dishes just as well as anyone born into an East Indian home. Josh's mother who firmly believed that the best way to a man's heart was through his stomach, had taught Amy how to make *Lonvas, Khudi, Frithad* and *Moile* among several other East Indian specialties.

Josh and Amy quickly breakfasted before Josh left for work. A few minutes later, the pressure cooker had whistled for the last time that day. Amy opened up the cooker carefully after running it under cold water to release the pent up pressure within. She checked the meat. It was tender. She was thankful for pressure cookers that made cooking so much quicker. She added the largely diced green pumpkin pieces to the pan. Then she added thick and creamy coconut milk, seasoned the curry with salt and allowed the curry to bubble on the stove.

A few minutes later the curry was ready. Amy covered the pan. She would steam rice to go with the curry later this evening. Maybe she would even fry a few *papads* (pappadoms) to go with it if she had a few minutes to spare. Maybe she would make vegetable cutlets to go with the meal, if she could get out of the office early. Though she knew it would be highly unlikely that day.

Thinking about having time to spare, Amy's mind flashed back to her experience with the women commuters in the second class compartment of the train she took daily to and from work.

Like the millions of daily commuters who traveled by Bombay's Railway System, Amy took the train to work every day. It was a short twenty three minute ride from Bandra to Churchgate Station, the last stop on the Western Railway Line. She usually bought a first class monthly train pass that allowed her to travel daily in the first class women's compartment.

The trains were always bursting to capacity, the general compartment (for men and women, but usually occupied by male commuters) and second class women's compartments filled to more than three times their seating ability. Commuters hung out of speeding trains barely holding onto the handle bars of the train compartments. If that wasn't dangerous enough, some travelers sat on top of the moving trains. Accidents, electrocutions and train deaths occurred all the time, but travelers remained undeterred.

Traveling by first class by no means assured Amy a seat on her commute, nor did it mean that the compartment had enough standing room. The compartment (much like those of the second class) was always packed during rush hour. If Amy was lucky, she could sometimes get a seat as the compartment emptied out along the way. But that didn't always happen.

The one saving grace about traveling first class was that the commuters were mostly civil and polite. One did not have to claw one's way to the front of the line to get on or off the train.

People did not push you out at a train stop or elbow you in the ribs trying to get ahead. The same could not be said for the commuters traveling in the second class women's compartment. They pushed and they elbowed their way in and out of the trains as a matter of course.

Among the regular second class commuters was a special posse of commuters. This posse of women was a breed unto itself. They were proprietary about their seats and their compartments and were possessive to a fault. They got on the same train everyday, selected the same compartment everyday and sat in the same seat everyday too. The posse was the ruling class in the compartment. They made it their business to know who was getting off when and where. They determined whether or not a commuter had the right to be standing where they were standing given their final destination. They went so far as to tell the person to move to another location if the current position did not meet with their self enforced code. And heaven forbid if things didn't go the way they wanted! The person who caused a disruption to the way they handled things, would have a very unpleasant ride to their destination. Amy found out the hard way.

Several years ago, a couple of months into her first job, her first class pass had expired and Amy had not had the chance to renew it. The lines were long at the ticket counter that renewed passes that day. In her haste to get home after a hard day at the office, she bought a second class ticket and waited at Churchgate Station for the fast train to pull into the platform. No sooner had the train pulled in, (it had not quite come to a complete stop) than hordes of women, (members of the large posse of bossy ruling class women commuters that plied the Bombay trains daily) picked up their sari hems by grabbing handfuls of the sari fabric at thigh height and ran forward, jumping onto the still moving train. They rushed to their self-designated seats and plopped down into them quickly, as though the devil himself was chasing them. The rest of the commuters then climbed onto the train and assumed the available positions, be it sitting or standing.

Amy had waited for the train to come to a complete stop before she boarded the train. She had stood off to the side in fear of being trampled upon by the herd of human cattle as they stomped their way forward, swarming the entrance of the train compartment. She hopped onto the train. It was already filled to standing capacity. Amy moved closer to the doors. If the train compartment was going to be this packed, then she preferred to be closer to the doors for some well needed fresh air. She picked her spot and settled in for the ride home.

The woman beside Amy nudged her none too discreetly. Amy turned her head to look at her.

"Which stop?" she asked.

"Excuse me?" Amy responded.

"Where are you getting off? Which stop?" the woman asked again.

Even though it was none of her business, Amy obliged her query and politely answered the inquisitive woman.

"Bandra Station. I will be getting off at Bandra."

The woman's countenance changed rapidly. Her vapid, bland expression was soon replaced by a frown of distinct displeasure.

"Bandra is ten stations away. Move inside. Don't stand by the door," she said rudely.

"I want to stand here," Amy said refusing to budge.

The woman looked around for fellow supporters to her cause. She found some.

"You'd better move," said one.

"Listen to her. Move away from the exit," said another.

You should find a place further inside the compartment," said a third supporter.

"It will be better for you," added the first.

They collectively urged Amy to move. Amy refused. The women were not happy with the annoying traveler who refused to abide by their rules.

At the next stop, under the pretense of being jostled by passengers getting off the train, two women pushed against Amy forcefully. Another dug her elbow into Amy's ribs. This was their not so subtle and unspoken way of letting Amy know that she was in the way and that she should do as they asked. Amy did not move. After the initial shock at the audacity of the women wore off and the ache in her ribs had subsided, Amy wondered if the actions of the women on the train had been deliberate or accidental. She had never been jabbed, jostled and poked on a train before today. When they elbowed, jabbed and jostled Amy again at the next stop, Amy knew for sure that there wasn't anything accidental about their actions. They were deliberately trying to intimidate her to heed their advice to move away from the doors.

She would deal with this herd of cattle. Amy geared up for the next upcoming assault. The train pulled into the next station. The women pushed and elbowed her again. But Amy was ready this time. She gave them a taste of their own medicine. She pushed and elbowed them right back. The nudging and pushing went back and forth for a couple more stations. They realized that the annoying passenger was not going to succumb to their bold tactics, so they soon tired of their punishment and left Amy alone. Amy was secretly triumphant with her win, but kept an eye out just in case their elbows got itchy again.

Even though the pushing had stopped, it was still stressful traveling in the second class compartment. People constantly jostled each other. The coconut oil soaked hair of many of the women brushed against Amy's white blouse leaving oil stains that would be any dry cleaner's nightmare. The fisherwomen who got onto the train with their huge smelly baskets were probably the luckiest of all, as passengers steered clear of them. But this was all still fairly bearable. What wasn't, was the smell of unwashed bodies and malodorous sweaty armpits of perspiring passengers that had never experienced the open end of a deodorant. The pungent odors mingled together, the resulting concoction potent enough to knock a skunk dead.

All in all, traveling by second class during rush hour was just too stressful and too unpleasant. It was no wonder the women who traveled the trains daily were as stressed and as catty as they were. Amy promised herself to be more diligent about renewing her first class pass in the future. In fact, she would head straight to the counter to renew her expired card once she got off the train at Bandra Station.

She had only a few more stops before she got off, but if these women wanted to do battle, then she was ready for them. They shot her dirty looks and snickered to each other, but for the most part they left her alone and did not do her anymore bodily harm.

She ignored them and looked around the compartment at her fellow commuters. She was puzzled by the scene her eyes took in over by the seating area. Some of the women seated were knitting, some were reading, some were peeling oranges or eating *channa* (roasted gram) and some were taking a short nap after a long work day. However, it was not these women that had grabbed her attention.

It was another group of women. Some of the women who had jumped into the moving train at Churchgate Station to secure their seats, had pulled out various vegetables and knives and were chopping up their produce in assorted shapes and sizes. There were at least six or seven women engaged in vegetable cutting on the moving train.

The lady standing next to Amy saw her puzzled expression.

"They are cutting vegetables," she said, stating the obvious.

"Yes, I see that. But why? Why would anyone want to cut vegetables on the train?" she Amy asked.

"To save time," the woman answered.

'What do you mean?" Amy asked. She was still puzzled by the bizarre behavior as the woman's answer did nothing to lessen her bewilderment.

"Many of these woman work very far away from their homes. They spend two hours, maybe more, on their way to work and then after a full day of work, they spend another two hours on their way back home every evening. Even though they spend four hours or so in travel everyday, they still have to go home and cook for their families. Cutting their vegetables on the train saves them some time. When they get home all they have to do is cook the *subzi* (vegetable dishes) and dinner is ready for their families," the woman explained to Amy.

Amy's heart filled with sympathy for these poor women. They didn't *want* to cut their vegetables on the train like she had first assumed. Rather, they *had* to cut their vegetables on the train. It's no wonder they rushed to get a seat. How else would they cut their vegetables?

Amy's thoughts returned to the present and to the task at hand in her kitchen. She touched the pressure cooker gingerly with her hand. It was still too warm to place in the refrigerator. She quickly left a note for her maid who came to her home around noon every day to do her housework. The maid would refrigerate the curry that would have cooled by then. Amy was thankful for the little comforts that she enjoyed. Thinking back to the vegetable cutting women on the train, Amy was thankful for so much.

She had a much shorter commute than they did. Her family was doing well enough that they could afford to hire help. She had an honest hardworking maid that in these days was very hard to come by. She could travel by first class and not be stressed everyday. But most of all she was just thankful that she didn't have to cut vegetables on the train.

Amy cast one final glance around her clean kitchen and headed to the bathroom that Josh had only just vacated a few minutes ago. Josh had left for the day, but she could faintly smell his cologne lingering in the air. Amy hurried into the shower. She had a lot on her plate at work that day. She had an important meeting with a client that morning and if she wanted to get to that 9:15 meeting, then she really needed to get going. She left her home a few minutes later and hailed a passing rickshaw.

Amy's rickshaw joined a horde of its brothers and sisters as it made its way down the final stretch to the Bandra train station.

The road had been dug up recently, the construction work narrowing the busy thoroughfare significantly. From an aerial view, the horde of black topped rickshaws resembled a teeming mass of cockroaches scurrying forward to converge on a narrow crack in their path, each vying for a better position than its counterparts. If the slightest opening happened to come up, at least five rickshaws from all directions revved their engines and surged forward to avail of the opportunity. Amy's cockroach pushed through the melee and found its way to the drop off point at the station. Amy quickly paid her fare and exited the rickshaw.

She passed the long line at the ticket booths and was thankful again for her monthly pass. She avoided the bustling main entrance, heading instead to the side entrance on the right. It would grant her direct access to the bridge staircase in order to catch a fast train on platform five.

Amy hurried to the entrance. Her regular fruit vendor stationed by the entrance, had a variety of luscious fruit on display on his wooden cart on wheels. Amy stopped to pick a couple of pieces of fruit for lunch almost everyday on her way to work. The vendor knew her well. Most days, she was so busy at work that she often worked through her lunch break. The fruit kept her going through the day and prevented her from frequenting the greasy food carts stationed outside her office building. She selected an apple, a pear and two bananas. Amy heard a little cry and turned to find a baby lying in a dirty cardboard box, its edges torn. The baby was alone.

"*Bechare*. Poor baby has been crying a lot," said the fruit vendor when he saw Amy's attention diverted by the baby.

"Where is the mother? The father? Who is with the child?" Amy asked, paying the vendor for her purchase.

"I don't know. I set up my cart at seven o'clock this morning. The baby was already here then," replied the fruit vendor, giving Amy her change.

"It's 8:20 now," said Amy looking at her wrist watch.

"The baby has been crying constantly. It's probably hungry," he said, packing Amy's fruit in a paper bag.

"Have you seen the mother? Maybe she went to get her baby some milk," suggested Amy, accepting the bag of fruit from the man.

"If she has, then I have not seen her since seven o'clock," he replied.

"That's almost an hour and a half," Amy said frowning as the infant's cry reached a higher decibel as if sensing it was the topic of conversation.

"Maybe someone knows where she is," Amy said, looking around for a likely possibility. People were milling in and out of the train station. Nobody paid any attention to the baby.

"Maybe some one knows, but I doubt it," returned the vendor.

"I'm sure the mother will be back shortly," Amy said to the man.

"Maybe," he replied as he turned to serve another customer.

Amy hesitated for a few seconds. Surely the mother would return for her baby. She was probably just delayed somewhere. The mother would return, Amy convinced herself as she purposely strode toward the staircase. If she didn't hurry, she would never make her client meeting in time. Amy stepped onto the platform, just as her train was pulling into the platform. She joined the other commuters as they prepared to enter the first class compartment. The sound of the baby crying kept ringing in Amy's ears. The 8:26 to Churchgate chugged out of the station.

Amy was not on it.

Amy found herself climbing the staircase again, but headed in the opposite direction this time. She raced past the throng of people on the bridge. When she got back outside, nothing had changed. The baby was still crying and the vendor was still selling his fruit. He looked surprised to see Amy.

"Did you forget your bag of fruit?" he asked looking around.

"No, no. I have it," she reassured the man.

"Did the mother come back?" she asked him urgently.

"No madam. I don't think she will be back," he replied.

Amy looked around. She was not sure what to do. The baby was crying hysterically, waving its arms and cycling its legs furiously.

"The baby must be hungry. I am going to buy the baby some food. I will be right back," Amy told the surprised fruit vendor.

All thoughts of making that 9:15 meeting vanished from Amy's mind. She knew her boss would be upset by her absence, but the baby needed to eat. Amy hailed a passing rickshaw and directed him to the row of shops on the other side of the station. She asked him to wait as she dashed into a general store.

A few minutes later purchases in hand, she climbed back into the rickshaw and directed the driver back to the station. On the very short ride back, Amy pulled out a feeding bottle, opened a tin of formula and scooped some of the powder into the bottle. She unscrewed a mineral water bottle and tipped its contents into the feeding bottle. She shook the bottle vigorously and waited for the rickshaw to come to a stop at the side entrance. She paid the driver. This was the shortest distance he had ever driven a passenger. People did all sorts of strange things. As a rickshaw driver he had seen his fair share of strange, though he had to admit this was the first time somebody had mixed up a bottle of milk in his rickshaw with no baby in sight. He accepted the proffered money and drove off. Amy hurried to the side entrance.

"Did the mother come back?" she asked the fruit vendor.

"No madam," he replied, coming forward to assist her.

She handed him the feeding bottle, as she bent down to pick up the wailing baby. It was a little boy. She gently nestled him In the crook of her left arm and took the feeding bottle from the fruit vendor. The baby wrapped his lips around the nipple of the bottle and lustily drank from it.

"You are a good woman madam," said the fruit vendor with tears in his eyes.

"The baby was hungry," she replied simply, meeting his eyes.

"Thousands of people passed this baby today, but only you stopped for him," he said, shaking his head sadly.

"People are busy. Everybody has their own life. I almost ignored him myself," Amy said.

"Yes, but you came back," he insisted.

"God will bless you abundantly," he said, pulling out a rickety wooden chair for her to sit on.

If only He would bless me with a child of my own, Amy thought to herself sadly.

She smiled at the man as she accepted the chair. She lowered her body into it, careful not to jostle the nipple out of the baby's mouth. The little child drank hungrily, making loud sucking noises, as he drained the nourishing liquid. He had probably been hungry for a while, Amy surmised. His emaciated little body was smeared with dirt and dust, the hair on his head was crusted and matted down to his scalp. There was dirt under his fingernails and toenails. Somebody had wrapped a piece of cloth around the child's groin and tied the ends together in a knot. The cloth was dirty and smelled of urine. It felt stiff to Amy, as though the child had soiled it several times and it had not been changed recently. The boy's pathetically thin body showed no visible bruises or scars. At least he had been spared that, Amy thought thankfully.

He finished his feed and Amy laid his head on her shoulder to burp him. He obliged in a loud and satisfying way. Amy smiled and placed him in the crook of her arm again. For the first time since Amy had picked him up that morning the little baby looked directly into Amy's eyes. He smiled. Amy's heart lurched in her ribcage. She hugged the little boy close as tears rolled down her face. Who would want to abandon such a sweet little boy?

God blessed some people with children and they didn't even want them. Other people craved the same blessing, but He denied them.

Life was just so very unfair.

After the infant had been fed, he cooed happily in her arms. He looked interestedly at the activity around him. Amy was not exactly sure what to do from this point on. Should she leave the baby in his card board box with the tin of formula and his bottle? What if the mother never returned for him? What would become of the little boy? Should she take him? What if his mother did return for him and found him missing? She would be devastated to find her child gone. Amy did not know what to do. She did the next best thing she could think of. She called Angela.

"Hello?" Angela asked as she answered the ringing telephone.

"Hi sis, it's me," Amy replied.

"Is everything okay? Are you at work already?" Angela queried look at the wall clock. Its long arm was still ten minutes shy of the ninth hour of the morning.

"I'm fine, but I am not at work. I'm still at Bandra station," Amy said hurriedly.

"Are the trains delayed this morning?" Amy asked.

"No, no. Just stop asking questions and listen to me," Amy said exasperatedly.

"Okay," Angela replied. She could hear the nervousness in her little sister's voice.

"Could you come to the station right away? With a diaper and some baby clothes and a wash cloth?" Amy said in a rush.

"Yeah, I guess so. Do you want to tell me why?" Angela asked, she was getting very alarmed by her sister's voice and her strange request.

"It's for a baby," Amy blurted.

"I figured out that much Amy. Whose baby? And why are you taking care of it?" Angela retorted.

"I found it," Amy said.

"Found it? You found a baby?" asked Angela incredulously.

"Yes. I found a baby crying at the steps of the entrance to the station. He was hungry, so I fed him some formula that I bought from the store, but he needs to be cleaned up. Oh Angela, I don't know what to do with him! I think his mother might have abandoned him. I was on my way to work when I saw him. My boss will be furious that I missed the meeting. It was really important that I make the meeting and now I haven't. But what could I do? The baby was crying. What do I do with this baby now? I can't leave him here and I can't take him with me either. I don't know what to do! Tell me what to do Angie, I don't know what to do," she sobbed into the phone. Amy's rambling words spewed forth in all directions like lava from a mouth of a volcano on the brink of eruption. It was obvious to Angela that her normally cool and collected sister was very stressed by the situation she had inadvertently put herself in.

"Calm down. I will be there just as fast as I can. I will leave Sophie with the neighbors. I will be there soon. Just try to stay calm Amy. Take a few deep breaths. I am coming to you," Angela soothed her sister.

Talking to Angela had the desired effect and Amy calmed down. She had been calm and methodical through everything up until this point. But the moment she heard Angela's voice, she felt like she had been hit by a ton of bricks. She had someone else's baby in her arms and she didn't know what to do with it, so she had panicked. She collected herself and resumed her seat by the fruit vendor's wooden cart on wheels. Angela was on her way and she would know what to do, Amy reassured herself over and over again.

Angela arrived shortly after with a bag full of baby paraphernalia. She hugged Amy first and then gently took the baby from her. They laid him on the seat of the chair Amy had vacated. Angela cleaned his thin little body all over with wet wipes. The boy had an angry red rash in his diaper area, in all probability from a dire lapse in hygiene and gross neglect. She applied a diaper cream liberally to the affected area that she had had the forethought to pack. Her own baby was due in two months and Angela had been well stocked on baby supplies. The baby needed a bath, but for now the wet wipes would have to do. They dressed him in clothes that were a tad too big for his little under nourished body, but at least he was clothed.

While Angela and Amy were busy at work with the baby, a crowd had started to gather by the fruit vendor. Curious eyes observed their every move.

"Does anybody know anything about this child? His mother? His father?" Angela asked the crowd. Nobody knew anything.

"What should we do now?" Amy asked Angela.

"This child clearly needs medical attention. Maybe we can take him to Dr. Krishna," Angela suggested.

"That's a great idea," agreed Amy.

Amy turned to the fruit vendor and said,

"We will take this baby to a doctor. If the mother returns while we are gone, will you let her know that we will bring her baby right back?"

"Yes madam. I will be here all day. If she returns I will tell her," returned the fruit vendor.

Dr. Krishna examined the baby as they recounted their story to him. The boy was definitely under nourished but beyond that he appeared to be healthy. Running some tests would reveal more information he could work with. Angela and Amy were relieved. They filled his prescription for vitamins and a medicated diaper cream at the pharmacy. They went back to the station, but no one had come looking for the child. They left a contact number with the fruit vendor just in case somebody did and Amy took the baby home.

When Josh got home that evening, he was surprised to see his wife feeding a little baby on their living room couch. Baby things littered the coffee table. There were bottles and jars, rattles and burp cloths. An opened pack of diapers lay on the rug of their usually pristine living room. Josh took in the chaos and his smiling wife amidst the mess. She seemed unperturbed by it all.

"Hi honey," he said enquiringly, his eyebrows raised slightly in question.

"Hi," Amy replied.

"Cute baby. Are you babysitting for one of the neighbors?" he asked.

"No, I am not baby sitting," she said.

"Okay, so whose baby did you kidnap?" Josh joked with his wife.

"I don't know," Amy said softly.

"You don't know? What do you mean, you don't know? Whose baby is that?" Josh asked a little more urgently.

"I found him," said Amy.

"You found him! And you took him? I was joking when I asked if you had kidnapped him! I didn't expect that you had, you had..." Josh looked flustered as he was unable to complete his sentence. They had wanted a baby, but resorting to kidnapping was not the way to do it. Was Amy losing her mind?

"I didn't exactly kidnap him, honey. Calm down and I will tell you what happened," Amy interrupted quietly, so as not to wake the little baby who had drifted off to sleep after a full feed. He probably hadn't had a full belly in a while, Amy thought to herself.

She explained the events of the day to Josh. He listened to Amy intently till she finished her story. He hugged his wife and counted his blessings that he had married such a compassionate person.

"Isn't he beautiful?" Amy asked her husband.

"Yes he is. Sleeping like a baby," Josh joked to lighten the situation.

"What should we do with Gavin?" she asked.

"Gavin? Whose Gavin?" asked Josh puzzled once more. Was there more to the story that Amy had left out?

"The baby," Amy replied.

"This baby? You've named him?" asked Josh.

"I've named him," replied Amy nuzzling his body closer.

"Amy my love, you realize this baby belongs to someone else, right? You know we can't keep him? What you did for him today was brave and courageous and very noble, but he is not ours to keep. You do realize that, right? Don't get too close to him Amy. You are only setting yourself up for pain when you have to give him up," said Josh cautiously, trying not to hurt his wife. She had been through so much today and he didn't want to upset her.

"I always wanted to name our son 'Gavin'," Amy said crying softly.

"Oh honey!" Josh said as he reached over and hugged his wife. "This is probably the closest I will ever come to having a child of my own, so I named him, 'Gavin'," Amy sobbed into Josh's chest.

"Gavin is a beautiful name for a beautiful little boy," Josh said, tears rolling down his face too, as he gently stroked Amy's hair.

They sat holding their baby for a long time, even though they knew they could not claim him for their own. Amy had forgotten about dinner. The rice remained uncooked, the vegetable cutlets and *papads* long forgotten, the once appetizing *Lonvas* curry lay congealing in the refrigerator. Their 'kidnapped' baby lay sleeping peacefully between them that night. Neither Josh nor Amy slept a wink. They watched over little sleeping Gavin till the sun came up.

Amy took time off from work to care for little Gavin. Her boss had been very understanding when she explained what had happened. For the next three days, on his way to and from work, Josh checked with the fruit vendor if anyone had come to claim the baby. No one had. If Amy hadn't stepped in when she had, the baby would've withered away and died. Now he was being loved and cared for and cherished, everything he had deserved but had not received, until now. He had been given a second chance.

On the third day, Josh and Amy took Gavin to an orphanage recommended by Dr. Krishna. They explained the situation to the person in charge. They also made clear their intention to adopt Gavin as their son. The paperwork went through and a few months later, they legally adopted Gavin.

Amy gave up her job to care for her boy. He had suffered so much in the first few months of his life, she had vowed that she would devote her life from this point on to make it up to him. Gavin filled their home with laughter and their hearts soared with joy. Their pristine home was never pristine again, but it was a small price to pay for the miracle of life.

God had given Gavin a second chance.
He had heard Amy's pleas after all and blessed her with a child.
He had given her a second chance too.

Chapter 9

Angela and Amy join Forces

Angela was sitting in her bedroom one morning reading the Times of India when she heard the pitter patter of little bare feet as they slapped the mosaic tiles in quick succession.

Thap thap, thap thap.

She smiled and turned to look as her little girl walking into her bedroom trailing her favorite yellow blanket on the floor behind her. Olivia jumped into her mother's lap almost toppling them both off the comfortable rattan chair that Angela had been sitting in. Angela quickly steadied the chair and hugged little Olivia back.

"Good morning, my little angel. Did you sleep well?" she asked of her two year old daughter.

Olivia nodded her head vigorously. She snuggled further into Angela's lap as she tried to get cozy.

"Are Sophie and Zack awake yet?" Angela asked Olivia.

Olivia nodded, still too sleepy to talk, rubbing her eyes with her balled fists.

"Okay then, little one, time to get the day started," said Angela, attempting to get up.

"Can we cuddle for just a wee bit longer mama?" Olivia asked, her eyes pleading.

"Of course my love we can," returned Angela.

She hugged her baby closer. Angela wrapped Olivia in her favorite blanket. It was a ratty blanket that had definitely seen better days. Olivia had grown attached to this blanket that had once boasted several large gingham appliquéd flowers on its buttercup yellow flannel background. Today, it was but a faint resemblance of its original beauty. The appliqué threads of the gingham flowers had either been pried off with tiny fingers that were able to find loose loops in the threads or they had been chewed off when Olivia gnawed on them as she worked her newly budding teeth.

The blanket had been washed so often that the brightness of its buttercup yellow had faded, giving way to a more dull and lifeless mustard-ish yellow. The one gingham flower that had stubbornly survived Olivia's prying fingers and gnawing teeth was now but a washed out replica with faint traces of blue, the checkered gingham pattern just barely visible. The blanket was definitely the worse for wear and practically begged retirement, but Olivia clung onto it fiercely, not quite ready to give it up. Angela let her keep her blanket. She knew Olivia would eventually outgrow it.

Sitting on the rattan chair now, they were both silent for a few seconds, before Sophie and Zack came bounding into the room.

"Good morning mummy!" they both said somewhat in unison as they jumped up on the rattan chair, each vying for the better location beside their mother. Somehow all four of them, mother and her three children managed to fit on the same chair as Zack and Sophie squeezed their bodies into the tiny space on either side between the chair and Angela. It got uncomfortable very quickly, and Angela had to coax them off the chair.

"Okay kids, who wants fish and frogs for breakfast?" she asked fully anticipating their response.

"Ugh, mummy!" said Zack making a face. Sophie made a face too. Olivia giggled at their funny faces.

"How about some snail's tails, then?" Angela needled them again.

"Ugh, ugh," said Zack, his funny face taking on another funny twist.

"Gross," said Sophie, imitating her brother.

Olivia was giggling even harder now, her brother and sister joining in. They had rolled off the chair and onto the floor. Soon they began tickling each other and they were all giggling uncontrollably. Angela joined in, unable to resist their infectious laughter. She tickled all three of them till they were all out of breath.

"Let's tickle mummy!" suddenly squealed Zack turning the tables on their mother. The three kids turned to Angela together and tickled her till she was rolling on the floor, trying to get away from the tickle fest.

"Okay, okay, stop! Please!" Angela pleaded with tears rolling down her face.

"How about some french toast for breakfast?" She managed to ask between tickles and peals of laughter.

"Yummy! Yippee! We want french toast!" shouted Sophie.

"With condensed milk, mummy! Please, please, please?" pleaded Zack.

"Pease, pease, pease," echoed Olivia, in her baby voice.

"Okay kids, let's have some breakfast and then Sophie and Zack, you both have to get ready for school," Angela said to them, still trying to restore her balance from their tickle onslaught. She loved the start of a new day, basking in their simple childish pleasures.

Zack and Sophie were finally packed off to school. Their neighbor on the first floor of their apartment building usually drove her own children as well as Angela's to school every morning and Angela drove all four of them back after school. It was a convenient arrangement that had been working very well for both families.

Mirabai usually showed up for work around 9:45am and stayed till noon. Her first task of the day was dropping Olivia off to a toddler care facility down the street. Olivia spent two hours there five days a week and was picked up by Mirabai at 12:00pm. The time in between gave Mirabai a chance to finish the house chores. She cleaned dishes, swept, mopped and dusted the Machado home everyday including weekends.

She had been with the family for sixteen years this November. She had started out with Lynette Pinto and had added to her work load when she took on Angela's home after Sophie was born nine years ago. Lynette and Angela had been very good to Mirabai and her family and she in turn had taken care of their homes and had become a part of their family. They had established an effective relationship that had lasted a long time, the bond growing stronger with each passing year.

For several years Mirabai had worked both homes. She had been happy to take on the additional work at Angela's home which also brought on additional pay to support her own growing family.

When Lynette and Robert had decided to sell their home in Bandra and move to Robert's ancestral home in Goa, Mirabai realized she would be out of one of her two jobs. Times were hard and her family needed the additional money. The extra money had helped defray expenses after her husband's accident at the factory that had rendered him immobile for several months. Things would be tight financially with only one job to support them.

But Lynette had not left Mirabai out to dry. She had placed her with her other daughter, Amy. Mirabai had been ever grateful to Lynette for helping her. Over the years, they had helped her family in difficult times. Lynette and Robert had paid for her son and daughter to go to a local school. After he was fully recovered from the accident, Josh had found her husband a job as chauffeur for the General Manager at his company. Angela and Frank had helped very generously with her daughter's wedding expenses. Over the years, they had all helped her out with clothes for her children, doctor's bills, school supplies and groceries. In addition they gave her children gifts at *Diwali* (The Hindu festival of lights) and sent home Christmas sweets for the family every year.

The family had been very good to her over the years. She had never forgotten their magnanimity. She had eaten the salt at their table of kindness and generosity and now she was forever indebted. She could never repay their generosity, but she would always be loyal to them. She worked herself tirelessly at all four weddings of the Pinto children and at all the other family functions- baptisms, communions, confirmations and even funerals. She had felt the loss of Frank *baba* deeply and had comforted Angela and her children. She helped out whenever she was needed, wherever she was needed.

Mirabai's own children were older now. Last year, her daughter married and moved away and her son's steady and unionized railway job as an out-of-station train driver, ensured that he was hardly ever home. Her responsibilities had eased off as her children grew older and more independent. She was able to give more of her time to Angela and her family of little children.

A few months ago when Angela had asked if she would like still more work, Mirabai had been happy to take more on. Her daily routine was hectic as it is, but she could never say no to Angela or turn down an opportunity to earn more for her family. She would have grandchildren soon and she liked the idea of having extra money to buy gifts and toys. She had never been in a position financially to afford such luxuries for her own children, but she was hoping to change that with her grandchildren.

Even though she was getting older, Mirabai never thought to slow down. Her day started at 5:30am. She cooked meals and cleaned her own home before she arrived at Angela's at 9:45am. She dropped Olivia off at her toddler school up the street, returned to perform household chores for Angela and picked Olivia up two hours later. She then went over to clean Amy's home for approximately two hours and returned to Angela's home by 3:30pm where she stayed and helped out for three hours or so before she headed home for the final stretch of her day. Mirabai had a long day everyday, but she enjoyed the work and the fruits her toil made possible for her family.

Today, she dropped Olivia off and returned to find Angela's head buried in a pile of books. She was busy crunching out numbers in an accounting journal on the table. Mirabai left Angela to her numbers and proceeded to attend to her designated daily chores.

Angela closed her book, the accounts up to date and moved on to making a list of things she needed to purchase for today's preparations.

Earlier that year, Angela along with her partner and sister Amy, had started their own catering business. They catered small private dinner parties. They set up custom menus with their clients, cooked and baked up enticing appetizers, succulent entrees and decadent desserts and offered excellent service and wait staff at the parties. Either Angela or Amy always supervised each party personally to make sure everything went off smoothly.

The business was only a few months old and it had taken a great deal of 'word of mouth' praise before they began seeing a stream of customers. After the first four or five months, they had almost called it quits as they were unable to generate much business. They would cater an occasional party once a month and wait by the phone for clients to call. It seemed like nothing was really working no matter how hard they tried or how successful each catered event was. It seemed as if the more blood and sweat they invested in the business, the less likely it was to get off the ground. Angela and Amy were frustrated and despondent. With their business sinking lower each week and their capital sinking still lower, they knew they needed a solid marketing plan, but neither had any experience in that department. They approached Mama Machado with their business plan and sought her advice on promoting their fledgling business.

Mama Machado had evolved over the years from the trusting wisp of a girl she had been when she first got married and moved to *Ranwar*, to a wise old woman, sharp as a tack. She had honed her business skills over the years when she had been forced to work to feed her family. Her drunkard husband flitted from one temporary job to another, unable to hold any for more than a few weeks, eventually giving up trying altogether. He sulked around the house or holed up at the local 'aunty's joint' that sold home brewed alcohol at prices significantly lower than the branded alcohol at the liquor shops.

'Aunty's joints' had cropped up all over the area in response to the enforced prohibition of yester years. The ban had long since been lifted allowing for the free trade of spirits, but the illegal businesses selling distilled country alcohol had flourished rampantly. The hole-in-the-wall 'aunty's joints' had continued to exist to pander to the addictive needs of incessant drunks that frequented their less than respectable locations.

The little money that Joe earned was squandered away on cheap booze. Money was tight and Mama Machado had to feed seven growing children.

She did what she had to do for her children.

Mama Machado started her own home based business, selling products from the one thing she knew how to do exceptionally well – Cook.

She cooked delicious curries and pickles everyday and she become famous. She made *Sorpotel* and *Vindaloo*, both pork curries, well loved and must-haves at most Christian celebrations and feasts. She also made spicy pickles of all varieties – green mango pickle, lime pickle, brinjal/eggplant pickle, carrot pickle, garlic pickle, chilli pickle. She also made *balchao* (prawn pickle) and dried fish pickle out of *Bombay ducks* (a type of fish found only in the waters around Bombay). The Bombay ducks which were really fish and certainly not ducks, were dried at *Danda*, an area just off Bandra's coast. An area that was visually and olfactorily recognizable instantly for its fish hung on wooden racks to dry by the salty ocean breezes coming in off the Arabian Sea.

By the time she was in her fifties, she had become indispensable to her community. Every one came to rely on Mama Machado's culinary capabilities. She had never been interested in growing her business beyond what she could handle at home. Her business had been a means to an end, nothing more. She made enough to care for her children and to put food on the table. Her family's survival depended on the money her curries and pickles brought in.

She needed the time to work and she could only do so if she could keep her husband happy. Joe was only happy when he was drunk. Sober, Joe got cranky and petulant and got in Mama Machado's way. So she gave him pocket money every day which he in turn used to feed his habit. The money disappeared into a bottle of home brewed 'country' faster than the blink of an eye. It made him happy to lose himself into oblivion and it made her happy to have him well out of her way.

Mama Machado kept her meager business going till all her children were grown and earning on their own. As she got older, she found it harder to keep up with the daily demands of her business. Her children never forgot their mother's hardships and what she had done for their family. They took care of her daily expenses and urged her to give up her business. Mama Machado had been glad to throw in the kitchen towel.

People still stopped by to see her regularly and that gave rise to a second 'career' for the aging Mama Machado. She had been the fertile soil that had nurtured her children to adulthood. She had taken care of them and they had their own lives now. With her children having flown the nest and her business having been wrapped up, Mama Machado found a good deal of free time on her hands.

So she opened her arms to others in need. Her doors had stayed open (literally and figuratively) all day as she constantly had a stream of visitors. She was always ready with her home made salves for cuts and bruises, a home cooked meal for a family returning from the hospital, her own special brew of *Khimad* (an alcohol concoction spiced with cloves, pepper and cinnamon) for coughs and colds, sometimes just lending a listening ear to worried neighbors or hugging those in dire need, a word here, a touch there, gently encouraging, hugely comforting. Everyone knew Mama Machado. They flocked to her for advice on marital problems, marriage proposals, picking names for their children, the merits of one job over another, resolution of family disputes to name a few. Sometimes, they came to her just to hear her stories.

Somewhere along the line she had become mother to everyone and anyone who needed mothering. She had become the doyenne of her community, a necessity in her neighborhood, the go–to person in times of need whose comforting arms offered succor and hope to the hopeless. She was loved and respected by the young and the old alike. Somebody in her community affectionately began addressing her as 'Mama Machado' and the name had stuck every since. It was more a title than a name change, one that was revered and well respected and adopted by all who knew her.

Knowing of her far reaching influence, Angela and Amy approached Mama Machado for her input to grow their business. Based on her advice Angela and Amy worked furiously to promote themselves. They decided to market their business more aggressively, sending out flyers and brochures, advertising in local newspapers, pitching to corporations and to schools and by word of mouth. Mama Machado spread the word around and asked the people she knew to do the same in their offices and gyms and clubs. Her influence was far reaching and their combined efforts at marketing and advertising finally worked.

Slowly but surely, clients started trickling in. Slow at first but gathering momentum with each passing month. The clients told others who told others and soon Angela and Amy were kept very busy. They whisked, chopped, stirred, blended, pureed, kneaded, flambéed, broiled, fried and grilled everyday to keep up with their business. They had to take on two additional part-time kitchen staff to stay on top of the work. Mirabai was one of them. She worked in Angela's kitchen for two hours or so every afternoon assisted by her niece who pitched in four hours a day.

Angela and Amy did all the cooking, baking, buying, ordering and menu planning, while Mirabai and her niece took on a more supportive roll. They followed orders and instructions. The four women worked well together and accomplished their daily tasks swiftly and efficiently.

The bulk of their events occurred on Friday, Saturday and Sunday, with an occasional weekday affair. They prepped Monday through Thursday and made sure that their parties were handled smoothly. Angela and Amy hired two wait staff on a free lance basis, who adroitly served up their delicious concoctions and creations. The business supplied its employees with crisp uniforms of dry cleaner starched white shirts embroidered with their logo on the breast pocket. They provided their staff with matching bowties, pressed black trousers, and polished black shoes. They dressed professionally and played their part to the hilt.

Angela or Amy or both (depending on the size of the party) supervised the kitchen at the party location and ensured that each course was served on schedule, piping hot or adequately chilled or invitingly warm depending on the requirement of the recipe.

Their business was off to a great start. The clients kept pouring in. They were working harder and the money was rolling in. They soon realized that Angela's kitchen was not big enough or equipped enough to handle their business. Neither was Amy's. They needed to find a bigger space to work in, more appliances, at least one more refrigerator, two would be ideal.

When Mirabai walked in that day, she saw Angela busy, her head buried in her accounting books. She was punching numbers into an oversized calculator and jotting down her entries on an open page. Angela was going through their finances, trying to figure out how much they had to invest in the things they needed to grow their business.

Angela, with help from those who loved her, had come a long way.

Chapter 10

Market Day

Angela closed her accounting books. She was smiling. The business had done better this quarter than she had expected. They had done well enough to buy the appliances and hardware they needed. A large chunk of the profits they earned went back into the business after salaries were paid monthly. They had done well so far, but they could use an additional bank loan to take the business still further.

Angela recalled the tough sell they had had to pitch to the bank the first time they needed a loan. Their initial business plan had been well written and well thought out but the bank had been hesitant to finance their business venture on account of their inexperience. They had worked very hard to convince the banking officials to lend them the money. In the end after all their persistence and using their own homes as collateral, they had received less than half of what they had requested.

They had been vigilant about making monthly payments on the loan and Angela was confident the bank would come through this time. Paying back the loan on time every month had served to build their credibility with the bank. Also, they had hard numbers of their escalating success to show the bank this time around. They had irrefutable proof that they were serious and committed to the business and conscious of their responsibility to make the loan payments.

Amy would set up an appointment with the bank to go over their plans to extend their business to include a rental facility. The second loan would take them further along. But this time around, Angela was not worried about being turned down by the bank.

She turned her attention to the menu she had put together last night after the kids had gone to bed. She needed Amy's input before she finalized it with their Saturday client. She picked up the telephone and dialed Amy's phone number.

"Hello?" Amy asked.

"Hi, it's me. I just got done with the books. It looks like we can have our extra fridge after all! Hey, we could have five if we want!" Angela practically shouted with joy into the receiver.

"That's just great! I will look at the accounts when I get there this afternoon. I figured we could swing it, but it always helps to know for sure. By the way, I set up an appointment with the bank manager for 10:30am on Thursday," returned Amy.

"We should both go to the appointment, don't you think?" asked Angela.

"I think that would be the best thing," said Amy.

"Right. That's settled then. For now, I need to go over the final menu for the Chopra party this Saturday. Do you have a minute?" Angela asked her sister.

"Yeah, go ahead," Amy replied, giving her sister her undivided attention.

"Okay. I thought we should start with a crab and sweet corn bisque served with mini garlic-parmesan bread sticks, followed by a lightly tossed red cabbage salad with a sesame vinaigrette dressing. For the main course, green masala mutton chops served over a bed of saffron pilaf with sautéed zucchini and asparagus drizzled with a creamy curried sauce on the side.

"Do you think Mrs. Chopra will be agree to the menu?" Angela asked.

"It sounds good except that Mrs. Chopra would prefer a fish entree. I left you a note. Did you get it?" asked Amy.

"Actually I didn't see it," said Angela rummaging among the papers on her desk.

"Aha, just found it. It somehow got buried under the accounting books. Anyway, that is a small adjustment. I can substitute fillets of fish for the mutton chops. What do you think?" asked Angela.

"I think they will like your selections," said Amy.

"Good. I will have to see what is fresh at the fish market today. The same with the veggies. I might swap out the zucchini or asparagus for something else depending on what I find," said Angela making changes in pencil to the menu.

"I've been thinking about dessert," said Amy, this being her area of expertise.

"Any ideas?" rejoined Angela.

"Yeah. The last time I talked to Mrs. Chopra, she had expressed a fondness for cheesecake. So I was thinking of doing a combination pre-plated desert- A wedge of raspberry swirl cheesecake with a ginger cookie crust with chocolate rum truffles on the side.

"Sounds yummy," enthused Angela.

"Great. Why don't I go ahead and talk to Mrs. Chopra to finalize the menu, so we can get started?" offered Amy.

"I will make up the shopping list and head over to the market. Call me if Mrs. Chopra wants to make any further adjustments to the menu," said Angela.

"I don't know if you recall, but she did add on two more guests to her list," reminded Amy.

"No, I had actually forgotten about that. Thanks for the reminder. I will take that into account. I'll see you later?" asked Angela.

"I'll be there around 2 -2:30 this afternoon," joined Amy.

It was a typical conversation between the two sisters, aspiring to keep their business afloat. They consulted each other on every issue to ensure that they were on the same page all the time. The effective communication had resulted in a smooth operation that was reaping immense benefits for them and for their families. Angela was able to support her children and Amy was happy to be working again. Gavin was older now and in school all day. Amy had discovered that she was not one to sit round all day doing nothing. When Angela had suggested the joint business venture to her, Amy had jumped at the opportunity.

Today was a good day. Their business was doing well and they were happy. Their client base was growing, but many of them were also return clients, a testament to their success. They were expanding steadily. Life was good. And it was going to get better as the holiday season was just around the corner. Their appointment book was fast filling up for private residential and corporate parties.

Angela quickly made up a list of the things they would need for the Chopra party. She added her list to another list of ingredients for the office party they were catering on Friday afternoon that week.

The Bandra Market was a hive of bustling activity. Vegetable and fruit vendors lined the streets with their produce, fresh off the farm or from the vendors at the *Dadar* wholesale market. They called out to the people walking on the street attempting to draw them into conversation over their goods. Angela enjoyed the brisk commerce apparent between vendors and customers. Business was business and they certainly took care of it, but they also found the time for light jovial conversations with their regular customers.

Over the years, regular customers built a rapport with certain vendors and tended to buy from them more often than not. Angela favored her own set of vendors too. They were always happy to see her because she bought in large quantities.

She had such a good relationship with her market vendors that they often set aside certain produce for her, knowing full well that she would need them in bulk and would pay good money for them. With her, they were practically assured a sale.

Once Angela made her selection, they would arrange to have her purchases delivered to her home directly. It saved Angela the trouble of lugging large quantities of market goods around as she made her bazaar rounds. They consolidated her purchases from several vendors for easy delivery. The vendors were happy to offer her the additional service for a few extra bucks. It cost them nothing to get one of their young assistants to ride a bicycle over to her house with her bagged purchases strapped to the carrier of the bicycle.

Angela in turn was good to these produce-toting boys as well. She always bought them a sweet *lassi* (yogurt drink) with a dollop of thick yogurt at the dairy store or treated them to ice cream cones or an icy refreshing drink of Coke or Sprite, depending on their preference for that day.

With some vendors at the Bandra Market, prices of goods were fixed. Like the shop that sold eggs and live chickens that were slaughtered, plucked and cleaned on site as per customer request. And the cold stores that sold bacon, ham and other pork products. And the dairy that sold yogurt so thick and creamy it had to be sliced off sideways with a big, flat serving spoon. Most of the meat vendors sold their goods at fixed prices too.

It was the fish vendors (the fisherwomen locally known as the *koli* folk) who were always up for a lively bargain. One could haggle prices back and forth till both parties were satisfied with the final price. It could even be said that they looked forward to the exchange of banter, expecting it with every sale, insulted if not engaged. Or so it seemed anyway.

The customers and fisherwomen knew that only the 'I'm-too-snobbish-for-my-own-good' elitist paid the actual asking price. Anyone out for a good deal *always* engaged in the bargaining process. This way, the customer felt assured that she or he received a good deal and had something to discuss with the neighbors the next time they met. Besides, nobody liked being labeled 'sucker'.

The fisherwoman for her part, felt that in return for the good deal she had so generously deigned to give, she would be assured repeat customers. It was a little song and dance enjoyed by all who chose to become engaged.

It was to the fish market that Angela headed first today. There was the indoor market and the outdoor market. She walked through the covered area first, briefly scanning the fish on display. This area of the fish market was nothing if not a long rectangular hallway with a sloping tiled rooftop. It was more like a long aisle with several symmetrical entry/exit points. A long and high built-in banquette about three to four feet off the ground, lined either side of the aisle, on top of which sat fisherwomen selling their husband's catch of the morning if they were lucky. The other fisher folk bought their fish wholesale from the fishing trawlers that docked at various locations on Mumbai's coastline.

The indoor fish vendors displayed their fruit of the sea in front of them on low white tables, a large basket with additional fish at the ready when their display had to be replenished. The height of the banquettes and fish display tables were cleverly designed to be just below the line of vision of the customers, but not so low that their customers would be inconvenienced to bend. They were about chest high or waist high to a standing customer depending on his or her height. Angela briefly scanned the indoor tables as she made her way to the outdoor market. She usually bought from a select few fisherwomen, but she was not past capitalizing on a good deal from an unfamiliar vendor every now and then. A deal was a deal after all.

The outdoor market was very different from its indoor counterpart. Firstly, the vendors here had no overhead protection from the scorching sun. To combat the sun's rays, they held umbrellas over their heads supporting the umbrella stems between neck and shoulder. Secondly, they did not have raised banquettes for their tables. Their white tables sat on the ground while the fisherwoman squatted down on over-turned wooden crates. The stray cats that canvassed the area were content with the discarded fish scraps that afforded them an easy meal they did not have to work for. Thirdly, their customers had to bend down to survey the fish displays that were most certainly not at a comfortable eye level.

Angela quickly took in the chaos around her at the outdoor fish market. Customers were milling around, some bargaining, some walking, some carrying large totes on tired shoulders. There was a great deal of noise as the fisher folk carried out their brisk trade. Today Sheila seemed to have fresh *pomfrets* at her outdoor post. Angela put her bargaining face on as she stopped by her table.

"How much for the pomfrets today, Sheila?" she asked looking uninterestedly, even though she was very interested.

"You like my pomfrets today, sister?" Sheila asked, also getting her bargaining game on.

"They look okay. I want some, but it depends on how much you want for them," Angela returned.

"Just look at them sister! They are fresh. Check, check for yourself," She invited Angela, pointing to her fish.

Angela examined a nearby sizeable pomfret (a much favored fish by Indians, found in the Indian Ocean. Related species are also found in the Atlantic and Pacific Oceans). Angela lifted the gills of the pomfret. They were a deep red. She prodded the skin with her forefinger. The slivery white fish skin bounced right back leaving no dimples. Next she proceeded to lift the fish by its tail. Tail down, head up, sightless eyes pointing to the sky. The fish stood up straight as if to attention. This was no flippy-floppy fish. It was definitely fresh. This was the freshest she had seen all day. Angela knew she wanted the fish. She put on a deadpan expression.

"See, didn't I tell you they were fresh?" reiterated Sheila, proud that she had vouched for her freshly dead fish and that they had stood up to Angela's fresh test.

"Yes, they are fresh," Angela conceded. She had to give credit where credit was due.

"So, you want them or not?" Sheila asked expectantly.

"How much for a pair of large pomfrets?" asked Angela, still visibly distancing herself from the fish.

"For you, only 1500 rupees, sister. For both," returned Sheila the fisherwoman.

"1500? That's too much! I don't want your fish," Angela feigned surprise. But Sheila was expecting her offer to get turned down.

"How much will you pay?" she countered.

"400 rupees," said Angela knowing that her offer would be rejected as well.

"400? For both? No, no. How can I feed my family if I give away the fish for next to nothing? You want my children to starve?" questioned Sheila rhetorically. She shook her head emphatically to answer her own question.

"Okay, how much are you willing to sell for?" asked Angela more seriously. She knew that the initial foray into bargaining was over. They were now in the thick of it. It was time to get serious. The first few steps of the song and dance had given way to a faster tempo.

"1200 for two beautiful fresh pomfrets," said Sheila, also getting serious.

"600 is my offer, otherwise I don't want them," countered Angela. She turned her back slightly to indicate disinterest and began walking away very slowly from the sale, even though she was still very interested.

"600? Are you crazy?" Sheila shouted to Angela's retreating back. Angela resolutely kept her back turned and began to show interest in a nearby fisherwoman's table, her ear still tuned to Sheila's voice that had pitched to a higher key as she raised her voice to be heard over the surrounding din.

"Okay, okay, come back sister. 800 is my final price. For two plump and juicy pomfrets," Sheila relented, lowering her price and the pitch of her voice. She knew she was about to close the sale.

Angela turned around and walked back quickly to the plump pomfrets.

"I'll take these two big ones plus that smaller one for 800," said Angela driving a hard bargain.

"What?" Sheila shrieked, caught off guard.

"Also, I'll buy four more large ones and two smaller ones for the same price," Angela added quickly sensing she might lose the battle. She needed about four pomfrets for the Chopra party, but she could always freeze the rest for another day or either she or Amy could make them for dinner that night. The pomfrets were really good today and Angela hated to let them go. By now she had developed quite an attachment to the dead glassy-eyed fish. She wanted them badly. Though looking at her poker-faced expression, one would never have guessed that to be the case.

Sheila looked back at Angela, cocking her heading backwards. She squinted, the black umbrella over her head not doing much to keep out the glinting sun at this angle.

"Okay. Take it. You are robbing me blind, but take it," she acquiesced, quickly picking out the fish and placing them in Angela's bag.

In return Angela counted out her money and handed it over to Sheila's eager fishy fingers.

Sheila pinched the money between the tips of her thumb and forefinger, so as not to get too much fish juice on the money. She quickly fanned the money out and held it over her table going methodically to all four corners and then kissing it, chanting prayers under her breath simultaneously. It was her first sale of the morning. It was a big sale and she thanked God for it, praying for the rest of the day to go just as magnificently. The fishy money quickly disappeared into the front opening of her sari blouse. The notes damp with fish juice seemed not to bother her in the slightest as they nestled between her breasts, mingling with the sweat there. The money drawer that had been cleverly added to the wooden crate she sat on, was used for small denomination notes. Notes that she would need to give back as change to customers. The larger, neatly folded notes were better off tucked into her bra for safe keeping.

Angela stopped by a few more fisherwomen's tables. She bought large tiger prawns, some Bombay ducks, a bucket of live crabs and some squid. At every stop, she employed highly honed bargaining skills that she had learned at her mother's knee. Lynette used to take Angela to the market with her every Saturday morning. She had learned the tricks and the subtle nuances of striking a good bargain and had surpassed her teacher's skills. Even Lynette would be astounded with Angela's skills in negotiation.

Angela checked off various items on both party lists and headed over to Ibrahim*bhai* her butcher, for a leg of lamb, Nitin*bhai*, her grocer for some rice, lentils, flour and cooking oil, before selecting her fruits and vegetables from Ashok*bhai* and Sunita*ben*. The yellow squash, asparagus and mushrooms looked very fresh today. Along with them, she picked onions and potatoes whole pods of garlic, stems of ginger, green chillies, *kothmir* (cilantro), okra, scallions and eggplant. Lila*ben* had some juicy pears today and Ramesh*bhai* had some deep red strawberries and firm bananas that would flambé beautifully for Friday's office party.

Everybody referred to each other as *'bhai'* (brother) or *'ben'* (sister). It was just the way things were done.

Ibrahim*bhai* had furnished Angela with a healthy leg of lamb. He had the dead and skinned animal along with its slaughtered friends, hung from high hooks for all to see. Once a customer made a selection, the butcher would cut out the requested part of the animal and wrap it up for the customer.

Beef and pork were never sold in the same shop as Hindus revere the cow and don't eat its meat and Muslims are prohibited by their religion from eating pork. The Muslim butchers tended to handle beef and mutton, while pork was usually available at cold stores or special pork stores handled by shopkeeper of other religious affiliations.

Angela made one final stop to buy three dozen eggs. She made arrangements with Amit*bhai*'s young assistant to bicycle most of her purchases to her home later. For his troubles, she bought the young teenager a refreshing sweet *lassi*.

She remembered to buy some for Sophie, Zack and Olivia as well. She only carried what needed immediate refrigeration with her as she made her way home.

Angela hailed a rickshaw and put her bags into the three-wheeler. She climbed in after her bags, thankful that most of her purchases would be delivered later by bicycle. If they got that bank loan, maybe they could buy a small vehicle for the business. They really needed one. On days they had to cater parties, Josh usually lent them his car.

Angela and Frank's car had been to the mechanic's shop so many times recently that she had finally sold it for parts to an auto body shop on Hill Road. She had not replaced the vehicle since then, using the very convenient public transportation to get around. Josh had let them use his car for their business needs, but it was definitely an inconvenience to him. Angela made a mental note to discuss purchasing a small van with Amy before the bank meeting on Thursday.

Angela reached her building, paid the rickshaw driver his fare. She unloaded her purchases and deposited her bags on the lobby floor by the elevator. She pressed the 'Up" button of the elevator/lift and waited for the elevator to arrive. Presently, it did. A few people walked out. Angela said a brief hello and took their place in the elevator.

Suresh, the liftman greeted her respectfully with a half-baked salute of fingertips that barely touched his temple, a demure smile with a quick flash of teeth, an imperceptible nod as his head bobbed from side to side like a pendulum with an imaginary cord, his eyes never quite daring to meet hers. The salute, smile, teeth and pendulous nod, all occurring almost in unison. He greeted all the building *memsahibs* and *sahibs* in this manner, considering himself subservient to their *sahibliness*. Angela smiled back kindly and asked after his little boy, Gopi. His son traveled from their little village outside of Mumbai to visit his dad in the big city every summer for two months.

The doors were just about to close, when Mrs. Pillai who lived on the second floor, stopped the automatic elevator doors from closing with her fingers. She needed Suresh to help her with her numerous bags. Suresh looked a little confused. Which *memsahib* should he assist first? Machado *memsahib* was already in the elevator and one of his assigned duties was to man the elevator. Pillai *memsahib* had tons of heavy bags and needed his help which was also one of his assigned duties. What should he do? He shuffled his feet undecidedly. Angela made the decision for him.

"Suresh, go help Mrs. Pillai with her bags. I will take the elevator up myself," she told the confused liftman. He smiled gratefully exiting the elevator.

Angela pressed the button to the eighth floor and rode up in the elevator. Her thoughts slipped back to the business and the tasks that needed to be completed today. Her mind was far away, so when the elevator came to a stop and the doors opened, she assumed she had arrived at her floor. She picked up her bags, holding one in each hand and proceeded to exit the elevator. At that very second, a neighbor from the fifth floor, Mr. Sharma chose to enter the elevator and Angela and her bags collided into him.

"Oh, I'm so sorry. I thought I was at my floor," Angela apologized looking at the floor indicator panel and realizing her mistake.

"It's no problem at all. It's not very often that a beautiful woman bumps into me in an elevator," he said looking directly at Angela.

Angela felt uncomfortable under his stare.

"I enjoyed it. Very much so," added Mr. Sharma reaching for the 'stop' button on the elevator control panel. The doors swished shut quietly. The elevator responding to the 'stop' command did not move.

Angela's head snapped back at the inappropriateness of his comment, only to find him staring lasciviously back at her. His eyes darted up and down her body, making Angela uneasy. He took a step toward her now that he had her attention. She took two steps backwards, feeling the cold elevator wall behind her.

The realization that she had nowhere to go caused her brain to panic. He took another step towards her, till he was so close she could feel his hot breath stir the fine hair on her horror-stricken face. Angela froze in her spot in the elevator corner. She knew she had to do something, but she couldn't move.

"Mrs. Machado. Angela. I have been waiting for you," he whispered into her hair, running his index finger down her cheek. She flinched. His massive body pinned her against the wall as his soft effeminate hands grabbed her breasts and squeezed. Hard. Angela body jerked from the pain, but still no sound came out of her throat.

"You must be so lonely these days with no man to warm your bed," he added as his hands continued to knead and squeeze her breasts, hurting her.

"So young and nobody to take care of you. Poor frustrated Angela," he mocked her.

He held the neckline of her dress with both hands and ripped open the fabric forcefully. The three pearl buttons of her favorite dress popped out of their stitching and fell soundlessly to the carpeted floor, their pinging sound going unheard.

As silent as the terrified scream that was lodged in her throat, refusing to come out.

"I will make you scream for more," he continued.

He held her captive with his forearm pressed against her neck under her chin and pawed her exposed breasts with one hand, attempting to urge the soft flesh out of the confines of her bra while at the same time his other hand lifted her dress and made its way up her thigh. His hands gripped her buttock and pulled her towards him. She could feel him through the thin cotton fabric of her summer dress. He ground his hardened groin into Angela's unwilling catatonic body, exciting himself further. His hand grabbed her panties and tore at the delicate fabric.

"You will be begging for more. Even Frank could not do better."

The fact that she had been docile thus far had been interpreted as encouragement by Mr. Sharma. It had emboldened him to push on as much as he could. He had accosted several other women in the past, to satisfy his sick thrills. He knew the drill. He had to work quickly before they managed to escape from his grasp.

He had once made the mistake of going after a woman with a husband and he had landed up in the hospital with a head concussion and a broken nose. Since then, he had learned his lesson. He reserved his advances for the kind of woman who needed a strong man (like himself) or one too meek to complain, like a widow or a lonely wife whose husband traveled, or a maid who worked for one of the families in the building. They were the easiest targets anyway with the least fall out for him. Usually they resisted him but he still managed to cop a few good feels before they got away.

Angela here on the other hand, seemed to be totally compliant and accepting of his advances. She probably really missed having a strong red blooded male around. He would really show her a good time.

He had waited patiently for an opportunity to present itself, to get Angela alone but it had been a long time coming. He had bided his time with Angela expecting an instant rebuff, but he thought now that maybe he had misjudged her. Maybe she had wanted this all along. Maybe she had been ready for him all along. Poor frustrated widow, burning with desire in her bed every night, and no one to put out her carnal fires.

Angela's panicked brain had gone into slow motion before it had screeched to a complete halt. She was cornered and she knew she had to do something. But she couldn't think of what it was that she had to do. Her mind had been absorbed by other matters and she had been caught completely unaware by the onslaught. Her brain had shut down. It had deserted her entirely. She was cognizant of every little detail happening as it occurred, but it seemed like it was happening in slow motion. The attack felt endless, like it had been going on for a while, when in actuality it had only been about a half a minute, maybe less.

Angela stood frozen in her spot, still holding her market bags, one in each hand. She could feel his sweaty, pudgy fingers as they groped her and she was repulsed by them. Her mind cried out in revolt, but no sound came through. She wanted to push back, but her hands seemed occupied. Her fingers had tightened so firmly around the handles of her market bags, that her nails left deep red indentations in her palms. Her knuckles turned white under the strain as her fingers locked into position around the handles of her shopping bags.

I am being assaulted by a predator in the elevator and what am I doing about it? I am clinging onto my market bags for dear life. Both my hands are unable to move. I am allowing him free rein of my body to maul as he pleases.

Whether it was the realization of the absurdity of her situation or the mention of Frank's name by her attacker, Angela did not know, but something (either one or both or maybe it was some other trigger entirely) galvanized her into action.

She uncurled her hands from the handles of the market bags allowing them to drop unceremoniously to the floor, their contents spilling on the carpet. She placed her suddenly liberated hands, palms flat against her attacker's chest and shoved him so hard, he fell backward hitting his head on the opposite elevator wall. Her tormentor was caught completely by surprise. None of his victims had ever fought back before. They wriggled and escaped out of his grasp eventually but no one had hit him before. Here, in the elevator, he was totally unprepared for her counterattack never having dealt with one before. He was at a huge disadvantage and his control over his victim dwindled rapidly. He was suddenly very frightened of Angela, his false macho bravado failing him instantly.

She jabbed her right fist into his eye and the left one into his solar plexus. She kneed him in the groin. Hard. Really hard. He was howling in pain holding onto his crotch with both hands, but she was not done with the scumbag. She scratched his face with all ten fingernails till she drew blood. Angela spied the leg of lamb sticking out of her bag. She picked it up with both hand and swung it like a baseball bat to the side of his head. The weapon made contact and he went down. Like a bowling pin. He lay in a crumpled heap on the floor, cowering and whimpering like a frightened rat before an anger crazed lioness.

"Take that you sick bastard. Try explaining those bruises to your wife. Come near me or my children ever again and I'll pluck your eyeballs out," she threatened.

Angela was out of breath from her fist fight. She jabbed the 'open door' button of the elevator. The contents of her market bags had spilled all over the floor, a few eggs had broken, some had even rolled away as if trying to escape the scuffle in the elevator, but Angela didn't stop to pick them up. She shot out of the elevator holding together the torn front of her dress and ran for her life.

Angela climbed the stairs two at a time and made it to her floor at break neck speed, the adrenalin surging through her body aiding her speedy exit. She entered her home and headed straight for her bathroom. She made it just in time as the bile and vomit gurgled into her mouth. She retched and retched till all the disgust was retched up, till her sides ached from the effort and she had to stop. Amy came running into the room. She had come in earlier than planned as she was ahead of schedule today. She was in the kitchen, when she heard the front door slam. She had called out to Angela, but had got no response. She had followed her sister to her room. She was surprised to see Angela throwing up.

"Angie, what's up? Are you feeling sick?" she asked concerned for her sister. She helped Angela get off the floor and saw the ripped fabric in the front of her dress.

"Oh, my God! Angie! What happened?" she asked, shocked.
"Angie, did someone try to hurt you? Oh, my God, your hands!
You're bleeding!" she exclaimed taking her sister's hands into
her own. Angela had punched the lights out of her attacker,
but she had come away with bruises too.
"Here, sit. Let me take care of the bruises," soothed Amy,
taking Angela to the rattan chairs in the room.

She took care of the bruises, cleaning them with antiseptic
lotion. She bandaged her sister's hands taking her time, giving
her sobbing sister a chance to collect herself. She muttered
soothing sounds and held her sister till she calmed down
enough to recount her disastrous encounter with the lecherous
Mr. Sharma.
They had all heard about his unwelcome advances and
exploits, preying on vulnerable women. The women of the
building gossiped and while neither Angela nor Amy had ever
been part of the gossiping inner circle, bits and pieces filtered
through to them from *memsahibs* who spoke to their maids
who gossiped with other maids, one of whom had mentioned
things on several occasions to Mirabai who in turn had
mentioned it in Angela's presence. Word got around.
Word of misdeeds *always* got around.
Angela took a long hot shower in an attempt to scrub off all
vestiges of her attacker. She lay curled up in bed with a hot
cup of tea at Amy's insistence. She had protested at first, as
they had so much to do for Friday and Saturday, but now she
was glad that she had listened. The surge of adrenalin had long
since worn off and Angela was sore in many places from her
attack. She knew she would have bruises on her body by
tomorrow. Her body ached all over, her brain devoid of any
coherent thought. She felt tired and drained.
He had violated her body.
He had invaded her mind.
He had plundered her sanctity.
Angela vomited again.

Thinking back to the attack, she couldn't believe it had taken her so long to react, so long to defend herself. She had been so preoccupied by her thoughts, she had failed to notice her surroundings. Frank was not here to protect her anymore she realized, but how she wished that he was!

Would Mr. Sharma attack her again? Had her actions enraged him enough that he would want revenge? Or had she scared him off forever? If not him, then weren't there others like him out there who lay in wait, poised to pounce on unsuspecting victims?

She needed to be more alert, for herself and for her children. If it happened again she needed to be more prepared. Maybe a class in self defense would not be such a bad idea, Angela thought to herself. She would enroll herself and the kids the first chance she got.

But for now she was very tired and needed to rest for a couple of hours. The kids would be home from school soon and she didn't want to upset them. The less they knew the better. She would use make-up to hide the bruises when they showed up tomorrow. Hopefully they would not be too bad, Angela thought.

Angela's eyes got heavy with sleep. She dozed, struggling to keep her eyes open. They had so much to do today, she could not allow herself a nap. But her eyelids were getting heavier and heavier by the second. Maybe she would close her eyes for just a little bit, Angela thought to herself. She could only afford to take a short nap. There was no way Amy could cope with preparations for two parties all by herself. She heard the doorbell ring as she was drifting off to sleep. Angela knew Amy would answer the door. She rolled over to her side, huddled up, hands joined under her cheek on the pillow and drifted off.

Frank, my love I really needed you today...

Amy returned to the kitchen with Angela's empty tea cup and her torn garments. Seeing Angela's clothes torn off her body, the reddened skin on her breasts and thighs where he had grabbed her flesh and her bloody hands with which she had scratched and fought off her attacker, had shocked Amy to the core. She herself had entered the house only a few minutes before Angela. It could have very well been her that had encountered Mr. Sharma. A shiver went down Amy's spine at the thought of a sexual assault. The thought of what he had done angered and frightened her at the same time.

But she had not the time to dwell on what might've or what could've happened to her when the stark reality of what really did happen to Angela was staring her in the face. She quickly burned the torn dress and undergarments, removing any tangible reminder of the incident and swept the ashes into the trash.

Amy had Josh who was a caring and protective husband. People knew that. Cowardly men like Mr. Sharma stayed away from her. But they also knew that Angela didn't have a man in her life to protect her. And one such individual had taken advantage of that fact today. He or someone else could strike again. She shuddered at the thought of it happening to either of them or their children. There were a lot of sick people in the world.

Today, their world had been touched by that sickness.

Amy had been surprised to hear that Angela had kicked and fought back. Her calm, sweet, delicate darling of a sister had stood her ground and had fought her tormentor. Amy was very proud of her. Frank would have been too, if he were here. He would have seen that Angela had come a long way since his death almost four years ago. His wife had moved on with her life. She had built a business on the rise and had taken responsibility for her life and her children. He would have been so proud to know that his Angela had fended off her attacker. They could all be proud of Angela. She had certainly shown them that she was capable of so much more than they had given her credit for.

Earlier, Angela had told Amy that she did not want to press charges. She did not want to file a police report. She just wanted to forget the whole thing. If it came out in the open, she would be devastated. It would get worse for everyone including the children. Especially the children.

Amy disagreed with Angela. She thought Mr. Sharma's debauchery deserved punishment. He deserved the shame and disrespect that would come his way with the exposure. But she also understood Angela's need to protect herself and her children from the gossipmongers and the school bullies who would twist and turn and embellish the actual incident to appease their cheap thrill seeking.

The doorbell interrupted her angry thoughts. She opened the door to a babbling liftman down on his knees. At first she thought Suresh had hurt himself and could not stand up.

"Suresh, what happened?" she asked.

"Sorry, *memsahib*, very sorry," he apologized, his hands joined in remorse.

"Sorry? What are you sorry for? What did you do?" she questioned.

"Very sorry, very sorry," he repeated, shaking his head, his head bent, his eyes staring at the floor.

"God will never forgive me. Please, please, I am very sorry," he ranted he joined his hands in apology.

"What's going on? What are you sorry for?" Amy asked again, trying to get a word in.

"I should never have left Machado *memsahib* alone in the elevator. What happened to her is my fault!" he explained.

The light bulb went on in Amy's brain. She realized that the poor groveling liftman somehow knew about the attack and had mistakenly blamed himself for it.

"It's okay Suresh. It's not your fault. *Memsahib* is okay. Nothing happened you hear. Nothing happened. She is just resting," returned Amy. She tried to allay the poor man's misplaced guilt while at the same time trying to respect Angela's wishes to ignore the incident.

"She dropped her bags in the elevator. Here they are," he said handing over Angela's market bags.

"She was feeling sick, so she rushed out of the elevator. She was in a hurry that's how she must've dropped her bags. Nothing else happened," Amy explained lamely.

Suresh handed the bags over, gave her his quick half-baked salute, a quick pendulous nod, no smile, no flash of teeth and walked quickly to the waiting elevator. He stopped mid stride suddenly remembering something. He had something in his pocket that he had meant to hand over. He stopped mid stride for a few seconds, he thought better of it and carried on his way. It was probably better that he didn't return them.

Amy knew from his expression that her on-the-spur-of-the-moment and not-very-believable excuse had not been bought by the liftman. She only hoped he would keep his mouth shut. If he mentioned it to Sonu, his 'secret' girlfriend who was also Mrs. D'Silva's maid, then there was no stopping the rumors from flying around. They would just have to deal with it if that happened. But it would be better for all concerned, if he would just keep his mouth shut tight.

Suresh had helped Mrs. Pillai with the last of her bags and had safely ushered her into the second elevator. He had waited patiently to resume his lift man duties as the first elevator he had been manning earlier that day returned to the ground floor. The automatic doors opened to a furious, disheveled Sharma *sahib* with bruises and scratches all over his face. He shoved Suresh out of his way, swearing out loud as he charged out of the elevator, raging madder than a bull seeing red at the *Pamplona Bull Run* in Spain.

Suresh managed to catch 'that mad bitch' as part of the expletives coming out of Sharma *sahib*'s vile mouth as he repeated it several times. Suresh cowered against the wall, till the raging mad bull stormed out of the lobby and silence was restored. There was no one else in the lobby to witness the outburst.

Suresh shrugged his shoulders, not sure what had happened. He knew enough English to include several words of profanity. He knew what 'mad bitch' meant. Sharma *sahib* probably had

had a really bad fight with his wife and was cursing out loud at her. He shrugged his shoulder again. He would hear the story on the building gossip grapevine by the end of the day. For now he was unconcerned. He turned his attention to his elevator and stopped dead in his tracks.

His clean freshly brushed carpeted elevator floor of this morning was peppered with packages that had apparently spilled out of the two shopping bags sitting in a heap on the floor. Three eggs had fallen out off their carton and had cracked open, their yolks and albumin seeping into the carpet fibers. Another egg had been shattered so severely that its shell had been crushed into a calcified powder that left a trail on the carpet. It had obviously been walked on. There were pomfrets and prawns, still in their cellophane bags strewn around. A leg of lamb was sticking out of its wrapping. It had somehow become separated from the other items as it lay docilely in a corner.

Suresh picked the food off the floor and placed everything back in the two shopping bags. One bag was moving away from him. It was the bag with the live crabs in it. He carefully picked the bag up and cautiously joined it with its relatives of the sea. He was careful to steer clear of their sharp pincers. Then his eye caught something else.

Three pearl buttons.

How very strange, he thought to himself, frowning as he picked up the little white buttons and looked them over. He deposited the buttons into his pocket. During the time he took to refill the bags, Suresh's mind was busy figuring out what had happened in his elevator just moments ago. It didn't take him long. Suresh was subservient, but he was not stupid.

Machado *memsahib*'s market bags, Sharma *sahib*'s scratched up face, his reputation with the ladies and the three pearl buttons. He had all the clues he needed to draw his own conclusion.

Those three buttons had their own story to tell.

Their inanimate quietude spoke volumes, nonetheless. Their irrefutable truth was as undeniable as the roundness of their shape.

Once he had the facts, he easily figured out how they factored into the equation. He surmised the 'bitch' in Sharma *sahib*'s rants had not been his wife as he initially suspected, but Machado *memsahib*. He had a pretty good guess so as to what had transpired in his elevator a few minutes ago.

He cleaned the mess out as best he could with a wet rag. He hoped nobody had noticed the altercation between Sharma *sahib* and Machado *memsahib* in the elevator. Even if they had, he would be powerless to stop the rumors. Nobody had been in the lobby when he had made the revelation himself. What he suspected had transpired here was a terrible thing. It was a shameful act. It was despicable beyond words.

He would not say anything to anyone about it if he was asked. He would not even say anything to Sonu, his girlfriend. He knew she enjoyed a good gossip just as much as the next person. If he told her about today's events, she would spread the word to all the other maids. So he would keep it from her. In any case their relationship wasn't working out and he was planning to end it anyway. So he didn't owe her anything. He would protect the good name of the poor widow on the eighth floor. He had not been in the elevator to protect her before, but he would protect her now.

If only Pillai *memsahib* had entered the lobby a few seconds later.

If only she had not stopped the elevator door from closing.

If only she had not needed his help with her bags.

If only he had manned his elevator like he was supposed to.

Then none of this would have happened.

If only.

Regrets. Useless, now after the fact. Suresh knew there was nothing he could do about it now. What had happened today had happened already. He could not change that. It had happened so quickly. It was his fault that the poor widow had suffered such degradation. It was his fault that she had been a victim of that *pig* Sharma's depraved lust.

When he carried Machado *memsahib*'s bags up to her door he could not stop berating himself for not manning his elevator like he was supposed to.

He handed over the market bags, but the three pearl buttons remained in his shirt pocket. Machado *memsahib's* sister said nothing had happened. He knew better. But if that's the way they wanted to play it, then who was he to question their decision?

Was it not better to just leave it that way anyway?

Chapter 11

Summer Vacation

School had let out early. It was the last day before summer vacation. Eleven year old Sophie was completing sixth grade while Zack four years younger, was at the end of the second grade. Little Olivia who had grown into a very fine and poised young lady of four years, was in nursery school.

Angela waited just outside the school gates for her children. She waited for them in their new van. It was not exactly a new van in the true sense of the word. Amy and Angela had been lucky to locate a second hand van that still had a number of good years left in it. While it was in essence, not a new vehicle, it was still *their* new van. They had finally bought it five months ago after securing the bank loan for their business. Since then, they had used it for all their business needs.

Angela didn't need the aid of the grocer's young assistants and their bicycles at the market anymore. She would load all her purchases directly into the van as she bought them from the vendors. The most important usage undoubtedly, was the use of the van to carry things back and forth for their catered events. Before the van, Josh had lent them his car on days they had events. It had been a necessary arrangement for the business but at a great inconvenience to him. Obtaining the van had been an expensive investment, but it had proven to be one well worth the money.

They had decided on painting the van in an unusual color in an attempt to brand their business. The brightly colored van was easily distinguishable on the road and was a great means of advertising for the business. It generated interest from other drivers who spoke about 'the bright purple van' they had encountered on the street. When they had decided on the unique color palette for their vehicle, Angela and Any had not taken into account the subsidiary benefits of doing so. They were thrilled to be on the receiving end of such curiosity nonetheless.

In addition to business needs, the van was also used five times a week when Angela or Amy picked up their kids from school. Angela waited patiently for school to let out. The kids had their last final exam today following which they would be on summer vacation for two whole months till mid June. Angela heard the school bell ring for the final time this academic school year.

Classroom doors opened and kids scurried out of its portals like droves of little mice drawn to pied piper's musical flute. They were talking excitedly amongst each other. Some were discussing the questions on the exam and hoping that their answers were right, others were exchanging phone numbers promising to call over the summer, others were discussing vacation plans. There was a palpable buzz of excitement and relief in the air. The final exams had been long and arduous and had been spread out over two weeks.

The children had worked hard all year long but harder still at exam time. Many stayed up late into the night burning the candle at both ends, hoping the extra time would better prepare them for the exam questions, get them extra points on the exam. They had crammed a great deal of information into their little heads, but now it was finally over. The weight had finally been lifted and they could breathe easy. They could forget about English readers, math and science books, dates in history and geography maps, Marathi and Hindi, grammar, syntax and gerunds for a whole two months. Two months. It seemed like a lifetime to the exam-driven-all-night-cramming students and they were happy to have forever. For however long forever lasted.

Angela did not rush the kids. The last day of school was the same every year. They took their time, they talked to friends like it was the last time they would ever see them again. They laughed with class mates and told each other 'knock-knock' jokes. She enjoyed seeing the tension ebb away from their little faces. Kids had it tough these days, Angela thought to herself. They had a heavy load of daily course work, they were bombarded with pages and pages of homework everyday, their poor little shoulders were weighed down by book bags that almost matched them in weight, but exam time was always the worst.

It was stressful for kids and parents alike. Children were pushed to excel in school from a very early age. Over zealous parents sent their kids, even the little ones, to prep courses and tuition classes to give their kids an edge over the others in the classroom. Children stressed because parents stressed. Parents stressed because schools stressed. School stressed because society stressed. Everyone stressed.

In a nutshell, excellence in school led to admission to better colleges which led to impressive resumes which led to better jobs. So everyone stressed high grades. The cycle was vicious and never ending. In the end, kids were over-stressed and their childhoods flashed by as they buried their noses in school papers and homework assignments. They hardly ever had time to play after school, some forced to forgo the pleasure altogether.

Angela was well aware of the pressures of society and the impact it had on their children. No matter what the homework load for the day, she always allotted play time for her kids. She believed, that play time was just as essential as study time for a well rounded, well developed mind and body. Often Sophie, Zack and Olivia would be the only kids playing in their building compound after school, but Angela considered it necessary. The children were only too happy to oblige. They rode their bicycles, played catch, ran around and made up outdoor games. It was nicer when the other building kids joined them, a rarity during the school year, but they were happy to play on their own if they had to.

The car door opened and the kids streamed into the waiting van. Sophie helped Olivia into the vehicle, while Zack and Gavin climbed in from the other side. They moved over to make place for Ritesh, a kid from their building who rode home with them every evening. It was a tight squeeze much like squished sardines in a tin.

"Hi kids. How was the exam?" Angela asked.

"Super! I think I am going to ace my math test!" Zack shouted exuberantly.

"Me too!" Olivia said excitedly.

"Livvie! You don't have math classes yet, silly!" Gavin returned.

"I don't?" said little Olivia looking very sad, as though she was missing out on something important.

"Nope. But you have the alphabet, right?" Sophie encouraged her little sister.

Olivia promptly nodded her answer. Then asked tentatively, "What's 'alphabet'?"

Everyone in the car laughed.

"It's your ABC's!" Ritesh, the neighbor's kid said.

"Oh yeah. I have those. I can write lots of letters," Olivia responded happy to be part of the team again.

"How did your History exam go, Sophie?" Angela asked her daughter.

Sophie had struggled with a few dates in her history book yesterday. Even though they occurred years apart, she kept confusing the dates of Gandhi's *Salt March at Dandi* with the *Jalianwala Bagh Massacre* in Amritsar.

"The paper was soooo long!" Sophie exaggerated, rolling her eyes.

"Really!" Angela retorted, well aware of her daughter's penchant for exaggeration.

"I just about finished the last sentence when the bell rang. I didn't have time to look the paper over for mistakes. But I guess I did okay," she replied.

"We'll have to wait and see when the results come out," Angela added.

Sophie shrugged her shoulders. The exam was done and she didn't want to think about it anymore.

"How about your exam, Gavin? You had Geography today, right? How did you do, son?" Angela asked her nephew.

"It went well, Auntie Angie. I wrote down all the answers, but I forgot the answer to one question on the world map diagram. So I am going to get that one wrong," Gavin replied.

"That's not so bad. You did try your best, right?" Angela asked.

"Yeah, I tried really hard but I couldn't remember where Morocco was," he replied.

"Well, that you tried is all that really matters then," she responded.

They arrived at the building within a few minutes, the school being only a half a mile away. The kids piled out of the car and headed home to begin their summer vacation in full swing. All thoughts of exams and books and school had receded from their minds. As they entered their home, their nostrils were treated to the aroma of fresh baking as it came wafting through the air.

"We have a special treat for you kids today," Angela said to four fast moving pairs of skinny brown legs as they followed their sniffing noses to the source of the delicious aroma.

"We can smell it mummy!" said Olivia excitedly.

"It smells like a bakery in here! What do you think it is?" asked Zack, sniffing appreciatively.

"Smells sweet. Like cookies," guessed Sophie.

"I smell chocolate," said Gavin.

"Cake. I smell cake. Orange, no wait, lemon. No, no, I think its orange," said Zack changing his mind back and forth in excitement.

"Go into the kitchen and you'll soon find out," Angela urged them.

They trooped into the kitchen to find an enormous cake sitting on the kitchen counter. A beautiful golden brown cake was cooling on a wire rack, having just been removed from the oven. Beside it sat its twin, also golden brown.

"Two cakes!" Olivia trilled.

Amy was vigorously whisking a fluffy white icing in a huge bowl. The messy kitchen was strewn with a variety pots and pans with syrupy spoons and sticky spatulas sticking out of them. She had on an apron covered in flour. Some had even got into her hair leaving a fine dusting.

"Ah, you are all back I see. How did the exams go?" she enquired planting kisses on all four heads.

"Fine, fine, ma. What cake is this?" asked Gavin.

"May we have some?" asked Zack.

"Who gets the second cake?" asked Sophie, assuming that the first one was theirs.

Olivia was busy trying to climb on to nearby stool, so she could get a better view.

"Kids, kids! Slow down. One at a time!" Amy laughed making eye contact with Angela. They enjoyed the moment, watching their happy kids impatient to get their eager little hands on some cake.

"You were all right. It is an orange peel cake with gooey chocolate chips inside," Angela answered the question at the top of their agenda.

"Why two?" asked Gavin.

"One cake is a treat for you all on the last day of school. The other cake is for your cousins when they get here tomorrow," explained Amy.

"What time will they be here, mummy?" asked Zack.

"By the time you kids wake up tomorrow morning, they will be here," offered Angela in response.

"Yippeeee!" shouted Zack and Gavin together.

"May we please have some cake now?" asked Sophie, unable to resist the tempting smells emanating from the cake in front of her.

"It's still very warm, baby. Auntie Amy only just took it out of the oven," said Angela.

"We love hot cake!" said Zack. Angela knew that to be true. They preferred to eat the cake warm out of the oven rather than cooled to room temperature, or maybe they were just too impatient to wait for it to cool.

"I'll tell you what. Why don't you go and change out of your school uniforms. In the meantime, Auntie Amy and I will serve up the cake. Go on all of you," Angela said, shooing them out of the kitchen.

Zack hung back a second after the others. He smiled impishly and asked,

"May I lick the bowl? Please mummy, please!" he begged eyeing the bowl that still had ribbons of cake batter in it.

Sophie heard her brother's pleas from the hallway and returned to the kitchen promptly, Gavin in tow.

"If he gets the bowl, then I want to lick the spatula," she half asked, half told her mother.

"Then I want the spoon!" piped in Gavin, also wanting some of the action.

"Okay, okay! Now off with all of you!" Amy hurried them out of the kitchen for the second time.

Sophie, Zack and Gavin trooped out of the kitchen. Olivia continued to sit on the stool. She had successfully climbed on to it, a telltale trace of frosting on the side of her mouth. She had stuck her finger into Auntie Amy's bowl and helped herself to the yummy whipped icing while the others had been discussing the assigned licking of cake bowls, spatulas and spoons. They had been too busy to notice her actions.

"And you missy? Don't you want to get changed?" asked Amy playfully of her little niece.

"Nope. I want cake first," returned Olivia, shaking her head.

"I don't think so missy," Angela told her little girl lifting her off the stool.

"Oh bother!" Livvie exclaimed.

Angela and Amy smiled at the look of exasperation on her small face.

"Off you go, little miss. Ask Sophie nicely to help you get changed," said Angela firmly.

"Okay, but I want lots and lots of whipped cream on my cake," Livvie added as she left the kitchen. She would do their bidding but not before they agreed to her conditions.

The kids enjoyed the cake and whipped orange cream that had been prepared specially for them on their last day of school. It was a great start to what was shaping up to be an awesome summer vacation.

They were going to Goa to see Nana Lynette. They went to Goa every summer for an entire month. They loved spending time with their grandmother and got to experience life in a small village that was so far removed from their life in the big city. This year was different though. They were still going to Goa this May, but they would not be going alone.

Nana Lynette was turning seventy-five this year. Her children had planned to spend her special birthday with her in Goa, along with their families. Alastair and his wife Gwen along with their two children, Candace and Ruth would be arriving in India early tomorrow morning from Canada. They were flying directly to Goa and would meet the rest of the family there in a few days. Adrian and Shayna along with their three children, Nicholas, Evan and Juliana were arriving in Mumbai tomorrow morning from New Jersey. Two days later, Adrian, Angela and Amy along with their families would take the train to Goa.

Their itinerary figured out, Angela and Amy had to get their families packed and ready to go, but they had one party to cater before the trip. The sisters looked forward to their well deserved break. They had been working round the clock for several months together. They were extremely happy and thankful to be busy but they were tired too.

Angela and Amy had discussed the possibility of taking on another employee to ease their work load when they returned from their vacation. In the meantime, they worked hard so that they could take a few weeks off to spend with their family. They resolutely refused to fill in their appointment planner for the scheduled four vacation weeks even though they were sorely tempted to accept the work. They had never turned away work before and it was a hard thing to lose that business, but they both felt strongly about family ties. It had taken a great deal of planning and ticket buying and resolving schedule conflicts on their part to make their mother's seventy fifth birthday trip a reality. So, Angela and Amy stuck to their guns and scheduled four entire weeks off.

Dadar train station was a hive of activity even at six o'clock in the morning. They were waiting on the platform for the train to Goa to pull in. The out station train terminal was crowded with people and their bags traveling all around the country.

Coolies were shuttling baggage to waiting train compartments, carrying most of their load on their heads. They didn't wear bright red turbans anymore, like they did during the days of the *British Raj* in India and for several years subsequent to that. The red turbans were really just very long scrunched up lengths of fabric that they wrapped around their heads before placing pieces of luggage on top. Some carried three maybe even four suitcases, their bodies performing a skilled balancing act as they navigated the crowded platforms. Nowadays, instead of the red turbans, the coolies carried thick cotton rope that was coiled into a ring.

Their own coolie had just deposited their luggage at their feet. They had a few minutes to spare before the train pulled in. Angela double checked the tickets to make sure that they were waiting in the right area on the platform while Josh counted the bags their coolie had just placed on the floor and tipped the man for his effort. Shayna rounded up the children and kept a watchful eye on the little ones while Amy stopped by a newspaper stand to buy reading materials for the journey.

The kids, all seven of them, were very excited. They had hardly slept the night before, staying up to talk about their vacation plans. They had finally fallen asleep from sheer exhaustion, but were bright eyed and bushy tailed first thing the following morning. There was time enough to rest on the train.

The train pulled into the station on schedule. It was a very short stop, so they hurried to get themselves and their belongings on the train. Angela and Shayna climbed in first and helped the children one at a time as Adrian hoisted them up, with Amy and Josh bringing up the rear. They quickly found their reserved sleepers and settled in, to a nine hour trip from Mumbai to Goa. Other passengers boarded the train and finally the *Konkan Kanya* (Girl of the *Konkan* region) chugged out of Dadar train station.

The steward from the train's galley passed around the compartment taking breakfast orders from the passengers. Their food arrived shortly after and Angela thought it was surprisingly good. Her past experiences with travel food had prepared her for the worst. So it was with much trepidation that she had ordered a meal today. Firstly, it arrived piping hot. The fact that their car happened to be adjacent to the galley car might have had something to do with that. Secondly, the food arrived in clean stainless steel containers on trays, yet another definite improvement from the past. Thirdly, the food was tasty and had obviously been freshly prepared. The fact that the railway service had cooks making fresh food on a moving train for hundreds of people was in itself an amazing feat. Their meal was followed by hot cups of instant Nescafe.

The family settled in for a few hours of peace and quiet. The past couple of days, since Adrian's family had arrived, things had been pretty hectic on the home front and on the business front as well. Angela, Amy and Shayna were talking quietly to each other. Josh was reading a newspaper and Adrian was playing cards with Sophie and Gavin. Little Olivia and Juliana were sitting beside their mothers. Olivia was playing with her doll and Juliana was coloring with crayons in her coloring book. Nicholas, Evan and Zack all more or less the same age had bonded very quickly with each other. The trio of cousins decided to explore the train car.

"We're bored mom. Could we take a walk up that way?" Nick asked his mother, pointing with his right hand.

"I don't see why not," Shayna replied looking at her eldest boy.

"Awesome mom!" Evan said enthusiastically.

"Just stay close. Do not leave this train car," She cautioned.

They walked down the aisle to their right. The other passengers were similarly engaged. Some were reading books or magazines, other were napping. They found a vacant sleeper by the window. They didn't have a seat like this one. It was a side sleeper that backed up to three windows, where in all three sleeper seats had a clear window view. They decided to borrow the seats for a little while, since no one was using it anyway. They knelt down on the sleeper, pressing their faces up against the bars on the window.

They looked out the window at the scenery as it whizzed by. They saw open stretches of land and grazing farm animals. They also saw a young girl walking on a dirt road carrying two large copper pots filled with water on her head, the water sloshing about as she walked. They saw mountains in the distance and endless green fields.

After a while the boys began to fidget. Evan turned around in his spot on the sleeper and sat on the seat. Zack and Nick were to his right. He looked around the train car casually taking the people in. That is, he looked around till he saw something he couldn't take his eyes off. A woman was seated to one end of the sleeper on his left.

It's not the fact that she was a heavy set woman that had his attention, or that this woman had breasts the size of watermelons. Rather, it was her nonchalant actions that had caught his fancy.

He nudged Zack with his elbow. Zack looked down at his cousin from his kneeling position on the sleeper.

"What?" he enquired.

Evan pointed discreetly to the woman. Zack looked. He took in the woman with the watermelons. He nudged Nick kneeling beside him.

"Yeah, what's up?" Nick asked his cousin.

Zack motioned Nick with his eyes to look at the woman.

They both turned around and sat beside Evan, gawking at the woman, their jaws hanging open.

She was as oblivious to their stares as she was to the fact that her scrunched up sari *pulloo* barely covered her ample bosom, a bosom that was practically falling out of her sari *choli* (blouse). The train was plowing ahead at full speed, causing her flesh to jiggle to its rhythm. She was munching on a *batata wada* (a batter fried potato ball). A few crumbs fell between the melons, nestling in a dark secret place. She didn't bother to fish them out. She munched on two more *wadas*, whose crumbs joined the previous crumbs. She then opened a paper cone of roasted *sheng-channa* (peanuts and gram) and proceeded to throw them into her mouth, one at a time. Her hand to mouth coordination was not as good as she expected it to be. Some of the pieces made their destination and she devoured them in an instant, some bounced off the melons and landed on the floor and some got diverted into the ravine between the melons and joined the previously deposited crumbs there. Next, she pulled a ripe peach out of her bag. She dug her teeth into the succulent fruit, its sweet juice tricking down her chin before it dripped into the valley to join the *wada* crumbs and *sheng-channa*.

Two drops. *Plop plop.*

"How much do you think she can store in there?" Evan asked, intrigued by the jiggling multi functioning melons.

"A lot I guess. They are so huge. Like cantaloupes," Zack answered.

The woman finished her peach, wiped her chin and neck with a handkerchief she had plucked out of her sari skirt. She then dabbed her bosom thoroughly, causing her flesh to jiggle even more.

"Not melons. More like Jell-O or maybe pudding," said Nick, watching the twin jigglers.

"Jell-O pudding," amended Evan.

"Caramel Jell-O pudding," added Nick.

"Yeah. Caramel Jell-O pudding in large water balloons," giggled Zack.

The boys had been whispering and nudging each other. They chuckled, attracting the woman's attention. Thus far she had ignored them completely. The boys were laughing now at their silly inferences, imagining jiggling water balloons filled with caramel Jell-O pudding flapping against each other. The woman was getting annoyed. She sensed she was the butt of their joke, but she didn't know for sure. She gesticulated animatedly with both arms asking them,

"What's so funny? Why are you laughing?"

Her actions caused still more jiggling. By now the boys had given up all pretenses and were laughing out loud.

'Get out of here, you silly boys! Go away!" she yelled, her reddening face an apoplectic parody.

Nick, Evan and Zack quickly retreated to their own seats, laughing all the way.

"What's going on boys?" Shayna asked, looked at the three boys. She could tell by the looks on their faces that they had been up to no good.

"Nothing, mom. Nothing," Nick answered for himself and the others.

"Uh huh. Then how come I don't believe you?" she asked.

But the boys wouldn't say.

Boys will be boys, Shayna thought as she shook her head.

The boy trio settled down after that, not causing much of a stir.

218 Three Pearl Buttons

The train stopped at *Panvel* station. Several railway vendors cased the train cars of the out station trains that stopped at the station. They hopped on to the train to sell their wares. There was a woman selling combs and clips and other hair accessories. She stopped in front of one interested customer who rifled through her goods. She waited patiently for the customer to make her choice. There was a *chaiwalla* (tea seller) selling hot cups of milky tea in little transparent glass glasses. There was, similarly a man selling coffee in little cups shouting, "Nescafe, Neeeyscafe!" in a nasal voice. Another vendor was selling hot *batata wadas* that got Nick, Evan and Zack chuckling again. A teenaged boy also got on the train with a huge box selling an assorted variety of cool drinks. The box was attached by a strong strap on either side that was slung around his neck, placing the box squarely in front of him. He called out to no one in particular,

"Tangola, Mangola, Pepsi Cola, Dukes!"

"What's a 'Tangola'? Is it any good?" Nick asked Amy.

"There is no such thing as 'Tangola'," Amy answered her nephew.

"But the man said there is," he returned.

"I know he did, but there isn't such a thing. My guess is that he just wanted to say something that would rhyme with 'Mangola'," Amy offered.

"Oh. Okay. What about 'Mangola' then, or is that just a made up word as well?' asked Nick.

"No, that's a real drink. Mangola is a really tasty mango juice. Would you like to try one?" asked Amy, looking over to Adrian for his permission.

"Sure, let's get some. I haven't had a Mangola in years. Not since I left India so many years ago," Adrian said.

The young seller pulled out five cold bottles of Mangola from his box. He took off the bottle caps with a metal bottle opener that showed faint telltale signs of once having been painted dark green. He inserted plastic straws into the mouth of the bottles and served up the cool drinks to his customers. Nick took a sip.

"It's really good, dad. You should try some Evan," he said offering his brother his bottle.

The vendor stood up with his box. He eased the strap around his neck again and adjusted the box for comfort. He would return in a few minutes for the empty bottles. He carried on into the train compartment calling out,

"Tangola, Mangola, Pepsi Cola, Dukes!"

He announced his drinks stock while simultaneously running his well used paint peeled metal bottle opener back and forth along the necks of the bottles, creating a sound that only metal on glass can make. It was much like tickling the ivories, except that the fingers were made of metal and the piano keys were made of glass. A jarring rendition of the delicate movement.

"Tangola, Mangola, Pepsi Cola, Dukes!"

"Tangola, Mangola, Pepsi Cola, Dukes!"

Chapter 12

Stuck with It

Lynette had been looking forward to their arrival for several months. She had been thrilled to learn that her family had wanted to spend her seventy-fifth birthday with her in Goa. Her children had kept her informed through the planning stages. It had seesawed back and forth quite a bit. One day their plan would work, another day it wouldn't. At one point Lynette believed the reunion didn't have a chance, on account of schedule conflicts. It was tough coordinating work and school schedules of seven adults and nine children across three countries, but they had eventually managed to pull it off.

It had been too long since their last family reunion. The last time they had all been together had been for Adrian and Shayna's wedding, almost eight years ago. The wedding had been held in America and while Lynette had gone to the wedding, it was not the same as having all her children and grandchildren under her roof.

Lynette mulled over the past eight years. So much had happened since then.

First of all, Lynette and Robert had relocated to Goa, setting up residence at Robert's ancestral home. After their children had married and moved away, Robert and Lynette had found life in Mumbai to be too fast paced for their aging minds and bodies. Life in Goa functioned at a slower pace, '*susaygaad*' as the locals called it. Returning to their roots had been an easy decision for Lynette and Robert, a chance to live out their final years in peaceful surroundings.

Second, they had settled into Goa but a short while, when Robert had passed away. He had gone to sleep one night never waking to see the next morning. He had died peacefully in his sleep. He had been strong and healthy and had not suffered before he took his last breath. This year would mark five years since his passing.

Third, Frank had followed him a year later. Angela had had to care for her young children and work at establishing her business with Amy.

Fourth, Alastair and his family had migrated to Canada. Lynette's eldest son and his family had moved far away, but at least Adrian was in America. They could visit each other every once in awhile.

Lastly, and probably the most important thing that had happened over the past eight years was that Lynette had been collecting grandchildren. She was the proud grandmother of nine grandbabies.

So much had happened. Their family had changed so much in these past eight years and they had so much to catch up on.

Alastair and Gwen had arrived two days ago with their girls, Candace and Ruth. Today the rest of the gang was expected to get here. It would be an exciting time for the kids. It was a chance for them to get to know their cousins better and a chance for the adults to catch up on the past eight years. Lynette was definitely excited. Her heart was filled with great expectations, a chance to make wonderful memories that would stay with her long after her children had returned to their busy lives.

In preparation for their arrival, she had cooked their favorite dishes, she had cleaned her home, hung new draperies. She had scrubbed the mosaic tiles so clean one could eat right off her floors. She had bought gifts for her grandchildren and she had informed the neighbors who were also expectantly awaiting their arrival. They looked forward to visitors to their little village, especially visitors from the big city of Mumbai and from far away countries abroad. They eagerly anticipated an exciting change to the humdrum of their daily lives.

The three taxis meandered through the narrow streets of Goa. They had hired three taxi cabs from the train station's taxi stand, to take them to their destination. Josh had negotiated a fair price with the taxi drivers eagerly awaiting a good fare from visitors as they disembarked from the train, hoping for a hefty tip at the end of the ride. Their group of five adults and seven children had piled into the yellow and black vehicles and headed to Nana Lynette's house.

They left the train station to a bollywood film title song sung by Goa's pop star Remo Fernandes blaring on the taxi cab stereo. The taxi driver was drumming his fingers on the steering wheel keeping tempo, as he sang along in Hindi for added entertainment – '*Pyaar Toh Hona Hi Tha.*'(Love just had to happen).

While the history of Goa stretches as far back to the Mauryan Empire in the 3rd century and it chronicles its Muslim rule in the fourteenth century among other governances in its history, the Portuguese occupation was one of the most prevailing influences of its time.

In ancient Vedic and Sanskrit texts, Goa had been referred to by many names- (*Goparashtra, Govarashtra, Gomanchala, Gove, Govapuri, Gopakpattan, Gopakapuri, Gomantak Gomant, and Gopakapattanam,*). The name '*Goa*' as it is known today, originated from the Portuguese. It has been said to have been derived from the Konkani word '*Goy*' meaning a tall patch of grass.

Vasco da Gama was the first European to land in India several hundred miles south of Goa. He landed at Calicut in Kerala in 1498, in search of a sea route from Europe to India. The Portuguese had been intent on controlling the spice trade from India and had been in search of a good trading seaport.

In 1510, the Portuguese fleet under the command of Alfonso Albuquerque landed in Goa. Goa was considered to be a highly suitable port of entry as it lay on the Konkan Coast of India, right off the Arabian Sea. The Portuguese were not easily able to overthrow the prevailing ruler, but after several agitations, they were finally able to assert their supremacy over the ruling Shah of Bijapur. They established Goa as a colony and naval base soon after. The territories of *Ilhas, Salcette, Mormugao and Bardez* formed part of Portugal's *'Velhas Conquistas'* or old conquests, which made up one fifth of the total area of modern Goa.

By 1543, Catholicism came to Goa via proselytizing Franciscan and Jesuit missionaries. Almost every catholic Goan has a characteristic Portuguese last name as a result of religious conversions where in they adopted a Portuguese name (usually that of the priest responsible for the conversion) or by marriage unions between the Portuguese and the local Indians.

Shortly after, King Sebastian of Portugal attempted to eradicate all traces of Indian customs via the Inquisition. However, many Christians of Goa were unwilling to relinquish their ancient Indian customs. They were forced to leave Goa and settle beyond Portuguese dominion. They fled to *Mangalore, Karwar* and *Kerala*, regions to the south of Goa and to *Malvan and Savantwadi*, to her north.

Later, due to a Portuguese fall out with the Jesuit order, conversions to Catholicism ceased and the Hindu majority was permitted the freedom to practice a religion of their choosing. Hinduism in Goa prevailed but not before a sizeable chunk of the population had been converted to Catholicism. The inhabitants of the *'Novas Conquitas'* or new conquest territories retained their Hindu identity and continue to do so as is evident in the large Hindu population prevalent in the region.

Under Portuguese rule, Goa became a vital trading port and its citizens were granted the same civic privileges as their counterparts in Lisbon, Portugal. The Portuguese brought to Goa, their meteoric trail blaze of power and ambition and the might of a Western nation at the apex of its imperial glory. It was regarded as the 'Rome of Asia' and the 'Pearl of the Orient'. Titles like 'Goa Dourada' or 'Golden Goa' referred not to Goa's acclaimed golden beaches but to the gilt altars in churches that were constructed of layers of real African gold brought in by the Portuguese.

In his 1839 novel titled 'Phantom Ship', English novelist Frederick Marryat described Goa during the Portuguese rule. An excerpt from his novel reads: 'The squares behind the palace and the wide streets were filled with living beings: elephants with gorgeous trappings; led or mounted horses with superb housings; palanquins carried by natives in splendid liveries; running footmen; syces, every variety of nation, from the proud Portuguese to the half-covered native; Musselmen, Arabs, Hindoos, Armenians; Officers and soldiers in their uniforms, all crowded and thronged together: all was bustle and motion. Such was the wealth, the splendor and luxury of the proud city of Goa – the Empress of the East.'

Portuguese influence can further be seen in the architecture of Goa. Most structures display an amalgamation of Portuguese, Moghul and Indian architectural styles. The Portuguese issued compulsory orders to residents to paint their homes every year after the monsoon season. It was mandated that the exterior walls of houses be painted in yellow ochre, Indian red, pale green or other similar earthy hues. The color 'white' could be used for architectural details like cornices, balustrades and window ledges of residential properties, but no building other than a church was allowed to be painted white all over.

The homes were characterized by a bust of Jesus or a cross at the entrance where the litany or the rosary was recited on feast days, a custom still very much in evidence. There were elaborately carved compound walls and gate posts. Most homes tended to possess a staircase leading up to a verandah or balcony. While bright colors adorned the exterior façade, the interior walls tended to be white or pastel in color. Almost every home had a false wooden ceiling and the roof was constructed of reddish country tiles more famously known as Mangalore tiles. The floors were tiled with elaborate patterns that had been brought in from Portugal and the windows were glazed with glass or oyster shells. A central courtyard was also a distinct feature of the Goan home and was often surrounded by coconut palms.

National Geographic Magazine compared Goa with the Amazon and the Congo basin for its rich tropical diversity. Goa's red, loamy soil, rich in laterites is very conducive to rice and coconut plantations. The alluvial soil is also beneficial to cashew, bamboo, teak and sal trees. Tropical fruit like mangoes, jackfruits, pineapples and blackberries grow abundantly.

Goa is considered to be India's richest state with a GDP per capita two and a half times that of the country as a whole, with the fastest growth rate in the country. Tourism is Goa's primary industry. The imposing Italian Renaissance Basilica of Bom Jesus (pronounced 'Bom Jesu', meaning 'Good Jesus'), draws millions of tourists to Goa every year. This world heritage site houses the mortal remains of St. Francis Xavier, the patron saint of Goa. Once every twelve years his body (miraculously still in existence) is displayed for veneration and public viewing. Goa's medicinal springs and more recently its foray into medical tourism assure the territory a continued supply of tourists.

While Konkani is the official language of Goa (as it lies on the Konkan Coast of India), Portuguese is still spoken by a few. Fish, rice and coconut are the staple foods of the Konkan people. The most popular alcoholic beverage in Goa is 'feni'. It is fermented and distilled from the fruit of the cashew tree or from the sap of toddy palms.

The three taxis wound their way through palm tree-lined streets of small towns and little villages. The children took in the rudimentary countryside and the simple ways of rustic living. The cabs zipped through the narrow tarred streets kicking up red dust from the laterite soil on the side of the road.

At one point, the narrow road curved sharply and they momentarily lost view of the approaching traffic. A large blue and white bus loomed upon them in a flash, forcing their taxi partially off the road. Their taxi screeched to a stop as the driver slammed on the brakes. The taxi cab lurched to an abrupt halt, its two left wheels off the road, its corresponding right ones on, causing the taxi to slant lopsidedly. Shayna's hand flew up to her throat in dismay as she watched the offending bus crammed with passengers zoom by within an inch of their taxi with no thought to slowing down at all.

"What is that crazy bus driver doing?" She screamed, as she instinctively grabbed her sleeping daughter's shoulder. Juliana woke up.

"He is going to kill us all!" she exclaimed nervously.

"This is the way they drive Shayna, calm down a little," Adrian soothed his wife even though he was suitably rattled himself. Shayna gave her husband a scathing look.

"Don't you tell me to calm down. That bus could've killed us all!" she yelled.

"Honey, they do this everyday. You are not used to this and I have to confess neither am I. I've been a way so long, that I had forgotten how they drive here," Adrian explained.

"The audacity of the man! He almost drove his bus straight into our taxi. He could have killed us or at the very least injured one of us!" she continued to rant.

Adrian knew when to keep his mouth shut. If he continued to argue when Shayna was this upset, the situation could get ugly.

It was better for them all if he allowed her to have her say. He couldn't help being immensely thankful that they were not taking the Volvo bus trip from Mumbai to Goa. Shayna would surely have had a lot to rant about that!

"Madam, don't worry. We are used to this," the taxi cab driver interjected nonchalantly not sure what the fuss was all about. But he did sense the husband's reluctance to answer his wife.

"I will get you to your destination in one piece, I promise," he added.

"He forced us off the road for heaven's sake! Why was he driving like a crazy man?" she asked the taxi driver.

"Everybody drives this way, madam. Don't worry, I can handle it," he assured his nervous passenger.

"Yeah, well I can't!" she muttered unintelligibly, but she did simmer down.

They encountered a similar situation a couple more times en route. Shayna began to realize what the driver meant when he said they all drove in this reckless fashion. Sometimes it was one of their taxi drivers that was the offender, but none of the other drivers who should have been offended, seemed offended in the least! They all drove recklessly and they all went their merry way, honking their horns at each other for good measure. Shayna realized that this do-as-you-please behavior would take some getting used to. She would have to make a concerted effort to quell her fears. But for now, this taxi ride from hell couldn't end soon enough for her.

The taxis finally pulled over beside a cottage with a sloping clay Mangalore tile roof. The main door flew open and two little girls, Candace and Ruth raced toward the taxis, followed by their parents and grandmother at a more sedate pace.

"They're here! They're here!" they shouted out loud.

Sophie, Zack, Gavin, Nick and Evan jumped out of their taxis and ran toward their cousins.

They hugged and they laughed, but mostly they jumped up and down holding onto each other as they squealed in welcome. There were hugs and kisses exchanged all around. The expectant neighbors came out of their houses to greet the latest party of visitors, extracting promises to visit and making offers to host lunches and dinners for the guests. The new arrivals were finally able to extricate themselves from the welcome committee and carried their bags into Nana Lynette's house.

"What's up on that hill, Nana?" Sophie asked her grandmother the next morning at breakfast. She helped herself to a slice of fresh papaya. The fruit had come from Nana Lynette's fruit and vegetable garden behind the house.

"Nothing much really, Sophie. Just fruit trees and lots and lots of open land. It's a good place to go for a walk though," said Lynette.

"Could we go for a hike up there before lunch?" Sophie asked.

"I don't see why not. I think you will like it up there Sophie," said her grandmother.

"Would it be okay to pick some fruit, Nana? What kind of fruit trees grow up on the hill?" questioned Ruth who was sitting next to Sophie.

She also sat by the plate of sliced papaya, but was not having any. She didn't really like the taste of the orange fruit. She chose a boiled egg instead. Nana Lynette's brood of chickens provided them with freshly laid eggs every morning.

"Of course you can pick the fruit. There are *karvanda* trees, *jhambul trees* and cashew trees," answered Lynette.

"What trees?" piped in Candace, who was sitting beside Sophie also enjoying a slice of sweet papaya. The local words were alien to her.

"I believe '*karvanda*' is a type of blueberry," offered Lynette.

"Oh, yummy. I love blueberries!" exclaimed Ruth.

"What about the other one?" asked Candace.

"*Jhambul*? I don't really know if there is an English word for it. Anyway, even if there is, I don't know it," confessed Lynette.

"What's it like?" asked Candace, curious about this unknown fruit.

"Well, it is purplish black in color. It's a bit sweet and a bit tart too," answered Lynette.

"The best part is that it turns your mouth blue when you eat it!" squealed Sophie in delight.

"A blue mouth? Now I really want to try it!" said Candace excitedly.

"We just have to try it!" piped in Ruth.

"Well, definitely pick some *jhambuls* then," laughed Lynette.

"What else can we pick off the trees?" Sophie wanted to know.

"There are cashew trees too. Tons of them," added Lynette.

"Cashew, as in 'cashew nut'?" asked Candace uncertainly.

"Yes, the same. The cashew nut grows out of a fleshy orange-red fruit about the size of a small apple. You have to pluck the fruit with the nut attached to it," said Lynette.

"Then what?" Sophie asked.

"The fruit can be eaten as is of course, but it has a pretty strong flavor and can be a bit scratchy on the tongue. Most often it is fermented to make *feni*. The cashew nut is fresh. It can be roasted or put into a curry. Either way, they are delicious," explained Lynette.

"If we bring some back, will you roast some nuts for us, Nana?" questioned Candace.

"Absolutely. And I will put some in the curry I am making for dinner tonight too," answered Lynette.

"What about the fruit of the cashew tree? Are you going to make feni?" asked Ruth as she placed her hands on her hips. She wondered if she would be allowed to taste the fermented drink if Nana made it.

"Good heavens no! I will give the fruit to Ignatius from the corner house on the street. He will know what to do with it," said Lynette.

"Let's go fruit picking! Come on Candy! Ruthie!" said Sophie picking her cousins up by each arm.

"Is it private property? Do we need permission?" Candace asked, getting up at her cousin's insistence.

"Actually, the hill in front of the house belongs to your grandfather's family," Lynette answered.

"Really?" asked Ruth.

"Yes, really. Now that he has passed on, I guess a part of it belongs to me," Lynette added.

"Cool, Nana! What will you do with it?" asked Sophie.

"I guess I haven't really thought about it. I am too old anyway for such ventures. When the time comes, I will pass it on to you kids," she said smiling at her grand daughters.

"I hope that will not be for a very long time, Nana," said Sophie hugging her grandmother.

"Not ever!" added Candace also putting her arms around Lynette.

"Please don't leave us, Nana!" said Ruth coming around to her grandmother's side.

"That day has to come, my angels. Everybody has to die and my day will come too. The one sure thing you inherit at birth, is death," said Lynette, hugging them back.

"Oh, Nana, don't say that!" said Sophie.

"You are right Sophie! Enough somber talk! Come on girls, round up the gang and go hiking! Go pick some fruit!" said Lynette as she urged her little granddaughters along.

"Girls, watch out for the foxes! And make sure you go up the hill with a grown up!" she called out to the retreating girls.

It had been a fun morning. They had rounded up the family and headed off to the hill. The kids had picked several baskets of fruit and returned to the house with blue mouths. Ruth didn't particularly like the slightly chalky aftertaste of the *jhambul* fruit. It had made her teeth squeak against each other. But she had very much wanted a blue mouth like the others, so she ate as many as she needed to color her tongue and lips blue.

Zack, Nick and Gavin had really wanted to see a fox. Nana had said that one could spot a fox occasionally. They had been on the look out for one, but had been very disappointed when none showed up. They took turns training Nick's binoculars on the area around them, but their attempts had been in vain. Maybe they would hike up the hill another day. For tomorrow they had plans to visit the Basilica of Bom Jesus during the day. And to celebrate Nana Lynette's seventy-fifth birthday, they had dinner reservations at a swanky restaurant at the *Fort Aguada Hotel.*

As they made their way down the hill, it started to drizzle lightly.

"Mom, look! It's raining!" Evan squealed in delight.

"Would it be okay for us to play in the rain? Mummy, please?" Sophie asked Angela.

The other kids seemed to think it was a great idea too and added their pleas to hers.

"Please, please, please!" they chorused.

"This is the first rain of the monsoon season you know," Amy said to them all.

"Yeah, yeah. Please let us play in the rain?" Zack echoed.

"Alright kids. But first take your baskets into the house," Shayna added.

All nine children pelted down the hill side carrying their filled baskets. They dumped the baskets on the porch, grabbed a couple of umbrellas from the stand in the corner and darted outdoors to play in the rain.

Their parents watched from the porch as the rain came down in sheets around them. The children seemed to be enjoying themselves. They splashed in the rain puddles and twirled their umbrellas over their heads more for fun than for protection from the rain. Josh and Shayna made little paper boats out of newspaper for them to sail in the little stream of water that was now flowing along side the sloping edge of the house. They placed the boats on the water which soon began to move downstream.

"Look at them go!" Zack squealed.

"That one is mine!" Evan shouted, pointing to the boat that had made it ahead of the others.

The children followed the sailing boats as they made their way to the back of the house. Then they picked them up to sail again, but they had gotten too soggy with the falling rain.

"We need more boats!" Nick exclaimed.

"Please make us some more!" Gavin exclaimed too.

"Come here and I will show all of you how to make your own boats. Come," Josh invited the gang of children.

"I had forgotten how beautiful the first rains were!" Adrian said nostalgically as he looked at the foliage around him.

The rain poured down in thick sheets, wetting and washing everything it touched. The children shed their inhibitions as they danced in the rain. Like so, the earth shed hers. The leaves on the trees shed their dust and grime of past months to reveal a rich healthy green surface underneath. The tree roots that that burrowed deep under the ground in search of moisture turned their attention upwards to ingest the droplets of sweet nectar as the rain seeped into the ground. The earthworms wriggled happily in their muddy habitats, thrilled that the monsoon season was here. The frogs croaked to the raindrops in merry welcome. The water washed away the soot from the colorfully painted houses and it divested the exterior corbels of their cobwebs. It cleansed the smog from the air and drenched the dust particles drowning them in the fast accumulating puddles.

But there were those who did not benefit from the catharsis of the falling rain. The birds sought shelter from the deluge in their nests and in doorways and cornices of nearby houses, ruffling their feathers in an attempt to be rid of the offensive wetness from the droplets. Little furry animals scurried down holes to escape heaven's mighty onslaught. The red ants were uprooted from their ant hills under the mango tree and were swept up in the building current of the flowing monsoon stream, carried to an unknown destination where they would have to set up house all over again. The bright flowers in the flowerbeds by the front of the house lay drooping, their faces low to the ground, as they took a beating from the merciless raindrops.

The smell of the earth after the first rains assailed their nostrils. They breathed the fresh aroma in. The monsoon season had definitely come to Goa. There would be more rain during the next few months. A lot more rain, if they had a good season. There would be times when it rained continuously for days or times when it rained intermittently for days. The sky would often be overcast with darkening rain clouds looming, threatening to open up at a moment's notice.

There could be droughts or floods depending on the whims and fancies of the rain Gods. There could be devastation of farm lands and destruction of properties if it rained too much. There could be illnesses and death from water borne diseases. Conversely, there could be times when it seemed like the rains had deserted them. There could be famine and drought if it rained too little. There could be death and starvation from the lack of adequate rain. Either way too much or too little, the rain could wreck havoc on the lives of the people.

But it didn't matter. None of it mattered. Not today. For today was the first day of the monsoon season. The rain brought respite from the sweltering summer heat. It brought relief to worried farmers who had seeded their land and prayed everyday for the rain to come. It washed away the dirt. It washed away the old. It brought with it, the promise of new life. It brought with it, the promise of tomorrow. One could smell it in the aroma of the fresh newly washed earth. They inhaled deeply, filling their lungs to capacity. They breathed in the promise of new life, the promise of tomorrow.

Sophie woke up the next morning before the others. The rain from the day before had continued well into the night. She had fallen asleep to the sound of the raindrops as they hit the roof tiles. She cocked her ear to hear the rain. There was no sound this morning. Some time during the night, the first rain of the monsoons had ceased.

She looked at her cousins sleeping beside her on the floor in Nana Lynette's living room. Several mattresses had been lined up to form one long rectangular bed. The girls were asleep on one side while the boys had the other side. Juliana and Olivia were asleep in the middle. Lynette' house had three bedrooms. One was being occupied by Adrian and Shayna, the second by

Alastair and Gwen. Amy and Josh were settled into Nana's large loft while Angela was sharing the third bedroom with her mother. The rooms were not large enough to accommodate all nine children, so it was decided that the cousins would sleep in the living room. The front room was the largest room in the house anyway. The cousins were thrilled to be sharing the same room. A giant sleepover, Candace had called it. They had pillow fights and wrestling matches. After Olivia and Juliana fell asleep, the older kids stayed up telling ghost stories late into the stormy monsoon night. They huddled under blankets and whispered to each other. They giggled and laughed till their parents hushed them to sleep.

Sophie looked about her. Her cousins lay sleeping peacefully. She rubbed her tummy. It felt a little weird. She rose from her bed silently and made her way to the bathroom, hoping to would relieve her discomfort. It didn't. Sophie came out a few minutes later to take fresh underwear from her suitcase. She washed out the used one, hung it to dry on the clothes line at the back of the house and returned to her bed.
She lay down silently but was unable to fall asleep. She could hear the birds chirping, announcing the arrival of a new morning. She heard a door creak on its hinges. Probably one of the grown ups waking up, she thought to herself. Presently, she heard Nana Lynette in the kitchen. A half hour later she returned to the bathroom. Her tummy still hurt.
The rest of the family was still asleep. Nana Lynette was preparing breakfast for her family on the wooden stove in her kitchen. She was stoking the wood fire, when she heard a sound. She was surprised to see Sophie walking past the kitchen.
"Sophie, is that you?" she called out.
Sophie traced her steps back and poked her head in the kitchen doorway. She nodded.
"Good Morning, Nana," she said softly.
"Good Morning Sophie. Is everything okay, love? You are up so early today," Lynette asked frowning worriedly. Her

granddaughter usually didn't surface till 8:30am. Sometimes even later.

"I'm okay," Sophie answered as she walked past the kitchen to the back door.

Lynette dismissed her concerns and focused her attention on preparing breakfast for her family. She could hear them stirring. Olivia came bounding into the kitchen.

"G'morning, Nana!" she sang out loud as she ran into her grandma's open arms.

Sophie picked at her breakfast, eating almost nothing. She was quiet and not really engaging in the lively conversation around her. A few minutes later, she got up. Nobody seemed to notice. They cleared up the breakfast dishes, taking them in to the kitchen to get cleaned.

"You okay Sophie?" Josh asked his niece. She had been unusually quiet at breakfast.

"Uh huh," Sophie nodded as she stepped into the bathroom.

"Is something wrong with Sophie?" he whispered to Amy.

"I don't know. Let me ask Angela," Amy answered back.

Amy found a quiet moment with Angela in the kitchen a few minutes later. The kids had gone out to play in the front yard. Adrian and Josh were helping them knock down mangoes off the huge *Alphonso* mango tree in the front of the cottage.

"Is Sophie okay? Has she said anything to you, Angie?" Amy asked her sister.

"What do you mean?" Angela asked.

"She seems out of sorts. I was just wondering if she was okay," explained Amy.

"No, she didn't say anything to me," Angela said to Amy.

"She woke up really early this morning. Before the other kids. Much before," added Lynette as she joined in the conversation.

"I wonder why? It's not like Sophie at all. She is the sleepyhead in the family," Angela mused.

"She probably just woke up earlier. Maybe a bad dream?" offered Amy.

"Probably. I'll ask her as soon as we put the breakfast dishes away," Angela returned.

A few seconds later, Sophie walked past the kitchen entrance on her way to the back of the house. She seemed not have not seen her mother, her aunt or her grandmother in the kitchen. She seemed far away, lost in her own thoughts. Angela, Amy and Lynette exchanged a silent look. Angela put down the kitchen cloth she was using to wipe the dishes. Amy and Lynette stopped working too. Angela was the first to follow Sophie, Amy and Lynette close on her heels. They followed Sophie to the back door. She was pegging a newly washed pair of panties to the clothesline. On the clothesline were seven other wet panties neatly pegged next to each other.

"Sophie honey, are you feeling sick?" Angela asked her daughter.

Sophie turned around to face her mother, her aunt and her grandmother. Her eyes were red and welled up with tears that were threatening to fall at any second.

"What is it, love?" tried Angela again.

"I think I am dying mummy," she said, as she burst into tears.

Angela rushed forward to comfort her daughter.

"Dying? What do you mean, love?" she asked, brushing back the hair from Sophie's forehead, so she could check her for a fever. Her forehead felt cool and dry to the touch. She led her to a chair nearby and sat her daughter down.

"I think I'm dying," repeated Sophie crying harder now.

"Do you feel sick?" Amy asked, kneeling in front of her niece.

"A little. Like I want to throw up," Sophie answered, hugging her tummy with both arms as she bent over.

"Would you like some lemon juice and honey or maybe some water?" asked Lynette.

Sophie shook her head.

"Does your tummy hurt?" Angela asked.

"Yes mummy. It hurts a lot. It really hurts a lot," sobbed poor Sophie.

"We can give you something for the pain Sophie, but we need to know what's causing it," said Amy.

"Do you have diarrhea?" Angela asked pointing to the eight newly washed panties strung together on the clothes line.

"No," answered Sophie.

"Then what is it love?" asked Lynette.

"What makes you think you are dying?" asked Amy.

"I'm bleeding, that's why! It was very little in the beginning so I thought it would go away. I keep changing my underwear but it won't stop! I don't want to die mummy! Please help me!" gushed Sophie.

Finally they had gotten to the root of the problem. Well not a problem really, more a situation. The three older women mobilized their energies into making Sophie feel better.

"First of all Sophie, you are not dying. Did you hear me? You are not dying," Angela assured her daughter.

"I'm not?" she asked as Angela wiped her tears away.

"No. You are going to be just fine, little one," Angela said as she took her little girl's face into her hands.

"I am going to make you a tall cool drink of lemonade. The lemon will help with the nausea," said Lynette, walking back to the kitchen.

"Getting your period, is the most natural thing in the world. When we were around your age, your mummy and I went through it too," said Amy.

"You did? You are here, so you didn't die," Sophie stated the obvious.

"Right. What's more, every girl has to face this at some time or the other. Some a little earlier than others, but all girls will, all the same," said Angela.

"When you return to school after the summer, don't be too surprised if other girls in your class tell you about their experiences," said Amy.

"All girls will bleed like me?" asked Sophie disbelievingly.

"Yes. It's like a right of passage Sophie," her mother said.

"Huh?" Sophie did not understand.

"You are advancing to the next phase in your life. You are leaving your childhood behind you and moving into womanhood," Amy explained.

"Womanhood? I don't want to enter womanhood. I like being the way I am. Nobody asked me if I wanted to go there," cried out Sophie.

"But your body is ready, love. Getting your mind to understand that, is what we are trying to do here," Angela said to her daughter.

"But why do I have to?" cried Sophie.

"Your body is getting ready to have babies," explained Amy.

"Babies! Who said I want babies? I don't want any babies! Mummy make it stop!! Please! Please make it stop!" pleaded Sophie crying again, her voice wobbling on hysterical.

"You are not having a baby right now, silly girl. Your body is changing. It is getting ready to carry a baby when you are ready to have one later in life. You might want babies then even if you don't want them now. In any case, I can't stop what's happening to you, honey," said Angela gently.

"I should have prepared you sooner for it. Then you would not have been so frightened today. I just didn't think you would get your period this early," explained Angela.

"It will pass Sophie," consoled Amy.

"Okay, so I'm stuck with it for now. When will this 'right of passage' be over?" questioned Sophie trying to come to terms with her predicament.

"In a few days. Five or six days more or less," answered Amy.

"Five or six days? That's so long! What am I supposed to do in the meantime? Live in the bathroom? Hide under the stairs? Shut myself up in a closet?" said an outraged and quite distraught Sophie.

"Don't be absurd. You can do anything you want, once we show you what to do to take care of yourself," said Angela.

"So after five or six days, I'll be done, right? Forever? It's not going to come back, right mummy? Auntie?" Sophie asked her mother and aunt expectantly.

Angela and Amy looked at each other. This was harder than they expected it would be. Poor little Sophie was in for a very rude shock. She had to be told, of course. There was no way out. Angela took a deep breath and said,

"Actually honey, you are going to get your period for about five or six days every month for many, many years to come," Angela explained to her dumbstruck daughter.

"Whaaaat!" Sophie finally managed to say as she reeled from the shock of her mother's words.

"Come with us, Sophie. It's not that bad. We will take care of you, love," soothed Amy.

Sophie sat sulking on the built-in seat on the verandah. This foreign thing between her legs that she had been made to wear felt alien. She was convinced that it made her waddle like a duck. The moment they observed her funny walk, the whole world would know what had happened to her today. How was she ever going to escape it? Tummy aches? Nausea? Bleeding? Waddling? Every month? For years and years? Her life sucked. She was not going to make it. She did not like this one bit! No way! Why did she have to get stuck with it?

Sophie planned to sit on the verandah seat all day and not budge an inch. She couldn't or else everyone would know. She could see and hear her cousins in the front yard under the mango tree. She wanted to join in the fun, she wanted to catch the falling mangoes, but she couldn't. And it was all because of her duck walk! It would be so embarrassing if they teased her. No, she was better off staying put on the verandah. She was missing out on all the fun, but what choice did she have? She couldn't let them discover the duck walk. She looked at her carefree siblings forlornly.

"Daddy, daddy, get that one!" squealed Juliana to her father, pointing to a big juicy mango.

"Which one?" asked Adrian as he followed his daughter's pointing arm. He stretched his arm out and tried to reach the mango with a long stick. He whacked the branch it sat on and a mango (not that one) fell.

Evan, Candace, Ruth and Zack were holding onto each corner of a large horizontal white bed sheet. They used it to catch the falling mango. *Thump!* The sweet ripe fruit fell into the waiting bed sheet. Olivia squealed, clapping her hands.

On the other side of the tree, Shayna and Josh were doing the same with their big sticks.

"Come on, Sophie! Don't be a wet blanket. Come and join us!" Gavin encouraged his sulking cousin as he ran over to her.

"No! I don't want to," Sophie said.

"Come on sour puss, you are missing out on all the fun," Gavin continued to urge.

"Go away!" Sophie yelled in exasperation.

"Another one, another mango!" yelled Zack.

"Okay. Have it your way. But you are missing out," said Gavin before he ran back to the mango tree.

"Watch out for the red ants, Livvie! They'll bite you," warned Nick as his little cousin bent down to pick a fallen mango.

"Why are the ants eating our mangoes?" Olivia asked, wiping her hand sticky from the mango sap.

"Because they are sweet. They eat the over ripe mangoes that fall on the ground and then they want more. So they climb the barks of the trees in search of more food," explained Josh.

"No wonder the ants are so fat!" giggled Juliana.

"Yup. They are plumping up on our mangoes," joined in Zack.

"It's okay. The tree has so many mangoes, we couldn't eat them all anyway," said Nick.

"Here, here! There's a big one on this branch!" exclaimed Evan.

Sophie sat alone on her verandah seat. She was missing out on all the fun under the mango tree. She was going to miss out on their day trip to the Basilica of Bom Jesus. She couldn't possibly go. How could she? Instead, she would sit on this bench all day, everyday till this awful thing had passed.

Her tummy hurt and she felt sick. Today was just the worst day ever! She sat sulking. Her life really sucked. And it was going to suck forever. She couldn't believe that she was stuck with this awful predicament for the rest of her life.

Angela came out to join the family. She saw her forlorn eldest child sitting by herself looking like her world had fallen apart.

She went up to her and put her arms around her little girl from behind.

"It will get better my love, I promise. It's really not all that bad once you accept it. You'll see," she soothed her. Angela bent to kiss her dejected daughter's forehead.

Sophie relaxed against Angela, as mother and daughter watched the plump ripe mangoes fall off the tree.

Chapter 13

One Time Too Many

The eighth day of September denotes the feast of Mother Mary, The Lady of the Mount. This day significantly impacts the lives of the people of Bandra specifically and the people of Mumbai at large. People from places far and wide make an annual pilgrimage to worship at the Basilica at the crest of Mount Mary's Road. The statue of Mary the Mother of Jesus is the focus of the Bandra Feast (as it is popularly known by the locals) and has a history all of its own.

The statue was brought to Bombay by the Portuguese in the fifteenth century. Records of the period indicate that a simple mud oratory had been constructed in 1566 by Portuguese Catholic priests to house the statue of Our Lady. The statue stayed in the simple mud hut at the top of the Hill for nine years till St. Andrew's Church was built in 1575. The new building was established as the parish church and the statue was subsequently relocated to it. However, the modest oratory was not demolished. To the contrary, it remained intact for several years to come and was enlarged later and used as a chapel by Portuguese troops stationed there. Unknown to the captain responsible for the expansion, he had laid the foundation for what was to become an iconic landmark, a Basilica, that continues to draw believers into its fold.

A century later the Marathas (of the state of *Maharashtra*) invaded Bandra Hill. They destroyed the little rustic chapel and threw the statue into the Arabian Sea. Devotions to the holy site ceased for the next twenty years or so and the area at the brow of Bandra Hill became isolated. No masses were said, no church bells tolled, no *ave maria* was sung.

The discarded statue was rescued by local fishermen and was taken to St. Andrew's church once again. In 1761 a new chapel was built and the rescued statue was taken in grand procession to its rightful home. Those devoted to Mother Mary resumed pilgrimages to her chapel. Every year the number of devotees grew till this third built structure, (the oratory and the chapel being the first and second structures) could not accommodate its burgeoning visitors. Extensions and porticos were added on but they too proved to be inadequate over time.

In 1902, the Basilica as it stands to this day, was finally commissioned for construction. Two years later, the imposing gothic Basilica was completed. The towering edifice faces the Arabian Sea, whose majestic turrets serve as a guiding beacon to fishermen out on their fishing boats.

While the *Bandra Feast* is primarily celebrated by the Bandra Catholics, devotees worshipping at the Basilica are by no means restricted to the Christian faith. Devotions at the Mount Mary's Basilica transcend all religions and all barriers. Hindus, Muslims, Parsis, Jains, Sihks and followers of other faiths can be seen venerating the statue of Our Lady. The faithful arrive by the hordes to pay their respects to the Holy Mother, to pray for graces and to thank her for granted wishes and miraculous cures. They set aside religious differences as they gather as one to hear masses, light candles and make offerings. The more devout, make a novena for the nine days leading up to the eighth day of September, the birthday of Our Lady of the Mount.

In preparation for the Feast Day, the volunteer committee at the Basilica works tirelessly to set up seating accommodation for the millions that pass through its portals. They line the courtyard of the church with rows and rows of seats, set up a massive outdoor altar on a raised platform, roll out red carpets and arrange for loudspeakers to carry the church services to the throngs that gather during the week. The flow of people in and out of the courtyard is facilitated by efficient and detailed planning. There is much to do and much that is done willingly every year in preparation for the week long celebration of the Bandra Feast.

The Feast Day is always celebrated on a Sunday. Probably for convenience to those traveling long distances, probably because Sunday is a holy day for Christians. Whatever the reason may be, the feast day is on a Sunday closest to the actual birthday of Our Lady (the eighth of September). Celebrations continue for a week and come to a close the following Sunday. The flow of people traffic is the highest on the two Sundays, but is still sizeable on the days in between. People usually pay their respects at the Basilica before heading down the hill to the Bandra Fair for the celebrations.

In preparation for the week long event, vendors set up thatched stalls adjacent to each other. The stalls begin at the foot of the Hill and line the street all the way up to the top where the Basilica sits. They sell religious trinkets, crosses and chains, or wax candles of assorted lengths to light at the altar and flowers and garlands as offerings. They even sell hollow wax formations of different body parts - an arm, a leg, a head, a hand, an elbow, a knee, a toe, a pair of eyes, a nose, among other similar body parts. Worshippers offer these body parts to Our Lady of the Mount either to pray for recovery from illness to one of these body parts or as a thank

you to express their gratitude for recovery from illness to one
of these body parts.

On the other side of the Basilica, vendors set up shop as well,
hoping to attract worshippers to their wares as they make
their way down to the Bandra Fair. Their stalls line the street
all the way into the fair at the bottom of the hill.
All streets connected to the Basilica are shut down to
vehicular traffic and open only to pedestrian traffic. Regular
routes are rerouted for eight days. Little rectangular plastic
laminated passes are handed out to the local residents with
vehicles of their own. An authorized pass on the dashboard
of a vehicle ensures easy entry to those who live on the
closed off streets. No visitor vehicles or any kind of public
transportation is permitted beyond the demarcated lines.

It was a tradition in the Machado family for all family
members to gather at Mama Machado's home after the
church services at the Basilica. This year was no different.
Mama Machado's children and grandchildren from Bandra
and the neighboring suburbs were gathered at her home for
the feast lunch. There was much excitement as they prepared
the noon repast.
Mama Machado's famous *Sorpotel* and *Vindhaloo* (both
spicy red pork curries) had center stage on the meal table.
There was an opaque glass bowl filled to the brim with
fugias (little golden fried dough balls just slightly smaller
than a ping pong ball). They were usually served with curries,
but the kids especially Sophie, was very fond of the slightly
sweet bread-like balls. A large platter of steaming basmati
pilaf garnished with nuts and raisins sat to one end of the
table.
Angela and Amy (whose family was invited every year even
though she was not a Machado) contributed to the feast
lunch with some traditional Goan dishes. They made chicken
xacuti (pronounced 'shakooti'), fried pomfrets stuffed with
rechaad masala and *sanaas* (little savory cakes made by

steaming small quantities of rice batter). A *kachumber* salad of diced cucumbers, tomatoes, onions and chillies accompanied the meal. For dessert they had a chocolate mousse made by Amy and a bread pudding with a brandy sauce made by Rowena, one of Mama Machado's many daughters.

The kids were impatient for the meal to end. It seemed like it would take forever. Once the family obligations were attended to, they were free to go to the Bandra Fair. At the end of the meal, they lined up to receive feast money from their aunts and uncles to spend at the stalls at the fair. Angela had promised to take her children to the fair and she could see the impatience on their little faces as they waited for lunch to be over. Finally it was time to leave. They kissed Mama Machado goodbye and bounded out of her house.

"Are we going up to the Mount, mum?" Sophie asked her mother, stuffing one last *fugia* into her mouth.

"Yes we are Sophie. Come along," Angela answered.

They crossed Hill Road just outside *Ranwar* and headed towards Mount Mary Road.

"Better stay close kids. I don't want anyone getting lost. There are so many people here, if you get separated from me I will not be able to find you," Angela warned, grabbing hold of nine year old Olivia's hand. Zack and Sophie walked just slightly ahead of their mother. As they walked past the stalls, the sellers called out to them.

"You want candles?"

"Aunty, please buy candles, aunty!"

"Flowers, garlands for *Saibini Mai!*"

"Please buy flowers for the Holy Mother!"

"Silver crosses and chains. Come see the rosaries! Two for the price of one!"

A little boy followed them, pleading for a sale.

"Please buy candle aunty," he said.

Angela looked at the little boy holding a bunch of thin white candles in his hand. She stopped to buy some.

"Thank you aunty. May *Gawd* bless you!"

"May *Gawd* bless your family!" echoed his mother who was keeping an eye on the sale from her stall.

The young boy pocketed Angela's money and turned his attention to another customer.

"Uncle, uncle, buy some candles!"

Angela and her children continued walking up the hill. They were stopped often by other candle sellers or flower sellers.

"Want some candles?"

"Make a wish to Our Mother. Buy a candle!"

"Fresh flowers! All colors! Make an offering!"

Every time a new seller came up to them, Angela waved her candles at them. They turned away from her. If she had already bought her offering, the possibility of her buying anymore were very slim. There was no point in wasting their sales pitch on her. They were better off pitching to a more viable customer.

They reached the Basilica and stood in line to light their candles, offering silent prayers beside other kneeling faithful. Sophie noticed a devotee with her hands joined in prayer. She walked on her knees from the back entrance of the Basilica all the way to the altar in the front, a good hundred feet or so. She lit her candles and made her offerings before she laid her body prostrate on the marble floor.

 The interior design of the structure boasted sweeping, lofty gothic archways that housed glass quatrefoils etched with religious symbols. The walls were painted with life size relief murals of holy scenes from the Bible and plaques denoting the various 'Stations of the Cross' at the time of crucifixion. The altar itself was imposing, the several towers and turrets and balconies displaying gold gilt accents. Two large chandeliers mounted from the ceiling on either side of the altar cast a pink glow on the devotees below as the lit bulbs emitted light softened through its rose colored glass.

The marble steps in front of the illustrious statue of Our Lady of the Mount were peppered with lighted candles, their flames flickering in prayer, much like the whispering lips of the devotees gathered around to pray. The statue itself was resplendent in robes of shimmering gold. A jewel studded crown sat atop the Holy Mother's regal head. She was carrying baby Jesus whose outstretched arms beckoned to all who sought His protection.

A few minutes later, offerings made and graces invoked, the Machado family headed down the steps leading into the fair. Unlike the candle and flowers vendors, the vendors on this side of the Basilica had set up food stalls. Angela and her trio stopped at the first stall to buy some boiled peanuts. The woman at the stall filled three large newspaper cones with the unshelled nuts and handed them over to her waiting customers. The kids munched on the cooked nuts as they took in the festive scene around them.

There were stalls selling spicy, dried Goa sausages, bottled pickles, jams and jellies, others selling traditional sweets from Goa- *kadio bodios* (gram flour and *jaggery* sweets that were dusted with powdered sugar or with a ginger infused sugar) were piled up not unlike little mountains, on large circular trays. The vendors skillfully packaged the sweets for customers, making sure that the sweet mountains didn't topple over in the process. The *peraad* (also known as 'guava cheese' made from boiling the flesh of the guava fruit with sugar) seemed to be disappearing very quickly. The sweet was colored a deep maroonish-brown and was cut into neat little diamond shapes. Angela stopped to buy some for the family. A woman was selling *bebik* (or *bebinca* is a baked sweet where in each layer of rich egg yolk batter is baked before the next layer is added for baking. This multi layered rich flavorful sweet when completely baked takes on a striped appearance.)

"Mummy, that lady there is selling *bebik*. Let's get some," said Zack, pointing to an old woman seated on a stool.

"Okay son, lead the way to her stall," Angela responded.

They approached the old woman who looked to be in her seventies at the very least.

"You want some *bebi*k, young man?" she asked Zack.

"Yes, we would like some," he answered looking for the largest one he could find. He was all but drooling over the beige brown sweet cakes neatly stacked on the table.

"They are all the same size son. Pick one," Angela said to Zack. She knew it was his favorite sweet.

"But they are not very big, mummy. They won't last very long," commented Zack.

"Your boy is right. It won't last very long. My *bebik* is very tasty. I made them myself!" added the old woman.

"Son, even if we buy all the cakes this lady has for sale, with you around they wouldn't last very long anyway!" Angela teased Zack. He grinned back knowing it to be true. The old woman smiled too.

"Alright, pick out two cakes," Angela said finally.

The family liked *bebik* too. So it would be a treat for them all. As the old woman packed up the two chosen cakes Angela reminisced,

"When you were little, you used to peel each layer off and eat each layer separately. I always wondered why you did that."

"It lasted much longer that way. I would still have my piece of *bebik* long after all of you were done eating yours," he offered in explanation.

"You still do it, Zackki even though you are twelve now," She smiled at him.

He smiled back. He bagged the two wrapped cakes. The old woman's wrinkles crinkled around her eyes as she smiled at the nice little boy who had bought two of her home made cakes.

Other stalls had a variety of sweets too – *dosh, cashew nut laddu, pinarg, dodol and peda*, but they didn't buy anymore.

As they walked through the fair they came across other vendors selling bubbles, yoyos, winding animal toys, dolls with bobbing heads and magnetic kissing-lips, dinky cars, toy guns, ceramic miniature tea sets, plastic spiders and bugs, colorful feather hats and whistles. Olivia wanted a pointed feather hat and a tea set. Zack wanted a scary spider, a blue car and a whistle. They pulled out their spending money to pay for their items.

Further up the road a *ghana juice cart* was bustling, its seller doing his best to keep up with the demand from his customers for the sweet and ice cold freshly squeezed sugarcane juice. The customers and the vendor seemed oblivious to the puddle of water near by. The stagnant water had attracted a family of mosquitoes, the female having bred an army of young ones in the few days that they had settled there. The family of mosquitoes buzzed noisily around the customers, searching for a suitable candidate whose blood they could feast on while the customers remained oblivious to the disease inflicting mosquitoes that were scoping the arena for their next malaria victim.

Angela hurried her family along. The candy floss/cotton candy cart further up the street was whipping up pink spun sugar that was wrapped around a wooden stick. Sophie, Zack and Olivia stopped to buy three sticks of the pink fluff.

They entered the 'Hall of Crazy Mirrors' and laughed at their funny reflections, they oohed and aahed at the crazy motorcycle stuntmen in shiny red suits as they whizzed by on the 'Wheel of Death'. Sophie entered a 'Guess the Weight of the Cake' raffle, but didn't win a prize. They ate 'Push Up' ice creams while they waited their turn in line on the Giant Wheel (Ferris wheel). They played 'Throw a Ring around the Object'. Olivia won a prize. She had to choose from an assortment of soaps (*Rin, Nirma* and *Lifeboy*). None of the prizes were of any interest to her but she picked a *Nirma* soap bar to be polite. Zack played 'shooting the balloons' with an air rifle and won a ball. While they waited in line for the merry-go-round (carousel), they watched a few contenders in the 'test your strength' game stall. The contestants had to punch a ball using all their muscle weight in order to win the jackpot.

It had been an exciting day, but it had also been a long one. Angela rounded up the kids from the various stalls.

"I'm tired mummy," said Olivia, yawning sleepily. The brightly feathered pointy hat sat at an angle on her head, its feathers drooping limply as though it too was tired after the day's activities.

"It has been a long day, Livvie. We'll leave in a minute," her mother agreed. Zack came over and joined his mother and sister.

"Let me carry the bag, mummy," said Zack chivalrously. He was only twelve but he always looked out for his mother. Angela smiled as she handed over her shoulder bag to Zack.

"Mum, I can stay a little longer, right?" Sophie came over too. She was meeting up with her junior college (eleventh grade) friends. They were getting together at the *'September Garden'* to watch the dance competition that had been scheduled for the evening.

"Yes honey you can. But only till ten o' clock," Angela returned.

"Ten o'clock? The competition will still be going on!" protested Sophie.

"Your curfew is ten Sophie," said Angela firmly.

"Mum, but my friends will still be here!" she tried again to win her mother over.

Angela gave her teenager a stern look.

"You have class tomorrow Sophie. If you cannot be home by ten tonight, then don't go at all," said Angela refusing to budge.

"Okay. I'll be home by ten even if it means I have to *drag* myself away from my friends and I have to *drag* myself away from all the fun," sixteen year old Sophie exaggerated.

She hugged her mother quickly and disappeared in the direction of the September Garden. Different events had been scheduled for each evening of the week. Sophie wanted to be there for the dance competition, but she definitely wanted to be there for the September Queen and the September King contests scheduled toward the end of the week. She had friends taking part in some of the events and they were counting on her presence to cheer them on. If she had to be home by ten o'clock tonight then she would be home on time. Knowing her mother, she would be grounded for the rest of the week if she didn't and she would miss out on all the fun. Fun till ten o'clock was better than no fun at all. Besides, if she was obedient today, there was an outside possibility that she could use it as leverage to convince her mother to let her hang out with her friends over the weekend past her curfew time.

Olivia, Zack and Angela headed home. Fifteen minutes later they entered their building. For eight o'clock in the evening it was surprisingly buzzing with life. Several people were gathered in the lobby downstairs. There was a police van parked beside an ambulance with flashing lights.

"What's going on?" Angela inquired of a bystander in the gathered crowd.

"There was a fight," somebody replied.

"Did anyone get hurt?" Angela asked.

'Yes. I think so. A man," the bystander replied.

Mrs. Patel, the building gossip, spied Angela in the crowd and came speedily over to her.

"Hi Angela. Did you hear what just happened here?" she asked, ready to share a juicy tidbit.

"Who got hurt?" Angela asked her neighbor from the sixth floor.

"Mr. Sharma did," Mrs. Patel answered excitedly.

"What happened?" Angela asked, knowing Mrs. Patel would have all the answers.

"He got stabbed," Mrs. Patel answered.

"Stabbed? Are you sure?" Angela asked, shocked at her neighbor's answer.

"Stabbed," Mrs. Patel confirmed smugly, crossing her arms in front of her.

"Is he alive?" Angela asked.

She craned her neck to get a better view of the foyer entrance where the maximum commotion seemed to be. The ambulance crew were setting up a stretcher and asking the watchman, Suresh for directions to the scene of the crime. A couple of police men appeared to be questioning Mrs. D'Silva, who was answering them animatedly, her hands flying in all directions. Her flabby upper arms wobbled unflatteringly and her double chin trembled from the effort of the agitated exercise. She appeared to be the center of the interrogation and seemed to be enjoying the focus of attention on herself. Her maid servant Sonu, was hovering by the lobby wall, watching the action. Her face was tear-streaked. Nobody was talking to her.

"Is he alive?" Angela asked again.

"The ambulance crews are still examining him," Mrs. Patel said.

"He appears to be still. Not moving," she added trying to get a rise out of Angela.

"Who stabbed him?" Angela wanted to know.

Mrs. Patel leaned over to whisper conspiratorially into Angela's ear, but her reply was designed to be loud enough to turn several nearby heads in her direction.

"His wife. Mrs. Sharma stabbed him."

She delivered her bombshell punch line with aplomb so masterfully skilled, that it would have put a *bollywood* superstar to shame, had they heard it.

Mrs. Patel certainly had Angela's attention with her last revelation. She had everybody's attention. Mrs. Patel beamed. Her chest swelled as the bystanders around her looked to her for more information on the crime.

As the story goes, Mrs. D'Silva had been baking a cake for her son's birthday. She had measured out the required ingredients whereupon she had realized she was short a cup of sugar. Rather than order the sugar and wait for the grocer's delivery boy to bring it to the house, she had sent her maid Sonu, over to Mrs. Sharma's house to borrow a cup of the missing ingredient. Mrs. Sharma had gone to a kitty party (card game session) with a group of her regular card playing friends.

Mr. Sharma had answered Sonu's doorbell. He invited the young maid into the house while he had offered to fill her sugar cup. Unsuspecting, Sonu had done as Sharma *sahib* had asked. He had quickly slammed the front door shut and had dragged the resisting girl into his bedroom.

Shortly after, Mrs. Sharma had returned home from her kitty party. She had returned home earlier than expected. She had lost some money at that afternoon's game, but she was sure that she would make it up on another day. She had decided to quit early, cutting short her losing streak. She had entered her bedroom to find Mr. Sharma lying on his stomach, spread eagled on the bed. For a second, she had assumed her husband was taking a nap. Within seconds however, her misconstrued notion had been dispelled as she saw a pair of thin arms waving frantically from underneath his body weight.

Like a flailing insect squashed under a big rock.

Mrs. Sharma had known about her husband's philandering ways and had even seen him sidle up to her women friends at social events, but she had dismissed it, convincing herself that he just had a roving eye.

Her wedding night had been a nightmare that she had not been prepared for, but she had quickly gotten over the shock as she calculated the advantages of her new marriage. Her life had been very comfortable after she had married her husband. They could afford luxuries that most could not. They could take vacations abroad, buy new cars, hire several maids, buy a vacation home. He bought her expensive jewelry and gifts and allowed her to come and go as she pleased. In return, he made bizarre and sometimes rough sexual demands in the bedroom, but it was nothing she couldn't handle. Besides, if she met his needs then he wouldn't seek an outlet elsewhere. He would continue to be faithful to her. No one else would know of his depravity. Their secret would be safe. The pros of her situation far outweighed the cons. She had put up with his needs knowing that she could live in the lap of luxury.

When she returned home that evening to find him assaulting Mrs. D'Silva's maid, something happened inside of her. She had endured his torturous sexual advances and she had suffered his bruises and beatings for years. She had done it for the sake of her marriage. She admitted she had also done it to maintain her cushy lifestyle. But over the years, she had given as much as she had taken. Her debt was paid in full. Humiliating her by assaulting a defenseless young servant girl in their own bedroom, in their bed, had been too much to bear. Had she not cried and nursed her own bruises in that very same bed? Had she not given in to every one of his base demands in that very same bed? Had she not endured it so that he would remain faithful to her? That he would stay away from other women? Had she suffered for naught? After today, their secret would be revealed to the world.

She snapped.

In a moment of passionate rage, she had picked up the pair of scissors that she had used earlier that morning to cut out a recipe for *Lahori fish fry* from the Sunday newspaper, and stabbed her husband in the back.

She stabbed it into the rock that was squashing the insect.

The insect was free.

Angela made her way to the front of the crowd, just as the ambulance staff carried Mr. Sharma's body with the pair of scissors still sticking out of his back to the waiting ambulance.

Her eyes met the liftman Suresh's eyes across the lobby. For a split second there was an exchange of unspoken thoughts, an understanding, a silent acknowledgement of that fateful day Angela had been alone in the elevator. A silent acknowledgement that today, justice had been served.

He knew. Now she knew that he knew.

For a split second she was not a *memsahib,* he was not a lowly watchman.

For a split second they were equals.

For just a split second.

Angela looked away first as she entered the elevator, for she *was* the memsahib. Suresh cast his eyes downwards.

The ambulance crew rushed Mr. Sharma to *Lilavati* Hospital a short ride away. When Mrs. Sharma had stabbed him, she had stabbed him in the spine, causing irreparable damage to his nerves. Unknowingly, she had paralyzed her husband from the neck down.

A predator, by a bizarre turn of events, had been laid to rest. He had assaulted just one time too many and now he was paying the price. The women of their building could rest easy. He wasn't dead, but it would have been a far better fate for him, if he had been. His quadriplegic body was reduced to a wheelchair. His fully functioning brain would crave the satisfaction of its depravity from his immobile paralyzed body, commanding him to act.

But he would be unable to do anything.

Because he could not do anything about it.

Except suffer in agonizing silence.

And burn in his own private hell.

Angela walked into her home with her children. She was calm. She was thinking about every woman he had assaulted who could now feel avenged. By her actions, Mrs. Sharma had vindicated them all. She knew it was un-Christian like, but she couldn't help thinking that Mr. Sharma had got what he deserved. Mrs. Sharma had all the money in the world to hire the smartest lawyers. Lawyers who would do everything it took to keep their client out of jail. They would plead temporary insanity or a crime of passion or some other equally convincing defense. Angela was sure Mrs. Sharma would be okay. As would all her husband's victims.

We will all be okay.

Angela slept fitfully that night. She opened her eyes and listened to the sounds of the morning around her. Birds chirping, car doors slamming, the newspaper boy delivering the morning paper. She heard the *thunk* as the newspaper slammed her front door first before coming to rest on the doormat, its gaining momentum abruptly arrested. It was time to get up. Angela rose from the bed and a few minutes later walked toward the kitchen for a cup of *chai*.

The children were still asleep. The house was quiet. Angela walked to the front door to collect the newspaper. It lay to one side of the door mat, neatly placed to face the front door. It was obvious that the casually thrown newspaper had been intentionally moved aside by someone. It had been moved from its original position to make place for something else deliberately placed in the center.

Angela's three missing pearl buttons arranged neatly in a row, lay gleaming innocuously on her front door mat.

Chapter 14

Together Again

Angela placed the last piece of clothing into her suitcase and snapped the locks shut. She carried her luggage out into the hall and placed it beside two other similar looking suitcases by the front door. She checked the locks on the other two pieces and found them to her satisfaction.

"Hurry up Livvie! We're going to miss our flight!" Angela called out in the general direction of her daughter's room. She received no response.

Olivia was probably in the shower and hadn't heard her. Angela let out a sigh of exasperation. She turned the door knob of her youngest child's closed bedroom door and walked into the room.

Angela's senses were instantly assaulted by what splayed out in front of her. The room looked like it had been ravaged by the unleashed fury of a hurricane. Pieces of clothing, belts and socks hung haphazardly off every possible structure in the room. It seemed as though the contents of the closet were anywhere but in the closet and yet Angela could see that that was not the case at all. A crack in the closet door revealed a pile of clothes just itching to cascade past its restraining doors.

The bedroom floor was another matter altogether. Books and magazines carpeted the floor exposing an occasional glimpse of the original tile flooring that peeked through the wall-to-wall spread. A stack of books served as a makeshift table for a plate with food remnants so distorted, they were hard to distinguish from a dissected specimen in a biology experiment. Posters hung on the wall behind Olivia's bed, the edge of one peeling off the wall and curling forward. Shoes of all sorts littered the room like designed accents placed with contrived casualness by her daughter's acute sense of teenage decor.

Olivia's favorite band was rapping through the tiny speakers of an old boom box plugged into the wall. The music box lay resting on top of a tall chest of drawers. The volume had been turned up high enough for its listener to hear the music through the closed bathroom door. The room reverberated with the sound of a drum set reaching a fevered pitch as Angela's eardrums resounded to the lead singer's high pitched crescendo. Angela strode quickly to the offending box and unplugged the noise maker from the wall, not bothering to use the buttons on the machine designed for just that purpose. An eerie silence descended on the room, but Angela couldn't hear it. Her eardrums were still ringing from the cacophonic onslaught.

"What happened to the music?" Olivia asked as she poked her frothy shampoo covered head around the door.

"I turned it off," Angela answered.

"You mean you yanked the wire out of the socket," corrected Olivia as her eyes fell on the boom box.

"I turned it off," repeated Angela.

"Why can't you use the buttons like everybody else, mum?" Olivia asked in exasperation, dripping shampoo froth and droplets of water at her feet.

"That would require me to look for the 'stop' button, which would take a few seconds longer than pulling the plug. By that time, I would be completely deaf!" Angela answered her daughter.

"You really do love to exaggerate don't you?" said Olivia, not really expecting an answer as she rolled her eyes upwards much like Sophie used to do at her age.

"Hurry up, we must leave for the airport soon," urged Angela.

"Okay," Olivia replied. She slammed the bathroom door shut, but opened it a second later and said to her mother,

"Oh mum, on your way out, could you please turn the music back on? It helps me to think."

"Think? What do you need to think about? You don't have time to 'think' right now, Livvie. All you should be concerned about is getting ready to leave," Angela said.

"Yeah, yeah. The music helps mum," returned Olivia winking at her mother as she shut the door once again.

"Don't dilly dally Olivia! There is no time for that today!" Angela said to the closed bathroom door.

Angela just shook her head in exasperation at her teenaged daughter. How could anybody 'think' with all that noise? Think indeed! Besides, Olivia didn't think. She just did! She did things without thinking most of the time! So what did she have to 'think' about today? Teenagers!

After dealing with Sophie and Zack through their teenage years, Angela had learned to accept what she could not change. Teenagers thought differently, they behaved strangely, they spoke funnily and they dressed weirdly. It was a fact of life. A button got switched on at thirteen and then switched off a few years later. Just like that. One moment here, the next moment gone. As though they were visiting Earth from an unknown planet for seven years, give or take a few.

Angela had wised up fairly quickly and had stopped trying to figure her teenagers out. She just did her best to ensure that they stayed out of trouble and did well in school. She had managed to get Sophie and Zack through *teenage hood* mostly unscathed and Olivia remained her last challenge.

Olivia would not make it easy for her, Angela knew, as her youngest was the most spirited of her three children. Olivia was almost sixteen and still had a long way to go. Angela sighed tiredly in anticipation of the years of rebellion ahead. She picked up the dirty plate of aged food specimen from the makeshift book-magazine table and plugged the boom box cord back into the wall. She pressed 'play' on the boom box. The music started up instantly. Angela quickly lowered the volume and left her daughter's room.

Angela washed out the plate and headed to her own room to get dressed for the flight. She slipped on a pair of trousers and a comfortable blouse.   She rummaged through the hangers of her closet looking for her cashmere wool cardigan. It would keep her warm in the chilly aircraft cabin. The garment was nowhere to be found in her closet. Angela tried the chest of drawers by the dressing table. She finally found it in the second drawer folded and put away a few months ago.

Mumbai weather rarely called for warm clothing and Angela had consequently dry-cleaned the garment and stored it away. She shook the cardigan free of its folds and looked over it with a critical eye. She had expected the soft wool to smell musty from lack of use, but it appeared to be in excellent wearable condition except for the third button that had come loose from its stitching and seemed to be missing.

Angela retrieved her sewing kit from the closet and pulled out a box from the top chest drawer. The box had little bits of ribbon, a reel of gold braid, lengths of lace and bric-a-brac, buttons of all shapes and sizes and other odds and ends leftover from past sewing projects and craft undertakings. Angela looked for a button to replace the missing one on the cardigan, but she did not seem to have any. She frowned unhappily.

Her fingers continued to search the box and came across a little round button stuck in the corner of the box. She pried it loose and stared at it as it lay in the center of her palm.

Angela looked at the little pearl button for the first time in years. Her mind was instantly assailed with memories of the past. She sat down abruptly on the bed, curling her fingers tightly around the little button. Her fingernails dug into her palms, but Angela was oblivious to the pain. For the next few seconds, her brain raced back in time as thoughts came flooding through her mind. Her heart thudded in her chest. Angela took a deep breath and calmed her nerves. Over the years, she had learned to deal with the unexpected. She had learned to get past the anguish it resurrected. Angela unfurled her fingers and looked at the little pearl button. The little round button gleamed in the palm of her hand.

The little pearl button had evoked Angela's memories. She touched the button gently with her forefinger. She remembered the day Frank had given her the dress with the three pearl buttons. It had been her birthday and she had been so happy that day. She remembered how happy their life together had been. She remembered being pregnant with Olivia and wearing the dress on the day she had been informed of Frank's death. She remembered wearing the dress when she had been attacked in the elevator. She remembered how the three buttons had mysteriously appeared at her doorstep a few years later.

They represented the happy as well as the painful experiences of Angela's past. They represented the fulfilling love she had known with Frank. They represented Angela's heart wrenching struggle to get past the curve balls that life that thrown at her. They represented her valiant attempts to get up when life had pushed her down. They represented her tenacious perseverance to embrace life no matter what lay in store for her and her family. They represented her well earned victory over strife and hardship. They represented the metamorphosis of a sheltered and protected young girl into a fiercely independent woman. A woman very much in control of her own destiny.

They represented the skeins that threaded the very fabric of her life.

The three little buttons were so inconspicuous in their existence and yet so powerful. Angela firmly closed her fingers around the tiny object. She stood up and rummaged through the box one more time. She retrieved the other two pearl buttons that had been buried and long forgotten in the intervening years.

Frank had bought her the dress with the three pearl buttons over twenty years ago. Her husband was long gone and the dress had been burned to ashes along the way, but the three little buttons had stubbornly survived destruction. They had been a part of the last twenty years of her life and Angela wanted them to be a part of the next twenty.

She cut out the stitching of the other two still perfectly attached buttons on the cardigan and purposefully sewed the three pearl buttons in their place. Angela smiled when she was done. She put the cardigan on over her blouse and looked at her reflection in the dressing table mirror.

The three little pearl buttons represented Angela's Past, her Present and her Future.

There were no demons that she could not face.

Angela looked up to see Olivia staring at her intently.

"Are you okay mum?" she asked concerned.

She had seen the far away look in her mother's eyes. Her mother never day dreamed. She was always bustling about either at home or at work. And when she wasn't working, her mother spent the rest of her time correcting her. No, her mother never day dreamed. She didn't seem to have the time for such pleasures. But here she was, actually day dreaming. Weird. Seeing her mother's distant gaze, Olivia felt like she had intruded on a private moment. Angela turned to face her youngest child.

"Mum? Is everything okay?" she asked again.

"Yes honey I am just fine," Angela assured Olivia, the nostalgia slipping away.

"It didn't look that way to me. You seemed so far away. Are you sure you're okay?" she persisted.

"Yes Livvie, I'm sure. I will explain it to you someday when you are older," Angela smiled to reassure her daughter.

"I am old enough now," She replied stubbornly.

"Let it go, Livvie. I promise I will tell you about it when I think you are ready to hear it, okay?" Angela smiled at her little girl.

"Okay, if you say so," acquiesced Olivia, reluctantly.

"In the mean time, we need to hurry. Why don't you finish dressing so we can leave?" queried Angela, suddenly all business-like. This was the mother Olivia was used to.

"I'm dressed. Let's go," replied her daughter.

Angela turned to look at her soon to be sixteen year old. Olivia had on a net-like fabric beige top. Had it not been knotted against her waist, it would have hung to her bony knees. The see through top did very little to cover the skimpy red top she wore underneath. A pair of opaque dark brown printed tights cut off at the shins and a red mini skirt boldly fraying at its hemline, covered the lower half of her body. A pair of open high heeled espadrilles laced up around her ankles. Her right arm was covered in an array of silver and gold chunky metal bangles and bracelets from wrist to forearm. Angela wondered how the right side of Olivia's body was not weighed down by the excesses of her fashion jewelry.

"Is that how you plan to dress?" Angela asked her teenager, her eyebrows raised in question.

"Yeah. Don't I look nice?" Olivia questioned.

"The niceness of your clothing is not in question here, Livvie. What is in question is its practicality," Angela answered diplomatically.

"What's wrong with it?" Olivia defended her fashion sense.

"Several things," Angela explained as she began to tick her objections off her fingers.

"What?" her child asked defiantly.

"Number one- you will freeze to death in that skimpy outfit when we get to New York. Number two- your toes will fall off your feet with frost bite, exposed in those shoes the way they are. Number three- the heels on those shoes are not exactly conducive to walking. You're likely to twist an ankle trying to manage yourself and lug your hand baggage on the long walkways at the airport. Number four- you will set off the alarm at the security checkpoint at the airport wearing all those bangles and bracelets. You will be made to take every one of them off before the security check and then put every one of them back on after you are through. Can you imagine how tiresome that's going to be for you? Number five- it's a sixteen hour flight. You want to be dressed comfortably. Number six-,"

"Okay, okay, I get your point! I'll change," Olivia conceded, raising her arms in defeat as she turned around and went back to her room.

"And take off some of that make-up young lady! You are not going to a night club!" added Angela, as an afterthought.

It had taken Olivia the better part of an hour to pick out her ensemble and get dressed today. Angela hurried along to her teen daughter's room. If they were going to make that flight tonight, Olivia would need to be urgently coaxed into comfortable clothing, urgent being the operative word.

They made it to the airport on time somehow and were waiting to board their flight to New York. It had taken Angela several years to muster up the courage to set foot on a plane after Frank's death. When her children had to get on a plane, she feared for their lives too. But she had learned to overcome her fears and quell the flutters within. How else could she get around? She had to live her life. Her children had to live theirs. She had *had* to get over her fears. It was as simple as that.

Their flight was finally called and Angela and Olivia boarded the aircraft bound for New York. Shortly after, the airplane taxied down the runway of *Chatrapatti Shivaji* Mumbai Airport (*Sahar International* Airport had been renamed in 1998, ten years ago). With a final burst of the engine's thrust, the aircraft soared upwards into the black night.

The passengers settled in for the long haul to New York. Angela and Olivia settled in as well. After the meal service, the lights in the cabin were dimmed and the window shutters were pulled down.

"It's nighttime. Why are the flight attendants requesting us to pull the shutters down?" Olivia asked her mother.

"In a few hours it will be light again. Most passengers will still be asleep and the sunlight will disturb them. If we pull the shutters down now, then nobody will be disturbed," explained Angela.

Angela had brought work with her. She had every intention of using a good part of the sixteen hour non-stop flight to catch up. She pulled out a laptop from her bag and immersed herself in her electronic files and folders. Olivia selected a movie on the flight entertainment system and donned an airline headset to follow the conversation. Angela was soon absorbed in her work.

Their little home based business had expanded rapidly over the past fourteen years. They had bought over the commercial kitchen they had once rented when Angela's tiny kitchen could not meet the needs of their growing business. They had expanded the new kitchen, bought three more delivery vans and rented space for a retail outlet in Bandra. They still catered parties both corporate and private in nature, but they also marketed their specially created products.

Their goods had been well received by their customers and had been written up in various magazines and newspapers. Their gourmet sauces, marinades, jams and dips flew off the shelves everyday. Their exceptional party platters and well packaged gift baskets along with their uniquely branded specialty products were in much demand.

They had recently introduced a take away and home delivery section. The food was prepared in their kitchens to order and delivered in their vans to their customers. Their work force had subsequently increased to accommodate their growing business. Angela and Amy had long since relinquished the kitchen reins to accomplished professionals, but they visited the kitchens everyday, sampling the food or trying out new recipes.

Their store was overseen by a very capable manager, but Amy and Angela still showed up everyday to talk with their customers about their needs and to build rapport with their employees. They paid attention to little details just as much as they did to the bigger picture. They had worked very hard to get to this point, but they never let up. They knew that only hard work and dedication would keep their business running smoothly. They had grown a successful business and they intended to keep it that way.

Their flourishing business had enabled them to pay for a college education for Sophie and Zack in America and Gavin in Switzerland. Olivia was soon to follow her siblings.

Adrian had applied for their permanent visas with the immigration authorities in America shortly after Frank's death. Their visas to the States had come through a couple of years ago. Angela had sent Sophie first and then Zack to live with Adrian and his family. They had quickly become accustomed to the way of life in a foreign country and had moved out into college dormitories before long.

Sophie had completed a graduate degree in Marine Biology and spent a great deal of time on expeditions around the world. Home was an apartment in Scarsdale New York, even though she spent most of her time away. She had recently returned from a trip to South America and was looking forward to spending some time with her mother and little Olivia before her next scheduled trip.

Zack who would turn nineteen in three weeks (four years younger than Sophie), was enrolled in an undergraduate degree program in Information Technology on the west coast. He was working on acquiring a much sought after internship with a company located in Silicon Valley in San Francisco. Angela had been concerned that Zack would be so far removed from his family in New York and New Jersey, but he seemed to be adjusting well to life in sunny California. Sophie and Zack visited each other at least once a year when their schedules allowed it. This year he would spend his entire Christmas vacation on the east coast with his family as Angela and Olivia would be there too.

Gavin, who was the same age as Zack, had opted to go to a culinary school in Switzerland. His program was among the best in the world in his field and Gavin was at the top of his class. Amy and Josh were proud of their son and his commitment to his education. They were thankful to be able to provide their son with an opportunity to excel at his endeavors. The little boy they had adopted into their lives and accepted into their hearts had filled their home with inexplicable joy. They often thought back to the circumstances that had brought him into their lives and Amy's role in it. They marveled at being given the opportunity to raise their own child and what they had collectively accomplished to date.

Olivia, the youngest, still resided in Mumbai with her mother. She was enrolled in a junior college science program in Mumbai, equivalent to the eleventh grade in America. Life at the moment was fun and friends, movies and hang outs. She had not yet decided on a college major and was toying with the idea of pursuing a career in either architecture or photography. At Sophie's urging she had promised to visit various campuses during her visit to the States in order to make up her mind. She would need to submit college applications next year and the urgency of choosing her path was looming large on the horizon.

Angela for the past couple of years had divided her time between America and Mumbai. She spent time with her kids when their schedules permitted, but she had taken advantage of her trips to further the business as well. She had met with suppliers and wholesalers in America and had established an import-export business. She bought gourmet cheeses, specialty oils and vinegars, cured meats and other food products from her contacts. They exported her selections to Mumbai. Amy and Angela sold the products exclusively in their store. Establishing a monopoly for the products drove demand up and they turned a healthy profit on their investment. Angela was always sourcing new products to add to their list. She was able to do that on her frequent visits to the States. They were exploring the exportation of goods from India to America as a new avenue and an added source of revenue for the business. Plans were in the works for another retail store in Mumbai. It was an exciting time for their business and Angela and Amy had been very busy.

Angela had sent her children to the States with her blessing as they began their new lives, but she herself had continued to make Mumbai her primary residence. She had not been able to relinquish her business, her ties to it too strong. They owed the success of their business to their blood, sweat and tears and giving it up for a new life in America had been unthinkable to Angela. She had chosen a happy medium, shuttling back and forth between the two countries.

Besides her business, she still had other responsibilities in India. Olivia had two years before she left for the States, for one. Secondly, Angela's mother, Lynette, had come to live with her a few years ago when she had been diagnosed with Alzheimer's disease. As the disease progressed, it had become increasingly apparent that she would be unable to live on her own or take care of herself. Her daughters had relocated their mother to Mumbai and had closed up her home in Goa. Angela and Amy cared for their mother as best they could, but there was not much they could do for her deteriorating brain cells and her lost memories. Every day was harder and longer for their eighty-six year old mother, her periods of lucidity decreasing with each passing day. It was difficult for them to see their mother wither away, now just a shell of the person she once was.

Mama Machado on the other hand, had stood strong and had been in complete possession of her mental faculties as the years progressed. While her body had succumbed to the natural pressures of aging, her brain had resisted all attempts at breaking down. Her movements had been restricted by painfully severe arthritis and she had been prescribed medication to control her high blood pressure and cholesterol, but her mind had remained as sharp as a tack till she passed away ninety-eight years after her birth.

Mama Machado had been a mere twenty years old when she had first beseeched God to take her instead of her unborn baby, but He had not heeded her prayers. Instead He had taken two more of her precious babies in the years to come. She had waited patiently and suffered agonizingly for seventy-eight years before God finally granted her wish. Mama Machado had waited a very long time to be united with her three dead children. At last, she could rest in peace. She was finally with her Violet, Annabelle and Frank. Her funeral had been well attended, her mourners and well wishers spilling out of the side entrances of St. Andrew's Church. People came from all over to pay their respects to a well loved woman, a mother to them all. They knew that there would not be another to replace her.

The aircraft touched down at John F. Kennedy international airport in New York. Angela and Olivia looked forward to the ten days ahead. Christmas had always been a special time for their family, a time for family reunions and for reliving memories and making new ones. This year they would gather together at Adrian and Shayna's home in New Jersey. Alastair, Gwen, Candace and Ruth would arrive from Toronto. Amy, Josh and Lynette would spend a few days with Gavin in Switzerland touring the Swiss Alps. The group of four would then fly out to New Jersey and join the rest of the family for the Christmas celebrations.

The family had attended the morning Christmas service in church and was now gathered around Adrian and Shayna's table for Christmas dinner. The table had been set with Shayna's fine china and her glistening polished silver cutlery. She had placed poinsettia arrangements along the length of the table, their red and white hues creating a striking contrast against the richness of the dark moss green table cloth. The table was invitingly festive and the air in the room was charged with merriment as the family members gathered around the table.

As head of their large family, Nana Lynette was given the seat of honor at the head of the table, but the import of the gesture was lost on the octogenarian's degenerative brain cells. Adrian and Shayna sat at one end of the table that had been elongated with add on tables to accommodate all eighteen dinner guests. The nine cousins (Sophie, Zack and Olivia, Gavin, Candace and Ruth, and Nicholas, Evan and Juliana) gravitated to one end of the table leaving their parents to occupy the other end. Adrian and Shayna had invited their neighbor, Lyle Preston to join them for the holiday meal. They bowed their heads to say grace, thanking God for his abundant blessings on their family.

"Praise the Lord and pass the sauce!" Zack exclaimed loudly after the prayer, his comment instantly breaking the somber prayerful mood, eliciting laughter from all gathered around the table.

Much later that day, Angela was seated in Adrian's living room. Her body was curled up in an armchair, her long legs tucked underneath. She wiggled her toes appreciatively at the warmth emanating from the lit fireplace. She was lost in thought as the flames danced across her luminous eyes changing them into limpid pools of amber brown. Sophie walked into the room with two mugs, one in each hand. She handed a mug to her mother. Angela's nostrils breathed in the cinnamon tinged apple cider. She wrapped her hands around the mug and took a sip of the warm golden liquid.

"Dinner was fun, huh?" Sophie asked her mother.

"Yes it was. Shayna really went to a lot of trouble. We are lucky to have such a wonderful family," answered Angela.

"Yes, we are," agreed Sophie, taking a sip from her cup too.

"Are you cousins having a good time?" asked Angela.

"Oh absolutely! We're planning on going to the movies later tonight. I'm meeting some friends for a quick drink before that," Sophie said.

"I am glad all of you get along so well," Angela smiled.

"So am I," smiled Sophie back.

Angela looked at Sophie in the firelight. She looked so much like her father, Angela thought to herself. She had his deep set serious eyes and his easy going affable nature. She had always loved being outdoors like her dad even when she was a little girl. She remembered Sophie walking around with band aids and juice boxes, dressed in a billowing silver cape that Nana Lynette had made for her. Her little Florence Nightingale was always ready to help those in need. She was all grown up now and still helping those in need. Only this time around she was helping animals instead of people. Sophie ran around the world saving dolphins and whales. Angela acknowledged that Sophie looked a lot like her too. Her daughter had her tall and slender build. She had her hair too. It fell to her shoulders like a thick velvet curtain softly framing her beautiful oval face in the glow of the burning embers. The flames of the fire shimmered as they danced on the thick silken strands.

"So what did you think of him?" Sophie interrupted her mother's thoughts.

"Of whom?" Angela asked, coming back into the moment.

"You know who. Lyle Preston," Sophie returned.

"Oh him. He's nice I suppose," Angela said noncommittally as she gently stoked the fire.

"Nice? That's so bland, mom. I think he's quite good looking, in a serious sort of way," Sophie replied.

"I suppose so," Angela agreed.

"He seemed interested in you," Sophie persisted.

"Rubbish! What an imaginative mind you have, Sophie!" exclaimed Angela.

"I think he is attracted to you mom," Sophie added.

"Don't be silly," Angela returned.

"And you know what? I think you are attracted to him too!" Sophie added with a twinkle in her eye.

"Now you really are crazy! Had too much wine at dinner, did you?" Angela queried.

"Come on mom, admit it. He does interest you, doesn't he?" Sophie said, not willing to let go.

"Okay fine. He is interesting," conceded Angela,

"And you find him attractive?" pushed her daughter.

"Maybe a little bit," said Angela growing pensive.

"There is nothing wrong with that mom. It's the most natural thing in the world," Sophie added quickly.

"Maybe for you child, but not for me," said Angela.

"What do you mean?" asked Sophie.

"I'm too old," replied Angela.

"I would hardly call forty-six old, mom!" retorted Sophie.

"What would people in India think?" Angela asked.

"What would they think? That a beautiful woman finds an available man attractive! That's what they would think! Besides, why should it matter what anyone thinks?" Sophie asked her mother.

"I'm not some spring chicken looking for romance, Sophie. I am a widow with three grown children who has never been with another man since we lost your father fifteen years ago," said Angela sadly.

"You don't go looking for romance mom. It finds you," said Sophie softly.

"It's been too long, Sophie. I don't think I can go down that road again," returned Angela.

"Of course you can!" insisted Sophie.

"It's not easy for me," Angela replied.

"Okay, so you haven't been with a man in a while," said Sophie.

"In fifteen years!" Angela exclaimed.

"So what? If anyone can get past this mental block, it's you mom. You should think about going on a date," Sophie said determinedly.

"A date?" Angela said 'date' as though it was the most bizarre and preposterous word in the English dictionary.

"A date," confirmed Sophie.

"A date. There is only one problem with that Sophie, one that you seem to have conveniently overlooked. No one has asked me out on a 'date'," returned Angela.

"Lyle might ask you out. He looked very interested in you. I saw him chatting you up at dinner," teased a smiling Sophie.

"He was just being a pleasant dinner companion," explained Angela.

"Yeah, right! By the way mom, he happens to be available," added Sophie

"How do you know whether he is available or not?" Angela queried.

"I asked Auntie Shayna," replied Sophie.

"You did, did you? Now what is she going to think of me?" lamented Angela.

"It's okay mom, I was discreet," Sophie said.

"I couldn't date him, anyway. I mean him being American and all," said Angela uncertainly.

"What's wrong with being American?" Sophie asked confusedly.

"There's nothing wrong with being American of course. I mean he is just different. Your father was my first and last boyfriend. I don't know how to date! An American man or any man for that matter!" exclaimed Angela ruefully.

"Oh mom!" Sophie said sympathetically.

"Besides, I doubt Lyle is familiar with Indian women either," added Angela.

"Men are men no matter from where, mom. Sure there will be differences, but that just makes it all the more exciting don't you think?" Sophie said.

"Hmm," said Angela noncommittally.

"If you are interested in each other I am sure you can find a way to make it work," Sophie replied.

"I suppose you are right about that," agreed Angela.

"I think I am. Anyway, If not him, then you should keep your options open," suggested Sophie.

"I am too busy to date, Sophie. I have the business to run, Nana Lynette needs me constantly, Livvie needs seeing to," Angela replied quickly.

"No more excuses mom. It's not like you have to marry the man! Or any man for that matter. Just have some fun, enjoy yourself for a change. All you've done since daddy died is take care of us and work, work, work. Maybe it's time to kick off your shoes and have some fun. Do something just for you," coaxed Sophie.

"I don't know about that, love," said Angela growing more pensive.

"At least promise me that you will think about it?" Sophie said, getting off the sofa. The doorbell had rung. Her friends had arrived to take her out.

"Okay, I will," promised Angela.

Sophie hugged her mother before she left the room.

"Sophie?" Angela called out to her oldest child. Sophie turned back to look at her mother.

"Do you really think he found me attractive?" Angela asked hesitatingly.

"I really think so mom," Sophie replied smiling.

"Okay," said Angela, taking a deep breath.

"Okay," said Sophie smiling at her mother.

"Go on now. Your friends are waiting. Be careful out there, the roads are icy. I love you baby," she said.

"I will. I love you too mom," Sophie came back to hug her mother once more.

"Oh, and one more thing Sophie. No alcohol for the younger ones. Livvie will do her best to get her hands on some!" warned Angela.

"Just popcorn and soda at the movies, I promise!" laughed Sophie as she left the room.

Angela reflected on her conversation with Sophie, as she lay in bed later that night. She *had* been attracted to Lyle Preston, Angela admitted that much to herself. She had also thought that he might have been attracted to her but she had been unsure till Sophie had pointed it out. Angela had decided to let the matter drop, but Sophie had thought to do otherwise. She had persisted like a hungry dog unwilling to let go of a meaty bone.

Angela had never imagined having a conversation of such a nature with her own daughter, and yet it had seemed like the most natural thing in the world. Mother and daughter talking like friends. When did her child get to be so wise in the ways of the world?

Sophie was obviously all for her going out with Lyle, but how would Zack and Olivia feel about their mother going out on a date? A date! Angela groaned. What did one do on dates nowadays? Where did one go on dates? She had not been on a date in so long!

What would Frank think? Angela knew the answer to that one. Frank would never begrudge her any happiness. She had been lonely for so long. Since his death fifteen years ago, she had never looked at another man. Her need to be physically loved by a man had quietly receded over time and had eventually disappeared.

Her days had been filled with work and taking care of the kids. She had had little time for anything else, leave alone a romance. A romance? Angela groaned again. She was too old for romance! Who would want to wine and dine a forty-six year old widow with grown children? Romance, Angela scoffed. She was not some silly school girl with her head in the clouds.

Then why was she feeling warm all over? Probably just the heat in Adrian's house, Angela dismissed, even though she knew that she could not explain away the butterflies in her stomach.

If her current physiological reaction was to be taken into consideration, Angela safely surmised that her physical needs had not completely disappeared as she had once thought. They had merely been pushed to the periphery of her consciousness, ready to burst forth at the asking.

Angela took a deep breath to steady her nerves. The man hasn't even asked you out, Angela and you are going weak in the knees, she chided herself. A sobering thought crossed Angela's mind. Maybe Lyle was just being polite when he appeared interested in her. Maybe he was just making pleasant conversation with her. What else could he do? She had been seated right next to him at the dinner table. It would have been rude if he hadn't talked to her, wouldn't it? Sophie could have misread the situation. He was probably not interested in the first place and here she was swooning like a Victorian heroine in a romance novel at the remote possibility of being asked out on a date! Angela rolled over and groaned for the third time.

Why had Sophie planted the seeds of possibility in her mind? Angela had been content to go on as she had for the past fifteen years. And now this! She had enough on her plate to deal with. 2008 had been a very busy year for her and 2009 just a few days away looked to be headed in the same direction. She didn't have the time to take on extra curricular activities. Did she really want this? Wouldn't it just complicate matters? How would her children react? Would they be angry with her? What about the rest of her family? Would they think she was insane to entertain such a notion? Was she insane?

If she was so crazy, then why did her toes curl in anticipation of what possibly lay ahead? Why did she feel like getting off the bed and dancing in the middle of the night? Why could she not contain the excitement bubbling unchecked inside her chest? Why did she feel a seed of hope germinating in the pit of her stomach?

Did she dare allow herself the chance to love again? Did she dare risk opening up her heart to another? Did she dare allow herself to hope? What about the pain and hurt that usually goes hand in hand with love? Was she ready for that? Did she dare open a door she had thought closed forever? Did she dare face her demon of loneliness?

Did she dare?

Lyle Preston called two days later.

"Hi Angela. It's Lyle Preston."

"Hello Lyle. How nice of you to call," she replied, holding her breath.

"I really enjoyed talking to you the other day. I was wondering if you might want to have dinner with me sometime?" he asked casually.

"I would like that very much," Angela replied, her heart racing at the rich timber of his voice.

"Awesome! There is an amazing little restaurant in the Village that I've been to a few times. They are usually very busy and the wait for a table can be long, but their food is superb. I could check if they accept reservations. Does Friday evening work for you?" he added.

"That's fine," Angela replied briefly, not trusting herself to talk. She barely heard a word he had said as her senses drowned in the sound of his voice.

"Is seven o'clock okay?" he queried.

"Seven o'clock sounds perfect," she just barely managed to say.

"Great! I look forward to Friday evening," he said softly.

"Friday evening," she echoed before hanging up the phone.

When Angela put the phone down, she was smiling from ear to ear. Sophie and Olivia were lounging on the couch in

Sophie's living room watching television. Zack was surfing the internet. They looked enquiringly at their mother.

"Judging from your reaction, I am guessing that went well?" Zack asked his mother.

"Lyle asked me out," Angela replied simply.

"That's great, mom!" Sophie said.

"I still can't believe it! I mean just look at me!" Angela said self deprecatingly.

"You know, for a forty-something year old, you are quite an attractive woman," Olivia quipped, smiling to take the bite out of her remark.

"Why Livvie, coming from you that is quite a compliment!" returned Angela ruffling her youngest child's hair playfully.

"Mum! My hair! You're messing it up!" Olivia said as she moved her messed up head out of her mother reach.

"Oh gosh! I just thought of something! I have absolutely nothing to wear!" Angela exclaimed, bringing her hands up to her cheeks in horror.

"Then I guess we're just going to have to go shopping tomorrow!" added a grinning Sophie.

The next day, they spent the day at the mall. They browsed through the vast array of stores and little boutiques. Angela tried on different ensembles. She thought one outfit suitable, Sophie liked another and Olivia had decided on a third. In the end, Angela bought them all because she couldn't make up her mind.

She felt a twinge of guilt for such excessive indulgence. She thought back to the hard times her family had been through financially after Frank had passed away and before her business had taken wings. They had been strapped for cash and had lived on a shoe string budget for awhile. She had just barely managed to make ends meet back then, stretching their money as far as it would go. And now here she was, spending like there was no tomorrow. How things had changed for them! Her children were studying and working abroad, their business was flourishing and she was buying three outfits for one date!

That evening, Sophie and Olivia helped their mother get ready for her first date in fifteen years. Sophie did her hair and Olivia painted her nails. Zack looked her new outfits over and made his pick. Angela decided to trust his choice. She opted to wear a simple calf length dress that flattered her slender curves with knee high boots that Sophie had absolutely insisted she buy. All in all, she didn't look too bad, Angela thought as she looked at her reflection in the mirror.

Sophie, Zack and Olivia had decided to leave the apartment a few minutes before seven o'clock that evening. They wanted to spare their mother any awkwardness when Lyle came over to pick her up. Angela was nervous and they did their best to put her at ease.

"You look beautiful mom! Have fun!" Sophie said as she slipped on her overcoat.

"Don't stay out too late! Remember your curfew or you'll be grounded!" Zack added mischievously, as he laced up his boots.

"Don't do anything you wouldn't want us to do!" Olivia exclaimed taking her cue from her brother's remark, as she donned a hat.

"Kids, you do realize I am the mother here, right?" asked Angela as she laughed with her children.

"Just be yourself mom. Go with your heart and do what you think feels right," Sophie said soberly, as she hugged her mother.

"I love you mom," Zack said hugging her.

"Me too," said Olivia as she joined in the hug.

"I love you too," Angela said to her three beautiful children as she put her arms around them all.

Angela was grateful for a few minutes alone to gather her thoughts. She looked out the window of the living room. It had snowed earlier that day and light, fluffy snowflakes had blanketed the ground. The trees and bushes were dressed in the same thick cold whiteness. Somebody, probably the building caretaker, had shoveled the walkway in front of the apartment building. It was the only surface not covered in the glistening white chilly splendor. The world looked so calm and so peaceful. So silent.

The snow magnified the silence as it absorbed the outdoor sounds, muffling them into their fluffy folds. The birth of a new day tomorrow would destroy the stillness. The sun would melt the fluffy snow to slush and the inevitable traffic would muddy the pure white snow, marring its blinding brilliance. But today would always be beautiful.

The air was thick with silence, a silence that lay quietly waiting for something to happen.

Just like Angela was.

Lyle walked up the shoveled path, bearing a box of chocolate truffles and a potted plant. She watched him walk up the path from the window. Her pulse quickened in anticipation as she opened the door. Angela smiled at Lyle. He smiled back.

"For you," he said.

She accepted the gifts and inhaled the sweet scent of an orchid already in bloom. She placed them on the hall table.

"Ready?" he asked.

"Ready," she replied.

Angela retrieved her overcoat from a nearby chair. Her eyes fell on the cardigan with the three pearl buttons that lay benignly beneath it. She touched the buttons lightly with her slender fingers. Angela smiled.

Her Past, Her Present, her Future.

She shut the front door gently behind her. Angela took a deep breath and strode confidently into the wintry white evening.

****

Acknowledgements

First of all, to you the Reader. Thank you for your support and the time you have spent in reading my work. I hope that it brought you much enjoyment.

To my dear family and friends who took the time to spread the word around, without whom this novel would have remained just my story.

To Marissa and her talented team at First Water, for ideating and executing an outstanding book cover design.

To the team at LSI, for making my book a tangible reality.

To Sam, for answering my many questions.

To Dale, my go-to person. For your diverse networking connections that simplified things.

To Iona, for your invaluable orientation to detail in proof reading my work.

To my Abe, who has yet to say 'no' to me. For your unwavering support in every venture that I have undertaken no matter how harebrained. For your constructive criticism, endless patience, attention to minutia and thoughtful insight as I wrote this story.

To my precious children, who made the biggest sacrifice of all, as I devoted endless hours to the completion of my debut novel. I live for the light that shines in your beautiful eyes.

Thank you from the depths of my heart.

References

1. Meningitis. (http://www.cdc.gov/meningitis/bacteria/faq/html)
2. Silverstein, Alvin and Silverstein Nunn, Laura. 'Symbiosis'. ISBN 0761330011
3. SIL International. *'Ethnologue report for language Isolate'*. (http://www.ethnologue.com/show_family.aspsubid=90087)
4. *'GM Crops Around the World- an accurate picture'*. (http://www.gmfreeze.org/uploads/GM_crops_land_area_final.pdf)
5. *Indian Census* (http://www.censusindia.gov.in/)
6. Mother tongues of India According to the 1961 Census. (http://www.languageindia.com/aug2002/indiamothertongues1961 aug2001.html)
7. India facts- Facts about India. (http://www.indianchild.com)
8. Sanskrit. (http://.en.wikipedia.org/wiki/Sanskrit)
9. Indus Valley Civilization. (http://.en.wikipedia.org/wiki/Indus_Valley_civilisation)
10. Symbols. (http://www.india.gov.in.knowindia/national_symbols.php)
11. 'Aryabhatiya of Aryabhata', translated by Walter Eugene Clark.
12. Bourbaki, Nicholas (1998). 'Elements of the History of Mathematics'. Berlin, Heidelberg and New York Springer-Verlag. 46 ISBN3540647678.
13. Britannica *Concise Encyclopedia* (2007), entry algebra.
14. Richardson, W. John (1994). *'Serious birdstrike-related accidents to military aircraft of ten countries: preliminary analysis of circumstances'*.
15. Damania, Ardeshir B. Dr. *'History of Mumbai'* - compiled and abridged from several sources.
16. Fernandes, Clarence, Rodrigues, Herman, Rodrigues, Denis. *'Ranwar'*. Article written for the Celebrate Bandra'05 Festival held in Bandra in November 2005.
17. *Bandra*. Excerpts taken from articles found in the Archives of the East Indian Association Silver Jubilee.

18. De Mello, Alfredo Froilano. *'A Summary of the History of Goa (2000BC-1500AD)'*
(http://www.goacom.com/culture/history/history.html)
19. *'Goa Inquisition'*. (http://en.wikipedia.org/wiki/goa_inquisition)
20. Marryat, Captain. *'The Phantom Ship'*. (1839).
21. Rodrigues, Sanford. *'Typical Goan Architecture'*.
(http://www.goavacationguide.com/goa-architecture.html)
22. Rodrigues, Sanford. *'History of Goan Catholics'*.
(http://en.wikipedia.org/wiki/History_of_Goan_Catholics)
23. Lobo, Joe. *'Goa and Mangalore'*.
(http://groups.yahoo.com/group/gulfgoans/message/10064. Indian Catholic Association of Florida.
24. Rodrigues, Sanford. *'Goan Catholic Research'*.
(http://www.goatoronto.com/images/stories/stock/catholic-goan-research-paper.pdf).

Printed in the United States
219839BV00001B/1/P

9 780615 297170